About t]

James Ellson was a police officer for 15 years, starting in London and finishing as a DI at Moss Side in Manchester. When he left the police he started writing, and has been writing ever since. He is currently working on the sequel to *The Trail*. He also mentors work in progress, and talks at writing groups and festivals.

James was a keen climber and mountaineer, and has visited Nepal many times. In 2004 he climbed 6,812 metre Ama Dablam, and in 2008 soloed the Matterhorn. He now lives on a smallholding in the Peak District with his wife, and manages their smallholding, which includes bees and an orchard. He offers tours, runs courses and gives talks on self-sufficiency and apples.

Super Patrons

Annette Alcock
Jamie Allan
Sally & Nick Archer
Lorna Ball
S Ball
Elon Bamforth
Helen Barnfield
Jim Blenkinsop
Samantha Boardley
Charlie Boardley
Peter & Lesley Boardley
Stephen Booth
Nigel Bowthorpe
Sarah Bowthorpe
Paul Brady
Mark Bray
Deirdre Byrne
Robert Cable
Duncan Cantor
Michael Conroy
Stephanie Cook
Mary & Michael Crawford
Tony Creely
Timothy David
Mark Davies
John Davy
Alison Dennis
Fiona Dewar
Alison Dewynter
Felicity Dick
Miss Drennan
Arabella Duffield
Bob Dulieu
Carl Edwards
Nick Ellson
Sarah Ellson
Philip & Helen Ellson
Max Ellson
James Emmett

Gareth Evans
Alison Foster
Greg Gaffney
Kuljit Ghata-Aura
Dan Gluckman
David Gouldthorpe
Susan Green
Chris Greensmith
Edward Griffith
Jane Griffiths
Margaret Haigh
Andrew Halls
Miranda Havelock-Allan
Mike Hazelton
Luke Heatley
Karin Heatley
Abigail Heatley
Olivia Heatley
Helena Heatley
Jonathan Hill
Lisa Hodgkinson
Tony and Juliet Holland
Peter Hooper
Nicola Hudson
David Hughes
Gareth Jeffery
Andrew Jeffreys
Charlotte Jolly
Thomas Jubb
Eamonn Keane
Peter Kendon
Felicity Kendon
Saj Khan
Dan Kieran
James Lappin
Philip Lee
Carolyn Lemon
Rosemary Mays Smith
John McCall

The Trail

James Ellson

unbound

This edition first published in 2020

Unbound
6th Floor Mutual House, 70 Conduit Street, London W1S 2GF
www.unbound.com
All rights reserved

ISBN (eBook): 978-1-78965-078-5
ISBN (Paperback): 978-1-78965-077-8

Cover design by Mecob

Printed and bound in Great Britain by Clays Ltd, Elcograf S.p.A.

For Sarah

1

War memorial 5 mins

Calix shoved the phone in his pocket, opened the car door and climbed out into the dark and the rain. In the distance he heard a burglar alarm and sirens, the muzak of Manchester.

On his face the cold rain felt like stabs of electricity. It suited him. Encouraged hoods up and heads down, discouraged hanging about. He looked around. Two lines of sardine-parked cars, spindly trees, and an army of wheelie-bins. A flickering streetlight revealed the slant of the rain. Behind the cars were small gardens and quiet houses. TV-blue seeped from windows.

No movement, no voices.

Too quiet?

On the car's passenger side he popped the small square flap and pulled it open. Instead of a petrol cap, there was a compartment half the size of a shoebox. Bespoke and expensive, but a business had to be invested in to be successful. In the compartment was a plastic bag. Smaller bags inside. He removed one bag and pushed the flap shut.

He walked around the back of the car, hopped up onto the pavement and headed for the meet. His last delivery of the

1

evening and so far no problems. No IOUs, no photocopied notes, no *these are my five mates from the football club.* The word delivery made him think of milkmen. Trudging around the streets clinking their bottles while everyone else got on with their lives. He was a modern milkman with a crap gig of a job. No holiday or sick pay, not even a Christmas party. A violent boss to answer to. But only temporary, and good money while he waited for something better to come along.

Maybe something just had.

A car splashed past. He pulled his hood up. Yes, he was a modern milkman, an oversized delivery boy, out in all weathers. Milkmen got to sleep with their customers.

No way was he doing that.

He reached the memorial, a cross above a great slab of stone. *Sacrifice* chiselled on the front and underneath, a long list of names. His john waited in the monument's deep shadow. The flare of a cigarette pinpointed him like the laser of a sniper's scope. A new john, friend of an old one. Second time.

Calix walked closer.

Ryan threw down his cigarette. It hissed in a puddle. He took a step forward. 'Alright?'

Calix nodded, sensing a problem. He liked to get it done quickly and without words. In and out, like a knife. 'Money.'

'Next week, okay?'

Calix stared at Ryan. Seventeen or eighteen, still at school or college. Under his charity shop trenchcoat was a Barry Manilow t-shirt. For fuck's sake. Ryan was trying it on, wearing a Barry Manilow t-shirt.

Credit meant more investment, a minder, and greater risk. Maybe when he came back from his trip, but for now he liked things as they were. Just him, no one else to stuff up. Once a week, meet The Big Red, a dozen deliveries. Easy.

'Okay,' said Calix, handing the bag over.

Ryan took it. He looked relieved, surprised even. 'Thank—'

Calix hit him.

An open-handed slap to the cheek. Not hard enough to put him on the floor, but hard enough to make him remember. 'Next week, double, plus next week, so that'll be triple. Sixty.'

He walked back to his car with its twin petrol flaps. Carrot and stick – basics.

2

A bee inside the veil was every beekeeper's nightmare. Going cross-eyed, Rick watched it crawl around on the mesh. She was annoyed and buzzing loudly. Keep calm, he told himself. He put down the frame of bees and pulled back a strip of Velcro which secured his hood and veil.

His phone rang.

Life would be boring, he thought, if incidents were doled out with fallopian frequency.

With a pincer-grip he extricated the phone from a pocket of his smock. He knew it would be work, even on a rest day. Still watching the bee, he prodded the screen with his gauntlet and held it up to his ear.

'DCI Castle.'

'Rick, it's Robbo, I've got a missing person enquiry for you.'

He closed one eye to see if it helped. It did. The bee was heading towards his left ear. 'I'll phone you back.' If anyone would understand it would be his boss because he'd given Rick his first nucleus.

'Soon as.'

He pocketed the phone. She'd disappeared.

Honeybees could tell if a keeper was nervous. He thought

of lying on a beach. Going to the cinema and eating popcorn. A meal out. Christmas with his parents and sister. Thoughts, not memories. He never lay on a beach – he hated them. He couldn't remember the last time he'd been to the cinema and he usually worked Christmas.

She was in his hair.

The sound as he ripped back the rest of the Velcro seemed to aggravate her and the buzzing intensified. Still he couldn't see her. He unzipped the smock, pushed the hood backwards and ran a hand through his hair. For a second he felt her vibrating body between his fingers, and then she was gone.

Ten minutes later, Rick had put the hive back together. Keeping it open, even on a bright spring day, wasted the bees' reserves.

He walked away from the hive, tapped a couple of keys on his phone and put it to his ear. He was worried he hadn't found the queen. She was longer than the workers and more spidery looking, and she was marked with a yellow dot. But despite all that, and checking every frame, he hadn't spotted her. Which meant problems.

'Why me, sir?'

'I know the missing's father,' said his boss. 'A war hero. Brigadier Coniston, David Coniston.'

'Iraq?'

'Falklands. Won the Military Cross.'

'Who's missing?'

'His son Calix.'

'Age?'

'Twenty-three.'

'Suicidal?'

'No.'

'Needs medication?'

'No.'

'Mentally ill?'

'No.'

'How long's he been missing?'

'Two weeks.'

In the pause, Rick could hear the M60, Manchester's orbital. Never at rest.

'I said you'd go and see the *brigadier* this afternoon.'

Rick put his phone, gauntlets and smoker into the box of beekeeping paraphernalia, heaved it up, and walked back through the apiary to his car. Pearl-grey clouds drifted across the sky and a hidden aeroplane droned. The air smelt of honey and grass pollen. Bees flitted amongst red and yellow poppies, bluebells, and the last of the daffodils. The scrub was wet and his socks felt damp.

Beekeeping was the perfect foil to police work. Honeybees behaved predictably, never complained, and cooperated for the greater good. Very rarely aggressive, even when they were stuck inside your veil.

3

'*Namaste*,' said the two small men in unison. They clapped their hands into the prayer position, and draped garlands of orange marigolds around Calix's neck.

'Welcome to Kathmandu,' said Amanda. The Nepal Adventures guide was tiny – not even five feet tall. Calix wondered how she'd shoulder her pack, let alone carry it for four weeks. He followed her through the teeming airport concourse to a line of taxis. Black with yellow bonnets. His rucksack wouldn't fit in the boot and he threw it up onto the roofrack. Amanda sat in the front and Calix, feeling like Gulliver, squeezed into the back.

The taxi set off, but only as far as the exit queue. Calix juddered the window down. The air was warm and humid – a welcome relief after the cold of Manchester – and stank of diesel. Beggars appeared from nowhere. A man on crutches, one of them broken and taped together, and a teenage boy with no arms and pine-needle legs. Two girls, no more than ten, one carrying a baby on her front. The baby bawled. Behind them were others. Hands crowded in through the window.

The taxi edged forward, and in the footwell Calix pulled notes from his wallet.

'You know that's real money?' said Amanda, watching him in the mirror. Her face was plain and freckly.

They drove to the hotel. The traffic was crazy. Lorries looking like carnival floats fought with legions of tiny cars – overtaking, undertaking, and veering off – as if it was the start of a race. Their taxi stopped at a huge junction. Standing in the middle, on a small pedestal, a dibble with long white gauntlets controlled traffic from five directions. Every vehicle honked and hooted. Moss Side on New Year's Eve.

Amanda turned around.

'Tomorrow there's a team meal in the evening when you'll meet the others. Twin brothers and a couple from London, a farmer from New Zealand, a writer, a couple from Ireland, a girl from Australia, and a Frenchman. Then a free day, and the morning after we'll leave for the trailhead. Any questions?'

Eleven people meant one of them didn't have to share a tent. Ideally that would be him, but requesting it might seem antisocial. He shook his head.

Calix was jet-lagged and got up late. The others had gone out. On the hotel balcony he ate a plate of *momos,* and watched parrots flitting around in the trees. Bird Bird would have kicked ass. He smoked a cigarette, and drank an Everest beer. He pushed the bottle around on the table, making patterns in the condensation trails. Beer at lunchtime was the definition of a holiday.

He wandered out into Thamel, Kathmandu's tourist district. Hundreds of people, a mixture of locals and tourists, packed the streets, along with tuk-tuks, bicycles and hand-carts. Dogs scavenged alone or roamed in small packs. The shopfronts were narrow, but the shops sold everything. Mountaineering equipment, linen, carpets, plastic containers of every size and shape, grey meat cuts covered in flies. Wafts of incense fought with the stench of sewage and diesel that choked the Kathmandu valley. A pig ran down the street, scattering people and knocking over a table of books.

His sister Megan would have loved the hustle-bustle, the throngs of people, the spice shops. The vibrant saris and pashminas. He had to experience it all for her. Since her accident, he had to live life for the two of them.

He bought a phrase book and a dictionary in a bookshop. Further along was a small hardware shop. He went in. It was crammed, floor to ceiling – nails to chicken wire to shovels. After a few minutes, he found what he was looking for, a small lock-knife with a wooden handle and a whetstone. He added a couple of other items and paid.

Next door, giant rolls of cloth leant against the frontage. As he entered, he heard sewing machines in the back.

'*Khaltis?*' he said, flapping at a trouser pocket.

'No problem, *sahib,*' replied the waistcoated assistant.

Calix explained what he wanted, and the man nodded. Calix took his trousers off and waited in his shorts.

Forty minutes later, they were ready. Calix tipped the assistant, and returned to the chaos on the street. He pulled out the map he had borrowed from his old man, and was quickly surrounded by hawkers.

'Tiger-balm?'

'Hashish?'

Calix walked on, stuffing the map into a pocket. Over his shoulder, he saw the man following. He entered an alley, and waited, wondering where the dealer stashed his gear – he was unlikely to have twin petrol flaps on his tuk-tuk. When Calix walked on he heard children shouting. He emerged into a building site where a dozen boys were playing football with a tennis ball. Shirts against skins, clothing for goalposts. Reminded him of school.

The boys stopped their game and crowded around. As shy as robins.

'Manchester United?'

'You, England?'

Calix grinned and nodded.

'World Cup?'

He walked away, back down a ginnel.

At the end was another boy, even younger than the footballers. He was looking around the corner and down the street. Shoeless and wearing only a filthy pair of shorts, the boy held a small branch like a rifle. He pointed it at Calix, and made the noise of a gunshot. Gasping, Calix clutched his chest with both hands. He staggered and fell back against the wall. The child giggled so much he got hiccups.

For half an hour Calix had forgotten himself, where he was, what he was doing.

The Kathmandu Kitchen was open air and busy with tourists. In a corner, a local band was setting up on the small stage. A warm smell of spices drifted through the open door of the kitchen, like bonfire smoke. Sporadic sounds of sizzling. Calix was starving.

Three tables were pushed together and he engineered himself a seat at one end, flanked by the twin brothers, Spencer and Barney. They didn't look like brothers, yet alone twins. Spencer was small with glasses, and weedy. Barney was tall and stocky with a week of stubble. He explained to Calix that he was growing his first beard to make it a memorable trip.

The twins ordered steaks.

Calix did too.

'You done anything like this before?' asked Barney.

'No,' said Calix. He double-swigged his bottle of beer. He was more than a touch nervous, which he hadn't expected.

'Not feeling good,' said Spencer. 'Where's the bog?'

'Small shed out the back. *Chirpi* on the door,' said Amanda. On her chair she had piled three cushions. When Spencer had gone, she turned to his brother. 'Is he alright?'

Barney puckered his nose. 'Main thing is his asthma.' He glanced at the back of the restaurant. 'I was wondering, Amanda, whether phones will work on the trek?'

'For most of it. Best thing is to buy a local SIM to avoid the cost of roaming.'

On the stage, the band started up. Two old men on small bongo-type drums, two women with recorders, and a younger man on a keyboard. It sounded like Calix's local curryhouse, but he quite liked it.

'Your father, Calix, he's a Ghurkha?' said Amanda.

'Used to be.' He turned from the band. 'He's at the MOD now.'

'One of our *sirdars*—'

'Sirders?' said Barney.

'*Sir-dar* – means chief guide.' Amanda looked back at Calix. 'This morning he was looking at the list of names for the trip. He saw your name and got a bit excited. Him, and a porter. Wouldn't say why.'

Dancers appeared. Brilliant red dresses, black hair covered with masses of golden jewellery, long necklaces. Clapping and dancing, side to side. One up on the Failston curryhouse.

'They've probably got confused,' said Calix, watching the dancers.

'Maybe, maybe not. The Sherpa villages who supply our staff also provide many of the Ghurkha soldiers. It's a much smaller world than you might think. In addition, all the soldiers are from Nepal. Only the officers are British.'

Calix shrugged.

Amanda turned away to talk to Vicky, the Australian girl. She had dark brown hair pulled back in a ponytail, and her nose was pierced with a stud. It looked red and she kept touching it and flinching.

Spencer sat down, wheezing slightly. He fished around in his pocket, and brought out an inhaler.

'Okay, bro?'

'I will be,' he said, shaking the inhaler.

The food started to arrive, the twins' steaks first. Calix ate a few of their chips. They weren't in France, but at least the chips were hot. His own steak arrived. He salted the chips, and ate them with his fingers, dabbing at the ketchup. When no one was looking, he stuffed a spoon up his sleeve.

The band stopped for a break, and Calix clapped with everyone else. The two brothers clinked their bottles of beer and turned to face him. They were still teenagers – Spencer had acne, Barney Brylcreemed his hair – and suddenly Calix felt nervous not only for himself, but for them, too.

'To Everest beer,' said Barney.

'To *chirpis*,' said Spencer.

4

The Conistons lived in three storeys of mock-Tudor in South Manchester. A gravel drive circled a well-tended rose garden, and in the centre stood a bronze statue of a heavy-breasted woman. The sky was pebble-grey, and black-bottomed clouds loomed.

Rick parked, and knocked on the front door, half-expecting it to be opened by the missing son. Only one person in five hundred reported missing wasn't found in the first month.

A rail-thin man greeted him.

'DCI Castle? David Coniston.' They shook hands.

The brigadier's face was a leathery deep brown, the legacy of a life spent in the field. He wore an olive cravat tucked into his shirt.

'Robbo said you were good,' said the brigadier. 'Underrated.'

There was a pause.

'Quite a rose garden,' said Rick.

'Everyone needs a hobby.'

'I keep bees.'

The brigadier nodded, already turning away.

Rick followed into the house. It smelt of furniture polish. He was left alone in the study, and he looked around. It was like a

13

military museum. Photographs, certificates, and, standing in a corner, a uniformed mannequin with medals. Above the desk was a framed photo of the brigadier being awarded a medal by Princess Margaret, and alongside it a newspaper article with the headline 'Falklands' Hero'.

He was reading the clipping when the brigadier returned carrying a kitchen chair. He was trailed by his wife. Also thin, she wore a knee-length russet skirt and black ward shoes. Her eyes were bloodshot and her fingers, in the brief fluttery hand-shake, icy-cold.

They sat down in a triangle, the brigadier behind his desk, his wife on a small green leather sofa and Rick on the ladder-back from the kitchen.

'Calix's been missing for two weeks?'

'He phoned us when he arrived, like we agreed. But nothing since. Said he'd contact us once a week.'

'You've phoned him?'

'Goes straight to voicemail,' said Mrs Coniston. 'But, I keep trying.'

Rick nodded. 'Where did he go missing?'

'Didn't Robbo tell you?' said the brigadier.

'No.'

'Nepal.'

'Nepal?'

'He won a competition,' said Mrs Coniston.

Rick shifted on the chair, making the wood creak.

'In January,' said the brigadier, 'Calix won a competition. The prize was a place on a trekking expedition in Nepal. He flew out two weeks ago, and since his phone call from Kath-mandu, we've heard nothing.'

'Tell him about Megan,' said Mrs Coniston.

'Calix is not our only child.' The soldier swivelled on his chair and glanced at his wife. Her eyes were closed. 'A year and a half ago Calix's younger sister Megan died in a road accident. She was cycling around Australia.'

'I'm very sorry to hear that.'

'As you can imagine, Pat was concerned about Calix going to Nepal. We only agreed if he promised to stay in touch. The trekking company, Nepal Adventures, told us that the cell phone network is pretty good now.'

'They have a sat phone as back-up,' said Mrs Coniston. Her eyes were open again. She sat stiffly on the sofa, ready to leap up at any moment. The phone or the front door. News of Calix. Calix himself. Rick expected it: it was usual. He was looking for unusual.

'They said phone calls would be possible throughout the expedition.'

Rick doubted it. Should, maybe. 'How did he sound on the phone?'

'Fine,' said the brigadier.

'Did he mention anything unusual?'

'No.'

'Did he seem concerned about anything, or about anyone else on the trip?'

'He didn't say so.'

'What did he say?'

'Not much. Said he had jet-lag, and the expedition guide was very small. Asked if Pat had fed his parrot.'

'Where should he be now?'

'On the trail to Mount Mera.'

'How do you know he's not? He's having such a good time that he's forgotten to get in touch? Maybe he's lost his phone or the battery's dead?'

'I'll be disappointed if that's the case.'

'How was he before he went?' Rick looked at Mrs Coniston. She looked at her husband, and Rick wondered whether it would have been better to interview them separately. He still could.

'I knew I'd worry,' said Mrs Coniston, 'but I thought going to Nepal would give him a boost. It's been quite tense here—'

'Listen,' said the brigadier. 'When I was Calix's age I was commanding thirty soldiers and had fought in the Falklands. He should be looking for a job, not swanning off on some holiday.'

'You've phoned the trekking company?'

'Of course. Buggers to get hold of, but yesterday afternoon they told me to stop fussing. Said he's halfway round the world climbing a Himalayan peak, not camping with the Scouts.'

The brigadier took off his old-fashioned watch. It had a large circular face with visible cogwheels and a black leather strap. The soldier held it across the palm of his hand, pulled out the small serrated knob with a nail and began winding. Long, slow, deliberate movements. He pushed the knob back in and refastened the watch around his wrist.

Mrs Coniston looked up. 'Are you taking this seriously, Inspector?'

'Of course.' Rick thought of the files on his desk. A spate of armed robberies, the arrest of a serial rapist, two lengthy reports for domestic murder for the CPS. His portfolio also included South Manchester's Missing Person Unit. Eighty-five people currently, including seven high risk. Calix was an adult, on holiday in Nepal, and had been missing for two weeks on a month-long trek. Not even medium risk.

'One stone at a time, Mrs Coniston.' He began to think about his bees. He needed to clean up his spare hive in preparation for the swarming season. 'Tell me more about Megan.'

'She was the adventurous one.' She worked off her wedding ring. 'The risk-taker.' She slipped the ring back on, and took a deep breath. 'From an early age, wandering round to the

16

neighbours, and on holiday, swimming in the sea whatever the weather. She had lots of friends. Wanted to be a travel writer, and was writing a blog of her Australia trip. Calix's always been more of a dreamer. Megan would go out and do things.'

'Were they close?'

'Not really,' said the brigadier.

'You didn't know, David. You were never here.'

'Mrs Coniston?'

'He dropped out of university.'

'He what?' The brigadier stood, leant forward, and rested his fingertips on the table. 'Pat?'

'After Megan's accident, at the beginning of his third year.'

'What the hell's he been doing then?'

'I don't know. Not exactly.'

Rick let the words hang. 'So, the two of them were close?'

Mrs Coniston nodded. She fingered a tissue from her sleeve and wept silently.

'Robbo promised us,' said the brigadier, 'that you would make this a high priority.'

Rick looked at the soldier. Short hair, clean-shaven. Probably the same haircut since the day he'd joined up.

'The chain of command doesn't really work like that in the police, sir.'

'Meaning what, exactly?'

'We have ranks, yes, but we think for ourselves.'

'Don't you mean, make it up for yourselves?' The brigadier's eyes fixed on Rick like a pair of cannon. 'From what I read in the papers, police officers don't stick to the rules, and never have. Hillsborough, Stephen Lawrence, De Menezes – hardly testaments to police professionalism. You're either covering up your mistakes, or making the face fit.'

'I'm sorry you think that.' Rick glanced at Mrs Coniston, who was staring into her lap. He stood up and walked out into the hallway with its polished parquet floor. Mrs Coniston followed and he turned to face her.

'You're not leaving?' She wiped tears from her eyes.

'No.'

The case was probably a dodo, but he wasn't leaving. He never left before he was done. Robbo knew that.

'I'm sorry about David.' She glanced back at the study. 'We're both rattled. He blames himself for Calix going in the first place, and I'm scared after what happened to Megan.'

'I'd like to see Calix's room.' Although Rick did feel for Mrs Coniston, he was no longer going through the motions. He had found something, something to dig into.

The competition.

A sixth sense. A detective's instincts. He could not really explain it. In itself it was nothing, just a fact, but it was unusual, and it had punctured his disinterest.

5

At the end of the second day the expedition reached Sete, famed for its abandoned Buddhist monastery. They were staying in the Bupsa Lodge in rooms of four. Calix unfolded the single blanket over his bed and laid out his sleeping bag. He was alone, the others drinking beer and eating Pringles on the sunny terrace. Even Mike. He lay down. The pillow was stained and the blanket scratchy.

He stared at the ceiling of rough beams. The builder's pencil calculations still remained, like hieroglyphics. His legs were tired. The walking wasn't as hard as he'd anticipated. The pace was slow and the breaks frequent. But there was plenty of up. He didn't mind. He felt good. From the trailhead where they'd left the minibuses, there'd only been paths. No roads at all – no smell of diesel, no clamour of beggars or hawkers. Following their porters, he and the others had walked through small villages with excited children. Threaded their way between tiny terraced fields. Above the fields were rhododendron forests, and in the distance loomed the shadowy ridges of the mountains.

He heard scratching from under the floorboards, and he sat up. There was a hole in the corner of the room, and he walked over to investigate. Small droppings like vermicelli. Mice.

Calix went outside, and walked the longer route to the back of the lodge, avoiding the terrace. He broke a branch from a rhododendron bush and returned to the room the same way. The wood was whippy like the hazel he used at home. From one of his new *khaltis* he took out a wire snare. A simple, free-running noose. He cut two forked sticks from the rhododendron, the size of golfer's pencils, and whittled them down. He jammed the sticks into gaps in the corner of the floorboard so they protruded one inch. He rested the loop of the snare in the forks, and tied the end of the snare to the nearest leg of the bed. Bait was unnecessary.

He took the knife out of his pocket and lay prone on the bed with his head protruding over the edge. He lay still, and waited. He could hear the others on the terrace. Barney telling jokes and making people laugh. Megan, he thought, would have liked Barney. She'd always gone for tall athletic types. And Barney would have liked Megan – everyone liked her. She was cute, even if she was his sister, but she'd also had nerve, and a carefree spirit.

Before she'd left for Australia, they'd argued. He'd borrowed her tweezers, and returned them bloody. Or so she said. It didn't matter: the very last words he'd said to her were bad-tempered. He was only in Nepal, doing what he was doing, because of her. Living life for both of them.

The mouse appeared. It paused, sniffed the air, and scampered back and forth. It paused again, whiskers twitching, and ran forward. The snare sprung, flinging the mouse in the air like a Roman catapult machine.

Calix counted to ten. He loosened the snare, removed the dead mouse, and reset it. He'd liked to have watched for longer, but there was a phone call he had to make, and he went back outside. He hurled the mouse into the bushes, and taking the same route as before, went in search of the monastery.

Villagers passed him, returning from the fields carrying baskets of firewood with tools strapped on top. They wore shoes more suited to a beach holiday.

'*Gompa?*'

The farmer pointed, and smiled with crenulated teeth. His feet were bare.

At the edge of the village, the *gompa* wasn't hard to find, and Calix entered its gloomy coolness. The rough benches were heaped in a corner, and it smelt like the back of a cave. On the walls stone slabs had been carved with what he assumed was scripture. He looked out of a broken window towards the village. There was no sign of Barney, who had been following him around like a new pup. The phone showed no reception, and he went back outside into the shafts of evening sunlight streaming through the trees.

The sky was milky blue. He sat down on a rock out of view of the lodges and put on his sunglasses. He felt like he'd gone back in time. He could hear cows lowing and the tinkling of their bells and the voices of their young herders. The twittering of birds. At home he could identify a dozen or more, but not on the trail. He practised his Nepali.

Ho, chaina. Yes, no.

Ek, dui, tin, chaar, paanch. One, two, three, four, five.

Mera jaane bato kata parcha? Which is the way to Mera?

He tried again with the phone, and this time he got through. 'It's me, Calix.'

Looking back at the village, he listened for a few seconds.

'We're slow,' said Calix. 'A French guy's hurt his leg. Day after tomorrow, or the day after that.'

Barney emerged from the shadows between two shacks, and headed towards the monastery. Calix pocketed the phone and watched the taller twin walking towards him. Six foot two-

and-three-quarters, Barney had told him. Brand new trekking gear, him and his brother.

'Phoning home?'

Calix nodded.

'What a place. The *gompa*, the scenery, everything. Amazing.'

Behind Barney, the golden sun was sinking. Staining the sky, as it went, with streaks of reddy-orange and yellow.

6

'Tell me about the competition.'

Mrs Coniston sighed, and sat down on the hall stool. 'I've started writing things down in the night. My doctor suggested it.' Next to her was a small oval table with a telephone base unit. The handset was missing. 'David calls it my worry book. Ironic thing is, I write about him in there too.'

'You left the phone on the sofa, Mrs Coniston.'

'Did I? Glasses on my head too, probably.' She patted her hair.

'The competition?'

'Sorry, the competition. A tourism initiative. Sponsored by Newcell? I think that's right. There's a letter in Calix's room.'

'Can I see it?'

'He has the attic.' She pointed to the stairs.

'While I'm up there, can you make a list of his friends and their contact details? I also need a recent photo and a toothbrush.' Rick started up the stairs, past a shelf of large hardback books.

'Thank you,' she called after him.

The attic smelt faintly – cat litter? He stood in the doorway of the huge room taking stock, like a lido swimmer dipping a toe. Every room he searched was different but few were surprising, and those that were kept their surprises well hidden. In false sockets or under floorboards or in furniture hollows. This one kept at least one of its surprises on show.

Suspended from the ceiling, like a model aeroplane, was an enormous bird of prey. Life-size, auburn and red feathering. Glassy eyes fixed on the doorway.

Rick took his time, trying to get a feel for the man who slept there. A double bed, a weights bench at its foot and a small table. Two desks, one with a pedestal underneath, and two chairs. A large bookcase, crammed with books and files. One wall covered in maps and paperwork.

He took some photos. On the shelf of the bedside table were four books. *Basic Taxidermy*, *How to Win Money at Texas Hold'em*, *King Rat*, *Being and Time*. Rick pulled out the hefty last book – Heidegger – and checked the envelope marking halfway. It was blank, and he put it back. He walked over to the desk with the pedestal. Locked. It took him five minutes to find the key on top of the doorframe. In the deep bottom drawer was a stack of files and paperwork. In the top drawers, a laptop, credit card receipts, and a slim notebook containing a column of coded names and numbers. They looked like drug deals. A reason to be missing? Not that Calix was missing. Just incommunicado, and probably intentionally.

On the second desk was an anglepoise lamp, and next to it a stand and clamp. Above it, a shelf of fauna – a blackbird, a smaller brown bird, and a squirrel. Rick switched on the lamp. At the back of the desk was a metal tray of implements, like a dentist's. Alongside, a needle and a spool of twine and a sharpening stone. A set of scalpels and two pairs of scissors, all stainless steel and spotlessly clean. Several more books, *Garden Birds & Animals* uppermost. A flutter of bookmarks. Underneath the desk was a large cardboard box; he pulled it out and opened the flaps. Inside was a black and white cat.

Rick pulled the box out further. The cat was standing, tail curled up and back across its body. Holes for eyes. He took a photo, closed the box and pushed it back. He switched off the lamp, and turned to the wall of paperwork.

Surrounding a large map of Nepal were newspaper articles, posters and printouts. He looked closer at the map. He had never seen so many contours and he ran his fingers across them, as if to feel the undulations. He liked maps, ever since a school geography teacher had brought in the Peters Projection.

To the right of the map were details of the expedition. Photos of Mera Peak, the itinerary and Calix's kit list, all ticked off. Rick crouched down. Under the map were newspaper articles on a campaign by Nepalese soldiers to improve their pensions. A photo with celebrities. 'Ghurkha champions hit back at Minister'. Several mentioned the role of the Ghurkhas on Mount William in the Falklands War.

In the garden, someone was trying hard to start a lawnmower.

More newspaper articles to the left of the map. 'Will Qatar's World Cup be built on a graveyard?' 'Increased death toll lays bare plight of World Cup workers'. '185 Nepalese killed last year – still no action'. He knew there'd been deaths, but had no idea of the scale. An official for FIFA, football's governing body, offered an urgent solution.

He returned to the letter from Newcell, Nepal's second largest mobile phone company, trying to become number one. He examined it again, then sealed it in an evidence bag.

Mrs Coniston walked in, and handed him a piece of paper. 'Calix's phone number, and the info you wanted. Contacting his friends won't take long as he only keeps up with a few.'

'Girlfriend?'

'I don't think so. Just Bird Bird.' She smiled thinly.

'Bird Bird?'

'A wild parrot. Flies to his window.'

'You said earlier, Calix is a dreamer?'

She sighed. 'Compared to Megan. Calix spends a lot of time up here. Very few friends, if any really. Good with his hands, and with animals.'

'Has he ever had a job?'

'A few shifts at the local pub.'

Mrs Coniston lingered in the doorway.

'Do you think he's okay, Inspector?'

The Nostradamus question.

Always asked.

Never answered.

Rick walked out to his car. He put Calix's laptop, notebook and other exhibits on the passenger seat and rummaged in his bag. As he drank from a bottle of water he checked his phone for messages. There were a clutch of work emails and a text from his sister.

Have you found someone yet? X.

At New Year, Becky had announced that she was getting married to Julian, a dentist. The date was set – Saturday 1 June – and she'd become obsessed with it. Last week it had been table decorations. This week, who was going to sit next to Dad.

He finished the water and pulled out the photo of Calix. He was striking a body-building pose. Short blond hair, a tattoo of an eagle on his biceps.

His phone beeped with another text. *Only six weeks!*

For Becky, or for him?

Rick pulled out of the drive and headed for South Manchester police station. As he drove away, he glanced through the window at the busty statue and the brigadier, mowing circles around her.

In the exhibits store, the lights were already on. A side panel of the photocopier hung down and Kate Saunders, the coroner's officer, was peering in. She wore tight jeans and a long black cardigan. Brown boots with buckles. Long red hair. He began to write in the exhibits book. Maybe he could take Kate to Becky's wedding.

'You're always here,' she said, glancing up.

'I'm doing a favour for Robbo. Missing person.'

'Favour?'

'A twenty-three-year-old called Calix who's trekking in Nepal, and hasn't phoned his parents for a couple of weeks.'

She looked up and scowled. 'Fallen into a crevasse?'

'More like his phone did. I've just been to see his parents. I think they were killing him.'

Her eyes flared. Horse-chestnut brown.

'Father's a soldier, old school, been away a lot, doesn't know his children. Worried about something, but, superficially at least, not Calix. Mother's paranoid since the death of their other child. I hadn't the heart to tell them, Calix is dealing weed.'

'You suspect the father?'

'Not really. I think Calix can't be bothered to phone. Statistically, if he is missing, then the father's the prime suspect. Only twenty per cent of male homicides are committed by a stranger.'

'Nepal seems odd.'

'If he is in Nepal.'

'Look on the bright side: you might go out there. I never go anywhere.'

'Do you need a hand?'

She shook her head and for a moment he studied her while she fiddled with the machine. She was attractive and funny, and also in her early thirties. He could ask her out without any more effort. She would understand that he worked a lot, and that he talked about death and dead bodies. She knew about his first set of nights as a DI. He closed his eyes, then opened them again. Exhibits book. Photocopier. Kate, looking at him.

'Sir, are you okay?'

He nodded.

She clicked the panel shut and stood up. 'I've got to go. Childminder.'

He'd forgotten she had a son. With a very long name. 'Richard?'

'Richard*son*.'

'Richardson. Like—'

'His father.'

Did she mean the boy's father was called Richard or they were both called Richardson? He didn't ask. Behind her, the photocopier whirred and powered down.

Rick went home. Thirty minutes, to his end-of-terrace stone cottage. On a good day he could see into the Peak District. Lyme Park was not far. He'd taken his parents there, and to Chatsworth. He thought about phoning them.

He phoned Robbo.

'Thoughts?'

'Four possibilities,' said Rick. 'One, Calix, is not missing – they just think he is. He's lost his phone or it's defunct.' He opened a drawer and pulled out some pasta. 'Two, he's been involved in an accident and is injured.' He stared out of the window above the sink. 'Three, he's ill or, four, something criminal.' The front fence needed replacing.

'If you had to pick one?'

The side fence, too. 'He's having a good time away from his parents, and forgot to call. But, one thing is bugging me.'

'I'm listening,' said his boss.

'The competition. Newcell are genuine, and the wording on the letter is okay. But the paper's too thick – as if someone's trying too hard. In the morning I'll go and see Nepal Adventures, the trekking company. Their HQ's local – Stockport.'

'Who do you need?'

'Three to take statements, plus a DS and Maggie on intel.'

Rick drained the pasta and tipped it into a bowl. He added pesto, but the parmesan was blue and lumpy and he put it in the bin. At the kitchen table, he forked in a mouthful and stared at the cloudy vase of bluebells. They were a good source of pollen and nectar for bees. He reached over to the shelf of books and pulled out *Hooper's*.

'How to find the queen'. He turned to the page, bent back the spine and balanced his phone on the left-hand page. Three methods.

After he'd eaten, he picked up the phone. He took a deep breath. It was best to get it over, then the evening was his. *Hooper's* flickered shut.

'Dad, it's me.'

'Who?'

'Me. Your son Rick.'

'Nick?'

If only it was a pun. 'Rick, Dad, *Rick*. Detective. I keep bees.'

'Bees?'

'Bees, bzzzz, bees. We looked at them together once, you wore a beekeeper's smock and a veil. Bzzzz.'

'Bzzzz, ha–ha, bzzzzzz.'

'Dad.'

'She burnt the toast. She always burns it.'

There was a pause, and muffled voices.

'Dad?'

'Rick, it's Mum. I didn't burn his toast, he didn't have toast. We had fish. It's not fair, Rick, he's not even sixty.'

'Mum—' Rick put his hand on the wall. It felt cold. His fingers slid down. The plaster was uneven.

'Rick, we need to talk. Not on the phone.'

He put the phone down. He felt hot. What was the point? Of anything? He should go and see them. Next weekend.

He washed up, and kept glancing at the fences.

The small lounge was cold, but he didn't light a fire. He drew the curtains Mum had made, and glanced at his birthday cards on the mantelpiece. Up since January, five of them. He wondered if other people counted. The room needed some art. Modern art, something to raise the spirits. It did have a plant, a banana tree, a present from Becky, and also two landscapes. Derbyshire quarries, bought on impulse.

He put on a coat and opened his briefcase. His dad had once found Rick using a briefcase for work as funny. Funny-odd, not funny-amusing. The distinction, let alone the comment, was long since beyond him. He pulled out some reading. 'Finding A Rapist: The Latest Analytical Techniques for Serious Sexual Offences'. Ten applications for the three trainee detective posts.

He switched on the TV and flicked through with the remote. He opted for radio – Classic FM – with the volume turned down. He thought about a beer, the drink he didn't have with Kate. What would he have worn? Said? He hadn't been on a date, one-on-one, for over two years.

Tomorrow was his next appointment.

He began to read. *Nilesh Khan. 7 years' service. 2 years in the Crime Squad. Personal Responsibility. Example one. I received information about a handler of stolen goods…*

7

Rick walked into the reception of Nepal Adventures. Posters of snowy mountains covered the walls, and a Moby album played from hidden speakers.

A middle-aged man in a wheelchair sat behind a table. He wore a green hat ringed with fishing hooks. He looked up.

'DCI Castle, South Manchester,' said Rick, showing his warrant card. 'I'd like to speak to whoever's in charge.'

'What about?' The receptionist's tone was abrupt.

It was the question everyone wanted to ask, but few people did. Asking was unusual, and unusual, like the competition, made Rick pause and consider.

'NA have a trekking expedition heading for Mount Mera in Nepal.'

'Yes, Amanda's leading it.' Avoiding eye contact, the man jabbed at a deskpad with a pen.

'Did you meet any of the clients?'

'One or two. Why?'

'Which ones?'

'Clients who live locally came in to hire kit. Sleeping bags and mountaineering boots.'

'Calix Coniston?'

'Yes,' said the man, slowly. He stopped doodling and looked up.

'What was he like?'

'Why do you want to know?'

'I'd like to talk to your boss first,' said Rick.

'He was a right pain in the arse, if you want the truth. Very demanding, wanting the newest kit, the cleanest sleeping bag.'

'Anything else?'

The man threw the pen on the desk, and moved back. 'I'll see if Russell's free.' He pushed into the central area, but turned back.

'He also wanted a list of who was going on the trip. A bloody list.'

'Did you give it to him?'

'No.'

'Why not?'

'It wasn't confirmed,' said the man, wheeling off.

Rick walked over to the Nepalese mountains and villages and colourful temples. Police questions made most people jittery, but the NA receptionist had seemed particularly uneasy.

He pulled out his phone and texted his sister. *Becks, do you think Dad's getting worse?*

She texted straight back. *They'd love a visit.*

The receptionist returned. 'Russ will see you now. He's the owner.' He pointed down the corridor.

'Thanks—?' Rick waited.

'Paul.'

Rick walked down the corridor stacked with tents and climbing equipment and into a large room.

The owner of NA stood up from behind a table. Six foot three, ruddy face and tidy beard, physique of a two-hundred-metre sprinter. On his slate-grey jacket was the company logo of an ice-axe and a pair of walking boots above a map of Nepal.

The mountaineer thrust out a hand. 'Russell Weatherbeater.' He wore a chunky yellow watch.

'Is that your real name?'

He grinned. 'I changed it by deed poll when I set the company up – I had the idea when a man tried to sell me double-glazing, and said his name was Bill Window. I don't know whether it helped us get established, but it still gets a laugh.'

Rick glanced across the table. Computer, desk diary, NA brochures, and a large glass jar. Screw-top, almost full of a colourless liquid in which floated five or six objects. Reminded him of sausage rolls. Looking up, he found faint amusement on the mountaineer's face.

'You've done Everest?'

'Five times. Hope I've got one more in me. Mountaineering is something that you get better at as you get older. 'Til you're as old as Bonington.'

'Explain.'

'You make better decisions. Young bloods get into trouble.'

Rick nodded. It was the same for policing. Racing around on Friday and Saturday nights was exciting but often self-defeating. Incidents made worse, or even started.

'How can I help?' said Weatherbeater, waving at a chair.

'The parents of Calix Coniston have reported him missing. He's in Nepal on your Mera trip.'

'Missing?' The mountaineer scrunched his thick eyebrows. 'Why do they think that?'

'He's supposed to keep in contact, but there's been nothing for two weeks. Since he left Kathmandu.'

'I spoke to Amanda about a week ago; she's leading our Mera trip. Here, I made a note of it in my diary,' he said, pointing with a finger. The next finger ended at the knuckle. 'The eleventh, a week ago exactly. Someone had twisted an ankle which was slowing them up, but otherwise everything was fine.'

'Calix?'

'No, a French bloke.'

'Why didn't you tell his parents?'

'I haven't spoken to them.'

'They phoned your office and were told to stop fussing.'

'That'll be Paul. Hang on a minute.' The mountaineer walked out.

Rick glanced around the room. There were more climbing photos and posters, and in a corner, a pull-up bar. On the back of the door hung a dartboard with three darts sticking out.

Weatherbeater returned. 'It was Paul – he's my office manager – who spoke to Mrs Coniston. He also gave me this.' The mountaineer passed Rick a photocopy of a cheque. 'Calix paid for the trip with a banker's draft which Paul thought was odd. So he took a copy.'

'Why didn't he tell me?'

'Paul can be a grumpy sod, and I don't want to make excuses, but—' The mountaineer glanced towards the door, and lowered his voice. 'He had both his legs amputated after a climbing accident.'

The glass jar on the table. Not sausage rolls.

'Yours is a crazy world, Mr—'

'Russell, please.' The mountaineer beamed. 'It's not for everyone, but we think having a taste is a good thing. That's why we don't want relatives phoning up to ask about an expedition's progress. Our view is that Calix, or whoever, will be back in the UK in a month's time having gotten away from it all. Away from social media, the internet, heating, relationships et cetera. Expeditions put stressful modern lives into perspective, and interruptions from home ruin that.'

Rick nodded. He thought that Calix was doing exactly the

right thing. Maybe *he* should go on an expedition. Last year he hadn't gone anywhere, and Robbo was moaning about the forty-seven days of annual leave that he'd accrued. No nice girlfriend to go with, he could hear his mother saying. He'd go and see them at the weekend. NA would be something to talk about with Dad.

'Can I take a brochure?'

'I'd take it as a compliment. Or should I be concerned about you investigating our small print?'

Rick let go a smile. He'd warmed to the mountaineer, and he didn't like many people he met. 'When will you talk to Amanda again?'

'Nothing pre-arranged. When she feels like it or if she's got a problem.'

'Can you phone her now?'

'Sure. Why not.' He picked up the desk phone, and pressed a key.

Rick waited, feeling his heart-rate quicken. One phone call could puncture the missing enquiry, or inflate it to headline news.

'Straight to voicemail.' Russell tried again, then clicked the handset back onto the base. 'Same. I'll keep trying, and let you know as soon as I speak to her.'

Rick nodded. He stood up, his eyes drawn back to the glass jar.

'Have a closer look.'

He picked up the jar – filled, he guessed, with a preserving liquid. Floating around inside were three or four toes and a couple of fingers. He turned the jar on its side, and the digits swam sideways. Like a macabre paperweight.

'Frostbite?'

Russell nodded. 'If I lose too many more I won't be able to hold my ice-axes properly. Or count to ten.'

Rick put the jar back down on the table and watched the contents settle. 'Calix Coniston won a competition, and the prize was a place on your Mera expedition.'

'First I've heard of it.'

'Really?'

'You think I'm lying?'

'Sorry, turn of phrase.' The truth was he didn't think so, but he couldn't be certain. 'But I will need details of everyone on the expedition with Calix, clients and staff, and everyone who works here.'

'Including me?'

'Including you.'

8

The expedition stopped on the football field near Kathara. Barefooted children kicking a football in the goalmouth stopped, and stared. Behind them a strew of twenty houses. Animated voices and the smell of woodsmoke drifted down.

While the porters put up the tents, the clients slumped on their rucksacks. Patrick wandered off to play footie. The rest of them sat in two groups. Calix with the twins and Vicky, and the others, whom the four of them called the Grown-Ups. The only client missing was Jean-Paul; shadowed by Amanda, he was some way behind on the trail.

Calix passed round his packet of sweets left over from lunch. He felt on edge. No one said much. Spencer moaned he wasn't sleeping, and dozed. Barney and Vicky whispered like teenagers. They were.

Movement caught his eye. He picked up his binoculars. On the far side of the field a house was being extended, and two carpenters wearing bobble-hats were hard at work. Cutting a tree trunk lengthways with a two-man saw. One carpenter knelt under the trunk, and the other man balanced on top, inching back as the work progressed. Next to them stood a stack of planks.

Looking as if she'd only recently got up, Amanda arrived with a heavily perspiring Jean-Paul. The Frenchman shucked off his pack and sat down. He coughed, lit a cigarette, and coughed again.

'*Merde!*'

'Right, listen in everybody,' said Amanda, standing on her rucksack. 'We're now at 2,800 metres so you should expect an altitude headache. Keep drinking, and it will get better. And – dun, dun, dun.' She imitated a drumroll. 'It's our first night in tents.' She glanced at Calix.

He'd been waiting for it, and stared back.

'Tent pairings. I've had a request.'

The Grown-Ups made jokes about swinging and spinning the bottle with car keys. Jason and Jean-Paul kept coughing, and they all drank water like rehydrating camels.

'Okay, here we go. Debbie and Jason. Kalin and Patrick. Jean-Paul and Mike. Ellen and Vicky. Barney and Spencer. Calix.' She paused and surveyed the glowing faces. 'Think yourself lucky – you don't have to put up with his snoring.'

He'd told her to say that. He tipped up the packet of sweets and ate the rest in a sugary rush.

Barney cleared his throat. 'Amanda, Spencer's not sleeping because of all the coughing. Okay to move our tent a bit further away?'

'Fine. Food will be in the dining tent at seven.'

Everyone stood and grabbed up their rucksacks. They'd not stretched off, and they moved like old people. Jean-Paul and Jason were still coughing, the others wise-cracking. It was a holiday – the trip of a lifetime.

'Can I ask a favour, Calix?' whispered Barney.

Calix knew what it would be. He could make the twin sweat, or ask for a sweetener, but he already had enough to think about.

'Okay if Spencer jumps in with you tonight? So me and Vic, you know, so she can help sharpen my ice-axe.'

Calix nodded, slowly, but didn't smile. He stared across the football pitch. The carpenters were still sawing the same plank. Beyond them the trail disappeared into waves of dark rhododendron. It covered the hillside for miles. Enough to conceal an army.

The rip of the tent zip woke Calix up. Opening his eyes, he was blinded by two head-torched Nepalese men staring in.

One held a pistol.

The other a cardboard sign: 'Quite'.

Calix's heart thundered like a waterfall and his ears rang. For a few seconds he heard nothing.

The second man crawled in with a roll of gaffa tape.

'Don't fight him, Spencer.' Calix whispered the words to help himself breathe, wake up and get a grip on himself. He needn't have worried about Spencer's reaction. He was a rabbit caught in headlights.

The guard gagged them both, and withdrew. A second strip of cardboard ordered 'Colect You Clothes'. The pistol pointed and waved, as if it had a mind of its own. Spencer pissed himself and broke his glasses. They dressed and Calix stuffed their rucksacks. They put their boots on inside the tent, Amanda's great taboo. Outside, they were hooded with balaclavas, face-holes swivelled to the back. Their hands were put in plasticuffs.

'Walk,' whispered a guard, shoving Calix in the back. His breath smelt of garlic and nicotine, and the command sounded more like *whelk* than *walk*. But Calix got the point. He was led across the football pitch. Then, ten minutes of stumbling along a path and five minutes of waiting. He hoped Spencer was okay.

His hood was removed.

The moon had risen, and the sky glimmered with stars. He saw he was in a line with Spencer, Barney and Vicky. They were also gagged and cuffed. Vicky was shaking with shock, Spencer sniffing. Barney stood in front of them. He was tall and muscular, but looked as if he wanted someone standing in front of him. Calix felt for them. There'd be worse to come.

For hours they stumbled along in the dark, keeping to the trail, heading for Mera. The guards kept their torches off, and the bone-coloured moon was only a sliver. Spencer walked more and more slowly, stopping repeatedly to press his inhaler to his lips. Barney strapped Spencer's pack to his and walked behind his brother. At the front Vicky was quiet. Calix stayed at the back.

Finally, they turned off the main trail, and a few minutes later reached an abandoned hut. An oil lamp was lit and hung from the ceiling. Their gags and cuffs were removed.

'*Khaltis*,' said a guard.

Calix recognised the word, one of the few he knew. He emptied his pockets, and signalled the others to do the same. Vicky and the twins followed his lead and didn't protest. The four of them were made to sit against the back wall. Their bags were searched. Cameras, phones and maps were taken. Another man entered.

Calix watched Barney's face contort with recognition.

The man was Nepalese, small and slim, with a neat goatee beard. He was dressed like the trekkers in decent outdoor clothing and expensive hiking boots. The guards called him Hant.

'Walk six, seven days,' said Hant. 'No try escape.'

Calix sensed Barney twitching. He felt for the stronger twin, genetically and culturally desperate to protect his brother and a woman. Maybe even his new friend Calix.

'Easy,' whispered Calix. 'Not now.'

Hant glared at him.

'If you sensible,' said Hant, pronouncing the word with an *a*, 'and other sensible, you four okay.'

'What do you want?' said Barney. He sounded loud and aggressive.

A guard held up the 'Quite' sign. The other men snickered, but Hant's face didn't flicker.

Calix grabbed Barney's shirt and held him down. His knuckles pressed the twin's flesh, which was hot and pulsing. He kept him down until Hant walked out, and like a dying fire Barney cooled and settled.

The lamp was turned down and the four of them dozed against their rucksacks.

Some time later, Calix woke up. His neck was stiff and he rocked it from side to side. He flexed his hands, and realised Barney was watching him.

'Did you recognise him – Hant?' whispered Barney.

Calix shook his head.

'It was him at the station.'

'Ssh.' Calix nodded at the guards by the door.

A guard mooched over. Without warning, and like a rugby goalkicker, he backlifted and followed through, hoofing Barney in the thigh. He wore desert-coloured boots. Barney's whole body lurched sideways, and he yelled in pain and surprise. When Calix began to stand he was pushed back down. He started to speak, and the guard who'd kicked Barney toe-poked his boots. Calix fell silent and still. A guard with a lazy eye tore the 'Quite' sign into small pieces, another grabbed Barney by the hair, pulled his head back and forced open his mouth. They stuffed in the cardboard pieces one by one, and made him chew and swallow. Barney tried not to cry.

Calix didn't go back to sleep. He watched the shadows become mauve-edged and then mauve and then dark blue. Outside, a bird stuttered and went quiet. The guard re-laced his sandy boots, and brushed mud from the toes. The other guards rose and readied. Calix's stomach heaved – you didn't have to be a savant to know it was only just beginning.

9

At the police station, Rick went to find Maggie, the new analyst in the intelligence unit. Already, she'd been there three months. He found her in a corner of the CID office. She was multi-tasking, tapping on a computer and talking on the phone. Crimping her brown bob was a headset. On the back of her chair hung a wicker bag with a book and a flask poking out. Around her, half a dozen detectives worked at their desks. Voices ebbed and flowed. Rick waited.

She finished the call and turned to face him. She wore a cream blouse and black trousers which hung tidily from the knee. She took her headset off and smiled.

'Yes, sir?'

'What're you reading?' He nodded at her bag.

'Three things, actually. A historical by Sarah Dunant. A biography of Agatha Christie, and a thriller.'

'I've been reading the same book for months.'

'Books take me away.' She twirled the ends of her hair.

He nodded. Sometimes his rank felt like a motte and bailey. He handed her the list of names to be checked against the police databases and briefed her on the meeting with the owner of Nepal Adventures.

She scanned the list. 'You don't really think Weatherbeater and his trek leader are in conspiracy?'

'I think Calix Coniston can't be bothered to phone his parents.'

Maggie smiled again. She had a smile that made you lose your thread. A slight gap between her front teeth. Around her neck was a silver choker.

Rick thought of Becky's wedding. Did Maggie go on dates? According to his last interviewing course, non-verbals accounted for sixty to ninety per cent of human interaction. He hoped it was wrong.

'Did you get anywhere with the Newcell letter?'

'I phoned their marketing department in Nepal. A man called Tarak thought he'd heard of the competition, and directed me to their special ops unit in Frankfurt.'

'And Frankfurt?' asked Rick.

'All in a meeting.'

'What about Calix's phone number and computer?'

'Telecoms said tomorrow. However, I've made a start on the notebook.' She handed him a sheet of paper. 'Some pages have been ripped out and the ones left are coded. The pages titled Fantasy Football look like drug deals. At the back are scribbled notes. I recognised Super Fast Pizzas, and I'll work on the others.'

Rick nodded, taking the sheet.

'One result, a negative. No usage on the bank cards since Calix left the UK.'

'Maybe he hasn't been robbed. Then again, maybe he has. Can you also make enquiries into this?' He gave her the photocopy of Calix's cheque. 'NA's office manager, Paul Parry, is responsible for their accounts. He thought the cheque was unusual, and photocopied it before paying it in. It's a banker's draft made out to NA for £2,790.'

Rick found himself staring at the carbon fibre wheels on her wheelchair. It was the second he'd seen that day. 'Maggie, Paul Parry at Nepal Adventures.' Maggie was always direct so he would be too.

'Yes?'

'He's in a wheelchair. Perhaps—'

'Perhaps what? That because I'm in a wheelchair I only want to socialise with other wheelchairs? That while this Paul Parry and I are making out in the house, our wheelchairs can share a cigarette in the garden?'

The office went quiet, and Rick felt the stares of the junior detectives.

'Maggie, I didn't mean—'

'Sir, I've got work to do.' She put her headset back on and spun around to face her computer.

He walked out. Behind him, the office hubbub restarted.

He chose the long way back to his office, down three flights of stairs to the ground floor, and back up the rear stairs. His usual policy was to avoid small-talk, and he wished he'd kept to it. At the gym he stopped and peered in through the glass panels. He could hear music and the clunk of weights. A public order unit were working hard and he felt like joining them.

He loosened his tie and unfolded the sheet of paper Maggie had given him. He was a good detective, always assessed the facts, considered pros and cons and made balanced decisions. But his social interaction was more haphazard.

Exhibit RC/1 – Calix Coniston's notebook
999
SFP   *0161 700 3333*
13?
Catra, 10th?

PP	*07973 581 048*
R.S.	*07831 871 116*
Crick Lane Farm	
Joe's bday ***	
NWRMG	*01457 366 129*
R	*07933 676 656*
A	*07816 223 254*
+3000	

Mergers & Acquisitions
Nov – sq.
Dec – b.b.
Jan – ct.
Feb –

PP – Paul Parry? A – Amanda? Who was Catra? Joe? Where was Crick Lane Farm? What were Mergers & Acquisitions?

Robbo was where he always was, behind his desk. The superintendent was putting on weight, his face losing its definition, the shirt tight across his chest. He closed the file of papers in front of him. 'Confidential'.

'Have you found David's son yet?'

Rick took a deep breath.

'Did you run here?'

'No.'

'There's a perfectly good lift.'

Which his boss should avoid. 'I've spoken to the owner of Nepal Adventures, Russell Weatherbeater. He last spoke to Amanda, the Mera expedition leader, on the eleventh, and everything was fine. That could mean Calix's only been missing for a week.'

'Could?'

'It's only Amanda's word that Calix was okay when Weatherbeater spoke to her, and only his word the call took place. Maggie's doing background checks.'

'Anything else?'

'Maybe. Calix's trip was paid for with a banker's draft, which is odd.'

'One more thing, Rick. We've had a Senior Management Team meeting, and I'm afraid you're not going to like what's been decided.'

On the desk, the phone buzzed.

Robbo picked it up.

Rick went to the window and looked into the backyard. The public order serial was climbing into a van. Occasionally he envied their simple shifts: physical training, refs, and a couple of call-outs to something adrenalin-pumping.

Robbo put the phone down.

'That was Superintendent Gaffney from the Met – Richmond Borough. Two brothers, twins, have been reported missing by their parents. They're on the same expedition as Calix Coniston.'

'Story?'

'You can ask him yourself.' He wrote a phone number, and pushed it across the desk.

'People watch too much TV.'

'Rick.'

At the door he turned to face his boss. Drink would explain the recent chubbiness, but he hadn't smelt anything. No telltale nose.

'Gaffney also said that one of the twins won a competition.'

Rick felt his pulse surge.

On his way home, Rick drove into the vast car park of the

shopping mall. Well lit, but almost deserted. He parked and walked across to the busy inner ring-road that ran alongside. Headlights lit him up as he waited to cross. He felt cold and put his hands in his pockets. For the first appointment he'd needed his A-Z. Up Kestrel Street, second right and into Opal Street.

At Magenta House he pressed the intercom. 'Rick Castle.'

The door buzzed open. He entered the old-fashioned lift – a cage on pulleys – and held the doors for a woman in a red trouser suit. He wondered why she was there. She looked normal.

Room 331.

Emma opened the door. 'Come in, Rick. How're you?'

They sat down. Rick on the couch, Emma on a chair near her desk, and a low table between them. Behind Emma was a shelf with a few books and files and a spider plant that needed dealing with. There was no fish-tank, no posters, nothing to distract him or anyone else. There must be others like him.

'I thought we'd continue from where we left off,' said Emma.

On the table was a box of man-size tissues, one sticking out. A white flag of surrender. He nodded.

10

In Barnes the tide was low and the muddy banks on either side of the kale-green Thames were exposed. Seagulls hopped about on the tarry sludge and wheeled around the dishwater sky.

Rick knocked on the door of the river-front house. As he waited, the seagulls' harsh squawks took him to other places and other times. The seaside, when he was young, Becky wandering off and a stranger bringing her back, Dad helping him catch crabs.

The door was opened by a short greying man with bare feet. Behind him rose a staircase.

'DCI Castle, sir.' Rick showed his warrant card.

'Terry Williams. Louisa's upstairs.' He turned, and padded up. 'Shoes off, if you don't mind,' he said over his shoulder.

Rick unlaced his shoes, slipped them off, and followed.

The first floor was open-plan. Mrs Williams sat in the lounge area, but stood as he entered. The room smelt of perfume, and the flowers on the dresser. Large windows looked over the river.

'Great view,' said Rick.

'It's the perfect place to watch the Boat Race,' said Mrs

Williams. She looked ten years younger than her husband. She wore a light-coloured dress and red suede shoes.

'Have you got any news?' Her tone was pained.

Rick shook his head.

While Mrs Williams made coffee, her husband talked about his job. He was a FIFA executive. He worked from home two days a week. He had married his secretary. He asked Rick if he was looking forward to the World Cup.

Of course he was.

Mrs Williams returned with coffee and sticks of shortbread arranged on a silver tray. She served, and sat alongside Terry.

'One of your sons won a competition?'

'Barney,' said Mrs Williams. 'Oldest by nine minutes.'

'And a lot heavier,' said Terry.

'In December,' continued Mrs Williams, 'Barney filled in a questionnaire at our local station. Barnes Bridge. A few weeks later, a letter arrived from Newcell stating he'd won a competition to go to Nepal. We decided to pay for Spencer to go, too. Two weeks ago they flew out there. We got a text from Kathmandu on the fourth, but after that nothing. The trekking company Nepal Adventures haven't exactly been helpful. The boys are only eighteen. We expected lots of WhatsApps – at least.'

Rick's phone beeped.

'Do check it,' said Mrs Williams. 'It might be important.'

Rick checked. Being allowed an intrusive phone was a perk of the job. It was a message from Kate to say her cot death meeting at the hospital had been delayed. He tucked the phone away. All the way to Barnes for a row in the car with Kate, and a conversation with stressed parents he could have delegated. But Robbo had insisted Rick come – *he's a vice president of FIFA* – and so Rick had come.

He shook his head.

'Sorry.'

'The thing is,' said Terry, 'no one else we know completed the questionnaire. I've also knocked the road. No one. Don't you think that's odd?'

'Maybe. Have you got a copy of the questionnaire?'

Mrs Williams shook her head. 'I did ask Barney, but he was pretty vague. Aren't they all at that age.' Next to her, Terry winced.

'Anything else?'

'No problem doing a press conference,' said Terry. 'Just say the word.'

Rick stood, his feet feeling the cold wooden floor.

The Williams's front door shut behind him with a hefty clunk. A second set of wealthy parents. Blackmail – for money, or something else – was a possible motive.

He walked out of the tiny front garden, across the road, and onto the pavement that ran alongside the silent churning river. It would help him think, like it always had. He headed towards Barnes Bridge, planning to cross the river, walk to the next bridge, re-cross and walk back. The symmetry appealed. He texted Kate to suggest she meet him, then jotted down questions for Russell about the Nepalese phone system.

A rowing scull slid past. At Nottingham, where he'd been a student, the river had been a place to run alongside, a place to escape the social and academic bombardment. Now, rivers were more complex.

Halfway across the bridge, he stopped and stared into the restless black-green water. An acidic smell made his eyes smart.

On the second night, seven bodies. Five joy-riders and two at the bus stop. Vauxhall Astra pulled from the Irwell. The girl in the mid-

dle of the back seat. Pearl. Windscreen glass in her mouth and up her nose. In her eyes.

Static in his head.

Made himself keep walking.

A rowing crew emerged from a boathouse. They carried the boat above their heads, arms extended, the boat upside down. At the river's edge the eight slapped the boat onto the water. His phone beeped with another message from Kate. *Meeting over.*

He walked on. It had seemed a good idea to drive down with Kate. A chance to get to know her without dressing up. Silences allowed. But she'd wanted to smoke in the car.

He spotted her.

A hundred metres away, hands in the pockets of her long coat, walking towards him. He waved, and she waved back. He hoped they could forget the journey.

On Hammersmith Bridge, the two of them stopped and leant against the rail. Two swans landed on the water, both marked with red tags. Kate tucked her arm into his. Rick glanced down at her boots. He wanted to say something, quote somebody.

'How about fish 'n' chips?' said Kate. 'I'm starving.'

It was his meal in Room 101, but he reminded himself of Becky and her wedding. 'Okay, but you can't eat it in my car.'

'Seriously?'

'It'd stink for weeks.'

'Oh, for God's sake. It's a metal box to get from A to B, not the Hadron Collider.'

On the journey back to Manchester, Rick pulled into a service station. The two of them had hardly said a word. Kate went off for a cigarette, and Rick walked around the car park to stretch his legs. The driver of a van and a woman in a fur coat were arguing loudly about a dent in her cabriolet. He sat on a bench checking it didn't escalate, and phoned Maggie for an update.

She'd spoken to the emergency contacts for the other clients on the expedition, but no one knew anything about a competition. The lab hadn't started on Calix's computer because of pressure from North West Regional. He asked about the checks on the NA staff.

'Weatherbeater has cautions for possession of cannabis, but Amanda Whittle and the part-timers are all clean except for Paul Parry. He's got one for deception, and served eighteen months.'

'MO?'

'Before NA he used to run Treks International, and before that Summits International, Trekking Dreams and Himalayan Summits. Each one offered a no-frills service: no shopfront in the UK, everything organised online. Book your own flights and meet the guide and other clients at the destination. Over a hundred people booked and flew out to meet their guide.'

'Let me guess: there was no guide and no operation. Parry just took the money, disappeared, and a few months later started over.' Rick watched the woman in the fur coat write down the registration number of the van.

'Right. His sentence was mitigated in light of his injury and PTSD.'

Rick wondered if Maggie agreed with the court's leniency. 'I'm surprised Weatherbeater hired him. Then again, he might not even know. I'll find out. In the meantime, pull Parry's bank accounts and let's see if he's back at it.'

'Anything else?'

'Would you eat fish 'n' chips in your car?'

'Yes. Why?'

'Tell you when I see you.'

The van wheel-spun away and the woman in the fur shouted after it.

Rick phoned Becky and told her what had happened with Kate. Nothing. It was the same old story.

'Work, work, work,' said Becky.

'I've got my bees.'

'You make time for them.'

Did she never listen? Beekeeping only required a couple of hours a month – twice that in the summer, nothing in the winter – and was a hobby even a DCI could manage.

Kate appeared. She sat down, heavy with smoke, and passed him a KitKat. Maybe, Rick thought, all was not lost.

They started driving again, and talking.

A telecoms van cut in front of their car, and Rick braked hard. He made a mental note of the registration. Another habit from his uniform days.

Manchester 43 miles. Under an hour. He switched on the headlights.

Weatherbeater phoned and Kate put him on speaker. She had long, graceful fingers. He glanced across at her, then back at the road ahead and waded in.

'Russell, did you know that Paul has a conviction for deception? Not just any deception, but conning trekkers and climbers.'

A pause.

'Yes.'

Another pause.

'I was in the rescue team when he lost his legs. He had some dark years and I gave him a chance.' The mountaineer's voice filled the car.

'I've seen him on TV,' whispered Kate.

'Do you trust him?' Rick asked Russell.

'I don't think he'd let me down, and I have a good accountant.'

Rick turned onto the M60. Stockport's area car overtook them at high speed, and he waited until its sirens had faded.

'Russell, did you also know that two more people on your Mera expedition have been reported missing?'

'No, I didn't. But the reason I'm calling you is Amanda has just phoned. Four of her clients have gone AWOL.'

'Four?'

'Calix Coniston, the one you asked about. Spencer and Barney Williams who are twins, and an Australian woman, Vicky Brant. They took most of their stuff.'

'When?'

'Three days ago.'

'Why the hell didn't Amanda tell you sooner?'

'She was embarrassed. Nothing like that's happened to her before, and she was hoping they would come back. To be fair to her, Rick, I've been running NA for fifteen years and nothing like this has happened to me either.'

'Did she give any more details?'

'They left a note, stating they weren't enjoying the forced march – their words – and had decided to go trekking by themselves. It was signed by Calix.'

After dropping Kate at the police station, Rick drove to Chesterfield, famous for its church with a crooked spire. The seventy-minute drive through the Peak District was dark, but beautiful under a starry, moonlit sky. Farm buildings and trees marked the horizon. Red-eyed dozy sheep lined many of the drystone walls. His parents lived on the far side, between the town and the motorway. Their drive and the large garden were steep, and impracticable. They hadn't always been.

Rick let himself in, and inhaled the familiar smell of wet boots and stored potatoes in the utility room. His parents were in the lounge with the TV on low. A small fire hissed in the grate. The thin silver-birch logs were damp and unseasoned. His mother sat on the sofa, a rug over her legs, a magazine on her lap. She got up.

'Rick.' She hugged him, and he pecked her on the cheek. She looked tired, felt cold. She turned off the TV.

'Hello, Dad.'

His dad sat in the armchair, the usual one, but it was covered in a dustsheet. There were tea-towels and cloths on the floor beside his chair. His shirt was stained. He still had a full head of dark brown hair.

'He's got so clumsy.' His mum sat down. She stood up again. 'Sorry, Rick, what can I get you? Coffee, something stronger? Thanks for coming.'

'It's alright, Mum, I'll get it. In a bit.' He went over to his dad. 'Dad.' He wanted to hug him but he stuck out a hand. His dad was a shaker not a hugger.

His dad looked at Rick's hand but did not move. 'Do I know you?'

That again. 'Rick, your son, Rick. Bees, bzzzzz. Policeman in Manchester. I lock up bad men.' Look for missing ones.

His dad turned to his mum. 'Do I know him?'

'He's forgetting my name now.' The voice was a stranger's: hesitant, fragile.

The two of them moved to the kitchen. Rick made a coffee and his mum poured small glasses of her sloe gin. They sat on kitchen chairs.

'How're you?'

'I'm fine. Fine. Really.'

Rick held her hands, which were calloused and scarred from the garden.

'I have to watch him all the time, and I can't sleep properly because he's started wandering in the night.' She closed her eyes.

Rick looked past her, across the window-sill with her jars of dried herbs from the garden, all proudly labelled, through the unshrouded window, and into the speckled sky. A dinner-plate moon.

Later, he sat in the car watching his breath fog the windscreen. He didn't have any answers. His mum was exhausted – she needed help and a break. He'd speak to Becky.

He drove home, back across the Peak. Past the red-eyed ewes and the cold stern walls. He wished he'd played golf with him. Just once or twice.

11

A kilometre beyond the small village of Dumghat, Calix sat down alongside Barney on a stone bench. Built at hip height so porters could rest without having to remove their loads, they were as common in Nepal as bus stops in Manchester.

He slipped his rucksack off, knowing it would be a while before Spencer and Vicky's group caught up. Two porters sat at the other end of the bench. Their excited murmurs and cigarette smoke drifted over.

Sweat soaked his clothes. He drank deeply from a water bottle and watched the three guards take up their usual positions. One scouted ahead, one stood close, one further away. Their tail was protected by the second group. Contact between the groups was made by mobile phone. The wonders of modern technology.

'Spence didn't even want to come,' said Barney, kneading his thigh with his thumbs. 'And I wish I hadn't asked Vic to share my tent.'

Calix rubbed the red circular grooves on his wrists, still not believing what had happened. He said nothing, but he too felt guilty.

He hobbled over to the signpost. Already, he was stiffening

up. It was a signpost for tourists: New York 7,500 miles, London 5,000 miles. No mention of Manchester. Local places were at the bottom, along with time estimates going downhill. Jiri, the trailhead, was a week back, but had taken almost twice that. Mera, a week ahead.

'Calix!' whispered Barney. 'A group of tourists just hit the skyline. Coming down, Mera direction.'

'Don't whisper,' said Calix, his heart-rate spiking. 'Look and sound normal. The guards can't understand us.' Slowly, he put on his sunglasses.

Barney nodded. 'There's four of them, no sign of any porters.'

Calix looked up the trail. A succession of enormous U-shaped valleys. Up a huge hill, and down the other side, up another huge hill and down again, the hills progressively higher. On the furthest hilltop, a corrugated iron roof glinted in the sun, and nearby, four people were descending. Rucksacks with rollmats. Westerners. Help.

'Got them.'

'What shall we do?'

'We wait. Pretend we haven't seen them. They'll soon disappear into the valley. Then they'll only be visible again on the next hilltop. Then on the one nearest us. We wait and we hope.'

'How far away do you think they are?'

'Well over an hour. Ninety minutes.' His heart pumped faster. It was a long time to remain nervous.

'And when they're close?'

Calix was silent for a moment.

'I'll distract the guards, and you make a run for it. Shouting and screaming.'

Calix forced himself to act normal. He pushed against the signpost, stretching his calves. He stared at the far hill until the four trekkers were out of sight. He looked across the terraced fields. Every shade of green and brown.

'Twenty minutes,' said Barney, looking at his expensive altimeter watch.

'What about your brother? And Vicky? We don't want to put them in danger.'

Barney frowned. 'We're trying to save all four of us. Might be our only chance.'

Calix looked back the way they'd come, trying to spot Vicky and Spencer's group. Usually, they were about an hour back. He couldn't see them.

'They're on the next hilltop,' said Barney, his voice twisting with emotion.

Calix jerked his head round. The four trekkers were larger – closer. Two men and two women, standing at a viewpoint. If Calix waved they could see him. He observed the three guards in turn. The last was staring up the trail, and shouted in rapid Nepali. The message was clear: the guard had spotted the four trekkers. A second guard made a phone call.

'We could wave,' whispered Barney. 'Shout.'

Calix shook his head. 'They'll think we're waving to say hello. Nothing more than that.'

The guards herded them back towards Dumghat. In the fields, scattered villagers worked bent over, oblivious. At the first house, the two of them were walked around to the back. Then through a field to a small shack. The *chirpi*.

Their hands were secured behind their backs in plasticuffs, and strips of gaffa tape put across their mouths. Barney was shoved through the door. Then Calix. A guard followed, and the door shut.

The *chirpi* was small and gloomy, and it stank. Worse than overflowing storm drains, worse than the Stockport sewage works. Silent flies flickered all round.

The guard took out his pistol, and motioned them to sit on the floor.

They sat.

The building was three metres square with wicker walls and a corrugated iron roof. A gap between roof and walls let light enter, and, in theory only, the smell leave. A basket of leaves sat in the corner. The middle of the floor was covered by boards with a letterbox-shaped opening. Squat, shit, wipe with leaves. A basic composting toilet.

The guard yanked up the boards so the opening was ten times larger. It revealed a mound of sludge like an anthill. He jabbed the mound with a stick. Flies rose, and the smell arrested the air. Calix and Barney gagged, but the guard seemed unaffected. He pointed at the two of them, and pretended to shout, then pointed into the hole.

Calix nodded.

Barney nodded.

Threat conveyed, the guard squatted on the far side of the hole.

Calix inspected the shack more closely. The rear wall of wicker was coming away from the corner post. A shoulder-barge and he'd be out. He observed their captor. Cheap boots, jeans, dirty woollen jumper. Pistol tucked into his trousers. Tufty hair like in a comic book, and a smooth, pale brown face. No sense of smell. A lazy eye roamed, but there was no doubt Calix was being observed back.

The guard stood and looked through a spyhole in the door.

Barney nudged Calix, and nodded.

Calix nodded back. They needed to develop a sign language, and quickly. He glanced up at the guard. Still staring out.

Calix nodded at the insecure rear wall, and Barney winked in conspiracy.

The guard sat back down. Took out his phone, and started twiddling. The glow of the screen lit his childish face.

Calix swiftly worked a plan. The most important thing was to time an attempted break-out to coincide with when the four trekkers walked past. He couldn't see a watch, so he'd have to estimate. Ninety minutes initially. About half had elapsed. So, count forty-five minutes, and make a run for it. He started counting. One thousand, two thousand, three thousand.

He counted a minute. Five minutes. The guard kept playing on his phone. Calix felt Barney getting restless, and he wondered if the twin was counting too. He worried the trekkers might stop for a rest. He was bound to underestimate, so to compensate he decided to count sixty minutes.

The guard tapped with both sets of fingers. Rainbows of light flickered across his face.

Calix lost count, but reckoned he'd reached thirty. Thirty to go. He kept counting, his pounding heart unrelenting. He shook his head to unsettle the flies. The smell not a tad muted.

Next to him Barney was increasingly fidgety. Like a child who needed a pee. Ironic. Calix's misplaced humour, the result of the pressure he was feeling. And building.

Twenty to go.

Barney nudged him, and nodded furiously.

Calix got it. The twin's question was, *now?*

Calix shook his head.

The guard stopped playing on his phone, and looked at his watch. He pocketed the phone, and stood, hand on pistol butt. Put his eye to the spyhole.

Barney elbowed Calix, and nodded like a wound-up toy.

Calix shook his head. Too early, and it would all be for nothing. He tapped his leg, slowly, trying to show Barney he was counting.

Ten minutes.

Barney nodded, his face pained. Calix shook his head.

Five minutes.

A shout from outside. Their tufty-haired guard booted the door open, then bent down and ripped away their strips of gaffa tape.

It stung Calix like nettles, hurt like a slap.

But for Barney, growing a beard, it would have hurt far more. The twin screamed, then shouted.

'Fu-uck! We waited too long. Fuck!'

Calix barged out through the back wall of the *chirpi*, out of the gloom and free from the smell. He'd over-estimated the time. The sheet-white sunlight bore down like a hammer.

12

Rick slotted in his pass at the back gate. The barrier started to rise, hesitated, and continued. He looked up at the police station. A PFI monstrosity, all red brick and lavender-blue steel.

Robbo's tinted-glass Range Rover pulled up, followed him to the marked bays, and parked alongside. Rick got out, and Robbo's window buzzed down.

'You found him yet?' The over-ripe smell of a fast food breakfast wafted from the dashboard. It reminded Rick of a farmyard, and made him faintly nauseous.

'He left a note. At least, according to Amanda the trek leader, four trekkers exited the expedition and left a note. Written by Calix. *Allegedly* written by Calix.'

Robbo picked up a greaseproof wrapper and unveiled the edge of a burger. He took a bite.

'If it's genuine, then it's odd behaviour from all four. But if it's a forgery, we know we have a case, and I'll need to get out to Nepal. I've asked Amanda to email a copy of the note, and I'll get the handwriting analysed.'

Robbo nodded, and took another bite.

'Seems very unlikely the four trekkers simply took off. So, if they didn't leave of their own free will, the alternative is they've been taken. The big question is, why?'

Robbo put the burger down, and dabbed ketchup from his lips. 'We had an SMT meeting.' He picked up a takeaway coffee, and took a sip. 'We're reshuffling the DCIs.'

'There's only me and Jack. And he doesn't want CID. He prefers the squads, intel, and informants.'

'We're getting a flyer – Chief Inspector Bransby – who needs CID experience.'

'He's not a detective?'

'He'll be made acting.'

A wad of reconstituted meat fell out of the half-eaten burger and slipped down the dashboard, leaving a greasy trail like a slug.

In his office Rick hung his coat on the door. Not yet seven, but through the glass wall he could see three detectives grouped around the night log. He turned on the kettle and dropped bread in the toaster. His door was open, and he could hear discussion of the overnight jobs. Above the toaster was a framed photo of his passing-out parade. Rick in full uniform – tunic, helmet, white gloves – and his parents all dressed up. So quick with Dad: less than a year since he'd stayed with his parents on the north Devon coast. The three of them had walked the coastal paths, eaten picnics, and in the evenings played Scrabble. Looking back, maybe Dad had taken ages to come up with a word. But hadn't he always?

The toast popped and he spread it with honey. Last year had been good: he'd taken fifteen kilos and still left twenty to sustain the bees through the winter.

At his desk he read the night log and started on his emails. A light knock on the door made him look up.

'I can smell honey,' said Maggie. She wheeled up to his desk. 'It looks different – lumpy.'

'It's honeycomb. Try some.' He pushed the plate towards her. 'I haven't got an extractor, so I chop the frames into small blocks.'

She took a bite, catching crumbs in her hand. 'Wow!'

'Beekeepers' secret.'

'I've brought you the report.' She paused, still chewing. 'Calix's phone number.'

'Anything?'

'Focus on N1, a new friend from October. If you've got any questions you know where I am.' She moved to the door and stopped. 'Almost forgot. Parry's in debt, heavily. Twenty K on his current account and another twenty on his cards. I'll email the details when I get them.'

Rick nodded and she went out.

He followed. More detectives were spilling into the main CID room and he ushered two into his office, Bennett wearing his round-rimmed glasses, keen but over-confident, and Woods, still in his anorak, before he started the day's Sudoku. They all remained standing while Rick explained the statements he wanted. All the staff at NA, starting with Parry and Weatherbeater.

The two men listened and scribbled notes. Rick sent them out again.

He finished his toast, pushed his keyboard aside and picked up the report on Calix's phone number.

Calix had flown to Nepal on the 2nd April. There had been two calls on the 4th just after four pm local time, or ten fifteen am GMT. A footnote from Maggie stated that the reason the time difference was five hours and forty-five minutes was because Nepal wanted to distinguish itself from India.

Second call to the Conistons' house, ten minutes in duration. The first, immediately beforehand, to a Nepalese pay as you go, five minutes. The Conistons had confirmed the second call as Calix, which made the first likely to be him too.

Two more calls to the same PAYG, on the 7th and the 15th. Calls made by Calix? If so, to whom? If not, had he been robbed? Why no more calls? Did Calix know anyone in Nepal? Had another person on his trip bought a local SIM card?

Laughter in the main office made Rick look up. Kate was talking to Maggie. He got up to shut his door. Sergeant Harris and three of his team walked by.

He sat down again.

Maggie had analysed the previous six months of call history.

Calix had made calls to seventeen different mobiles. A bar graph showed the frequency to each number. Thirty-three calls to N1, nineteen to N2, thirteen to N3, the others ten or fewer. N1 was a UK PAYG; calls to it averaged twenty minutes.

Maggie had gone back another six months. Calls to N1 only started on 13 October. What had Calix done on that day? Where had he been? Who had he met?

Telecommunications' reports always posed more questions than they gave up answers.

Final section, the analysis. Maggie had entered all the mobile numbers into the police databases. Three, including N2, produced hits for the same person. William Redman, also known as The Big Red or TBR. A local cannabis dealer who regularly changed his phones. Calix phoned Redman once a week.

Links between Calix's phone number and his notebook. Eight calls to Super Fast Pizzas. Two calls to the NWRMG – the North West Raptor Monitoring Group.

Two calls to A. Amanda?

Ten calls to PP, starting December. The last call, two days before Calix left for Nepal. Paul Parry?

Mid-morning, Rick drove to Stretford for the monthly meeting on organised crime groups. Each division sent a DI or a DCI, and it was his turn.

On his way back, lunchtime, he detoured out to the apiary. Half an hour.

Pale clouds swept across the coin-coloured sun, but it was warm enough to open the hive and look for the queen. He geared up but didn't light the smoker because he wanted to start by watching the bees returning home. The horseshoe of hives was in a woody glade, next to an arable field. A perfect place for an apiary. The air was busy and noisy with bees.

In Manchester there was an image of a honeybee on every litter-bin. The worker bee, the symbol of the city. Hard to believe, he'd always thought.

He approached his hive from the side. Bees were coming and going. At the entrance, one was doing the famous waggle dance. Waving its tail to indicate where pollen and nectar could be found. If a queen was present in the hive, then she should be laying eggs, up to two thousand a day. The young bees needed pollen. So, if she was laying, the workers would be collecting pollen. They carried it in hairs on their legs, which made it very easy to spot. Different-coloured bulges, depending on the source. Yellow for willow, orange for dandelion, red for horse chestnut.

Two or three minutes passed. He couldn't see any pollen sacs, which was serious. No laying queen or no queen, there was not much difference.

He waited another ten minutes, but only counted five bees

bringing back pollen. Not nearly enough. Potentially, the colony was lost. He decided against opening the hive for another inspection. Opening them twice in a few days wasn't good practice, and he should get back to work.

He unzipped his veil and walked back to the car, pulling off his leather gauntlets. There were things he could do. Find another queen. He'd ask Robbo, maybe email the club.

At the police station, he made a coffee and considered the two actions from the organised crime groups meeting. But he couldn't concentrate: he kept thinking about the report on Calix's phone. It was possible that N1 was a new number for someone Calix already knew. Maybe Redman.

He heard Maggie in the corridor, and he asked her to pop in. She wore a necklace of chunky black beads instead of the choker.

'We need to ask the Conistons what Calix did in the week leading up to the thirteenth of October.'

'Just spoken to Mrs Coniston. The twelfth of October was a Saturday and Calix was in London attending a taxidermy lecture.'

'Where?'

'UCL – he studied there. When he returned home she said his face was shiny, as if he'd met a girl. But he didn't say anything.'

'Did you ask her about the notebook?'

'She couldn't help with the Fantasy Football list. A bit on the other stuff. Joe is Calix's grandfather. Everyone calls him Joe, even Calix. It was Joe's birthday on the thirtieth of March. But she doesn't know Catra. Nor heard Calix mention her. And she'd never heard of Crick Lane Farm.'

'What about Paul Parry or Amanda Whittle?'

'I wanted to check with you before I asked.' Maggie began to play with her hair.

'Let's wait until I get the NA statements from Bennett and Woods. Have you contacted UCL?'

'On my list.'

He nodded, and ran his hand through his hair. Short, black, wiry. His gesture had unconsciously mirrored hers – did that mean something? Becky was right, he had to actually ask someone, not just think about asking someone. Maggie had liked the honeycomb, and she was in a wheelchair. How could she refuse?

'Is there anything else?'

'Do you fancy a drink later?' He could go in his work suit, pretend he hadn't had time to change. Talk about wheelchair access to public buildings – he knew a bit about that. Bees of course, he could bore her to death with them.

'What do you mean?'

'A glass of wine somewhere.' His stomach felt concave.

'I know what a drink is,' she said. 'I meant, why? Is it an apology?'

'No,' said Rick. 'I mean, yes. I don't know. It's what people do.' He couldn't tell her about Becky's wedding but it wasn't only that. It was Maggie herself. No one at the police station seemed to know what had happened to her. Only rumours. An incident which led to her changing her name and re-training as a police analyst.

'Well, do you?'

'No.'

'Is it because I'm the DCI?'

'No, it's not because you're the DCI.'

'Why then?'

'You just don't get it, do you?'

71

He stood up and followed her to the door. Watched her wheel away down the corridor. *Get what?*

'I'm not The Bearded Lady.' A yell, as if she'd heard him.

Bennett walked up, looking awkward. 'I've got the NA statements, boss.'

'Parry's?'

'Yes.'

Bennett followed Rick into his office and handed him a sheaf of statements. Paul Parry's was at the top. They remained standing while Rick read through it. He looked up, half-hoping to see Maggie at the door. She'd changed her mind, and she did want to go for a drink.

'He signed the financial consent form, no problem,' said Bennett. 'He told me he was in debt, thousands and thousands across all his bank accounts and credit cards. But he said he'd been hacked – in February. Been in dispute with the banks ever since. He said he's about to hire a lawyer.' Bennett pushed his glasses higher up his nose.

'You don't believe him?'

'No. He'd not reported it to us although he said he'd tried. But not just that. No embarrassment, no mistakes, no hesitation. Spieled it all out like an actor.'

'Did you ask if he knew any of the clients on the Mera expedition?'

'Said he didn't.'

'Mobile number?'

'Not the same as the PP in Calix's notebook,' said Bennett. 'But he could have two phones.'

'Anything else?'

'Right at the end I got into the weeds. He said he'd recently remarried his first wife after she'd divorced him for having an affair. You'll never believe who with.'

Rick looked up from the statement.

Bennett prodded his glasses again. 'Amanda Whittle, the leader of Calix's trip.'

'Has he been in touch with her since they left?'

'Said he hadn't.'

'Where does his climbing accident figure in all this? Let me guess, it put an end to his affair and his wife came back to him?'

'Hole in one, boss. Do you want me to bring him in, officially? Search his house et cetera?'

'Not yet. Go and update Maggie.' Maggie, Maggie, Maggie. What a mess. 'Tell her to chase the banks as a priority.'

When Bennett had left, Rick looked out of the large window into the backyard.

Waiting at the loading dock was a police van, rocking side to side with an angry prisoner. Nearby, an Alsatian and its handler waited patiently.

What had he been thinking – asking someone out in a wheelchair? An analyst, the equivalent of three ranks below him. At the same station. What did he have in common with her? Of course Maggie was going to say no.

13

Calix's group turned off the main trail, and after twenty minutes arrived at the hamlet of Kanjar. A scrawny dog ran about barking, then yawned and lay down. Two mud-spattered boys peeped around a wall, and ran up to one of the guards.

He picked them up, one in each arm, and kissed them on the cheeks. The lead guard walked on, and Calix and Barney followed, along the path of uneven stones through the houses to the central courtyard. It was covered in light brown cobs drying in the sun. Food for the goats, or the people if times were hard. The small shop sold RaRa noodles, toilet rolls and cheap butter biscuits, the wrappers of which littered the trails.

Calix and Barney were directed to stop. They sat on a wall, next to trays of red chillies.

A woman appeared from the back of the shop and stood in the doorway, alongside the counter. She was tiny. Her ears and nose were heavily ringed. Wrapped around her body were countless layers of colourful cloth. She was thin, but the folds of material made her look plump. She could have been thirty. Or sixty. Around her ankles were more layers of cloth, like puttees. Her feet were bare, her toes splayed and dirty.

The lead guard let the children down, and held a confab

with his goons. He spoke to the woman, and shook two empty baskets. She pointed around the back, and he walked off. The tufty-haired guard from the *chirpi* and the second guard retreated to the edge of the square. Calix sensed them relax.

'It's their village. They're picking up supplies.'

Barney nodded. 'Maybe the others will catch us up.' He looked back to the main trail, but no one was in sight. He took off a boot. The scrawny dog sauntered closer. A mongrel, dirty-brown and lean. Hungry, like all the dogs.

'Get away,' said Barney, and waved his hand.

The mutt backed up. Barney pulled off his sock, and Calix held up his fingers, as if he was concealing something.

Looking hopeful, the dog approached again. It was two feet long, a foot high, and had a decent tail. 'Okay, boy,' said Calix.

'Careful,' said Barney. 'Might bite.'

Calix nuzzled the dog's ears, and it let out a low whine. 'Animals like me.' He pushed the dog away, and it trotted off.

A young girl appeared, and grabbed a fold of the woman's skirts. She buried her head in the cloth.

'Here I go,' said Calix.

He walked over to the counter, glancing over his shoulder at the guards. His breathing quickened. The guards were sharing a beer, and watching him. A pistol was stuffed into each of their waistbands. Carried as casually as a pencil behind the ear.

He turned to the woman.

'Cigarettes?' He pretended to smoke.

She nodded, and pulled a basket from a shelf. He pointed at a dusty packet of Marlboro, and she threw them on the counter next to a mobile phone. He handed over a few of the coins the guards had let him keep, and lit up with her matches. Breathed out a sharp funnel of smoke. He'd not expected them to take everything, even if they'd said he'd get it all back.

The tufty-haired guard strolled over. He picked up the pack

of cigarettes, and blew dust from it into Calix's face. 'Okay,' he said, snickering.

Calix stayed at the counter, smoking, and trying to enjoy the bumps of nicotine. The casual man about town, except he was anything but. He glanced at Barney, who'd got off the wall and was sitting on the ground in front of it, his eyes closed.

He lit a second cigarette from the first. Megan had taught him to smoke, and they'd shared the occasional illicit cigarette at home. The first time – he'd been about twelve so Megan only ten or eleven – in the woods at the top of the garden, puffing at fag butts he'd stashed in a perspiring plastic bag. And as they'd got older, leaning out of the attic window, and keeping a lookout for their old man.

The two muddy boys returned. 'Rupee?' the older boy shouted. The younger one threw a stone, laughed and ran away.

Calix sputtered on his cigarette.

'Pen?' shouted the older boy. 'Pen, pen, pen.' His nose was snotty and his shorts were on inside out.

The girl left the woman's side, her hand holding onto the skirts until the last moment so the skirt was pulled up into the air. She approached Calix, holding out her hand. In it was a small piece of wood in the rough shape of a heart.

It probably wasn't the right thing to do. The right thing was to teach them some English or maths. Or make a donation to their school – if they went to school. The right thing was to play noughts and crosses, or to teach them checkers, or chess.

He dug in his pocket.

'*Ek*,' said Calix. He held up a finger.

He placed all three coins on the palm of one hand, and the children walked up to him, one by one. The older boy first. Then the younger boy. He snatched a coin, knocking the third one onto the floor. Calix picked it up and watched him run away. The girl came. She took the last coin, her tiny fingers cool against his skin.

'*Namaste*,' she whispered.

Calix turned to the woman behind the counter, and leant in closer. Felt his stomach cramp.

'Phone?' He pointed.

She wagged a finger, and called out to the guards. This time, the second guard stood up, walked over.

He prodded Calix in the chest. Instinctively, Calix knocked the arm away. The guard stood his ground, and without warning and scant drawback, punched Calix in the stomach. The air rushed out of him. Gasping, he bent double. Sank to his knees, and onto all fours. As he concentrated on breathing, he watched the desert-coloured boots take the man back across the square.

He understood: carrot and stick. Basics.

But he wouldn't forget.

He crawled back to the wall.

'You okay?' said Barney.

Calix nodded. He looked up the valley. It was steep-sided with a mixture of scree and scrub, snow patches, and the odd miserable tree. At the end, in the V left by the plunging valley sides, was a postcard mountain. Mount Mera. It had a wavy snow-line, like the sauce on a Christmas pudding. He closed his eyes, and again thought back to what Amanda had said about his surname at the restaurant in Kathmandu. He should have asked the guide to explain, but it was too late for that now.

'I want to know *why*,' said Barney.

'We've talked about that,' said Calix. 'Money.'

'I think it's about the competition.'

'Vicky didn't win one.'

'I don't think she should be here.'

'So you keep saying,' said Calix.

'What does your dad do in the MOD?'

'I'm not sure exactly.'

'Our dad works for FIFA.'

'You said.'

'I can hear them coming,' said Barney. 'Vicky's dad's in oil.'

'There you are then,' said Calix, opening his eyes.

A guard from Spencer and Vicky's group appeared. Barney stood, and Calix hauled himself up onto the wall.

They heard Spencer before they saw him. Gasping like an emphysemic. The twin walked up slowly, Vicky behind him. He collapsed on the ground next to the wall. A hole in one knee of his trousers. The porters dumped their loads and the guards took up positions.

'You've done really well, Spence,' said Vicky. She leant her poles against the wall, and looked at Barney. She gave a small shake of the head. Her pink top was wet with sweat. The poles clattered to the ground.

Barney fumbled through his brother's pockets until he found a blue inhaler. 'Practically empty.' He scowled. Spencer slumped forward, head between his knees. Barney shook the inhaler up and down, and put it in his brother's hand. Spencer raised his head. His face was pale. He took a pathetic puff. 'A couple more,' said Barney. He put a hand on his brother's head.

Vicky undid her ponytail and shook out her damp hair. Already, it was blonder. 'He's fallen over a bit. He can't see too well.'

'I've fixed them,' said Calix. He pulled Spencer's glasses from a pocket. 'We're going to be okay. All of us.' The twins and Vicky looked at him, and Vicky squeezed Barney's hand.

Behind them, Hant prodded a guard in the chest.

'Spencer needs a doctor,' shouted Barney, letting go of

Vicky's hand. He rolled his shoulders like a limbering athlete. 'Aargh!'

Hant walked closer.

Barney straightened up.

'Half people Nepal need doctor,' the Nepalese leader said quietly.

'Easy,' said Calix, tugging Barney's shirt. He stepped in front of the twin. 'How much further, Hant?'

'Two, three day. Soon we cross snow.'

Calix looked up the valley. Mist had descended, like a blind, and Mount Mera had disappeared. He wondered when he'd be going home. He thought about his parents, Bird Bird, TBR. Whether his parents had done anything – he wasn't due back for a couple of weeks. How Bird Bird was faring without him. Who was doing his milk round.

Somewhere in the mist-cloud came the whining of a small plane. It got louder, but he couldn't see it. He wondered if it was looking for them.

14

Rick got up early. He ran, showered, and drove to work in the pouring rain.

At the police station, he waited at the barrier. Water dripped from the roof of the sentry box, occupied if the threat level reached severe.

Thoughts, like dogs, chased each other around in his head. Paul Parry and his huge debts: had he been hacked? If not, what was he up to? Rick had been unsure about the NA office manager ever since meeting him. Uneasy and awkward, then helpful, but disingenuously so, he suspected.

Calix Coniston and his mystery phone calls. Who was he calling? Parry?

He wondered what Maggie thought. Maggie Nash. Maggie Nash and her parting comment. As soon as she'd said it he knew what she meant. *Roll up, roll up, fifty pence to see The Bearded Lady, all the fun of the fair.* He thought she'd have been desperate to be taken out, but he couldn't have been more wrong. Would he have asked her if she hadn't been in a wheelchair? He wasn't sure. And what now?

The barrier rose. He drove in. The barrier clanged down. Dad. Should Rick and Becky arrange for a carer? Visit them every week? Becky's wedding reception. Was he making any progress? His bees. Should he just hope that the queen would start laying?

In his office he hadn't even reached the kettle when his desk phone rang. A second later his mobile started up. A cat chorus joining the racing dogs.

Woods and Bennett appeared at the door. Woods, his damp anorak half-unzipped, and Bennett, pen behind an ear and clutching his daybook. Like ghosts of CID Past and CID Yet To Come.

'Ten minutes,' he said to the two detectives.

Bennett hovered but Woods yanked his arm. They walked off. The desk phone went quiet. He switched on the kettle, and answered his mobile.

'You start early,' said Rick.

'Midnight's early for climbers,' said Russell Weatherbeater. 'I've had a call from a friend who runs another mountaineering company. One of their expeditions is also doing Mera Peak but started a few days later than ours. The trip leader phoned him an hour ago to say they've found the body of a trekker.'

Rick shut his eyes. Not Calix Coniston. Robbo would kill him. 'Who?'

'The body was in a river, but they managed to get it out. A woman.'

'Victoria Brant?'

A sigh echoed down the phone. 'Looks like it. She was wearing a rucksack and a hotel receipt was in it.'

'What happened?'

'Don't know,' said Russell.

'Any valuables?'

'Don't know any more than what I've told you.'

'I'll get Kate to help you with family liaison and a press statement. But first, I need phone numbers for Amanda and your friend in the other company. And, while we're at it, all the numbers you have for Paul Parry.'

'Why?'

'I'll explain in person.'

Rick wrote everything down. 'Last thing, how good is the Nepalese phone network?'

'Coverage on the popular trekking routes is good. Away from them it's patchier. All our expeditions carry a sat phone for emergencies – of course, they're not infallible either.'

Rick's desk phone started ringing again. 'Thanks, speak soon.' He changed phones.

'Are you ignoring me?' said Robbo.

'No, sir.'

'I'd like an update on Calix Coniston.'

Bennett and Woods arrived back at Rick's door. The anorak was finally off.

'Five minutes, sir,' said Rick.

He put the phone down, and looked up. 'Sorry.'

The detectives walked away, and Rick ordered his thoughts for Robbo.

Was Vicky's death an accident? If so, why had it been discovered, not reported? Were Calix and the Williams twins okay? Where were they? Why weren't they with Vicky, and why hadn't they been in contact? Had they gone walkabout, or had they been snatched? If Calix's note was a forgery, and the four of them had been kidnapped, Vicky's death could have been an escape attempt gone wrong or she could have been murdered. Was Paul Parry involved?

Rick smile-acknowledged Elaine, Robbo's plump PA, and walked into the superintendent's office. He remained standing to brief his boss.

'You need to get out there, pronto.'

'I'll need a second.'

'Take Kate.'

'She's the coroner's officer. What about one of the DSs, Khan or Harris? Even DC Bennett.'

'Kate'll handle all the next-of-kin matters and get the body sent back to Australia. She's also level three victim liaison.'

'We don't know that Calix is not okay.'

'That's just it – we don't know that, or much else. That's why I need you out there. You and Kate.' Robbo removed his glasses. Rolls of skin bunched up behind his wedding ring. Even his fingers were putting on weight. 'Until we know the cause of death, this is a missing persons enquiry. You are *looking* for Calix Coniston and the Williams twins. Vicky Brant's death may be an accident.' He huffed into the lenses and began to clean them. 'It stinks, but until we know for definite we won't bother the Nepalese authorities.' He put his glasses back on. 'You'll need an interpreter.'

'I could ask Russell Weatherbeater, the owner of Nepal Adventures. I'd know what I was getting, and he knows his way around.' Rick wondered whether Robbo's bulkiness was linked to his recent failure at the board for chief superintendent. Too many biscuits as he prepared? The stress of failing?

'Can he be trusted?'

Rick thought of Russell's five Everest summits. The jar on his desk. The mountaineer's comments on over-ambition. 'Out there, I'd trust him more than anyone.'

'We can only pay his expenses. Go and see him. I'll speak to Kate.'

Rick didn't move. 'The reshuffle.'

'Effective when you return from Nepal.'

'Move Jack. I'll take the squads.'

'We're not moving Jack.'

'Why?'

'It's not because you're not good.' Robbo paused. 'The others don't even realise you detectives aren't all the same.'

'Why then?'

'It's because you've got lots else going on.'

'Meaning what exactly?'

'Your dad.' Robbo paused. 'Then there're the sessions with Emma. There's a feeling that you're not coping, and it would be better if you sat somewhere with less pressure. Less stress.'

Rick stared at the file on Robbo's desk. The red capital letters, the yellow rubber band, the list of signatures and dates.

'We think it's in your best interest.'

'Who does?'

'We took a vote and the SMT's unanimous.'

'Including you?'

'You know I've always stuck up for you.'

'And this time?'

Robbo paused. 'I abstained. It was all I could do. We read Emma's reports.'

'I thought they were confidential.'

'They are.'

Rick walked to the door. In the bin were a damp supermarket bag and jam-stained doughnut wrappers. He turned round. 'You know, Robbo, you've become a fat man.'

The high street at the front of Nepal Adventures was busy, and Rick parked in a small municipal car park. He threw the police logbook on the dashboard and glanced up at the back of the shops. Three storeys, a mixture of flats and businesses. Lights, here and there. Steaming boiler vents.

From a window on the top floor a man was climbing out.

Rick reached for his police radio, automatically preparing

his *Suspects On* message. Male, white, forties, five foot ten. Blue outdoor jacket, blue jeans. His fingers gripped the short antenna.

On the window ledge, the man held onto two shiny handles attached to the wall. He stepped down with his right foot until it met a protruding brick. It was lighter in colour. He lowered his left foot onto another similar piece. He dropped his hands onto more pieces and continued climbing downwards. His legs were jerky, but he moved quickly, as if he'd done it before.

He had done it before. Rick relaxed his grip on the radio.

A metre from the ground the man stopped, looked over a shoulder, and started traversing to his right. A battered estate car drove up alongside, stopped, but kept its engine idling. The front passenger door was flung open. The man climbed down from the wall and into the car, not once touching the ground. The door slammed shut, and the car drove off. A woman – Mrs Parry? – at the wheel.

Rick locked his car and walked up to the rear of Nepal Adventures. The light-coloured pieces of brick covered the whole of the windowless ground storey, and continued, in a ladder formation, up through the second storey to the third-storey window and its two shiny handles.

He went to find its owner – via the front entrance.

Weatherbeater was behind his desk, wearing the same clothes as last time. A fleck of white in his beard. Next to the jar of fingers and toes a half-eaten bowl of porridge.

'Just seen Paul Parry going home.'

'Out the back way?'

Rick was getting to know that grin. 'Down.'

'Or up.'

'He seems to have made a miraculous recovery.'

'Thank God, or rather, thank the people who've repaired his prosthetics. He's so irritable when he's in a wheelchair.'

Rick wondered if it was the only reason. And why Maggie didn't use prosthetics.

'I know what you're thinking. Have health and safety seen the climbing wall entrance? They've been all over us. Literally – they brought a man in a helmet and a harness. We're legit.'

'I wasn't—'

'Our postie loves it, she's—'

'Russell.'

'—been on one of our trips…' His voice petered out.

'Russell, listen. Forget health and safety. You might not have a business at all if it turns out that Vicky Brant was murdered in a conspiracy involving your staff.'

The mountaineer's huge frame jerked up.

'I'm flying out to Nepal to find out what's going on. I'd like you to come with me.'

Five pm, Rick sat at his desk with a mug of tea and a banana. Outside, it was raining again. He scrolled through the day's crime reports – robberies, burglaries, a carjacking. No firearms and no gang incidents, which meant he could concentrate on the Coniston enquiry. He typed *vaccinations for Nepal* into Google, and thought about the press statement for Vicky Brant. He wondered where his passport was.

He looked up. Bennett stood at the door.

'Saw you come back, boss.'

'Woods gone home?'

Bennett nodded.

'Well, what've you got for me?'

'Maggie's looking at the Conistons and the Williamses, and she asked us to focus on Parry and on Coniston's notebook. So earlier we was wondering about surveillance on Parry.'

'He's a person of interest,' said Rick, 'but it's a bit thin for surveillance. His previous is deception, not kidnapping, and no violence. We don't even know if a crime's been committed. Instead, submit the PP mobile number to Telecoms and find out who PP has been phoning. Hopefully, his gran. Then we'll have a solid connection between Coniston and Parry.'

'Cunning.'

'Do the same for A in the notebook.'

Bennett nodded. 'I also had a go at Crick Lane Farm. There are seven in the UK. Closest is in the Peak District, Buxton way. It's been up for sale for eighteen months. I spoke to the land agent.'

'What're you thinking?'

'Cannabis factory. Hydroponics.'

'Any connection with Nepal or Parry?'

Bennett shook his head. 'Nothing substantive. It might explain Parry's debts,' he said. 'I'm following the money.' He looked hopeful.

'Tomorrow,' said Rick, 'I'm revisiting the Conistons with Maggie, but you and Woods make an appointment with the land agent. See what you can see. Or smell.'

Propped up by two pillows, Rick read in bed. On the wall in front of him, the TV showed the BBC news. He'd adjusted the volume so that he could read, but would know to turn it up if a headline caught his interest.

The volume remained low.

He was ploughing through the last three detective applications – he would have to email his assessments from Nepal. Karen Downcliff's was particularly turgid. *In interview I used clever questions to trap AFZAL into admissions that meant I could charge him with lots of multiple offences. The victims was over the moon.*

'The disaster in Nepal,' said the BBC anchorman.

Rick jabbed the remote.

'Nineteen Sherpas have been confirmed dead in what is thought to be the worst disaster on Everest since climbing began.' The TV showed pictures of a massive avalanche and tiny figures disappearing. Rick wondered if Russell knew anyone. After a couple of minutes he turned the TV back down. Downcliff's application was woeful and he couldn't face any more. He swapped it for *Hooper's* and read about the consequences of not having a queen.

In the summer, worker bees only lived for six weeks and, to keep up numbers, the queen laid up to 2000 eggs a day. Without a queen the hive could not function. Not simply a dwindling population and no honey, but the dystopian problem of laying workers.

Some of the workers, all female, realising that there was no queen, would start laying eggs. However, the eggs were unfertilised and the hive would slowly fill with male bees and become as useful as an unlocked prison cell. Drones had one purpose and that was to mate with the queen; in a hive of 30,000 bees, there would usually be only a few hundred. Although there were solutions to laying workers, the colony was probably doomed. The best cure was prevention.

Rick sighed. There was no time to find another queen – he was flying to Nepal the day after tomorrow. As he'd thought, he'd have to hope there was a queen and she'd start laying. And he had no choice but to ask the fat man to check while he was away.

He turned the TV volume back up. The anchor was still talking about Nepal. 'There has been more bad news today for the Kingdom of Nepal. Three more Nepalese workers have died on Qatari building sites.' Rick turned the volume up another notch. Calix Coniston's attic wall had several newspaper cuttings on the issue. 'Four years ago,' said a TV reporter, standing in front of a vast building site crawling with helmeted workers, 'Qatar was awarded the 2022 World Cup by FIFA. As you can see, the construction of football stadiums has begun in earnest. The men are migrant labour, including many from Nepal. But, with poor working conditions and temperatures that reach fifty degrees Celsius, it's a dangerous job.' The TV cut to a blazing sun, then back to the studio. 'Last year there were almost two hundred deaths of Nepalese workers alone. Today's deaths have brought further pressure onto FIFA and its president, Sepp Blatter, to do something about it.' A picture of Blatter. 'In local news—'

Rick turned it down, but not off. There was always the possibility of seeing a colleague making a mess of a press conference.

He picked up his papers. *The victims was over the moon.* What a way to finish the day: in bed with Karen Downcliff.

15

Rick waited in the Conistons' hallway while Maggie dried her hair on a pink towel. Rain was still lashing down, and water pummelled the front door. In the car he'd explained how he wanted her to sift through all Calix's paperwork. Confirm a connection with Paul Parry or even Amanda Whittle. Or dig up something else. A Nepalese connection. Something substantive before he flew out there. Tomorrow, all confirmed: Russell, Kate and him. At home, DS Harris would coordinate and Maggie would remain on intel. He'd found his passport and didn't need vaccinations as long as he wasn't bitten by a rabid dog.

She offered him the towel, and looked up the stairs. Tried to stifle a smile. 'I thought detectives were supposed to be good at working things out.'

'We concentrate on making sense of the past. I'll have to carry you.'

'If David was here, he'd help,' said Mrs Coniston in the kitchen doorway.

'I'm not helpless, just different,' said Maggie. 'Imagine if we all had wheels, not legs. There would be no stairs.'

'Wheels?'

'Evolution doesn't plan ahead. It just happens. Eyes are incredible but elbow joints could do with more R and D.'

'Maggie, will you let me carry you up the stairs?'

'I don't have a choice.'

Rick took off his jacket, tucked in his tie and squatted. He leant forward, and Maggie clasped her hands behind his neck. As he squeezed his hands under her bottom he began to understand her procrastination. He straightened his back and legs, and Maggie, even if it was what she feared in her worst nightmare, fell gently against him. Around her neck was a leather band with a moonstone. Her breath was minty. Their heads touched, his right ear buried in her brown hair. It was still damp.

'You've got to breathe,' she said.

He nodded. 'All aboard, this train is now leaving.' She smiled, and he stepped onto the first stair. She wasn't heavy. Obvious. After two flights he wanted it to last longer, to the top of the Penrose Stairs.

In the attic he briefed her on his previous search. Locked pedestal, stuffed cat in the box under the second desk. Three places for paperwork: the pedestal, the bookcase, and the wall. Sift and seize.

Maggie started on the deep bottom drawer, and Rick walked up to the wall of paperwork. Something had been nagging him. He started with a couple of newspaper articles he'd not read last time. They all needed reading, every last column inch. He glanced at Maggie. Focused. That's what his dad said about him. Used to say – anyone's guess what he'd say now. Or, was Maggie thinking about being carried up the stairs? He read an article on the tiny Ghurkha pensions paid by the British state. He read two more articles. And there it was.

The something.

He unpinned one of the newspaper cuttings.

Maggie looked over. 'What about the photos?'

'I'll put it back. Listen to this: *FIFA official promises an urgent solution... FIFA executive committee member, Terry Williams...*'

'The twins' father?'

'This is the connection between Calix and the twins.'

'A connection or a coincidence?'

'Coincidences are connections waiting to be unravelled.' He paused. 'Maggie, I need to think for a moment. I'll be in the car. I'll be back.'

He detoured via the kitchen. Mrs Coniston had her hands in a mixing bowl, rubbing butter into flour. Her watch and rings lay alongside. It reminded him of his mother in her kitchen.

She looked up. 'I'm making rhubarb and ginger crumble, Calix's favourite. Stupid really, but I wanted to think about him.'

'When will the brigadier be back, Mrs Coniston?'

'Six.'

'Do you mind if I ask you some questions?'

She shook her head.

'How did Calix get interested in taxidermy?'

'At university. He found the red kite in a junk shop but the others are all his handiwork.'

'Where does he get the animals?'

'He finds them.'

'Do you know what's in the box under his desk?'

'Our neighbours' cat. Run over.' She looked up, her fingers not stopping. 'He's doing it for them. Nice of him, don't you think?'

'Did Calix have any enemies?'

She didn't answer immediately and he watched her fingers. Rubbing away at the implication. She shook her head. 'Not that I know about.'

'Was he caught up in anything – drugs, maybe, or anything where people might want to hurt him?'

She washed her hands, and picking up a tea-towel, turned to face him. 'He didn't go out much, as I've told you. But every Friday afternoon he disappeared for several hours. Said he was visiting Megan's grave.'

'But you didn't believe him?'

She dried her hands on the towel. 'I wanted to.' She hung the towel on the oven. 'Once, he came home with a black eye, and said he'd been robbed. He was adamant that he didn't want to report it.'

'What did the brigadier say?'

'David was away.'

'Did you tell him?'

'No.'

'Why not?'

'Because he was *away*.' She paused. 'Sorry, it's hard to explain.'

Rick nodded. 'So what did you think Calix was up to?'

'I don't know.' She took the towel from the ovenfront, and dried her hands again. 'Calix didn't seem any different. Didn't look any different – apart from the eye that one time. Didn't look as if he was taking drugs.' She slotted the towel back on the oven. 'Is he mixed up in something? In drugs? Do you think he's gone to Nepal to buy drugs?' She frowned. 'But he won a competition.'

'Maybe he didn't. '

'Oh, God.' She went to a drawer, and took out a strip of tablets. She popped a couple out, and swallowed them.

'Do you know Terry Williams?'

'No.'

'Last question.' He decided he'd have to return later with Kate, and tell the Conistons together about the missing twins.

'When I was here last time, you mentioned your worry book. You said you wrote not only about Calix but also about the brigadier. What have you written? If you don't mind telling me?'

'I don't mind because that's just it: David's not telling *me*. He used to tell me everything. It was part of the attraction: on the surface, bluff and uncompromising, but underneath he's… well, he's a good man. Anyway, he's stopped talking to me. He's bottling something up.'

'For how long?'

'Months, maybe a year.'

Rick went out to his car. The rain had stopped and the statue in the centre of the rose garden was steaming.

16

Crude marks of charcoal adorned one wall of the cave. They showed stick men around a fire. Drawn by Victorian explorers or hunter-gatherers? Lost mountaineers? More likely, thought Calix, the guards doing a recce.

Or previous hostages.

His stomach cramps returned.

In front of the cave was a car-sized rock, and, bolted to it, a chunky metal ring. Three ten-metre chains led down from the ring and twisted along the ground to the end shackles and the legs of the three prisoners. Calix's shackle was fixed just above his left boot, and already his skin was sore and itchy.

He sat with Barney and Spencer on flat rocks in a small circle. A council of war without any soldiers, without any guns, without any ideas.

In the ocean-blue sky the sun glared like a welder's flame. But the air was cold and they wore woolly hats. A stream ran down from the cave, close enough to shuffle alongside and snatch an icy drink.

'We shouldn't have left her there,' said Barney. His eyes were red-rimmed, and he looked thinner and older.

'We had n-no ch-choice,' said Spencer. His voice was weak, his eyes, without spectacles, staring. Like a frog.

The brothers glanced at Calix.

Despite her crampons, Vicky had slipped on a snow slope. She'd dropped her ice-axe and careered downwards. Spun around and hit a rock head-first. She'd called out, making no sense, then slipped hundreds of metres below.

'It was an accident.'

'Makes no difference,' said Barney. 'If we hadn't been kidnapped, she'd still be alive.'

'You're right.'

Calix picked at the scabs on his wrists from the cuffs. Picking hurt. He wanted it to hurt, and he kept teasing and tearing. Until now, he'd never seen the attraction of self-harm, but Vicky was dead. He *deserved* the pain. The scabs began to bleed, and he put his tongue to the blood. The metallic taste made him feel sick. He thought about Megan, and her accident. Vicky was a similar age, also travelling alone, thousands of miles from the people who loved her.

'What're we g-g-going to do?'

Calix looked over his shoulder, back at the cave and the three orange tents. Their tent, Hant's tent and a larger one for the five guards. The porters had all been paid and sent away. Paid extra, Calix assumed, for their discretion. He daydreamed of an overheard conversation, a bilingual guide from a trekking company, a two-plus-two moment, a dramatic rescue. Headline news.

Calix took out the knife he'd bought in Kathmandu, and placed it on the ground between the three of them.

'How come they didn't find it?' said Barney.

Calix shrugged. 'I know you're both scared. I'm scared, too. But we mustn't lose hope.'

'F-f-fight?'

'I've done some kick-boxing at school.'

'Okay, Barney.' Calix was older than the twins, and knew he had to lead them. His heart thumped. 'Maybe not fight. But we should be prepared.'

Outside the cave, Hant sat on a rock talking on the sat phone. It had a distinctive stubby aerial – Amanda had one. Every now and then, Hant glanced in their direction. Nearby, three of the guards were crouched down playing cards. They were able to remain in that position, rocked back on the flats of their feet, for hours. Calix stretched around further, to the fourth guard, the one who'd kicked Barney. The one with the sandy reinforced boots.

The guard stared back at Calix.

There was no sign of the fifth guard, but he was probably asleep. The nightwatchman.

The cave was at the back of a hanging valley, a couple of hours uphill from the main path. The valley led nowhere, the ground getting steeper and steeper until it met snow slopes reaching down from a vast mountainous ridge. Large boulders were the grassy valley's only features. It was remote, and austere, and he would never forget it.

'Prepared for what?' said Barney.

'I don't know. An opportunity.'

A series of high-pitched shrieks made Calix look up. A little way down the hillside, marmots were running about. Occasionally, one stopped, stood on its hind legs, and let out a warning cry. Their burrows were everywhere, one only a few metres away, partly hidden by heather-like scrub. He delved into the baggy pocket on his knee, and pulled out a plastic bag. Warburtons Thick Sliced Wholemeal. Another world, another lifetime. He thought of his mum in the kitchen, cooking. His old man cleaning shoes, or pressing his uniform. Wondered if they were missing him.

From the bag he pulled out bits of *naan* that he'd been saving. He ripped them up and tossed the pieces around the entrance to the burrow.

'I keep hearing Vic's head hit the rock,' said Barney. 'I really liked her, you know.'

Calix was hearing it too. Starting with the gasp as she fell, and the scream as she picked up speed. A moment of silence. A garbled shout, then a dull thump, like running over a cat in the car. Then more, deafening, silence.

'P-p-prepare, h-h-how?'

'We can start by practising Nepali.' Calix pulled out his phrase book.

Garam chaa. It's warm. *Jaaro chha.* It's cold. *Paani parchcha.* It's raining. *Thaahaa chha.* I know. *Maile bujhina.* I don't under-stand.

'Right, you two, repeat after me. *Jaaro chha.* It means, it's cold. *Jaaro chha.*'

'*Jaaro chha.*'

'*J-j-jaaro ch-chha.*'

'Good. We'll all be fluent by the time we get back.'

On the hillside below them, a figure appeared.

'We've got company,' said Calix.

He watched the figure approach. Whoever it was had done the hard bit, the steep section, and had reached the flatter ground. He was following the river, as they had done the day before, and occasionally crossed it to keep to the easiest route. An easy, fluid gait.

He walked closer. He was carrying a large yellow rucksack. He was only a boy, and on his own. He looked about ten but was probably older, thirteen or fourteen. It wasn't the cavalry.

A greeting was shouted by the guard on the rock, and the boy stuck up a hand. He wore Western outdoor clothing.

Calix stared.

The boy stopped and stared back. *'Namaste!'*

'Namaste!' said Calix. *'Timro nama ke ho?'*

'Ram.'

'Ram nama ramro,' said Calix. He stuck a thumb in the air.

The boy grinned. *'Tapa im?'*

Calix guessed at it. 'Calix.'

'Licks?'

'Kall-icks. Kall-icks.'

Ram said something else, grinned, and walked on.

'You see, Spence?' said Barney.

In the entrance of the cave, Ram took off his rucksack. He squatted down and drank from the jerrycan. In loud, rapid Nepali, he spoke to Hant. Calix watched and listened carefully, but he understood one word in a hundred.

Ram unloaded his rucksack. There were cabbages, a dead chicken, and at least a dozen bottles of beer. *Chhang.*

Calix tamped down the bloody scabs on his wrist. Then ripped them off again, and watched the blood pool until it overran, and trailed down his arm, and dripped into the scrub.

17

Rain dripped off shadowy trees. A motorbike accelerated hard down the road, revealing, as it sped past the end of the Conistons' drive, a glimpse of leather and shiny chrome.

Rick tapped out a text to Becky. *A possible plus one, don't give up on me.*

The FIFA connection had set his brain turning. He opened his policy book and wrote the date. The car was stuffy and he lowered the window further. A bee rested on the bonnet. Not a honeybee, but a bumblebee. Larger and hairier, abdomen like a guardsman's bearskin. Only their queens survived the winter. Maybe when he retired he would get some more colonies, become a serious beekeeper. Learn more about bumblebees.

His phone beeped with a reply from Becky. *Police?*

Yes and no, he texted back.

Another beep, another message from Becky: *???!!!*

He put his phone on silent and turned it over.

He thought back to his SIO course. *Put your foot on the ball, and ask yourself the four big questions.* He'd lost count how many times he'd followed that advice.

What do I know? Calix Coniston and Barney Williams had won a competition to go to Nepal. For six months beforehand,

Coniston phoned a new associate, or he'd increased contact with an old one. Coniston and the twins had not contacted their parents from Nepal when they said they would. The three of them and a fourth trekker, Vicky Brant, had unexpectedly left the expedition, and Coniston or someone pretending to be Coniston had left a note explaining why. Brant had subsequently been found dead. In Coniston's attic, a notebook with lists of drug deals and contacts.

Paul Parry, Weatherbeater's office manager. Previous for a similar-ish deception, probably in debt, possibly the PP in Coniston's notebook. Reacted oddly to Rick's questions.

What are my hypotheses for what happened? Hypothesis 1: no crime – a genuine competition sponsored by Newcell. The four trekkers had decided to leave and Brant had an accident. Hypothesis 2a: kidnap then murder, but with what motive? Drugs? Hypothesis 2b: kidnap then demands in return for the hostages. But kidnap by whom, and why? Parry, and others?

The most likely was hypothesis 2b. The target was not Coniston or the twins, or even Brant, but a third party connected to them – a person, a company, or a government. Coniston and the others were bargaining chips. Motivation was financial or political. Terrorism crossed his mind, but he was reluctant to even write the word down. Technically, he should report even a suspicion.

The trees had stopped dripping, and the bumblebee was still on the bonnet.

Same spot, not moving. Bumblebees had a tendency to overload and overheat. To conk out, and be unable to make it back to the nest, like a marathon runner hitting the wall and failing to make the finish-line. She needed help. He rummaged around in the door pocket and in the central console. He opened a sachet of sugar and poured it into the cap of the de-icer can. Added water and stirred with his finger. He got out of the car, and using a scrap of paper, picked up the bumblebee and floated her on the sugary pool. She had two yellow bands and a white tail.

He sat back in the car, and picked up his notes. He watched her for a few seconds but she still didn't move. But then nobody did anything when they were being watched, especially by a policeman.

Money seemed unlikely as a motive. Although the Conistons and the Williamses were well off they were not *Sunday Times* rich list. Brant hadn't won a competition. Rick made a note to ask Maggie to chase the Australian police for her background. Some madcap political goal? Nepal had been in civil war for years, but he was unsure whether tourists had been killed or kidnapped. Another point for Maggie to research.

The key was the link between Coniston and the Williams twins. His light-bulb moment in the attic: the FIFA connection. Terry Williams was on the FIFA executive committee, and the article on Coniston's wall mentioned him – he'd promised to improve the working conditions of the Nepalese workers. There was the second, and obvious, connection, too. FIFA was connected to Nepal, via Qatar and the World Cup, and Coniston and the twins were in Nepal.

Two connections, two coincidences. For a detective, the equivalent of measles.

If the twins had been kidnapped because their father worked for FIFA, maybe Coniston had too? Did a relation of the Conistons work for FIFA?

He dropped back a stage in his thinking – what about Brigadier Coniston? He worked in Whitehall for the MOD. It was possible that Calix Coniston had been kidnapped due to his father's military knowledge. But it still didn't explain a connection to the Williams family.

Rick glanced out of the window, at the plastic de-icer cap sitting on the bonnet. Empty. He got out of the car to check.

The bumblebee had gone – buzzed back to the nest, he hoped.

Try to think outside the box was the SIO course instructor's advice when stuck. Outside the car would have to do. If the Williams family was connected to the Coniston family it was one case. If the two families were *not* connected there were two cases. Someone was trying to kill two birds with one stone. And if the competition was genuine, Vicky Brant would make a third. A Mr Big trying to kill three birds with one stone.

Both scenarios seemed unlikely.

He was stuck again. *Take your clothes off, stand on your head, do whatever it takes.*

Collateral. Maybe Coniston was collateral. The kidnap was aimed at the twins. Or maybe the twins *and* Coniston were collateral, and Vicky Brant was the target. Or, all four of them were collateral and the kidnap had been aimed at someone else, and had been bungled.

The answer was there somewhere.

Or it wasn't.

He looked up at the attic, where Maggie was sifting the paperwork. He drummed his fingers on the roof of the car. There were always connections that he hadn't seen. Next to the house was a greenhouse, white-washed for the summer. Shadows of plants inside. He got back in the car.

Calix Coniston. He underlined the name and ringed it. Calix had lied to his parents about his job in the pub, but that wasn't unusual. He'd been deeply affected by his sister's death and had dropped out of his third year. He was an odd mix of university intelligence and low-level drug dealing. Connected to William Redman – The Big Red. Taxidermy for a hobby, and a parrot for a pet. The neighbour's cat – a kind gesture, or was he responsible for its death? Calix's phone calls: who was his new acquaintance, what had they talked about, and who had he phoned in Nepal?

He'd got ahead of himself. Maybe Maggie was right: there wasn't a connection between Calix and the twins, and the FIFA connection was a coincidence.

What else do I need to know? Whether the competition was genuine; whether the note had been written by Calix; what Amanda had to say; how Vicky had died; more on Calix, the twins, and Vicky; Calix's computer results; and background on FIFA, Qatar and the 2022 World Cup, and Nepal and its civil war.

How can I find the information I need? Fly to Nepal. DS Harris, DCs Bennett and Woods and Maggie would follow the lines of enquiry in the UK.

He'd lost track of time, and he glanced up at the house. Hanging from one of the attic windows was a white, longish piece of cloth.

A bra.

He reached into the car and turned over his phone. Five missed calls and three texts.

Twenty minutes later they were sitting in the car.

'Some message.'

'Worked though,' said Maggie.

'Sorry.' Rick looked across at her, at her purple shirt, and at the empty footwell. He put his keys in the ignition.

They spoke at the same time.

'Maggie, why did—'

'Robbo's ordered—'

'You first,' said Rick. The car keys tinkled as his hand fell away.

'Robbo's ordered a sat phone and asked me to brief you. Unless you've used one before?'

He shook his head.

'A cellphone picks up signals from phone masts, a sat phone connects to satellites. Similar functionality: phone calls, texts, email, internet. They work anywhere on the planet – in theory. Used by journalists and the military – anyone working in remote areas.'

'Downside?'

'They're expensive, and don't like being indoors – obviously.' She paused. 'Are you listening?'

He was, but he was also wondering whether waving the bra meant he should ask her again. He could make a logical case. She had rejected his suggestion of Parry because he was in a wheelchair, and Rick, because he wasn't. Which left an empty sea. He could make a joke, and say that he wanted to shave the Bearded Lady, to uncover the real Maggie.

He said nothing. Nor did Maggie.

At the side of the house was a huge pine tree, the grass underneath covered in cones. Next to the garden wall stood a rusty roller.

Did he want to go out with someone in a wheelchair? A Catch-22 question: he could only know whether he wanted to go out with her if he went out with her.

They couldn't keep sitting in silence. Mrs Coniston might come out, might call the AA. One of them had to say something, or they should drive back to the police station. His thumb and index finger reached for the ignition key.

'Rick, you were about to say something.'

'Was I?'

'You want to know why I turned you down?'

His hand relaxed. He sensed her looking at him.

'I'll tell you.'

Rick turned towards her.

'Being in a wheelchair is humiliating, as you just witnessed. Humiliating and frustrating. I'm different to everyone else. My eyes are level with people's groins. The only people who don't stare down at me are children. Only they seem to accept me for who I am, not my ability to see over a hedge or ride a bicycle. I'm not just different, I'm unwanted. Like a burglar – invisible most of the time, annoying when I appear. At least burglars get to go burgling. What do wheelies get? Wheelchair marathons – great.

'It's painful, Rick. My stumps hurt, I get huge sores, and horrible back pain. And there's no escape. No break. I go to sleep, and I wake up still the same. Not even when I go on holiday – then it's all of that but ten times worse.'

'Prosthetics?'

'I've tried them – long story.' She sighed. 'I wasn't always like this, Rick.'

He nodded. A robin landed on the handle of the roller, a worm dangling.

'That's me, Rick. Now, tell me about you, your stuff.'

'My stuff?' Did she know about his stuff, or did she mean she could tell he had stuff? Or everyone had stuff? His hand reached for the ignition key again.

'Your stuff.'

Quid pro quo.

Rick took a deep breath. 'There were seventeen bodies in my first week of nights as a new DI. Seventeen dead people.' He started the car and drove around the statue. At the end of the drive, he slowed, indicated and pulled out onto the road.

He took another deep breath. 'On the Sunday night, Maggie, there was only one – a primary school head teacher, hanging in his garage.'

He accelerated, selected third gear.

The stretched neck. The smell of urine. Under each nostril, a blob of congealed blood.

One day it would be him. The one thing in life which was certain. The end. Nothing. Oblivion.

A post office van went past flashing its lights. Rick braked for the corner. The car keys clinked as they swung around.

Rick's phone woke him up, but not quickly enough for him to answer it. He rolled over and looked at the clock radio.

Four am.

Calix Coniston and the Williams twins had been found… dead? He picked up the phone and pressed for the message. 'Rick, are you there?' said his mum. She was in tears. 'I'm at the hospital with Dad.' He turned on the light and sat up.

He phoned back but her phone went straight to voicemail. He caught his reflection in the TV. His hair was sticking up. He tried a second time, then called Becky but without success. He tried to wait. He stared at his pyjama top on the floor. Accident? Collapse? Dying? Chesterfield hospital? Was there one? Should he know that?

Finally, she answered. 'Mum, what's happened?'

'I'd dropped off to sleep when I heard Roger screaming.' Her voice juddered with shock. 'He'd gone downstairs and put the kettle on.'

'Take your time, Mum, you're at hospital now.'

She sucked in some air. 'I told you I've to watch him.'

Rick's dream came back to him: he'd found Coniston and the Williams brothers in a Nepalese jail.

'He made a cup of tea and dropped it,' said his mum. 'All over himself. He was naked.'

'Burns?'

'Stomach, and down there. Screaming, he was.'

'I'm coming.'

'Don't be stupid, Rick.' She sounded better. 'You're flying to Nepal tomorrow. Today. Becky's coming.'

Rick hauled himself out of bed. His taxi to the airport was due at 5.30. As he showered he could still hear his mum's cracked voice, until recently so strong. Becky was going. He wasn't. In the kitchen he stood at the window, staring into the half-light, at the green–black shadows and the smear of yellow growing in the east.

18

From the breakfast terrace of the Jyatha Temple Hotel, steps led down to a walled courtyard. Monkeys chattered in a line of gnarled trees and in the distance snow-capped mountains spangled in the sunlight. Taking it in turns, the monkeys climbed down, ran across the courtyard and approached the hotel guests. If they got close, a strategically placed groundsman chased them away with a stick. It begged the question: what if two monkeys approached together?

Rick's head thumped, and his eyes tried to pull shut. The waiter with the coffee pot was nowhere to be seen. He swallowed two ibuprofen, and picked up a leaflet. The hotel had once been the hunting grounds of kings of Nepal and home to large herds of deer. In their place was now a golf course, a swimming pool and a business centre.

He logged on to the Wi-Fi, but there were no messages from home.

A couple walked past his table, holding hands. The woman wore a black dress with red whorls, and her partner a brown suede jacket. They sat at the next table, and watched the monkeys.

Amanda wasn't due until later so he had time to read Maggie's briefing pack and the remaining crime squad applications. He should have read them on the plane, but he was a terrible traveller. And he'd been worrying about Dad.

There were four slim files: 'Nepal'; 'Qatar & the 2022 World Cup'; 'FIFA'; and 'Life in a Wheelchair'. The first of the remaining application forms was 'Trever' Sinclair's. Surely there wasn't a typo in his own name? Either way, Rick couldn't face him without breakfast. He opened the FIFA file.

FIFA runs football tournaments, including the World Cup. Set up in 1904, membership of 209. Mind-boggling wealth: in 2013 FIFA reported an income of a billion dollars, a profit of 70 million, and cash reserves of 1.5 billion.

Outrageous, thought Rick. FIFA ran competitions for people who wore shorts to work.

FIFA is run by a president (Sepp Blatter), a congress (each country supplies a member) and an executive committee who make decisions. The executive committee includes eight vice presidents. Terry Williams is the current VP for the whole of the UK.

Terry Williams had told him some of it a few days earlier, but he hadn't mentioned the money. Rick skim-read the rest of the document. Two pages on corruption issues, including the election of Blatter and the awarding of the 2018 and 2022 World Cups. FIFA were as bad as the Police Federation.

Still no messages.

Breakfast arrived. Coffee, juice and toast. He could have had curry or waffles. As he ate, Rick assessed Trever Sinclair. *Trevor is a tremendous asset to B team, and we would be sorry to lose him* wrote his line manager, Sergeant Blanchard. *He works hard, turns up on time. Four arrests in the last month.* Sinclair was neither a spellchecker, nor a thief-taker, and Blanchard was *not* sorry to lose him.

Still no messages from home.

Rick turned to the Qatar file.

FIFA awarded the 2022 World Cup to Qatar. A country at the bottom of football rankings, summer temperatures of 50 degrees and a population, almost uniquely, who couldn't care less about football. The result, a shopping list for a dozen football stadiums. Currently being built not by the Qataris, but by overseas workers, including many from Nepal.

Paragraphs followed on working conditions, employment rights, *kafala*, passports and living conditions. He read the conclusion. Two hundred Nepalese deaths the previous year, three hundred in total, many more injured. Similar information to the articles in Calix Coniston's attic.

At the next table, the woman pushed back her hair, and laughed at something her partner said.

Rick sipped his coffee. Perhaps he should learn some jokes. And buy a suede jacket.

He checked for monkeys, and opened the Nepal file.

The Kingdom of Nepal lies between Tibet and India and includes a large slice of the Himalaya including 8 of the world's 14 mountains above 8,000 metres. A honeypot to swarms of mountaineers. Ancient history, strong religions, incredible scenery, friendly people and some of the best walking on the planet.

It was a cut-and-paste job, but with a sprinkling of Maggie. The metaphor especially for him? He flicked through the other pages. History, geography, economy, climate, flora and fauna, language, religion, food and drink, misc. He stopped at a table.

	GDP per capita ($)	IMF ranking
Qatar	145,000	1
US	53,000	10
UK	36,000	28
Nepal	2,200	159

Nepal was poor, he knew that. Qatar was wealthy, he knew that too, but the scale was staggering.

The final section was highlighted in yellow.

Although Nepal has been a monarchy for much of its history, it became a republic in 2008. Five years of civil war followed as the Congress Party struggled for power with the Maoists. Earlier this year a new prime minister from the Congress Party was elected. During the civil war the Maoists kidnapped two Italian tourists (March 2012).

If Calix and the others had been kidnapped by Maoists, why had there not been any demands?

In front of him came the moment he'd been waiting for: two monkeys approaching the terrace together. The groundsman must have seen it hundreds of times, but the old man dithered. *Throw the stick.* Rick could hear the waiters sniggering. The old man took off his flip-flops and threw them at the first monkey, then lolloped after the second. The invaders scampered off, and the couple at the next table burst into applause. Suede jacket stood up, walked over to the groundsman and pulled out his wallet. The waiters stopped sniggering and the old man bowed.

Rick watched the old man collect his flip-flops and slump back in the chair. He wondered whether it was a set-up.

It was still early back home, but he couldn't wait any longer, and he took out his phone.

'How is he?'

'It's five to six, Rick.' Becky's yawn echoed down the phone.

'Is he still there?'

'Yeah, home tomorrow or the day after. I'm going to stay with them for a few days.'

'I was thinking, Becky, about a stair-gate.'

'Got one. Julian put it up.'

'Thought he was a dentist.'

'He's good at that stuff.'

He should have done it. *His* dad.

He picked up the last file. Inside, there was only one piece of paper. In large letters, Maggie shouted up at him.

IT'S SHIT!

He got it.

He stared at the array of files. They were all pointless. The case was pointless. Solve it and there'd be another one. Maybe he should go home, check the stair-gate was up properly. But what then? He had to do something between getting out of bed and getting back in again.

Robbo knew he wouldn't go home. Becky knew he wouldn't. *He* knew he wouldn't. He had witnesses to interview, two scenes and a body to examine. A job to do: find Calix Coniston and the Williams twins and take them home.

Familiar voices made him look up. Russell and Kate stood in the open French doors to the dining room. Russell talking, Kate listening, standing together, like a couple. Kate scanned the tables on the terrace, and caught Rick's eye. Her long red hair was wet and shiny. She waved and he forced a smile.

Maybe he should get a dog.

He shuffled up his files.

They walked over, Russell towering over the waiters. He

was halfway up Everest before he'd even started climbing. Several people recognised the mountaineer and started whispering.

'Amanda's going to be late,' said Russell. 'Some time tomorrow.'

Kate peered over Rick's shoulder at his notebook.

Stair-gate?

Suede jacket?

Dog?

He snapped the book shut.

19

At the front of the cave, a guard put another tree root on the fire. Wood was scarce at that altitude and nothing was wasted. Sparks tumbled over each other on their way skywards. An oil lamp burned, and the smell of roasting chicken hung thickly.

Calix held his palms towards the fire, and squatting next to him, Barney did the same. Amanda and the Mera expedition, with its dining tent, under-table heater and three-course meals, were long gone. The twin nudged Calix and raised his eyebrows. 'Now?' he whispered.

Calix shook his head.

On the other side of the fire, the guard who doubled up as cook tended two large stainless steel pans. Around him, hunkered down, were the rest of the guards. One of the chickens delivered by Ram, the boy with the yellow rucksack, had been plucked and gutted, the scrawny remainder mounted on a spit. At random intervals, the cook-guard rotated it. The smell filled Calix's nostrils, excited his stomach, played with his head – the Kathmandu Kitchen, chicken 'n' chips at Failston Fry, dinner at home with his parents. Home.

Fat from the chicken dripped into the fire and the flames hissed and flared.

A tent zip pulled.

Calix turned around, but the tent he shared with the twins was still. A chain snaked in through the door, one end attached to Spencer, and the other to a bracket bolted to the cave wall. Three brackets, three chains. For Spencer, it was overkill: he couldn't go anywhere, even if he wanted to. Even now, he was coughing. The other tents were at the back of the cave, and from the gloom, Hant emerged. The guards made room for him at the fire.

'I'm going to ask him,' said Barney. He stood up. His chain rattled, and he yanked it with his boot. The chain held fast, and the low murmurs of the guards stopped. They looked over, the flickering flames picking out their round, similar faces. Weathered, impassive, a dusting of stubble.

Calix grabbed Barney's trouser-leg and pulled him down. 'Let's eat first.' Barney kicked at the chain but sat down. The noise echoed around the cave.

Hant produced a beer and flipped off the lid. There was no need for a fridge. Calix watched him drink the first feel-good mouthful. He looked away, not wanting to make it any better.

The food was ready. *Dal baht*, the Nepalese staple. Rice and lentils, and a spicy sauce to go with it. Nandos five-chilli spicy. *Piro*. The cook-guard ladled portions onto orange plastic plates like frisbees. Hant first, guards, prisoners. A pecking order, even in a cave high in the Himalaya.

Calix took his plate, and watched the guards start to eat. They used their hands, didn't wait. Hant took his plate, swigged his beer and put the bottle down. He glanced up, caught Calix's eye and held it. Calix tried to read the Nepalese man – *I can do this for a very long time*, he seemed to be saying. The leader looked the same as he'd done a week earlier, not tired or sunburnt or unshaven. His goatee beard was tidy, his movements deft and unhurried. Hant looked at home. He put down his beer, and began to eat with a fork.

Calix felt into a trouser pocket for his spoon from the Kathmandu Kitchen. He found it, their one communal digger. The rice was stodgy and the lentils bland but they were hot and calmed his stomach.

Barney sat down beside Calix. 'Says he's not hungry, but I left his plate anyway.' Calix passed him the spoon, and watched him eat. As a Cub Scout he'd been told to keep five things in his pocket – a clean kerchief, a 50p coin, safety pins, two others he'd forgotten. Even then, he'd found much of it childish – the Akela nonsense, woggles, games of crab football in the hall – but the self-reliance had stuck.

The guards passed around a jerrycan of water, taking it in turns to drink. Each man held it a few centimetres from his mouth. After a nod from Hant, the tufty-haired guard passed it to Calix. He drank – the water was clear but cold, and made his teeth hurt. Barney's turn, and he lifted and poured, but too fast, and ended up coughing and spluttering. The guards snickered.

The cook-guard started on the chicken.

All the men's eyes followed his progress. He slid the roasted bird onto a plastic plate and tore it apart into pieces. Wings, legs, lower legs, chunks of breast. He licked his fingers several times. Finally, he broke the carcass into pieces. The smell of hot fat, of cooked chicken juices, of meat – they hadn't eaten meat for a week – was mesmerising. Torturous. Calix hadn't realised how much he liked chicken. The cook divided the plate up. Five guards, including the cook, Hant and three of them – nine. Enough for at least a piece each.

The plate was passed to Hant, who took a leg, a wing, and some breast. Pecking order. Barney sighed, and Calix sensed the twin getting twitchy. 'They're divvying up the chicken,' he shouted at his brother in the tent.

'I can smell it,' Spencer shouted back. It set him off coughing and wheezing.

Barney scowled and stretched out his bad leg. He flexed his fingers, first one hand, then the other. He was a tall man, a sturdy man, but he was still young and unsure what to do with it all. Calix slapped a fist down on Barney's thigh.

'Easy.'

The chicken plate was passed around the guards and they each grabbed some of the meat. It was placed back on a lidded saucepan, a few pieces still left.

Calix forced himself to look away. He ate another mouthful of gloopy rice and passed the spoon to Barney. The twin held it up, twisted it and sighed. He stood, his rattling chain announcing his movement. This time, Calix didn't stop him.

'Spence needs a hospital, Hant. Needs to go back to Kathmandu. You've already got Vic on your conscience.'

All eyes were now on Barney.

Hant forked in a piece of chicken and chewed.

'Hant, answer me, Spencer might die. Dad'll pay, however much.' Barney kicked at his chain. 'For fuck's sake,' he shouted.

A guard stood up, put a hand in his coat pocket and semi-circled around behind him. The other guards continued to eat.

'Sit,' said Hant. 'Sit, and we talk.'

Barney sat down, pulling noisily at his chain.

'Not about money,' said Hant, shaking his head. He put down his plate and prodded at his teeth with a toothpick. 'You see news TV?'

'Yes,' said Barney.

'Nepal?' said Hant. A guard picked up the leader's plate and crunched on the ends of the bones.

Barney shook his head.

'Qatar?'

Barney frowned.

'After World Cup Russia, World Cup Qatar.'

The guard with Hant's plate threw the bones on the fire. He ran his finger around the plate and licked it clean.

'So?' said Barney.

'Qatar people no like football, no big place watch football. But Qatar very rich country. Nepal very poor country. Nepal people build very big place so Qatar people watch football.'

'Isn't that a good thing?'

'Maybe good, yes. But no. Bad, very bad. Work one hundred hours in week. Very, very hot. Live very small place. Money very small.'

The cook-guard collected the plates, scraping the bones onto the fire.

'Two, three hundred workers Nepal dead. Ten, twenty, thirty hundred injured.'

'I'm sorry for the Nepalese people,' said Barney, 'but, why don't they go home?'

'They no leave. *Kafala*. Employer keep passport. If try leave police arrest.'

Barney was quiet, and Calix picked at the scabs on his wrists.

'So, that's why we're here?' said Barney. 'Because Dad's in FIFA?'

Hant nodded. 'FIFA very bad. No do nothing. Like porter who drink much *rakshi*. You and Spencer... make FIFA change.'

Barney threw his plate onto the fire. The plastic slowly sagged and dripped. The fire hissed and a toxic smell replaced the fading chicken.

'I still don't get it. Why's Calix here? His dad's a soldier.'

'Newcell competition real, Calix win real.'

'Still doesn't make sense. Why's he at the cave? Why kidnap

him – and Vic?' Calix stopped picking at his scabs and looked up.

'You fault. You change Vic-key you tent. Vic-key no you tent, Vic-key still—'

Barney lunged for a stick in the fire but Calix moved faster, stamping his boot on it. Barney scowled. 'He's a sick fuck.' He jabbed a finger at Hant. '*You're* a sick fuck.'

When Barney finally crawled into the tent, Calix clanked to the edge of the cave. The guards had moved closer to the fire, and were smoking and laughing. One guard hawked into the flames.

Calix stared out into the blackness of the valley, his freezing breath marking the air. Two or three lights were visible, but miles away. Miles and miles. His wrists throbbed. He looked up into the starlit sky and wished he knew the names of some of the constellations. Something familiar.

20

In a shady part of the hotel garden, wicker chairs had been set out around low glass tables. Wooden trellising formed a cage overhead, and small pink roses climbed up. Their sweet fragrance filled the air. Russell and Kate sat at a table opposite a short woman. Between them were bottles of Everest beer and large burger-filled baps with Nepalese flags sticking out. The bowl of chips was huge. All three were laughing.

'Rick, this is Amanda,' said Russell. 'Amanda, Rick.'

Rick nodded. His plan was to interview Amanda before dinner and view Vicky's body in the afternoon.

Amanda smiled up at him. Her face was freckly and un-made-up. Her hair was short and wiry – tomboyish. Next to her chair was a small rucksack with a teddy bear tied to the top. She saw him staring. 'That's Brad. He's stood with me on the summits of three eight-thousanders. Lucky.' She paused. 'Until now.'

'Pull up a seat, Rick,' said Russell.

'We can't talk here.' Rick glanced around at the nearby tables. Two couples and a large family group. 'I've booked a room in the business centre.'

'We've just started eating,' said Kate. She picked up her beer.

'This isn't a holiday,' said Rick. 'I'm sure Amanda will understand.' The guide took an unladylike bite of burger and stood up. Rick turned to go, but turned back. 'Need you, too, Russell. Thanks. And, Amanda, you've got the note?' She nodded, still chewing.

The room was basic but functional. A table and six chairs, and a computer on a desk in the corner. No windows. Rick sat alongside Russell, and opposite Amanda. She'd brought her beer with her but he let it go. Behind her was a large painting of Cho Oyu.

'This feels very formal,' said Amanda. 'Do I need a solicitor?'

'No.'

'I was joking.' She laughed, nervously, and sipped her beer. She wore grey fingerless gloves.

'You're not under arrest, you don't have to say anything and, of course, you're free to leave at any time. I only want the truth.' He knew the whole interview would be inadmissible, but he only had to give the impression that it would be played in court. He put his Dictaphone on the table, and switched it on. 'That's so Russell doesn't have to take notes.'

Amanda forced out a smile. She put her beer on the floor.

'Rick, is that... all this... really necessary?' said Russell.

'Vicky Brant is dead and three men are missing, so, yes, it is. It won't take long.' A white lie. 'Amanda, can you start by telling us what happened?'

'Well, nothing really. We were camping on a football pitch near Kathara. People stayed up—'

Rick raised his hand. 'Hang on, Amanda. I thought you were camping near the village of Katt-har-er?'

'No, Kathara.'

'How're you spelling that?'

'K–a–t–h–a–r–a.'

'But pronounced Catt-rer?'

'More or less. Why?'

Rick shook his head. 'Carry on.' The name in Calix's notebook, *Catra*. He'd thought it was a girl's name but was it Kathara?

'As I was saying,' said Amanda, 'after dinner, people stayed up for a bit, then, when it was getting cold, they started drifting off to their tents. Spencer was one of the first. Vicky and Barney not long after – they'd become a bit of an item. Calix, one of the last. I had a final walk around and then turned in myself.'

'Porters?'

'Cook team, *sirdar*?' added Russell.

'They all sleep in the dining tent. I read for a bit, and heard them talking. I've asked them, and they said they didn't hear anything.'

Rick nodded. 'And?'

'That's it. In the morning two tents were empty and the four of them had gone. The tea which the cook boy leaves outside each tent lay untouched, and when I went to check, no one. Just the note in Calix's tent. No one heard or saw anything, and believe me, I have asked.'

'We believe you,' said Russell.

'Anything to suggest the four of them were going to leave? An argument with the others?'

She shook her head. 'No, nothing.'

'Anything unusual happen the day before?'

'No. A normal day at the office.'

'What about the whole trip?'

Again, she shook her head. 'I've led the Mera expedition seven times, and I know the route and all the campsites better than the ones around Sheff.'

'Who knew the route?'

'It's on our website,' said Russell.

Rick nodded. 'Ah.' That may have ruled out his dad, but not many other people. 'Anyone following you, Amanda? Any sign of the Maoists?'

'No, the Mera route's been clear for a while.'

'Nothing odd at all? Think back.'

'Every trip is different. This one was very slow as Jean-Paul hurt his ankle.' She paused. 'There was one thing. When the *sirdar* and one of the porters read a list of the clients they got a bit excited about Calix Coniston. It was back in Kathmandu, before we'd started.'

'Why?'

'They wouldn't say.'

'Where are they now?'

'Escorting the rest of the expedition back to Kathmandu, still a few days away.'

'Russell, we'll need to speak to the two of them as soon as they get back. And the other clients.' Russell nodded. Rick would have to sort him out with a notebook. If the mountaineer was going to ride shotgun, then he'd have to pack a pen. 'What about the other trekkers, Amanda?'

'Eleven clients. Two couples from the UK, a Kiwi called Mike, a Dutch woman called Ellen, Jean-Paul, and the four who went missing. Vicky, Calix, and the twins, Barney and Spencer, one alpha male and one about xylophone. Spencer was asthmatic, not outdoorsy and probably didn't want to be there. But if anyone stood out, it was Calix. He didn't say much, liked going off with his binoculars. He was very keen to have his own tent. First mentioned it when I met him at the airport.'

'I thought you said only two tents were targeted?'

'Yes.'

'Three of them in the other tent?'

'No, Calix had started sharing with Spencer.'

'Why?'

'Well, it all started with Spencer complaining about not sleeping because a few clients had developed mountaineer's cough. So, two tents were moved away from the others.'

'When?'

'The night the four went missing.'

'Two tents?'

'At the same time, Vicky moved in with Barney. So, Spencer moved out, and in with Calix.'

'Why Calix, and not whoever Vicky had been sharing with?'

'She'd been sharing with Ellen. But I don't know.'

'Did that not strike you as odd? Calix the loner, Calix the odd one out, agreeing to share a tent after making a big deal of having his own one, and with someone like Spencer.'

'I suppose.'

'Whose idea was it to move tents?'

'Spencer's... I think.'

'You're not sure? Think, it's important.'

'Easy, Rick,' said Russell. 'I'm not sure where this is getting us. Have you got many more questions?'

Rick stood up. 'Russell, a word outside. Sorry, Amanda.'

She shrugged.

Rick shut the door. They stood like teacher and pupil, DCI and trainee 'tec. Alongside them was an enormous mural of the Annapurna region.

'I'm sorry, but—'

'Listen, Russell. You may be the expert up there.' Rick jerked his chin at the mural. 'In the snow and ice, and on the mountain trails. But, in there –' and he tapped the door with his foot – 'is my territory.'

'Amanda's done nothing wrong.'

'You may be right, but we don't know that. This might be a murder enquiry, and Amanda might be a suspect. Imagine if Vicky was your daughter.'

'You think they were kidnapped?'

'Maybe.'

The two of them went back in and sat down.

'Amanda, why didn't you report the disappearance immediately?'

Her face coloured. 'I should have done. I thought... I hoped they'd come back. That it was a joke or something. I can't believe Vicky's dead. I'm sorry. Very, very sorry.'

'Rick, I explained this all to you, back in England. What's happened is very unusual. Unheard of, and I've been in this game a long time.'

Rick glared across at Russell, then turned back to Amanda. 'Let's have a look at the note.'

From her daypack, Amanda produced a plastic wallet containing a single piece of paper. She passed it over.

The note was written on a page ripped out of a book, originally just bearing a footer with the book's title. *Concept of Time: Heidegger.* There was another Heidegger by the bed in the Conistons' attic.

Amanda

The 4 of us r leaving the expedition. 2 much like a forced march. We're going 2 do our own trek at a more relaxed pace. Hope u understand. Nothing personal.

Calix

Rick passed it to Russell to read.

'Was it a forced march, Amanda?'

'Hardly. As I said, Jean-Paul had hurt his ankle. We were taking twice as long as usual.'

'Any other thoughts, Russell? You too, Amanda.'

'It doesn't feel right to me,' said Amanda. 'The whole thing. I mean, where are they now?'

'You say it doesn't feel right. But earlier you said you hoped they'd come back. Which is it?'

'I don't know, you've confused me.'

'Take your time, I only want the truth.'

'What the hell's that supposed to mean?'

'Steady, Rick.'

'Stay out of this, Russell,' said Amanda, glowering at her NA boss.

'Calm down, both of you.' Rick wondered if he should swap Russell with Kate.

'I am calm,' said Amanda.

'Well, answer the question, did the note seem odd, or not?'

She picked up her beer from the floor, looked at Rick and put it down again without drinking. 'Both, I suppose. At the time I hoped they'd come back, but in retrospect, the note does seem odd.'

Rick let it go. He'd rattled her, which was enough for the moment. Rattled both of them, which was a bonus.

'Russell?'

'I agree, the note's definitely odd,' said the mountaineer after a pause. 'What's the alternative? The four of them wander off, have a row, Vicky goes off by herself, and the three guys get lost? Spencer doesn't sound like the next Bonington.'

'So, if you're both right?' There were a lot of alternatives – in various combinations – and one was sitting with him in the room.

There was a knock on the door. Kate poked her head in. 'Got a moment, sir?'

Rick didn't want to leave Amanda and Russell together, but he had no choice. He left the door open and ushered Kate down the corridor. 'Ssh.'

'What's happening?' said Kate.

'I don't know, but something's not right.'

'This'll add to it. Maggie's been in touch. The Newcell competition's a fraud. Thought you'd want to know asap. I got her to forward the email.'

Sir

The competition IS A FRAUD. Newcell's Special Operations Unit in Frankfurt hadn't heard of it, and I checked back with Tarak but he couldn't add anything. They seemed a bit left hand right hand, so I spoke to their head of security – I should have started with him really. Ex-Job. Phoned me back after 24 hours; he'd spoken to every office, checked every database, and studied the letter. Definite fraud, a good one: perfect copy of their letterhead and style-wise very similar to a competition they ran early last year. Except – paper's too thick.

'Yes!' Rick punched the air.

At last, the enquiry was taking shape. Possibly a kidnap but nothing to do with Maoists, or Vicky. It was back to his theory of two cases, or one case and a connection. The follow-up question remained: why drag the three missing out to Nepal?

'Kate, phone Maggie, ask her to repeat all the checks on Russell and Amanda. Include their financial records. And get her to confirm with Vicky's family that she didn't win a competition. Didn't *think* she'd won.'

'Russell?' said Kate. She looked like her dog had died.

'Look, the job's on, and I want to be sure about him before we go much further.'

'Earlier, Rick, in the garden. I'm sorry if it looked bad; I was trying to relax Amanda. It's been traumatic for her.' Rick could smell the beer on her breath. He nodded.

She walked off, and he went back into the room. Russell and Amanda weren't talking. 'The competition's a fraud.'

'No!' said Russell.

'Amanda, prior to this trip, did you know, or contact in any way, Calix Coniston or the Williams brothers or either of their families?'

She frowned. 'No.'

'When I searched Calix's room, I found a notebook. In it were phone numbers, one belonging to someone referred to as A. 07816 223 254. Is that you?'

'No. Surely Russell has told you that?'

'Do you have a second phone?'

'Course not – what is this? You think *I'm* involved? I promise you I'm not.'

Next to Rick, Russell shifted in his chair and cleared his throat. Rick ignored him. 'Paul Parry.'

She held his stare. 'We had an affair. I'm not proud of it.'

'Why did it end?'

'Rick, you can't ask her that.'

'I can. I have.'

'Amanda, you don't have to answer.'

'It's alright, Russ, he's only doing his job.'

'No, it's not alright. You've had a time of it.' He turned to face Rick. 'She's done nothing wrong.'

So the mountaineer kept saying, thought Rick. 'Amanda, do you know about Paul's conviction for fraud?'

'No.' She looked away, and took a deep breath. She looked back. 'I mean, yes.'

'Amanda!' said Russell. 'Fuck.'

'Can I get a glass of water?'

Rick got the hint. 'Russell, can you get Amanda some water?' The mountaineer left the room.

Amanda threw Brad into the bin. 'He's fired.' She smiled weakly, and nodded at the door. 'Does he know?'

'About what?'

'About Paul's criminal record. I don't want Paul to lose his job.'

'Did Paul ever suggest to you a scam like Trekking Dreams, or Summits International?'

'No.'

'Did you know about the fake Newcell competition?'

'No.'

'Have you contacted Paul on this trip?'

'A couple of texts.'

One of them was lying, Parry or Amanda. Possibly both. 'Have you any idea what happened to Vicky?'

'No.'

'Where the other three are now?'

'No.' Amanda took a deep breath. 'God,' she yelled. 'I've not done anything. Nothing. And I'm not saying anything else. Not one bloody word.'

'Okay,' said Rick. 'Okay.'

'Get Russell back.'

Rick stood up, and leaving the door open, went out to find Kate. She was waiting down the corridor, in a doorway to the garden. No sign of Russell. She stubbed out her cigarette and dropped it in the metal tray.

'Not sure,' said Rick. 'About either of them.'

'I'm sorry again, boss, about earlier.' She repeated her explanation. 'I was trying to win Amanda's trust, so if she did have anything to say, she'd say it.'

'Okay.' He paused. 'How's Richardson?'

She looked surprised he'd asked. 'He's got a bit of a cough. Missing his mummy.'

Rick nodded. He would if he was Richardson. He almost said as much, but the moment passed. 'Go back in there, Kate, and try to smooth things over. We still need them, both of them.' She turned to go. 'And Kate, no more drinking during the day. We're here to work.'

Smoke curled up from the tray, and Rick strolled further into the garden. It was lush with growth, and full of sound. Beds of bright flowery shrubs, and behind them rhododendron bushes with huge pregnant buds. He sat on a chair. Ancient trees, trunks wrapped in creepers. A hidden chorus of birds.

He picked up a menu from under the chair, and beckoned a waitress.

'Yes, sir?'

'Apple pie, and cream. Thank you.'

She walked away, and he replaced the menu under the chair.

He picked up the bag with Calix's note. It didn't seem likely that Calix had written it. To make sure, Rick took a photo on his phone and emailed it to Maggie – she could show it to Calix's parents to see whether they recognised the handwriting.

He had another thought, remembering an input from a detective superintendent on a training day. The super had spoken for half an hour on his pet project, 'Victim Notes left for the Police in case of Suicide, Kidnap and Ransom'. The talk opened with a video of a US soldier blinking Morse code when paraded on TV by the Viet Cong. The super had even mentioned an episode of *Homeland*. The advice was twofold: not to underestimate either the victim's ingenuity to hide a message, or the victim's confidence in the police to find it.

The super's focus was on an ordinary Joe Public hiding something quickly, and he'd stressed it was often a message that only someone familiar to them would be able to decipher. He gave a few examples – an incorrect middle name or date of birth, a pet they didn't own – and the letters or numbers that shouldn't have been there spelt out a car registration number, or an address, or some other crucial information.

The waitress brought a thick wedge of apple pie. The plate was cold and flecked with cinnamon. Rick paid, and added a generous tip.

He ate it, staring at Calix's message. Even if he'd been made to write it at gunpoint, Calix might have been able to slip something in. He opened his notebook and began to scrutinise every word, every number, every space.

4/r/2/2/u – Morse code? some other code?

forced march – why underlined, some kind of anagram?

4/2/2 – numbers?

After half an hour he had a page of numbers and letters but nothing more. He emailed Maggie again, asking her to show the note to a handwriting expert, a code-breaker, the superintendent who had given the CPD input and the CID office, including the applicants for the detective posts. He'd eat his shoe if Downcliff cracked it.

He turned to his hypotheses.

Hypothesis 1 was out – he now had a crime. Hypothesis 2a, kidnap then murder, and hypothesis 2b, kidnap then demands, were both still possible. Calix's note was likely bogus, but he still needed confirmation. He also needed another hypothesis, one that caught everything except H2a and H2b, one where there was still hope for Calix and the twins, even if they had been kidnapped. He settled on H3, missing in Nepal – maybe they'd escaped or the kidnap attempt had been botched. If they were missing then they should come to notice very soon. Over a week had passed – Calix's note had been left on 16 April and it was now the 25th. H3 did seem very unlikely even in mountainous, undeveloped Nepal – unless they also were lying injured or dead somewhere.

Was the Catra in Calix's notebook a reference to Kathara, a Nepalese village, and close to where the four had gone missing? Or been kidnapped. If it was, then had Calix known what was coming? How, and why? The date in the notebook was the 10th, not the 16th, but the expedition had been slow because of Jean-Paul hurting his leg.

Had Paul Parry concocted something with Calix Coniston?

Behind the huge trees were glistening mountains. Somewhere between them were the answers.

21

Kathmandu Central Morgue was a large grey building next to a bridge over a river. The sloping riverbanks were made of wide stone steps and stretched into the distance. Several groups of women were washing clothes in the river, and laying them to dry on the steps. Two men arrived, their baskets piled high with logs. They dumped them next to a concrete plinth that was like the foot of a statue. After lighting cigarettes, the men walked off.

Rick stood on the bridge, waiting for Russell and Kate. He felt better. He'd had a decent night's sleep. He felt less— He wouldn't even think the word. According to Emma, that was half the battle. He looked around for his colleagues. He was impatient to get on: view the body, then interview the trekkers on the Mera expedition.

The men returned with more wood. They unloaded and arranged it on the plinth. A neat stack about two feet deep.

Russell and Kate arrived, the mountaineer's size and Kate's long red hair attracting stares. A group of children appeared, and watched in silence. Rick's feeling of wellbeing disappeared.

'Have you got the letter?'

Kate nodded.

On the steps of the morgue, more people were hanging around.

Men holding hands, family groups, quiet children. The reception area was busy and there were queues at two windows, as if they were buying stamps. Two uniformed and armed police officers stood at the door.

Russell spoke to one of the policemen, and he let them through a security door. The mountaineer strode off, and a few minutes later came back with an overweight Nepalese man. He was dressed entirely in black: black baggy trousers, a black gilet and several black shirts, the collars in a mess. He looked stressed.

'This is the morgue superintendent.'

'*Namaste*,' said Rick. He showed him the letter.

'You friends of family?'

Rick nodded. The superintendent frowned and walked off. In the reception area, a woman started wailing. A small tree in a giant pot was dying. A circle of curled brown leaves surrounded it. The air smelt of smoke.

The superintendent came back. He shook his head. 'Very sorry, *sahib*. Very very sorry. The body Miss Victoria Brant go today morning. To Tribhuvan, airport. Miss Brant go home Australia. Very sorry, *sahib*.'

Rick wasn't surprised. He'd expected it, and, in a way, he was relieved. Morgues were not places for anything to go right. 'Can we have a copy of the death certificate?'

The superintendent looked pained. He walked off again. A brown leaf floated down from the tree in the pot, and settled amongst the others.

The three of them waited in the entrance to a courtyard. A grieving family walked past and disappeared through a door that led out of the yard. More leaves fell off the tree. Kate and Russell chatted in low voices. Every now and then, Kate laughed and pushed her hand back through her hair. Rick smelt incense in the smoke. The grieving family reappeared and walked back.

After thirty minutes the superintendent returned. Rick knew

what he was going to say – the same tactic was used by the front office at South Manchester. The longer someone was kept waiting, the more relieved they were with a negative answer. The superintendent shook his head. 'Very sorry, *sahib*, not find it.'

'Can you look again?' said Rick.

The three of them went back outside, and stood on the bridge. Kate lit a cigarette. The wood on the plinth was now three feet deep, and a pile of logs lay alongside. Rick heard more wailing and a small column of people came into view. Thirty adults and children. Some of the men carried a stretcher made from thick bamboo poles. On the stretcher was a man's body. The men laid the body over the logs on the plinth and arranged more logs on top. Fuel from a can was splashed over the pyre. The funeral party chanted and threw handfuls of rice-like bits.

'They're Hindu,' said Russell. 'Most Nepalese are. They believe in reincarnation – the soul is immortal and is reborn, time and time again.'

A Western couple in wide-brimmed straw sunhats walked onto the riverbank. They stopped and took photos.

'Same as the Buddhists,' said Kate. Holding her cigarette, she jabbed at a piece of tar on her lip with a finger.

'Yes, and no,' said Russell. 'Buddhists also believe in reincarnation but they believe in an end state. *Nirvana* is the end of suffering, of needs, of desires. And it's *karma* that leads you through the cycles. *Karma* is a rule of cause and effect – what you do in this life decides who or what you will come back as in the next life, and what you will live through.'

One man in the funeral party lit a torch, and walked around the pyre, setting fire to it. Rick wanted to leave, but like a moth to a candle he stayed. He didn't believe in reincarnation, or in anything. One life, and this was it. In the morgue he'd held it together, but only just. The fire took hold of the pyre and smoke began to billow across the river, over the bridge. The mourners chanted and wailed louder. More tourists stopped and one man took a video. Rick smelt burning flesh.

He was back there.

That week. Body number seventeen, the last one.

Thursday, the day after the sibling jumpers. A fire in an old people's home, the residents too frail to get out of bed. Firefighters had carried them out, but it'd been too late for one woman who was laid out next to his car. Her face had melted away, and her body was badly charred. Pieces of pink cardigan had fused with her skin. Days later, he could still smell her burnt flesh.

'Rick, are you okay?' said Kate. 'You look like you've seen a ghost.' She threw her cigarette butt into the river.

It was the smell. The smell of burning human flesh, in his hair, his clothes, inside his nostrils.

He nodded towards the morgue. The superintendent was walking towards them. In his hand was a piece of paper. 'Found, *sahib*.' He handed over a copy of the death certificate. Rick scanned through the Nepali to the English translation.

Cause of death: Cerebellar haemorrhage following major blunt trauma to front (upper) of head. Results of investigations awaited.

On the ceiling of Rick's ground-floor room, a huge fan lumbered round and round. The double doors were closed, but underneath them a column of ants marched in, and disappeared down a crack in the skirting board.

On the dresser sat two bottles of drinking water and a basket of fruit. The dresser was large enough to house all the clothes he owned. He washed an apple in the bottled water and sat down at the desk. Above it was a sign on the wall. 'Please, no smoke in room'.

Biting into the apple, he fired up his laptop. Half a screen of unread emails. He tapped up a report of the interview of Amanda and the fiasco at the morgue, and emailed it to everyone on the missing persons enquiry. Then he looked at his emails. Two were from Maggie, the one Kate had showed him and a second one.

Sir

Analysis of documents in Calix's attic room

I've copied and analysed the 35 documents on his wall. 5 on Mount Mera, 3 on Nepalese soldiers & the British pension, 8 misc, 19 on Qatar & 2022 World Cup.

Basic findings: 57 named people, 97 place names, 15 specific dates, 23 private companies, 9 countries.

Sepp Blatter had 23 hits, David Cameron 9, and the only person, I think, of interest to you, Terry Williams, 5. Attached are copies of the articles which mention him.

Five mentions of Terry Williams, the FIFA exec and father of the missing twins – chance? On the desk, an old-fashioned phone rang. Its cord was tangled and it had curved ends like a dog bone.

'Rick Castle.'

'You're now connected, Miss Nash,' said a Nepalese woman.

'I've a queue of people wanting to speak to you, sir,' said Maggie on the phone. 'Simon,' she said, raising her voice, 'it's the DCI.'

Bennett came onto the phone. Rick pictured his chewed-down

nails. 'Boss, you'll never believe it. Never.' Bennett garbled his words, but Rick got the gist. Bennett, Woods and a drugs dog had discovered a cannabis factory at Crick Lane Farm. Three Vietnamese illegals tending 1,500 plants. Sacks of dried leaves estimated at £2.5 million. The story had made the headlines on the local news, and been mentioned in the national papers. The chief super and Robbo were delighted. Rick wondered whether Bennett's nails were better or worse.

'Any connection with Parry or Calix Coniston?'

'Not yet,' said Bennett. 'Illegals said nothing and are now with Immigration. Got a sack of paperwork and a phone. So, I'm hopeful.'

'Is the report on the PP phone number back yet?'

'No. Telecoms can't find the paperwork so I've had to re-submit it. Time to bring Parry in anyway?'

'I'll have a think.' Surveillance was also an option, but with Amanda and Calix in Nepal, it was unlikely to reveal anything.

Maggie returned to the phone. 'I've sent Simon to get Robbo.'

Rick told her more about the interview with Amanda.

They discussed her emails.

There was so much he wanted to say.

'Maggie.'

'Yes?'

'Your fourth folder.'

'Yes?' said Maggie. *It's not shit. It's not that shit. What did he know?* 'Sir?'

'Rick.'

'Rick?'

Above him, the fan wobbled round and round. It was covered in cobwebs. The whole thing needed taking down, cleaning and fixing back up, properly. He'd likely make a mess of it, but no doubt Julian wouldn't.

I'm sorry for you. For what happened. But he didn't know what had happened, and anyway the comment would sound weak.

'I got it. I *get* it,' said Rick. There was no reply. 'Maggie?'

'No, it's Robbo. I've read your email, Rick. Things are moving this end, too. Vicky's death has been picked up by the press – her parents have been on TV. I've been in touch with the Aussie Old Bill and they're sending out a team to investigate. Here, the chief constable's bagman has been on the phone. I've had authority to send two more to help you, a DS and a DC. Harris and Bennett?'

'No, leave them on Parry. I'll take Khan and Emmett.'

'Okay. You ever had a stye?'

'You need to eat more fruit and veg, Robbo, and take more exercise.'

'You sound like Janice.'

'And stop using the lift.'

'You're also getting a liaison officer – Nepalese police. I managed to fudge an admin cock-up for the absence of liaison until now. So, in summary, keep doing what you're doing, play nicely with the Aussie boys, liaise with the liaison officer, and no talking to the press. Clear?'

'Yes.'

'No questions?'

'The reshuffle, Robbo. I'll get on top of things. The sessions with Emma are helping, just give me a bit more time.'

'We're giving you some time: Bransby will only be here six months. The decision's made.' The superintendent paused. 'Vicky Brant's death didn't help.'

'I can't work miracles. She was dead before I flew.'

'Maybe you should have flown sooner, not hung around for your dad. Is there anything else?'

'You haven't had a chance to look at my bees?'

'Jesus, Rick.'

22

A line of icicles crashed to the ground at the side of the cave. They formed overnight in the weep down the wall, and melted during the day. A diurnal cycle as reliable as the sun rising and setting, as reliable as *dal baht* for lunch and for dinner. As Hant arguing with the guards during the day and humiliating them in the evening.

The egg-yolk sun battered down, but still it was cold. Calix sat with Barney and Spencer, and inspected their injuries and complaints. Spencer was breathless, his face ashen. The sickly twin's feet were semi-frozen. Calix manipulated the toes, which felt like pebbles in a stream. He examined the chafing from the leg shackle; Spencer's ankle was swollen and plum-purple. Like Barney's, like his own. Swelling made the shackles tighter, and Calix worried about an infection from rust. The bruise on Barney's leg was fading, but he'd developed a cough and had a gash on his leg from a careering boulder. A bright red groove, the edges oozing. It wasn't healing, and Calix sprinkled salt he'd pilfered from the cook-guard, then dabbed it with his wet kerchief. Akela would have been proud. Barney needed antiseptic and stitches, Spencer his asthma drugs, and they all needed antibiotics. They were going downhill, and quickly.

'Are we going to be okay?' said Spencer. He sat with his feet drawn close, clasping his toes.

'As soon as they get what they want, they'll let us go.'

'V–v–icky.'

Calix nodded, hearing the thud of her head on the rock. He felt very alone.

'Spence needs his brown inhaler,' said Barney, coughing.

Calix rummaged in his daysack. He found Megan's chess set, recovered from her panniers in Australia. He handed it to Barney.

'Try and distract him.'

He watched them set up. Somehow, it was like having Megan alongside him. She wouldn't have given up. She never gave up.

Ram trekked up from the suspension bridge carrying a full rucksack. He stopped when he reached the three of them, and shucked off his rucksack.

Calix scratched a large X in the dirt with a stick. Ram bent down and drew an O with his finger. At the top of the boy's trouser-leg was a pattern of intricate stitching – large stars circling the letter R. Around his neck he wore a red and white bandana. He smiled up at Calix.

The game ended in a draw. They played another which Calix let Ram win. He winked at Barney, who whispered to Spencer.

The two of them sat down on the flat rocks, Calix's leg chain clinking as he moved and making him grimace. They stared at the huge rock, and at the metal ring and the three chains leading down. Calix cast around for more ideas. What would

Megan have done? Ram's yellow rucksack leant against a boulder. He checked his dictionary.

'*Thapa saag?*' More greens?

The boy nodded. '*Ra thapa biyara.*' And more beer.

Up at the cave, Hant talked to the cook-guard who was lighting the fire. Calix jerked his chin at them. 'Hant, *buwaa?*' Father. Calix had revised that word earlier.

Ram shook his head, and looked away.

Calix had caught something in the boy's eyes, in his face. Ram was young, not yet used to masking his emotions.

'*Hant, daai?*' Brother.

'*Chaina.*' The boy grinned. No.

Calix shrugged.

Ram thought for a moment. '*Aamaa daai.*'

Aamaa daai. Mother brother. Mother Brother. Uncle. Calix picked up his dictionary and looked up the word. '*Mama?*'

'*Ho*, Hant *mama.*' Yes, Hant uncle.

Calix nodded. '*Buwaa*, okay?'

Ram stared at Calix for a few seconds, then looked away. '*Chaina.*' He looked back and stuck his tongue out, closed his eyes and lolled his head over.

'*Mero buwaa, Ghurkha.* Soldier.' Calix mimed someone firing a gun. 'Ram *Buwaa*, Ghurkha?'

'*Chaina,*' replied Ram. No.

'*Mero buwaa naam ho* David Coniston. Con-iss-ton.' Calix wrote his surname on a scrap of paper from his pocket. Amanda's *sirdar* knew the name, and one of her porters. '*Chineu?*' Recognise? He'd looked that up too.

'*Chaina.*'

Calix sighed. He wasn't getting anywhere.

'Ram!' A shout from the cave. From Ram's *mama*. His uncle Hant.

Ram scowled and jumped up. He crouched in front of his pack, threaded his arms through the sweat-stained straps and straightened his legs. He lurched off.

Calix shoved a jacket behind his shoulders and leant back against a rock. Barney and Spencer were frowning at the board. Calix closed his eyes. An aeroplane is high in the sky. Ghurkhas parachute down, his father among them. The plane becomes the red kite – he's at home, in bed, staring at the ceiling. The Finchams' cat in the box under his desk needs finishing.

Something banged Calix's leg and he opened his eyes. Ram sat down, the lid of his empty rucksack flapping on his back.

'*Thik chha?*' Okay?

'*Thik chha,*' replied the boy. His eyes were watery, and on his cheek was a red weal which hadn't been there an hour previously.

'Hant hit him,' said Barney. The chess set was packed away, and Spencer sat holding his toes. Rocking slowly back and forth, humming to himself.

At the cave entrance, Hant stared down at them. 'Ram!' More words in Nepali followed with the angry flapping of his arm. He walked down the slope towards them.

Calix rummaged in his pocket within a pocket, produced a wrap of cannabis and threw it at Ram's feet. The boy looked up and Calix put his fingers to his lips and pretended to inhale. Ram's eyes widened. He picked up the wrap, and stood.

'Go on now,' said Calix. 'Go.' He waved a hand.

The boy hurried off.

Hant walked up, smoking a cigarette. His goatee was trimmed and his clothes were clean, as if they were living in a hotel. On his head was a fleece hat. A hotel in Norway. The two of them watched Ram run-walk down the valley, jumping several times over the stream. Marmots shrieked in alarm and dived into their burrows, then reappeared when he'd gone past. He came to a slide of large rocks and boulder-hopped his way through.

Hant squatted down next to Calix, and offered him the cigarette. Calix took it, and inhaled deeply. He handed it back, glancing at the twins. Barney was throwing stones at a balanced rock.

'Ram said you are his uncle, his *mama.*'

'Ram my sister son. Father taken Maoists, ten year. Think dead. I now boy father. He good boy. Strong boy. Very strong. Nepali: *baliyo.* Ram *baliyo.*'

The boy had disappeared down into the steep section. Low cloud was billowing up from the valley bottom, and the temperature was dropping. 'He's going to Saklis?'

'Yes, three hour, three half hour.'

'After dark.'

'He okay.'

Stones clattered as Barney's target collapsed.

Hant glanced round. Spencer was still rocking back and forth, still humming, his eyes now closed. Hant turned back, smirking. 'Spencer weak boy, not Ram. Not *baliyo.*'

'Calix,' said Hant, dropping his voice to a whisper, 'You say Barney and Spencer. Tonight.'

The long thin village of Ghandar had been built on the flank of a hill. A staircase of rocky steps ran up through the middle and there were houses and huts on both sides. Trekkers stayed in the many guesthouses.

Rick sat at a table on the rear terrace of the Tranquillity Lodge. His legs ached with the previous day's walking, and he had nothing but admiration for the hundreds of Nepalese people he'd passed on the trail. Schoolchildren in immaculate uniforms, young men in jeans and leather jackets, women in traditional costume. Families carrying loved ones to Kathmandu for medical attention, and porters hefting huge loads. A Nepalese army officer with a thin moustache, two boys with a blaring radio, and a *sadhu*, naked except for a cloth around his waist, his body dusty, his hair matted, carrying a trident.

The trek from Kathmandu had been like travelling on a motorway and being able to see into the other vehicles. He poured another cup of tea, and chewed the last crust of *roti*. The sky was a perfect cobalt.

Through a wooden balustrade, he looked down onto three houses and their communal backyard, the earthy surface baked hard in the sun. A wall of cobs was drying. Two old women sat in a corner, weaving baskets. They gossiped more than they worked, coughing and cackling with toothless grins. Dogs, chickens and young children ran about.

On the other side of the terrace, Russell and Kate were interviewing the first of the NA porters.

Two trekkers sat down in front of Rick. 'Debbie and Jason,' said the woman. Long blond hair and a touch of lipstick. Jason was tall and lean. Both wore sunglasses. Rick looked at his briefing sheet from Amanda. Debbie was a management consultant, and Jason a swimming instructor. She was thirty-four, Jason thirty-one.

'The night the four of them went missing, did you see or hear anything?'

'No,' said Debbie. Jason shook his head. He wore a red t-shirt over a blue long-sleeved top.

'Earlier that day, did you see anyone following you on the trail?'

'No,' said Debbie.

'Before then?'

'No.'

'Anything unusual?'

'No.'

'Jason?' said Rick.

'No.'

'How was Amanda?'

'Lovely,' said Debbie. 'Organised, relaxed but not too much. Interested in us. Professional, knew her stuff on flora and fauna, on altitude sickness, on group dynamics. Exactly as we'd hoped.'

'And when the four of them had gone?'

'Bemused, confused, increasingly worried. Upset. Jason?'

'Couldn't agree more – with all of it.'

'What about the four missing? Barney and Spencer, Vicky, and Calix.'

'What about them?'

Rick shrugged. 'Anything.'

'Spencer wasn't very well. Asthmatic, and slow. His brother, Barney, was one of the fittest. Good-looking, too. Vicky liked him. Then there was Calix. Cal. He hated being called that.'

'Did he?' said Jason.

'Look, Inspector,' said Debbie. She took off her glasses. 'The four of them were a bit younger than the rest of us. It wasn't a problem or anything but we just naturally migrated apart.'

Rick nodded. 'You saw the note – it referred to a forced march. Was there any indication that the four of them were going to go off?'

Debbie shook her head. 'Nope. And it was hardly a march. Jean-Paul was a hop-along. Forced dawdle, more like.'

Jason laughed. His sunglasses were still in place. 'Looking back now, I wonder whether we were drugged with something. It seems odd that no one heard anything.'

'What with?'

'I don't know. Something in the tea. I read a book about it once.'

'Anything more definite?' said Rick. 'Other symptoms, odd-looking urine, headache, sleepiness?'

'No, nothing that I didn't have before. It's just speculation, really. Sorry. Have you spoken to Mike yet?'

'No, you two are the first.'

'Here's Jean-Paul,' said Debbie.

They walked off and Rick annotated Amanda's sheet.

On the other side of the terrace, Kate and Russell were still talking to the same porter. Kate caught Rick's eye, and gave a quick shake of the head.

'Good morning, Inspector.' Rick motioned at a chair. Jean-

Paul took a final drag on his cigarette and stubbed it out. He was a big man and overweight. Forty-five. An engineer from Toulouse. He eased himself carefully into the hot seat. 'Everything go wrong on this trip. Even start again cigarette.'

'How's the leg?'

'*Comme-ci, comme-ça.*' He turned, and coughed repeatedly.

'That night, what did Amanda do?'

'She think a joke to begin. We search some hours. As time pass, joke disappear, sometimes she worry and sometimes cross. I was quite please. I not like Calix. He only talk Spencer and Barney.'

'Anything else?'

'Yes, yes. I injure leg day two or day three and then slow. Very slow. I walk last with one porter. Calix always look me with... *jumelles*... I don't know English.' He rolled his hands into tubes and looked through them.

'Binoculars?'

'I think, yes,' said Jean-Paul. 'Always look me, *jumelles*. Why not he look mountains? No. Just me. All time. I not like Calix. Not like.'

'Thank you, Jean-Paul. You've been very helpful. *Merci beaucoup.*'

The big man hauled himself to his feet. He lit up another cigarette, and strolled away.

In the yard below the children were squabbling. One boy in shorts pushed another boy to the ground. The second boy, smaller, and naked, started to cry. A dog ran up, barking. One of the old women whistled. The dog froze, and limped off. The boy on the ground stopped crying, and stood up. A miracle.

Rick beckoned over the second couple of NA trekkers. By deduction, Kalin and Patrick. Kalin's hair was tied back into a ponytail and she had huge teeth. Hunter-gatherer teeth. She'd been stretching off while they were waiting. Patrick was short with a messy beard and biro marks on his neck. Rick looked at his sheet. Irish, twenty-nine and thirty-three. Another consultant, and a designer.

'What do you design, Patrick?'

'Chairs,' said Kalin. 'He's pretty good, he's got one in a museum in Belfast.'

Her accent was strong and he had to concentrate. He looked around at the chairs on the terrace. Wood, four legs, flat bit. 'Okay,' said Rick. 'Anything you want to tell me?'

'No,' said Kalin.

Rick went through his questions, and like the first couple, Kalin answered them. Short, negative answers.

'What about the four who went walkabout?'

'Vicky was good *craic*,' said Kalin. 'The two of us talked a bit. I didn't say much to the other three, nor did Patrick. Have you been to Ireland, Inspector?'

'No.'

'You'd like it there.'

'If you think of anything else, you or Patrick.'

'Of c.' She stood up. 'Have you spoken to Mike yet?'

'No.'

'He'll probably show you his map.'

'He'll *definitely* show you his map,' said Patrick. The first words he'd said.

Debbie reappeared at the table. 'Sorry to interrupt, but I forgot one thing about Calix. I saw him steal a spoon.'

'*Really?*' said Kalin. She smiled. All teeth.

'A spoon?' said Rick.

Debbie nodded. 'It was at the team meal in Kathmandu before we left. I saw him slip it up his shirt sleeve. Very smoothly, like a magician. Like he'd done it before. It's probably nothing, but I thought I'd tell you.'

'It all helps,' said Rick. The three of them walked off, the two women chatting.

Nearby, a woman wearing earphones was waiting. She took out the plugs. 'Are you ready for me? I'm Ellen.'

She sat down. Thirty-five, Dutch, a writer.

'Fiction or non-fiction?' Her face was rounder than long, slightly pudgy with very full lips. She was sucking a sweet.

'Novels. Thrillers. I used to be a research scientist in the Arctic, so they're set on ice-breakers. Amongst the icebergs. Miss Smilla used thirty words for snow, I do the same for ice.'

Rick nodded – knowingly, he hoped. Maggie had probably heard of Ellen and Miss Smilla, but he hadn't. Ellen's English was as good as his and he was tempted to ask if she'd solved his whodunit.

'You shared a tent with Vicky?'

'Yes,' said Ellen. 'The Bad Girls' Tent.'

'Go on.'

'Vicky moaned a lot about her nose-stud, but she was good – how-do-you-say in English? Good laugh?'

'A good laugh.'

'A good laugh. We begged a few fags off Jean-Paul, showed each other our tattoos, and discussed the men on the trip. She ended up sharing a tent with one of them.'

'Barney.'

'Yes, Barney. Although I can't believe Calix gave up having his own tent for the two of them.'

'Why's that?'

'Vicky hated Calix. We both did, really. Not a team player, never helped putting up the tents or shared his snacks. And he was creepy, always wandering off by himself, always checking his phone.'

'Anything else?'

'He liked petting the local animals – cow, goat, dog, it didn't matter. Always prodding and patting and mumbling. I didn't see him do it, but he reminded me of my brother when he was three or four and pulling the legs off spiders. Arrgh.' She shivered. 'As I said, creepy.'

'What about the twins?'

'They were okay. Spencer wasn't well, shouldn't have been there. But Barney was top value and looked good in a t-shirt. Do you want a sweet?'

Rick shook his head. Ellen unwrapped one and popped it in her mouth.

'If you think of anything else.'

She sucked her sweet. 'Have you been told about Mike?'

'No.'

'He's a bit... well, you'll see.' She stood up, re-inserted her earpieces and walked away down the side of the lodge. As if on cue, the three people at the second interviewing table stood and walked over.

'This is Pemba, the expedition *sirdar*,' said Russell.

'The one?'

'The one.'

They all sat down, Pemba opposite Rick. The guide's sunglasses were pushed up on his head and his hands tucked inside a grey fleece gilet.

'You speak English?'

'Of course.' He grinned. A gold tooth flashed in the sun.

Rick moved through his questions. Pemba may have been an expert on mountain navigation but he was almost blind to Western social relations. He knew who Mike was, Jean-Paul, and Calix, and Debbie when prompted with an imitation of lipstick application. But he confused the others.

'Okay?' said Rick, nodding at Russell and Kate. Cries of children fighting on the mud-baked backyard had drawn their attention. They all watched for a few seconds. Rick cleared his throat. 'Pemba, in Kathmandu, you saw a list of clients for this trip and recognised one name. Yes?'

Pemba nodded.

'Did you recognise the name Calix or the name Coniston?'

'Coniton.'

'Coni-*ton* or Con-*iss-ton*?'

Pemba shrugged. Russell shrugged.

'Why do you know the name?'

He shook his head.

'Pemba, this is very important. Vicky is dead. The girl with the nose-stud.' Rick tapped his nose. 'I am a Scotland Yard detective.' He wasn't, but Pemba wouldn't know. He pushed his badge across the table.

'Understand important. Difficult say.'

'Try.'

'My village Saklis. Many, many Ghurkha soldiers. My brothers, my father. Me, no. Me like mountains. Coniton big Ghurkha soldier. He bad Ghurkha.'

'Why a bad Ghurkha?'

Pemba mimed an explosion. 'Ghurkha dead.'

'Who?'

Pemba shook his head.

'It's very important.'

'Understand.'

Rick took Russell over to the balustrade. The children had disappeared, and one of the old women smiled up at him. 'I think, Rick, that he probably doesn't know much more. Feels like second-hand information.'

'But to know the name?'

'I hate to say it, but he may have got the name wrong.'

They sat down again. 'Pemba, why didn't you explain this to Amanda?'

'Bad luck before *puja*.'

Russell leant forward. 'The *puja* ceremony, Rick, usually happens at base camp. Offerings are made to the gods to bring good luck to the expedition.'

'But there was bad luck,' said Kate.

'Might have been even worse.'

A middle-aged trekker in an enormous woolly jumper approached their table. 'I was told twelve, midday.' He tapped his watch. 'It's twelve, midday, and three seconds.' The man didn't make eye contact.

'You must be Mike?'

'And you're DCI Castle.'

'Two minutes and I'll be with you.'

Mike retreated a few metres. 'Russ, Kate, can you finish up with Pemba? Tell him we might need to have another chat a bit later.'

Rick beckoned the farmer over. 'So, Mike, who's looking after your cows?'

'Herd's a hundred and fifty-three girls. Pride of North Island. Agnis, Ama, Amy, Anna, Aunty, Beatrice, Bee, Beth, Bethany, Bethesda...'

Rick let him finish. One of his neighbours at home also suffered from Asperger's. The farmer wore a jumper with snow-ploughing skiers. His hair was a mop. Rick glanced down at the yard. Jason was kicking a small ball with the kids and Debbie was taking photos.

'...Weenie, Wendy, Xanthe and Yaw.'

'Very impressive. Mike, the night—'

'We're here,' said the farmer. He pointed with a large hairy finger at a map. 'Ghandar.'

Rick relaxed. The interview was clearly DIY. With his neighbour at home, his tactic was to listen for five minutes and then walk away, politely, but definitively. With Mike, that option wasn't available.

'Twenty-five places on this map begin with the letter G. Gallat, Ganger, Ghandar, Ghandruk—'

'Mike, is it okay if I ask a question?'

'Seventeen more, Officer Castle.'

'Who else have you talked maps with?'

Mike thought for a moment before answering. 'Amanda, Jean-Paul, Spencer, Kalin, Patrick and Calix.'

Rick did not doubt the accuracy of the list – Mike was the world's best witness. And the worst – open questions were risky. 'What did you and Calix talk about on the map?'

He grinned. 'Everything.'

Rick thought of a better question. 'What did you talk about the most? The top three.'

'Mera Peak, Mount Everest and a village called Saklis.'

The hairs went up on Rick's neck.

'Saklis?'

'It's a Ghurkha recruiting village not far from our trekking route. Our intended trekking route.' As Mike detailed everything he knew about Saklis, Rick imagined he was Calix listening. Listening, just possibly, in Ghandar – Mike would probably know, but Rick didn't want to interrupt again. His neighbour was unpredictable like that. Didn't seem to mind someone walking off but interruptions were different.

Twenty minutes later, Mike and his snowploughing skiers wandered away.

Rick glanced down at the yard. Jason and Debbie had gone, and a child was wrestling a stick from a mangy dog.

24

Rick sat on the cement roof of the Tranquillity Lodge under a precarious bamboo shelter. Lines of washing criss-crossed from protruding metal rods. The lodge owners, a friendly ex-Ghurkha with only one arm and his heavily pregnant wife, had told him that reception was better up there.

He leant against the chimney and fired up his laptop. There was an email from Maggie, titled 'Good and bad news'.

The email wouldn't open, and he glanced up at the satellite dish above him. It looked okay. What did he know.

He stood up, and walked around the roof holding the laptop like a water diviner. The email still wouldn't open, and he rested the laptop on a corner of unfinished wall. Tied to an eyelet was a wheelie-bin overflowing with plastic bottles. Someone had lugged it from Kathmandu; someone else, the kitchen sink. He looked out across the valley. A band of pink cloud stained the pale blue sky.

The laptop squealed.

Skype opened, and there on the screen were Becky and Dad. He looked so much older, all of a sudden.

'That's Rick, Dad,' said Becky. 'He's in Nepal.'

'Paul?'

156

'*Nepal*, Dad,' said Rick. 'I'm in *Nepal*.' A Skype call wasn't quiet: everyone at the Tranquillity Lodge would be able to listen, but at least the NA trekkers were staying somewhere else.

'He's not deaf, Rick.'

'Sorry. I'm in Nepal, Dad, the home of Everest, the tallest moun—'

'—Everest, 8,850 metres. First climbed on the twenty-ninth of May 1953 by Edmund Hillary and Tenzing Norgay.'

'Yes!'

'Do you know what's really interesting, Philip?' His dad leant closer to the screen. 'What's really interesting is that news of the ascent arrived in time for the coronation of Queen Elizabeth the Second on the second of June. All the newspapers split their front page. Now, I bet you didn't know that, did you?'

'I didn't.' He did. Dad had told him many times before.

'Right, I can't sit around here all day. I'm going to cut the lawn. Blasted grass won't stop growing.' His dad rose and disappeared from view.

'I take it he's better?'

Becky nodded, looked away, and back at the screen.

'He's not going to cut the lawn, is he?'

'What do you think? He keeps going out to do it, but I've removed the mower's spark plug so he can't. Yesterday, he went down to the shed two or three times because he forgets.'

'That's a bit cruel.'

She sighed. 'You take time off work and come and look after him. He's like a five-year-old, and it gives him something to do. Anyway, it's not cruel. He doesn't know.'

'For a moment there, I thought he was back.'

'He's still pretty good with history, with dates and stuff. But rubbish with faces and the present.'

'I wish he'd call me Rick. Just once.'

'He might.'

'You mean if he goes through enough names?'

Becky nodded, and waved.

Rick stared at the empty screen. He hated goodbyes, always fearing the worst. What if he couldn't get back home? All planes were grounded due to a wave of terrorism worse than 9/11. Countries had sealed their borders and suspended flights and public transport. He'd have to climb fences, cadge lifts, and walk. It would take months, but he'd do it.

He sighed, inhaling deeply through his nose and smelling the newly familiar, and not unpleasant, whiff of Nepalese villages. A commingle of woodsmoke, all-day simmering stew, wild flowers, human waste, and animal dung.

He tried Maggie's email again.

Sir

Banker's Drafts

Good and bad news. Each Newcell letter came with two banker's drafts, one for £2,790 made out to Nepal Adventures, and one each to Calix Coniston / Barney Williams for £200. Bought with cash on 20 January. The suspect's ID was a driving licence in the name of Joe Mount. It's a false ID, and I've requested the bank's records. They've promised CCTV but I won't believe it till I see it. Failing that, I'll try to speak to the cashier and get a description.

Calix's computer

I've been through Calix's emails. Took me hours. Only two are relevant, both on 14 October, two days after the taxidermy lecture at UCL.

'Arhant, good to meet. Something to get my teeth into. Calix.'

The reply was an hour later: 'Speak me now. Hant.'

Interesting, eh?

Maggie x

Rick put the laptop down and opened his notebook. Hard-backed but still dog-eared, and three-quarters full. A sticker at the bottom: 'Keep Bees, Get Stung'.

He flicked through his notes on victims, persons of interest, motives. Then read through his hypotheses.

H1 no crime
H2a kidnap then murder
H2b kidnap then demands
H3 missing in Nepal
And started thinking.

Who was *Hant*? What was he? Was it possible that Calix and this Hant had cooked up the whole thing? The competition to lure the twins to Nepal, and a kidnap?

Three reasons he could conceive. He raised a thumb – Calix's phone calls following the taxidermy lecture. His index finger – the email from Calix to Hant. Middle finger – the false ID used to obtain the banker's drafts, an ID that might have been concocted by Calix.

It was likely Calix had met Hant at the taxidermy lecture, and possible they'd remained in regular contact until Calix had left the UK.

Raising money for a Nepalese school, or some other charitable enterprise, *could* fit that pattern of communication.

But, he didn't think so.

In the yard children were playing hide-and-seek. A boy had

hidden behind a *chirpi*, but a dog was barking and giving him away.

Rick twiddled his pen, mulling the new information from Maggie. If Calix and Hant were building a school, or a sanitation plant, or something similar, they would need to discuss everything. Location, fundraising, the tools and equipment they needed. And so on. There would be hundreds of emails.

But there were only two.

Across the valley the snow covering the mountains was turning a pinkish gold.

25

In the tent, Calix woke abruptly.

He lifted his head and listened. He thought he'd heard a gunshot. But there was just the crazy breathing of Barney and Spencer. Shallow breaths alternating with deeper ones. Amanda had warned them Cheyne-Stokes was a symptom of altitude.

'Barney, did you hear that?' He shoved the twin's lifeless torso.

'What?'

Two more gunshots echoed around the valley.

Calix did his best to sit up, his movement constricted by the tent roof, and by his leg chain. A rescue? He'd seen planes and he'd dreamt before about Ghurkha parachutists. He imagined an SAS team surrounding the cave.

Another shot rang out.

'Have they f-f-found us?' said Spencer.

Calix struggled out of his bag. 'I'll find out.' It didn't sound like a gunfight. No sounds of panic from the guards, only Hant shouting in Nepali. Spencer took a puff from his empty inhaler. 'Keep down,' whispered Calix. 'People die in these things.' He crawled out of the tent, his heart thumping.

Hant stood fifty metres from the cave, firing into the air. Calix turned through 180 degrees but could see no one else shooting. Guards were sitting or crouching as normal. Maybe they were quieter than usual. They watched their leader walking about, kicking stones, shouting to himself, and firing sporadically.

Barney thrust his head out of the tent.

'Only Hant,' shouted Calix.

He shuffled to the lip of the cave, squatted down like the guards, and waited. His leg throbbed from the shackle, and he yanked the chain for some slack. It was the best time of the day, according to his old man. As he watched, the bright orange sun climbed the porridge-white sky. Every second, the day got warmer.

Underneath Hant's folding chair were the sat phone and a small cardboard box. Calix shuffled along to the chair and sat down. He pulled out his sunglasses from the knee pocket on his trousers. The box was half-full of bullets. He put on his glasses.

The cook-guard busied himself with the fire. He cleared away the embers with a small shovel, piling them at the side of the cave. He collected handfuls of kindling from a pile and laid them next to the fire. He took out a knife and shaved pieces from a stick. He built the cookfire, starting with the shavings, then erecting a wigwam of twigs and sticks.

Hant walked back up to the cave. The cook-guard stopped working on the fire and withdrew into the shadows. The Nepalese leader reached underneath Calix's chair for the sat phone and the box. He put the phone in a pocket and slotted unused bullets back in the box. He put the box in his jacket.

'You want sit my chair, you say Barney and Spencer. You say or me say.' Hant patted his hair but it was unnecessary. His hair clung like a helmet.

Calix started to stand.

'No,' said Hant, and waved Calix to sit.

Calix sat. His throat was dry and he needed some water.

'Say what?' said Barney. The twin crawled out of the tent, and stood next to the wigwam of sticks, coughing and itching the gash on his leg.

The sun was almost up. A perfect orange globe. No wonder people believed in a sun-god. Calix couldn't stop the twins knowing, just as he couldn't stop the sun.

'You father problem,' said Hant, looking at Barney.

'What is?' Barney swivelled around. 'Spencer, you'd better come out here.'

Calix shuffled the chair sideways, so he could see both Hant and the twins. Spencer's head appeared in the tent flap. He spluttered, and wheezed. Calix felt like an Olympian. Spencer crawled out of the tent.

'Two my friends die yesterday Qatar. *Ramro* friends. Yash, Himal. Friends long time, from baby. You father problem, you father FIFA. You father *naramro*. FIFA *naramro*.'

'*Ramro*, good, *naramro*—' started Calix.

'I get it,' said Barney. He looked at Hant. 'FIFA employs many, many people.'

'You father big man FIFA.'

'Maybe,' said Spencer, 'but he's nothing to do with Qatar.'

Hant laughed. 'You West people. Always run, hide, always other people problem. Never you problem. Never. We say you father, stop die Qatar, or...' He slid a finger across his throat. Then snapped his fingers, and pointed at Calix's leg.

A guard came forward, unlocked Calix's manacle and yanked back the chain. Calix bent down and rubbed his swollen leg.

It wasn't meant to happen like that. He'd begun to hope it might not happen at all.

Everything was going too fast.

'Calix?' said Barney.

'Time, friend,' said Hant. He laughed. 'Time they men.'

'What the fuck, Calix?' said Barney. Behind him, Spencer's mouth gaped.

Calix stood up.

'Calix!' Barney yelled, 'Look at me. Look at me and tell me that Hant's messing with our heads.'

Calix walked out of the cave. He kept on walking, down the valley, his legs stiff after the days of sitting around. A stone whizzed over his head, another hit him in the back. He began to jog until he was out of range.

Behind him, Barney was still screaming.

Calix stopped by the stream that ran down the valley. He washed his face in the icy meltwater. He cupped some in his hands, drank, and let the rest slip through his fingers.

Hant had promised not to tell the twins of Calix's role. They'd agreed it wasn't necessary. The kidnap would take place, FIFA would do what they were told and Barney and Spencer would be released. No one need know about him.

But Vicky had died, and now Hant had blurted out Calix's involvement. Suddenly, he was in the spotlight.

He chopped the water with his hand. Hant! Fuckwit! And himself for thinking that it could have been straightforward. Anger turned to panic. He was doomed. Life imprisonment at Belmarsh, or he'd be left to rot in a Nepalese jail. He picked at the scabs on his wrist, then lurched over and opened his mouth.

Did Nepal practise capital punishment?

The bile only reached his throat but the taste made him retch again, and again.

Stepping through his lengthy shadow, Calix returned to the

cave. Barney and Spencer were still chained to the car-sized rock at the front. They were throwing stones at a target – a lump of rock wrapped in Calix's balaclava.

Spencer spotted him first and nodded at Barney, who looked around. They whispered. They threw more stones.

Calix stood watching.

He picked up a stone and threw it at the effigy. It missed.

'Fuck off,' said Barney.

The two brothers stopped throwing but kept collecting stones. 'Do you want something?' said Barney, finally. He knocked a couple of stones together.

'Will you let me explain?'

'So we can understand,' said Barney in a sarcastic tone. He threw another stone.

'Know, then.'

'Vicky's dead because of you.'

'That was an accident,' said Calix. He paused. 'Spence?'

'D-d-don't Spence me.' He took a deep breath, then inhaled on his useless inhaler.

Barney hauled on his chain. 'Look at us.' He threw more stones.

Calix glanced at the fireball sun, and for a moment was blinded. His vision reduced to sharp triangles of blood-orange and yellow.

'I didn't start this. Hant recruited *me*.'

'I want to know,' said Spencer quietly.

'Barney?'

The brothers nodded at each other.

'How did you even meet Hant?' said Spencer.

'I met him at a taxidermy lecture in London. A famous taxi-dermist. Professor Steinmann, over from the US.'

'Bollocks!'

'It's the truth,' said Calix.

'Barney, let him speak. He's looked after us since—'

'He's been feeling guilty,' said Barney. 'Guilty as Judas.'

'I felt scared.' Calix hadn't meant to say that, but it was the truth. More scared than he'd ever felt in his life.

'Coniston,' said Spencer.

'Okay. Hant was doing a course at the Institute and had seen a poster for the lecture. Ticket sales were poor and students were offered a free reception if they went along.'

Barney scowled.

'That's what he told me,' said Calix.

'Keep going,' said Spencer.

'After the lecture, Hant started talking to me in the bar. He told me he was from Nepal, the first person from his mountain village who'd been to university. After graduating, he got a job in the Nepalese telecoms industry and was sent to the UK. I asked him about Nepal, which I'd read about in the paper.'

'Was anyone else there?'

'The bar was packed.'

'Anyone else talking to Hant?'

'No.'

'And you expect us to believe this shit?' said Barney, throwing another stone.

Calix shrugged. 'Hant told me about life in his village called Saklis. My old man had talked about the Nepalese people and the scenery, so I had an idea. Hant described the transformation that the mobile phone companies were bringing about. The landline system was being bypassed, and for most Nepalese people their first phone was a mobile. A friend's mobile, their family's mobile. A village mobile.'

'Did he ask about you?' said Barney

'I told him I was an entrepreneur.'

'Ha!'

'We drank several beers. I said, the future seems bright for

Nepal. Hant didn't like that. Stared at me with his intense brown eyes. He got quite heated, and told me things that my old man hadn't. Life in the villages was basic, the villagers poor. There wasn't enough work, and lots of men worked overseas for very low wages. Some were in Qatar building football stadiums. Two hundred and sixty-seven of them had died.'

'Two hundred and sixty-seven,' scoffed Barney.

'I didn't believe him either, and while Hant was in the bog, I looked it up. It was true. The UK or the US would have gone to war.'

'Calix is right,' said Spencer.

'Shut up, Spence.'

'Hant offered me a cigarette and we went outside to smoke. He told me more about Qatar. The poor working conditions, the heat, the injuries, and the deaths. *Kafala.* Then pointed the finger at FIFA.'

'And?' said Spencer.

'Hant said he wanted to ask me something, and we agreed to meet in the morning.'

'Why not then?'

'I don't know. I had no intention of going, but in the morning, on impulse, I flipped a coin. Heads I'd meet him. Tails, I'd go home.'

'And, surprise, surprise, it was heads.'

'Why would I make this up? The next morning, we met in a café. We sat outside on the street, watching the double-deckers and the cabs bumper to bumper. We drank coffee, and smoked cigarettes, and I waited. Hant didn't mention the lecture, just talked more about FIFA.'

'But you stayed.'

'Wouldn't you? I was intrigued to know what he wanted. Finally, he asked me. Hant was going to stop the deaths in Qatar, and he wanted me to help him.'

'And you agreed to a kidnapping in Nepal, just like that?'

Calix hadn't needed to think or to toss a coin. He didn't want two up, two down, or two point four, nor did he want to be a milkman for The Big Red. Hant had offered him a chance to do something real. To be a player. Megan used to say, you only live once. So, he had said yes, and he and Hant had gone to the nearest pub and drunk Bloody Marys. But he didn't tell the twins that.

'No, that took six months of detailed planning. But the decision to get involved, yes. It seemed the right thing to do.'

'The right bloody thing!' said Barney.

'Yes, the right bloody thing. The death count for Nepalese workers in Qatar is now over three hundred and fifty. All for what? A World Cup in a country that doesn't like football. FIFA could have done things differently – *can* do things differently.'

'Dad's just a cog,' said Spencer. He wore the glasses that Calix had repaired.

'Exactly.' The stones clinked in Barney's hands. In the distance, marmots shrieked like pigs at the abattoir.

'Do you know how many deaths are predicted in Qatar?' asked Calix.

The stones kept clinking.

'Four thousand,' said Calix. 'Your old man might only be a cog, but stopping him turning stops the system. Saves over three thousand lives.'

'You feel strongly about something?' said Barney. 'Then go on a fucking demo. Wave a fucking placard. Kidnap? You're out of your mind.' He threw a stone.

Calix watched it land, watched it roll downhill, waited for it to stop moving. 'Direct action is the only answer – look at the Arab Spring. Force is the only thing that works.'

Barney pulled his arm back. 'You're away with the fucking

fundamentalists.' He let go. A large rock exploded across the balaclava.

Calix walked away. Behind him, stones clattered down as the twins scatter-bombed the target. He thought of his old man storming through Argentinean lines in the Falklands. He had wanted to live for Megan, and now he was. He had wanted to be a player, and now he was. But he was playing for the world to see, and that was very different. Purple-black thoughts crashed around his brain, and he broke into a run, not knowing or caring where he was going.

26

The front terrace of the Tranquillity Lodge looked out onto the main trail. Villagers were returning from a day in the fields, as many women as men. They carried machetes, tucked into waistbands or swinging in scabbards. Some held hoes, and they all lugged baskets of firewood. Children ran up and down the irregular stone cobbles, shouting and giggling. A dog ran with them, barking. As always, woodsmoke hung in the air.

Russell pushed two wobbly tables together and Rick spread the map across them.

'How long to walk to Saklis, Russell?'

Kate tapped dead her cigarette. 'Aren't we going to wait here for everyone else? Khan and Emmett, the Aussie team, the LO?'

'No, we'll wait for them in Saklis.'

They bent down to the map. *Shorong / Hinku, 1:50,000.* It showed an area south of Everest, Mount Mera in the top right quarter. Large white patches with blue contours.

'They're glaciers,' said Russell, pointing with one of his remaining fingers. 'Permanent masses of snow and ice. The snow can conceal crevasses, some of which can be huge and reach the foot of the glacier.'

'Like *Touching The Void*,' said Kate.

'We'll avoid the glaciers completely.'

'And, if we do?' Rick nodded at the map.

'A week to ten days of hard walking. Altitude, distance, cold.'

Kate made a face.

'There is another option.'

'Helicopter?' said Kate.

'Plane.'

'Talk us through it,' said Rick.

'Okay. The map is centred on Lukla, here.' Russell jabbed with a finger. 'It's got an airport and it's the main trailhead for trekkers going to Everest base camp. Lukla is in a river valley running north-south. Here. About fifteen kilometres to the east is another, parallel, river valley – follows the Hinku river. Amanda's Mera trek, and us in their footsteps, started at a different trailhead. Jiri. Here. That trekking route runs east to Ghandar – where we are now – and into the Hinku river valley where it turns north and towards Mera.'

'With you so far,' said Rick. 'Two trailheads, two trekking routes, one to Everest, one to Mera.'

'I wish I was fitter,' said Kate.

'You're fit enough,' said Russell, his eyes twinkling.

Rick looked down at the map. The three missing were there, somewhere.

'There's a trail between the two main routes. The route to Everest runs north from Lukla but there's also a trail that runs east and meets the Mera trail at a suspension bridge – a long one. There's an abandoned village called Mosom Kharka. The village of Saklis lies along that route, a day or so from Lukla.'

'That gives us two options,' said Rick. 'One, backtrack to Jiri and Kathmandu, fly to Lukla and walk to Saklis. Two, keep going for a week, up to Mosom Kharka and west to Saklis.'

'I know where my vote's going,' said Kate.

She didn't have a vote, but Rick said nothing. The first option meant getting to Saklis quickly, the second, slowly, but via the scenes of the kidnap and Vicky Brant's death. Leads to the location of the three missing were possible in all three places. But which was the most likely?

His phone rang. He still couldn't get used to it working in a place where there weren't any roads. He walked away from Russell and Kate.

'Rick Castle.' He stared out across the village and into the hills. Line after line of them, as far as he could see.

'Sir, it's Maggie.' She was still calling him sir.

'How're you?' He pictured her in her chair, twirling her hair. The silver choker or the chunky black beads, or the leather band with a moonstone around her neck.

'What do you mean?'

He wasn't sure. Well, he was – he remembered carrying her up the Conistons' staircase, his ear in her hair, the kiss sign-off on her last email – but he wasn't sure how to put it. She should know what he meant, women were meant to be intuitive. 'How's the incident room?'

'Robbo saw my spider plant, and told me not to get too comfortable. I told him that I sat all the time, and I was always too flipping comfortable.' She paused. 'Guess who paid in the money for the banker's drafts.'

'Calix?'

'I hope you're more fun at Christmas.'

He probably wasn't – he liked giving presents but hated receiving them. Christmas with Maggie? What would he wrap for her?

'Well, you're right. All four were obtained at Lloyds in Bramhall. I've watched the CCTV and spoken to the cashier. Calix helped invent the Newcell competition.'

'The question is *why*?'

'To fool someone about the reason he's in Nepal – his parents?'

'Maybe. If Calix and whoever, this Hant most likely, had already invented the competition to lure the two Williamses to Nepal, then it would have been easy. Less hassle from the brigadier.'

'I've been to see him and his wife. They thought the note was in Calix's handwriting.'

'Anything else?'

'Lots. First, the Conistons. Mrs C is now on sleeping pills, the brigadier, as you would expect, is more stoic. Mixture of anger and bafflement. *What the devil's going on over there*, that kind of thing. Threatened to get on a plane. I calmed him down a bit, laughed about the stairs, talked about the Falklands.'

'You didn't tell them about Calix inventing the competition?'

'Of course not.'

Mist or low cloud was rolling up the valley. The temperature was dropping. 'Hang on, Maggie.' He went to find the duvet jacket in his room. He put it on. A hat, too. He felt ridiculous. Back outside, the reception was better than indoors but the hills had disappeared. Russell had folded up the map and Kate was reading. 'I'm back, Maggie, what else?' He opened his notebook.

'I hit the jackpot with the CCTV at Barnes Bridge station. The Barnes DC has been really helpful. She re-interviewed Mrs Williams, who worked out the date and time when Barney filled in the questionnaire. One Asian-looking male who even smiled for the camera. She sent me a colour head-and-shoulders.'

'It's possible that's Hant. Well done, Maggie.'

'Maggie's handed me the phone, boss,' said DC Bennett. 'Me

and Woodsy took that image and the photo of Calix to London, to his old halls of residence. We showed it to the head porter, who remembered Calix. He helped us track down some of the bar staff who were working on the evening of the taxidermy lecture.'

'And?'

'We managed to speak to three of them, but none recognised the pictures. There were two more bar staff – we'll chase 'em up. While we were there, I pulled Calix's records. On the off-chance. It turns out he didn't simply leave in his third year – he was kicked out.'

'For?'

'Drug dealing. The cops weren't called provided he went quietly. The college say they wrote to his parents, but I take it they never mentioned that. It was his third offence – they have a three-strikes-and-you're-out policy, even if nothing's proved. No smoke without fire and all that.'

Rick scribbled a few notes. 'What were his other offences?'

'In his second year he stooged for a first-year student in the exams – for money. Calix's a bit of a clever dick, apparently. The other one was a vague but increasing suspicion of kidnapping animals. The two college cats went missing and then the principal's dog. Nothing was proved but his room was searched a few times. It was well known he was interested in taxidermy.'

Rick immediately thought of the cat in the box under Calix's desk. A neighbour's cat, which Mrs Coniston had said had been run over.

'And how's Crick Lane Farm?' Opposite him, Russell pulled up a chair.

'Died a death. The three illegals are likely to be deported and I've finished sifting the paperwork. No links to Calix or Paul Parry.'

'What about the PP number?'

'The report came back, finally. But no joy there either. PP turns out to be Phil Palmer, some student at Manchester. You were right about who he called. His mum *and* his nan. My guess is he bought weed from Calix. Super's had another idea about Parry, though. I'd better hand you back to Maggie.'

There was silence for a few seconds, then muffled voices through a covered handset.

'Sir?' said Maggie.

'What's this about Parry?' said Rick.

'I'm having a drink with him. Robbo suggested it as we've still got nothing substantive on him. He thought I might learn something.'

'You're having a drink with Paul Parry?' repeated Rick. His daydreams backtracked towards reality. *A drink with Parry.* He'd once suggested it.

'Anything for the Job, you once said.'

He'd said that too.

Rick pocketed the phone.

'One more thing, Rick, which I forgot to say about Saklis,' said Russell from across the table. 'No phone reception. You're okay in Lukla but after that it's the sat phone or nothing. I assume we're going to Lukla?'

'We are.'

'I'll tell Kate,' said the mountaineer.

Rick nodded.

'Are you okay?'

Rick stood up, the tables jitterbugging and the crockery rattling. 'These bloody tables!'

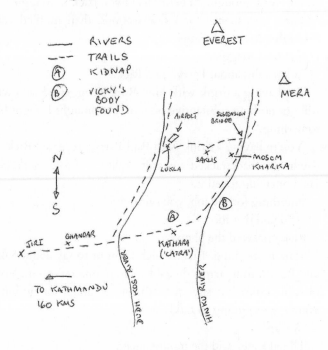

SKETCH MAP OF MERA TREKKING TRAIL

DCI Rick Castle

Rick went to his room and closed the door. He drew the flimsy curtain, lay on the bed, and stared at the ceiling. Through the window, he could hear the voices of children playing.

If the CCTV image was Hant, then he *was* linked to the competition. At last they were making some progress.

He revamped his hypotheses. H3, missing in Nepal, now ruled out. H2a, kidnap then murder, was unlikely, which meant he should concentrate on H2b, kidnap then demands. Hant and Calix had invented a competition to lure the twins to Nepal. They'd met for the first time, or had increased their contact, at the taxidermy lecture in London, and had been in touch ever since.

A possible motive was Qatar: Hant was probably Nepalese, maybe aggrieved about his countrymen dying in Qatar. The kidnap could be to put pressure on the twins' father, Terry Williams, a vice president of FIFA, to change things. That was a workable hypothesis.

He rose from the bed, walked over to the window and peeked round the curtain. In the half-light, the children were being scolded by their mother. He phoned Robbo.

'Can you make this quick, I'm in a meeting.'

'Did you suggest Maggie have a drink with Paul Parry?'

'Yes.'

'Parry's still a person of interest.'

'That's the point, Rick.'

'Maggie's not a UC, and it's against both policy and procedure.'

'She's done a crash-course.'

'Nicknamed, sir, for a reason. Anyway, the UC det super and HQ won't like it.'

'They won't know.'

They would know if I told them, Rick thought. 'She might get hurt.'

'It's not your decision, it's mine.'

Rick pulled open the curtain.

'Is there anything else?'

'If Jack's staying with the squads, what am I getting?'

'I'm not doing this now. The chief super's tapping the table.'

'Just tell me.'

'The crime desk.'

'That's a sergeant's role.'

'The chief super's under pressure from HQ about South Manchester's performance. He wants change. Make a difference, and you'll be in his good books.'

Rick threw the phone onto the bed, and yanked the curtain wider. It caught, and he yanked again, the stopper clattering away and the curtain spooling to the floor. Gripping the empty rail like a primate, he stared out into the gloaming. There was no longer any sign or sound of the children, and the village animals were quiet. He could hear a stream. The darkness confused the perspective, and the hills had become black lumps without distance or definition; he waited there, staring, until his pulse began to slow.

27

The four of them stopped at the long ropebridge they'd crossed a few days earlier. A giant sag across the Hinku river which crashed along below. Four wire cables held the wooden floor-boards above the water, two under the floor, and two for the handrails. Metal rods and chicken wire completed the sides. The undergrowth on the steep riverbanks was damp, and a fine spray drifted up. It reminded Calix of running around with Megan on a pier, dodging the wave spurts, and being scolded by their old man. Nothing to worry about – then.

He slipped off his pack and drank. The water tasted of chlorine; he was down to his last strip of purification tablets. Hant, Ram, and Kelsang stood in a line and urinated. Kelsang wore the waistcoat and trousers of a tweed suit, and his desert-coloured boots.

On the far side of the bridge a footpath snaked up a steep hillside. After a hundred metres the path disappeared, guillotined by low cloud. Somewhere in the cloud was Saklis, Hant and Ram's village, where Ram had been collecting supplies. Hant wanted to speak to the families of Yash and Himal, and he wanted Calix to meet some of the men injured in Qatar. Calix hoped it would boost his resolve and dispel his feelings of complicity – anything was better than staying at the cave with the twins.

Hant pulled a bunch of small bananas from Kelsang's basket, and handed them to Calix. He dumped his rucksack at Ram's feet, and spoke Nepali. The boy replied, and Hant cuffed him. Kelsang scowled, picked up his basket, and climbed the short ladder onto the bridge. Hant followed, and with the bridge swaying, the two of them walked across.

Ram stuffed Hant's pack inside his rucksack and strapped it down. He muttered Hant's name and saluted. Calix mimed a talking mouth with his hand.

Ram grinned.

'Banana,' said Calix, tossing one over.

'*Kero*,' replied Ram.

'*Ek kero*,' said Calix, waggling his thumb. He grabbed Ram's banana skin.

Ram got the idea. '*Dui kero*.'

They crossed the rocking bridge, Calix staring down through gaps in the boards into the roiling water, and started up the hillside. He counted in Nepali, and encouraged Ram to join in. *Ek, dui, teen, char, panch, chha, saat, aath, nau, das*. They counted ten bananas, and then in tens to a hundred bananas.

'*Panch biyara*,' said Ram. Five beers. He staggered for a few paces, burped loudly and fell over.

Calix forced a smile. '*Das biyara*.' He pretended to retch. He tried to think of something else to say. '*Kati bajyo?*' What's the time?

Ram shrugged and showed Calix his bare wrists. Calix looked at his own watch. '*Das*.'

'*Das bajyo*,' said Ram. Ten o'clock.

They stopped at a small shrine. A rough shelter of stones protected a god wielding a sword. A saucer held a few small coins.

'*Manjushree,*' said Ram, pointing.

Calix nodded.

'Calix, *sahib?*' The boy put his fingers to his lips and smoked an imaginary cigarette. He crossed his eyes, and lurched. A joint.

Calix shook his head, and they climbed on. The trail steepened, and Calix focused on the back of Ram's legs. He had the calves of a racehorse. The boy tapped a rhythm with a length of bamboo.

Hant was waiting in a clearing. He sat motionless, facing the sun with his eyes closed, like a lizard. He rose as Calix and Ram approached, ushered the boy ahead, and fell in behind Calix.

The two of them walked for a while in silence, Calix conscious of his heavy breathing. His heavy guilt. Rhododendron roots like giant bird claws criss-crossed the path. Three porters with empty baskets scampered down the trail.

Calix turned round and stopped. 'You agreed not to say.'

'Keep walk.'

Calix stumbled on a tree root, but walked on.

'Not think,' said Hant. 'I very upset my friends.'

'You promised.'

'I sorry.'

'Now, everyone will know. My old man, the police, the whole world.'

'I say sorry.'

'Sorry!'

Calix stopped by a stand of bamboo. He bent a piece to the ground and stamped down with his foot. He wrestled the cane back and forth with increasing violence, but it wouldn't come away. Hant waved him back, took out his *kukri*, and chopped. He measured the severed pole against Calix, chopped twice more, and handed the pole to Calix.

'You said, we would discuss everything. Work together.'

'Difficult, you pretend Barney, Spencer. Now, easy. Like cut bamboo with *kukri*.'

'When are we going to make the demands?' The quicker it was all over, Calix thought, the better: Spencer would see a doctor, and the twins would go home.

'I make demand.'

'When?'

'Yesterday.'

Calix stubbed the bamboo in the ground. 'What are they?'

'Like end *kafala*, end seize passports, good dollar for injury. Then release you and brothers.'

'Me? Don't you get it?' Calix felt sick again. The twins hated him, and he couldn't trust Hant. Everyone would soon know he was a kidnapper. He felt his stomach hollowing out and he swished the bamboo pole against a tree. It broke and the end flew into the undergrowth.

Three hours after leaving the cave, they arrived at Saklis. The cloud had lifted, and the large village was visible for the first time. Hundreds of buildings, all steaming in the morning sunshine. Light rebounded from windows and villagers hustled about.

Calix felt them staring. He was completely alone, as if he'd been beaten up and left at the bottom of a ditch.

Outside the village was a *chorten*, a Buddhist monument, twice the size of an English village war memorial. The comparison flashed Calix back to giving Ryan a slap. It had worked: Ryan hadn't tried it again. The image gave him a small wave of energy.

Each side of the *chorten*'s tower was painted with a pair of large colourful eyes. Above the tower rose a pyramidal spire with steps leading to a crescent-shaped moon and a spike. Local people had left vegetables and coins at the base of the *chorten*, and, as Calix walked past, it seemed that a set of eyes was following him. Accusing him.

They were greeted by a pack of village dogs, and an equally energetic group of children. The youngsters clamoured around Hant and Ram, chanting their names and pulling at their clothes.

One dog, wilder than the rest, jumped around in circles, barking loudly. It snapped at the children, and the younger ones hid behind the others. It growled at Calix. He threw it a piece of *roti* and while it was eating stroked its head. It stopped barking but remained frisky, its back legs swinging around. Calix stretched his leg over the dog so it was beneath him, and felt down the back of its head to the base of the skull. When he found the spot he pushed down hard with his thumbs. The dog stopped swinging about, and sank to the ground with a low whine.

Lying with its head on the ground, the dog looked dead.

'Is dead?' asked Hant.

'No,' said Calix. 'But if I'd pressed harder, it would be.'

Hant nodded. 'What about people – same?'

The question was a coincidence. Calix had been debating the issue. He'd seen YouTube clips where soldiers did something similar to sentries. Theoretically, he could.

'The bone is too hard,' said Calix, knocking on his head.

Hant grunted.

With Hant leading, they worked their way through a maze of narrow streets to a small square, centring on a water tap. The children tagged along, chattering with Hant and Ram. At the tap, the four visitors took it in turns to wash their faces.

A small woman walked into the square. She wore a red checked shirt and a headscarf, and scowled at Hant. She pointed at Calix, and muttered in rapid Nepali.

'*Chaina*,' said Hant. The woman spat on the ground, turned on her heel and walked back the way she had come.

'What did she say?'

'She say, you no god.'

'Why?'

'You not make donation *chorten*.'

After bowls of RaRa noodles, Calix and the others made their way deeper into the village. The group of children followed. An old man tended a herd of goats and two women washed clothes at another tap. Most villagers were working in the fields. They entered a large square dominated by Saklis's largest building. In contrast to the rest of the village, the square was quiet. Most of the children vanished. Only two remained, holding onto Ram's long shorts. Even the ubiquitous dogs avoided the place.

The square looked like the grounds of a makeshift hospital during a world war. In front of the building's double doors sat or lay a dozen young men.

Calix pulled Hant back.

'Listen, I've been thinking: we must release Spencer when we get back. He needs a doctor.' Releasing Spencer would help expunge his guilt, and curry favour with the dibble if he was caught. He was going to be caught, he had no doubt. Hant might be able to melt away into the mountains but he couldn't.

'No. Sick man make strong demands.'

'Yes, but we can't risk another death. This is about holding a multinational to account.'

'I no understand.'

Calix scowled. 'This, this thing, this kidnapping, is about forcing FIFA to treat Nepalese workers better. To prevent deaths. But Vicky died, and Spencer is very ill.'

'I sorry. But hundreds Nepalese die. Thousands injure. Now, you see.' He waved at the men in the square.

'I thought we were deciding things together?'

'No, you help me.'

'Fuck, Hant!'

The Nepalese man stared at Calix with his glossy brown eyes. Depthless, unreadable, like a dog's eyes. Calix looked away and picked at his plasticuff scabs, puffy and bruised purple.

'Come,' said Hant.

Calix followed him to two men lying on hessian mats. Their eyes were closed and they seemed oblivious to the flies. Others sat on plastic chairs. They sat in twos and threes, but there was little conversation. Two sat in wheelchairs, the first Calix had seen in Nepal, and one man knelt on the ground. The men looked tired or bored, or both.

The square might have looked like the grounds of a hospital, but it didn't smell like one. No antiseptic or bleach, just the odours of dressings needing to be changed, of urine and shit. He wasn't surprised that children avoided the place.

Calix looked more closely at the last man. He wasn't kneeling, but standing on his stump ends on a metal tray. The man slid across the courtyard towards them, as if he was on a magic carpet. The tray had small wheels and the man paddled the ground with his hands. When he reached Hant, he hugged his legs and Hant folded his arms over the man's head.

Hant turned to Calix, and beckoned him closer. 'These men from Qatar. Build football stadium. This, Ashok Limbu. Brother my friend, Himal, who dead.'

Calix reached down like Hant, and the man hugged his legs and mumbled in Nepali. The hairs went up on the back of Calix's neck.

'Ashok say my friend is friend Ashok.'

'What happened?' said Calix.

Hant picked up a lump of cement from the foot of a wall, and mimed it falling. 'Very big. Break Ashok legs. Ashok eighteen, seven brothers. Three brothers work same football stadium Qatar.'

Ashok retreated by paddling backwards, and Calix and Hant walked towards another small group. Ram had disappeared, along with the children, and Kelsang sat smoking near the courtyard entrance as if the injured men were contagious.

'What is this place – a nursing home?'

Hant scoffed. 'No. Only big house. Family take turn cook and wash. Small medicine.'

They stood next to one of the men lying down. His eyes were closed, and flies crawled over his face. Calix flicked them away. Hant told him that Dipesh had fallen off a stadium roof and broken his back, and that he was lucky not to have died. Dipesh was married with five children, and his eldest boy of fifteen was now head of the family.

They moved to the next man, sitting in one of the chairs. He was blind and his face badly disfigured. Hant explained that he'd been one of seventeen men injured in a fire in a chemical store. He was married with a child. He received forty dollars of compensation from the Qatari employer.

Calix felt like the queen inspecting a hospital. What did she say? He had to say something, and he wanted to say it in Nepali.

'*Sano Nepali.*' He duplicated the message with his thumb and forefinger.

Hant said something about Calix to the blind man.

'*Namaste. Mero naam* Calix *ho.*'

'Shyam.'

'*Chorachori?*' Children?

'*Ek chhora.*' One son.

'*Naam?*'

'Trilok.'

'*Trilok cha ramro.*' Calix wanted to tell the man that if he ever had a child he would call it Trilok. A lie: he would be calling his son Calix, but it was the best he could think of. He asked Hant to translate.

The man grinned, exposing stained teeth and contorting his disfigured face even more.

That evening, Calix laid out his sleeping bag, and wormed in. The room was basic: one small window, unfinished walls, and a ceiling of rough beams. Above them he could hear scratching. He lay on a dirty mattress on the floor, but it was comfier than the thin mat in the tent.

He imagined the injured men in the large house, on their dirty mattresses. The screams in the night. The smell. Their nightmares.

The men were like the ones in the newspaper articles on his attic wall. The reason he'd got involved. Part of it.

The kidnapping would change things – make a difference. Protest, as he'd tried to explain to Barney, was toothless. A middle-class way of expunging guilt. To get anything done, you had to get your hands dirty. What he hadn't said, hadn't realised, was you had to expect a reckoning.

28

The small plane lurched, and Rick's stomach lurched in tandem. He shut his eyes, glad of the cotton wool balls in his ears.

Despite them, the two straining engines sounded as if they were inside the cabin. He sucked on the boiled sweet handed out by the air hostess along with the cotton wool. The sweet helped cope with the unpressurised cabin. He thought it surprising there were cabin crew on a plane so small – thirty people, including the hostess and the two pilots. He assumed the pilots had eaten different meals beforehand, that they knew things like that.

He opened his eyes and looked out of the small oval window.

Kathmandu's dense urban centre was somewhere behind them. Below, the houses and shops were lower. Half-built in many cases, metal rods sticking up into the air, waiting for another storey. Piles of garbage, everywhere. Groups of schoolchildren. A school: long low buildings around a dusty yard. Children looked up, and waved. Fields, dotted with bent-over people. Hoeing, weeding, planting. Toiling. Two oxen pulling a plough. In the next field a tractor. Houses and fields gave way to hills. Line after line of them, higher and higher. Patches of fields, green, and yellow, and brown. More bent-over people. Toiling.

Life was hard. Rick closed his eyes again. Would they find

Calix Coniston and the Williams twins in Saklis? He imagined an underground prison, its trapdoor in the rough floor of an animal shed. Like the ones he'd seen in Vietnam War films.

He could smell Kate's perfume. She sat directly behind him, next to Russell, whose long legs stretched alongside Rick's aisle. Russell was talking – he never stopped.

Across the aisle sat a group of four trekkers about to set off for Everest base camp. Four young guys with short haircuts, bulging forearms, and identical boots. Plummy British accents. They oozed confidence and cheeriness, and were foisting it on everyone else. The plane's luggage included military-style Bergens, and Rick guessed they were Sandhurst recruits.

'You're Russell Weatherbeater, aren't you?' said one of them. He half-shouted so he could be heard above the engine noise.

Rick could sense Kate nodding and smiling. She was proud to be with him. Damn it – Rick was proud to be with him.

'I am,' shouted Russell.

Rick could hear the four talking. 'Five times,' said one. 'He runs the company with the climbing wall for a backdoor,' said a second.

'Were you on the hill in ninety-six?'

The others cackled.

'I was lucky enough to be at base camp. Helped out in the aftermath.'

Russell began to explain what had happened. Rick tuned out. He'd heard the story on the flight over from the UK.

He didn't much like planes, definitely not a small one that had the wrong engines fitted. It was both the height and the motion. Once, only once, he'd been up in the police helicopter above Manchester – part of his SIO course. Not only had he been sick, but he'd sweated so much in his suit that it needed dry-cleaning. The motion in a plane was smoother, but closing his eyes still helped.

The right-hand engine made a different noise to the left. Spluttered more. He wondered how often a plane crashed, and wished he had a parachute. But parachutes failed, even reserve ones. Then what?

A soggy mess of blood and bone.

Like stew.

A Wednesday. Nothing much happened on Wednesdays, but it had that week. That week of seventeen deaths. Two on the Wednesday. Jumpers. A brother and sister who'd just learnt their family secret. They were Chinese and tiny and they'd jumped from the twelfth floor. Holding hands, a witness had told him. Parts of them would be together for ever.

Rick could feel himself getting hot, and he undid his seatbelt. Despite what the Nepalese thought, there was only one life. The Chinese siblings had given their lives away. It made no sense. It was something he needed to talk more to Emma about. He took off his jacket, and unzipped his base layer.

Rick felt a tap on the shoulder.

'We're getting close,' said Russell. 'You can see Saklis.'

Rick looked out of the small window. In the distance was a village, smoke curling from chimneys. It was set on a steep hillside, only a few houses visible.

'The hill leads down to the Hinku river valley. Mosom Kharka, the abandoned village I told you about, is at the bottom of the hill. Follow the river south and you'll eventually get to Ghandar, where you interviewed Amanda's trekkers, and Jiri, the trailhead.'

Rick pulled out his sketch-map.

'Wow,' said Kate.

Rick looked up. A perfect chocolate-box mountain shimmered in the strong sunlight. Enormous, steep on every side. A background of white peaks, as far as he could see.

'That's Ama Dablam,' said Russell. 'Known as the Matterhorn of the Himalaya.'

'You climbed it?' asked the loudest of the four.

'He's soloed it,' said Kate.

Rick looked up at the four soldiers, who were crowding onto his side of the plane. It couldn't be good for stability. He sighed, not wanting to be a spoilsport. 'Point out something on the other side,' he whispered to Russell.

How did Kate know Russell had climbed it? Soloed it? How did she even know the word?

'Recognise that one?' said Russell, leaning over Kate's shoulder, and pointing.

Rick looked out of his porthole. A vast mass. Black rock, with countless small patches of snow and ice. A squashed point of a summit. It was a far chunkier mountain than Ama Dablam, and without any of the clean steep ridgelines. Like an uncut diamond.

Kate shook her head. 'No idea.'

'That's Everest.'

'But it's not the highest.'

'Perspective.'

Rick turned from the window. Diagonally across the aisle was a small Nepalese man sitting sideways on his seat. He was Amanda's *sirdar* Pemba, whom Russell had co-opted for their trek to Saklis and wherever else, possibly as far as Kathara. Pemba also flashed him a smile. The prominent gold tooth brought back the discussion at Ghandar. Rick leant forward.

'Pemba, in Ghandar you said Coniston was a bad Ghurkha. And another Ghurkha had died. Have you remembered a name? Who died?'

Pemba smiled again. 'You ask Saklis, *sahib.*'

'Do you know when it happened?'

'Ask Saklis.'

'Where?'

Pemba shook his head.

Rick turned to Russell. 'Does he understand?'

'He doesn't like to say no. None of them do, so they just grin.'

'You don't think he knows, but doesn't want to tell me?'

Russell shrugged. 'Maybe.'

Seventy minutes after take-off from Kathmandu airport, Rick could see Lukla. A messy village with an army barracks at the top and a huge river valley at the side. He checked his seatbelt. The plane began to descend, and he closed his eyes, then opened them again.

'Russell, where's the runway?'

'That's it, there,' the mountaineer said, pointing. 'Between the river and the town. A couple of planes are parked up.'

Rick closed his eyes again. He'd seen the stationary planes but assumed they were on the taxiing and parking area.

The Sandhurst recruits yabbered. The runway was 460 metres long, one of the world's shortest. It had a twelve per cent gradient and due to the plunging drop at one end and mountainous terrain at the other, had no opportunities for go-arounds. No second attempts at landing. A History Channel documentary had declared the airport the most dangerous on the planet. Rick stuck his fingers in his ears, along with the cotton wool.

They landed. The things he did for the Job. The plane taxied to the side, stopped with the others and the lawnmower noise died away. However long it took, he was going to walk back to Kathmandu.

29

In a sun-dappled clearing next to the trail, three men were laying the foundations for a house. The undergrowth had been chopped back and collected into a heap. A fire smouldered next to three piles of stone. Gravel, rounded stones and rectangular blocks. Propped against the blocks stood a pickaxe and a sledgehammer. Two of the men were digging, and the older man was fixing up a plumb line. A radio played and a wailing female voice filled the site. One of the younger men whistled along.

Calix sat on the ground and ate some biscuits. He didn't mind the wailing, and if Ram had been there he'd have asked him what he thought. But the boy had stayed in Saklis.

Hant and Kelsang sat next to the piles of stone. Kelsang squatted, cursing as he tried to light a cigarette. Hant sat on a stone block, his large white dog by his side. It had a leonine face, and thick rings of fur around its head.

Hant directed Kelsang, who stood up, scowling and puffing at his cigarette. He walked to the stack of undergrowth waiting to be burnt, and pulled out a small branch. He threw the stick for the dog.

The dog padded off.

Hant waved the cigarette packet.

Calix took a cigarette. He lit it, inhaled, and pocketed his lighter. '*Kukur?*' Dog?

The Nepalese man nodded. 'Himalaya Sheepdog. Name Chet. Family *kukur*, like UK.'

'Why're you bringing it back to the cave?'

'Bite child.'

Calix blew a smoke-ring, aware Hant was watching him. Chet ran up with the stick. Calix took out a piece of the morning's *roti*, and let Chet snuffle it from his hand. He threw the stick again, and Chet raced off.

'In the UK, if a dog bites a child, the dog would be put down.'

'No understand.'

Calix drew a finger across his throat remembering, as he did so, the knife he'd bought in Kathmandu. Safe in its custom-made *khalti*.

Chet returned with the stick and sat at Calix's feet. Calix laid the cigarette on a rock, and stroked the dog's ears. From the base of each ear to the tip, over and over. 'Easy, boy, easy.' Chet stretched out his front feet and lay down. Closed his eyes. His head slumped. 'Good dog, good *kukur*.' Calix's fingers pressed into the glossy concave hollows.

'Not too hard,' said Hant, his face set, his eyes staring.

Holding Hant's stare, Calix stroked Chet's ears, base to tip, slowly, and again, base to tip, slowly, then picked up his cigarette.

Two porters arrived and unloaded more stone from their wicker baskets. They exchanged a few words with the house-builders, then scampered back down the path.

Calix smoked, and watched the three men working. Father and sons. Father handing down skills and know-how, and sons setting out on their life-journeys. He watched the older man explaining the plumb line. Where was *his* journey going? What had he got himself into? If he couldn't go home, where would he live? Could he build a house?

He thought of the drama which would be unfolding back in the UK – his nerve-wracked mother and his raging old man, the twins' worrying parents, the involvement of dibble. Soon, FIFA would be drawn in, and then the government. Newspapers, the TV news people.

He took a final drag on the cigarette, and ground it to nothing on a rock. This was what he thought he'd wanted: this was playing.

After re-crossing the ropebridge, Calix rested on the porters' platform in the shade. His legs ached from the long downhill. Hant walked on with Chet, the dog bounding ahead as he chased whistling marmots. Calix waved Kelsang to follow, but the Nepalese man shook his head and unleashed a stream of Nepali.

'*Sano Nepali*,' said Calix. Not much Nepali.

Kelsang waggled his finger. 'Hant.'

Calix shrugged. It made no sense: it would have been difficult to get lost, even if he'd lost sight of his former guard.

He picked at his scabs, the fine spray from the river again reminding him of Megan. He couldn't just give up and let fate take over. She wouldn't have done, and neither would he.

His fingers curled around his knife. Think, Calix, think, he told himself.

False identity, false passport. Become someone else.

That was more like it.

A year or two in Nepal, grow a beard, obtain a false passport, move to Spain, maybe even plastic surgery. If he ever saw Bird Bird again, she might have little Bird Birds.

He stood, hefted his daysack, and walked into the bright lemon-coloured light.

As he neared the cave, he couldn't see Barney or Spencer. Not in the cave entrance, and not chained to the rock at the front. The ground surrounding the voodoo rock was littered with stones, like a golf driving range, and only fragments of green fleece remained of Calix's balaclava.

It meant the twins had to be in the tent.

The guards squatted in their usual positions: smoking and observing, but they weren't talking. Not one of them. Not even Ved the cook. Hant sat facing into the cave, Chet at his feet. The only noise was the short shrill shrieks of marmots.

Calix walked the last fifty metres. He was tired, thirsty, hungry. He had a blister on his heel and every step from the bridge had hurt.

He stopped at the lip of the cave.

'What's going on?'

Chet stood up, yawned, stretched, and trotted out to meet him. Calix rubbed the dog's mouth.

'Hant?'

There was no response.

Barney sat against a wall of the cave, his legs stretched flat across the front of the tent. The tent flaps were tied open.

'Barney?'

The twin didn't reply.

Calix glanced inside the tent. One sleeping bag had been pushed up against the side and the other was laid out flat.

'Where's Spencer?'

Still no one spoke.

Calix looked again inside the tent. At the unfurled sleeping bag. He reached out towards the end of the bag, intending to lift a corner.

'Don't you dare.'

Calix withdrew his arm as if he'd been bitten. Barney's eyes were bloodshot, his face blotchy and unshaven. He looked in Calix's direction but through him, focusing on something behind him.

Calix turned. 'Hant?'

'Barney not talk. But cook say Spencer much cough in night, difficult breathe much hours.'

'Spencer's *dead*?'

Hant nodded.

'Barney, fuck, I—'

'Don't even start,' said Barney, his voice echoing in the cave.

'Barney, I—'

'*I said, don't start.*' His voice and the echoes clashed around the cave. 'I said, don't fucking start. I said—' He picked up a stone and threw it across the hideout. It ricocheted off the far wall and skittered along the floor. The stone slowed and petered out, the echoes subsided, and slowly there was silence again.

Water dripped down from the roof of the cave.

A puddle had formed by Barney's outstretched legs. The twin wore his boots but had not tied them up, and long orange laces trailed into the water. The puddle shimmered dark orange like the eyes of the Finchams' dying cat.

30

The bulging oily-black stomach, large as a sack of rice, slithered out of the dead cow's ribcage and onto the hessian mat. Clouds of flies rose and resettled. Three barefooted villagers leant over the carcass, their t-shirts and baggy shorts bloody and stained. They heaved the wobbling stomach to the side, then used *kukris* to hack the meat into lumps to take away.

A stench of entrails filled the air, but no one in the crowd of a hundred seemed to notice. Most stood but some sat on the walls bordering the small yard. Behind the three men with knives was an army of small children. The older ones with a keener look.

'Why so many people?' asked Rick. His shirt was damp with sweat and he was tired after the hike from Lukla. He wiped dirt from the top of his water bottle and took a long drink.

'Killing a cow – a *gaai* – is a rare event in remote villages like Saklis,' said Russell. 'Against their religion, so there will be people here from other villages who've come to get a share.'

'Why the exception?'

Russell spoke to a man on the edge of the circle. Both laughed.

'This cow had an accident,' said Russell.

'Explain,' said Kate.

'I'm not sure I can.'

The children near the dead cow started whispering and filing away. They threaded their way back through the crowd and stood around the newcomers, jostling and shouting words in English. 'Hello.' 'Sweet.' 'Pen.' One girl in a white vest and denim skirt reached up to touch Kate's long red hair.

Russell rebuked the girl, and all the children stepped back a few metres.

'It's okay, really,' said Kate.

Rick dug around in his bag. He took out the photos of the three missing and of Hant, and a packet of chocolate éclairs. The kids surged at him as if he was Willy Wonka.

'Russell, tell them they can all have a sweet, but first they must look at the photos.'

Rick passed around the photos of the three missing. Calix, blond hair and quiff, tattoo. Barney, tall, beefy, in his rugby kit. Spencer, glasses, eating a burger, the runt of the three. He wondered what they were doing at that moment.

The younger kids glanced at the photos, and snatched them from each other, giggling. An older child in a red football shirt with Rooney on the back lingered with the photo of Calix. Rick was hopeful.

Russell spoke to the boy, who shook his head and laughed. 'Manchester United?' said the boy.

'The adults might be better,' said the mountaineer, 'but we'll need to wait for the meat to be divided up.'

Rick retrieved the photos of Calix and the twins, and replaced them with photos of Hant. Hardly had they left his hand than the group erupted in delight. Furious whispering turned to pointing and they handed the photos to the boy in the Rooney shirt. He looked at the photos, and said a few words in Nepali.

'He lives here,' said Russell.

'Where?' said Rick.

There was another exchange in Nepali, and more shy laughter. 'He'll show us.'

Rick handed Kate the sweets. 'You stay and see if any more kids turn up.'

A posse of children swarmed around Rick and Russell as they set off. The lad in the Rooney shirt led through the network of narrow pathways, and Rick and Russell followed, Rick feeling like the Pied Piper. Uneven cobbled paths between stone walls two metres apart. Down one side of the cobbles was an open gutter with a dirty trickle of water, but no sewage. A man overtook them carrying a lump of butchered cow, bloody and dripping.

Gradually, they worked their way diagonally across the village. A squawking chicken ran across their path, followed by a rooster. It was silent in its chase. Rick peered over the wall into a brushed yard and watched the rooster pin the chicken to the ground. It took only a few seconds. The chicken scuttled away, its back bleeding, and the rooster raked the ground with its claws.

A woman appeared in the dark doorway of the house.

'*Namaste*,' said Rick. The children laughed and one threw a stone at the rooster.

At a water tap, Rick filled his bottle and added a purifying tablet. Twenty minutes before he could drink.

The children stopped at a small shack. Some of them pointed and there was more laughing. Russell knocked on the door and Rick went around the back. Habit. Suddenly, he needed ten detectives.

'Rick,' shouted Russell.

'Rick, Rick,' shouted the children.

He returned to the front. Russell was talking to a woman at

the door of a neighbouring shack. A baby was strapped to her chest and a second child held her skirt and looked up at Russell as if he was from another planet.

'Hant doesn't live in Saklis any more. Hasn't done for years. Just his mother.'

'Father?' said Rick.

The woman pointed behind them, and they turned around. A woman in a headscarf and a red checked shirt walked up. She was short with a lined face, and looked about fifty.

'Hant's mother,' said Russell.

'*Namaste*,' said Rick.

The woman scowled and launched into a stream of Nepali. The children retreated to the path and Russell tried to intervene, but the woman's yabbering only strengthened. She walked around them, and issued instructions to the woman with the baby.

'Telling her not to talk to anyone from the government.'

'We only want to speak to her son. Tell her we're British, and not from the government.'

Russell tried again but the woman started yelling. The children disappeared, and the two of them walked away. 'Wasted trip,' said Russell.

Rick shrugged. Russell was wrong. Hant's mother knew what was going on.

'We'll try some house-to-house on the way back.'

'Shack-to-shack,' said Russell. The two of them walked back down the greasy cobbles. Several children reappeared, chattering non-stop. A man approached carrying a large slab of beef. A *kukri* was tucked through his belt.

They stopped again, and knocked on a stable door. The top half was open and cooking smells wafted out. A young woman appeared, a chunky comb in her hair. She looked at them as if they were ghosts. Rick showed her a photo of Hant, and Russell asked some questions. When did you last see Hant? Do you know where he is? From behind them, there was a burst of bad-tempered Nepali. They turned to find Hant's mother. The young woman disappeared into the gloomy interior.

'She's furious about something,' he said, as they walked away for a second time. They speeded up, backtracked, and using Russell's uncanny sense of direction, walked a large circle through the maze of paths. They tried again at another open door. There was no sign of Hant's mother.

A teenage boy, fourteen or fifteen, wearing a grubby t-shirt, came into view.

'*Namaste*,' said Russell. Rick produced the photo.

The boy scowled, and shook his head. Word had gone around.

They walked the ten minutes back to the square where they'd started. The carcass had disappeared and so had most of the people, including Kate and all the children. Surrounded by flies, two of the barefooted butchers were tidying up. The hessian mat was covered in a thick paste of gritty, lumpy blood. Pieces of bone and scraps of skin lay scattered about, and two buckets held entrails. A warm, abrasive smell clogged the air.

Three old men sat on a wall. They wore traditional Nepalese *topi* hats, and one of them was missing an arm to the shoulder. Rick had noticed them before. Sitting, watching, smiling, saying the occasional word. Like old men everywhere.

'Try them, Russell. I'm going to find Kate.'

Rick found her, several backyards away. She was sitting on a plastic chair in front of a wall, and at her feet were thirty cross-legged children. A few of them were whispering but most were quiet. Two stood behind her, plaiting her hair. One small boy held her trouser-leg. The wall had been plastered flat and Kate was using it as a chalkboard. A map of the world, arrows for England and Nepal. France, Germany, Italy, the

USA, Canada and Japan. The G7 by luck or judgement, Rick wasn't sure. *Kate* in large letters. Several of the kids' names.

'You're wasted as a coroner's officer,' said Rick. 'Any luck with the photos? I take it you have shown the photos?'

'I have. Two boys not only recognised Hant but also recognised Calix. Both of them were here a few days ago.' The two girls continued plaiting her hair. Concentration on their faces. Kate held her head still, like a model.

'Really?'

'Really.'

'Calix?'

'Yes! The boys' father came looking for them, and he spoke some English.'

'Are you sure they didn't just say they recognised Calix?'

'Not a hundred per cent.'

Kate pointed out the two boys and Rick beckoned them over. Their plimsolls were cheap and their t-shirts and shorts were grey from too much scrubbing. One wore National Health-style glasses. Rick knelt down and pulled out his phone. He shuffled some of the photos around and created two new folders: ten photos of white men including Calix, and ten photos of Asian men including Hant. With sign language, he explained what he wanted the boys to do. The three of them exchanged a thumbs-up. He felt Kate watching, assessing his performance.

Rick started with the Hant folder, and showed his phone to the boy with glasses. The boy picked out Hant without hesitation. The boy without glasses borrowed those of his friend, and did the same. Rick moved onto the Calix folder. The boys grinned, loving every second of the gringo's game.

Again, both boys picked out Calix without hesitation. Thumbs-up, all round. The identifications weren't PACE-compliant but it didn't matter. Only the result mattered.

'Rick.' Russell's voice. 'You'll want to hear this.'

Rick turned around. Russell stood in a gap in the wall of the yard. It had fallen down and the mountaineer stood on the stones. Behind him, snow on distant mountains sparkled in the sunshine.

'What?'

'The old men, they're Ghurkha vets. You need to talk to them.'

He nodded, but first he had a call to make. At the side of the yard he righted a plastic chair, knocked off the dirt, and sat down.

He'd not used a sat phone before, but Maggie had said he could contact anyone on the planet. He phoned her.

As he waited for it to connect, he pictured her sitting in a pub garden. Twirling her hair. Across the table is Parry. He's making her laugh with mountaineering stories. She twirls her hair some more. Parry goes to get refills. From the table he climbs onto a stone wall, and without touching the ground climbs along the wall to the pub building. He climbs along the side of the building, using a window frame for his hands. No footholds. Other customers start to watch. Parry arrives at the door. There's the sound of clapping. Maggie is clapping.

How would *he* entertain her, and make her laugh? Not climbing, like Parry. He'd have to talk to her, tell her things. Not funny stories, or tales of derring-do, like Russell. He'd tell her stuff about bees. About detective work.

'CID, South Manchester Police,' said Maggie. 'How can I help?'

'It's Rick. I'm on the bat-phone.'

'Where are you?'

'Saklis, took us two days' walk from Lukla. It is Hant's village, and we're getting close – Calix and Hant were here a few days ago.'

'The twins?'

'Not seen here – at least, not by the people we've spoken to. Doesn't mean they weren't here.' He took a deep breath. 'How'd it go with Parry?' He waited, heart beating like a teenager. Crazy.

'He's not involved. I'm almost certain.'

'Why?'

'Too much going on in his life. He drank mineral water all evening. Said he was a trying-to-recover addict, both alcohol and gambling. Said he'd lied about being hacked because he was embarrassed about his gambling. He gave me the names of an online bookmaker's and a local one. Both have confirmed Paul's story – off the record. He's in GA and AA. His first wife, second time, and his two teenage daughters soak up the rest of him.'

Rick nodded, only half-listening.

'Rick?'

'Yes?'

The question mark hung in the air, like a tethered balloon. She'd used his first name again, as if she was deliberately teasing him.

'Almost forgot. Simon and I went round to see the Finchams, the neighbours of the Conistons. Thought it was best in person. We asked them about their cat. They said they were glad they hadn't found Riley after he'd been run over, and it was lucky Calix found him.'

There was no proof that the cat had ever been run over.

'Anything else?' said Maggie.

He wanted to ask whether she was seeing Parry again. But he couldn't. She had to tell him. 'I don't know, is there?'

'No.'

Rick pocketed the phone and stood up. Under a pink-tinged dome of sky, he walked towards the square, kicking a stone.

31

A large crow flapped its wings, and landed on the pile of earth. In the brutal sunlight, the crow's feathers wore a purple sheen. It let out an abrasive squawk. A second crow landed, and together, they pecked and raked the freshly dug soil.

Calix stood at the edge of the shallow hole, watching Barney dig.

'Do you want any help?'

Barney propped the mattock, and climbed out. With his back to Calix, he drained his water bottle and threw it down. He grabbed up the spade by the shaft, and turned around. His beard was unkempt and his t-shirt sweat-stained and soiled. The pale blue veins running down his biceps stood proud. He looked like a wild man, and could easily have been holding a thunderbolt or a scythe.

Calix took a step back.

Barney snorted, and jumped back into the hole.

Calix retreated to a nearby boulder, climbed onto it, and sat down. Kelsang and the guard with the garlic and nicotine breath sat on another boulder, watching like vultures. They'd removed Barney's chain so he could dig, and feared he might escape.

Calix lit a cigarette.

Snowy mountainous ramparts bore down on two sides. Frozen waterfalls glimmered, and issued sharp cracks like gunshots.

He pondered his situation. Spencer wasn't meant to die, nor was Vicky. If he stopped, when should he tell Barney? *What* should he tell him?

Barney's spade rang as it hit a stone. Calix watched the twin work away the earth to reveal a boot-sized lump, then lever with the spade and pull down hard. The rock rose up and beached on the bottom of the hole.

Two people would have made it easier, but Calix held back.

He lit a second cigarette from the first. He now had his own pack, a present from Hant, and he looked past the two guards, back towards the cave where Hant sat in the chair. Calix held up the cigarette, and nodded.

Hant did not move or speak.

Barney heaved out another rock from the hole. Rocks were the killers, Calix knew from experience. Earth was easy, just keep going, but hitting a rock delayed things. You couldn't guess the size of a hidden rock, and they were always heavier when buried. He thought of the graves he had dug for animals where capture or mounting had gone wrong. He thought of the TB-crazed badger he had killed with a garden fork. A mercy-killing. The screeching and the thrashing around had been unnerving. And the mess. Natural deaths, clean kills were better as his method of acquisition. The Finchams' cat, for example.

Chet padded up.

Calix held out his hand, his fingers curled. The dog nuzzled the fingers aside but his hand was empty. Chet whined, and Calix pushed the dog away. He watched Barney throw some of the smaller rocks back into the hole, and climb in again. He walked over, and peered down at Barney. The twin was on his knees, fitting the rocks together like a mosaic.

'No one's going to see the floor.'

Calix waited for a reply, but none came. He stubbed out the cigarette. 'Water?' He held out his bottle.

'No.'

Barney turned a stone over, tried it in the pattern, frowned, picked it up again, and tried it another way. He tried a third way. A fourth way. They were going to be there all night.

Calix understood about the mosaic, even though no one would ever see it. He always did something: a decent hole, a marker of some kind – a shaped stone, a stick, but nothing his old man might notice – and a moment of reflection. He liked animals, they liked him, but man was at the top of the food chain. Some men, higher than others.

He'd still not made his decision. If he stopped, he could probably get out of it somehow. Yesterday or the day before, he couldn't remember which, he'd over-dramatised about Belmarsh and capital punishment. He'd just say he'd been coerced, forced, threatened at gunpoint, he'd make something up – he had before. He'd always managed to wiggle his way out of situations. Never say much, that was the key.

Calix followed Barney back to the cave to collect Spencer's body. As the two of them arrived, Hant was crawling out of Barney's tent. Calix now had his own.

'What the hell are you doing?' said Barney.

'Check,' said Hant. He stood up, his eyes like stones, his face unreadable.

'Hant?' said Calix.

The Nepalese man ignored him and walked off.

Barney disappeared into the tent and Calix tied back the

flaps. Barney secured a sleeping bag around Spencer's stiff body. He then backed out, hauling the rollmat, and Spencer.

'I could help,' said Calix.

Barney scowled. Looking over his shoulder, he began dragging the rollmat down the slope towards the grave. Three shifts got him there.

Calix followed behind.

'You can't do this bit by yourself.'

'Fuck off.'

Calix returned to his boulder, sat down and lit up. Chet chased marmots down the hillside, but they were quick, and the dog scattergun in its approach.

Barney struggled to unpeel the cocooned, rigid body from the mat, gave up and shoved them both into the grave. He threw a book on top. A breeze had picked up and the pages fluttered. Barney walked to the end of the grave, and stood looking down. He took a piece of paper from his pocket.

Calix slipped off the rock.

The paper flapped in the wind. Barney pulled it taut, and cleared his throat. He was shaking. Calix put out a hand, and slowly withdrew it.

'Today, Spence,' said Barney, his body shuddering and his voice trembling. 'I am 6,760 days old.' He took a deep breath. 'Until three days ago, I spoke to you on every single one of those days.' He paused. 'Every single one.'

The pages of the book flickered back and forth.

'I'm sorry, Spence. I know you didn't even want to come on this trip. You did it for me.'

Barney fell to his knees, soil cascading into the hole. He cried out, and pushed in more soil. He slapped the soil with his hands, over and over.

'God!'

Behind Barney, Calix walked closer, his heart beating.

'Our Father,' said Calix.

'Our Father,' repeated Barney through his tears. He stood up, soil falling from his trousers. 'Who art in heaven.'

They said the words together. When they'd finished, Calix turned around and rubbed away his silent tears. He felt sick, and guilty, and scared. He felt for Barney, and wished he could hold him. But the tears weren't only for Barney. Calix knew he was responsible for Spencer's and Vicky's deaths, and the guilt would remain with him for ever. And he was scared. He'd waded out of his depth, and he was starting to panic.

Barney shovelled more earth on top of the sleeping bag, some catching in the pages of the book. The sleeping bag slowly disappeared. The twin didn't stop until the heap had gone. He piled the rocks on top, then picked up a crude wooden cross and jammed it amongst them. He glanced at Calix, but didn't speak.

The two guards jumped to the ground, and knocked out their cigarettes on the rock, pocketing what was left. Barney picked up the tools and set off towards the cave. Behind him, the two crows flew down and perched on the cross.

Calix stood up.

He'd decided.

The crows took off and wheeled away into the darkening sky.

Low cloud welled up in the valley and slowly covered the land. The light faded. The vegetation around the cave became uniformly drab, all dark greens and dark browns. Above the hidden valley slopes, the snowy mountain peaks remained resplendent. Poking up through the rising cloud, they caught the last of the day's sun. The white snow patches and rocky ridge lines looked thousands of miles away. Unreal. A moon-scape.

Gradually at first, and then with great speed, the snow patches changed colour. Yellow, orange and finally reddy-purple as they merged into the sky above.

The light went.

Darkness.

Hant unscrewed the tops from two beer bottles, and handed a bottle to Calix. He sent the bottle tops spinning into the dark. They walked down the slope to the rock, Hant swinging an oil lamp. Chet brushed past his legs and disappeared.

Calix leant back against the rock and swigged his beer. A yellow glow emanated from the cave, and, somewhere, a bird was calling.

'You said, Hant, no one would get hurt.'

'I said hope no people injure.' He adjusted the wick on the lamp.

Calix picked at the label on the beer bottle. He peeled it away and rolled it into a tube. Flicked it into the blue-black gloom.

'Two people are dead. *Dead*, for fuck's sake.' Chet emerged from the murk, and lay at Calix's feet.

'Two accident.'

'No kidnap, no accident,' said Calix. Barney's argument. Barney was right.

'Four hundred Nepalese dead Qatar. You think one West people same two hundred Nepal people?'

'No,' said Calix. Chet nuzzled his hand.

'Spencer not strong man,' said Hant.

Calix finished his beer, and rested the bottle at his feet. The unseen bird stopped calling, and only the low chatter of the men by the fire remained. He picked at the scabs on his wrists.

They were healing, the centres pinky-red but the edges still a translucent white. The colour of bumblebee eggs.

'Hant, I'm not doing this any longer.'

'I not stop.'

'Hant, I'm going back to Kathmandu, and I'm taking Barney with me. It's finished, Hant. I'm sorry.'

Hant threw his bottle out into the night. Chet raced off. There was the sound of breaking glass. 'Not finish. Barney stay here. You stay here.' He stood, and shouted up at the cave.

Kelsang and the lazy-eyed guard ran down the slope. They pointed torches and pistols.

Calix looked at the pistols and the men holding them. At Hant's impassive face, caught in the yellow torchlight. 'I thought—'

'You wrong, my friend. Not only Nepal people dead Qatar. *Mero buwaa. Mero buwaa* dead.'

Buwaa. Father. Hant's old man, dead.

Calix ripped off the scabs on his wrists, one by one. Felt the flashes of pain. And watched his dark red blood begin to flow.

32

In the square, the three old men in *topi* hats still sat on the wall. They were passing round a half-bottle of a colourless liquid, and as Rick and Russell walked up one man proffered the bottle. His breath smelt of alcohol.

Rick took the uncapped bottle and sniffed it. 'Ahhh!' He handed it to Russell. 'What is it?'

'*Rakshi*, the local hooch.'

Rick shook his head, and the men laughed with toothless mouths. Russell took a swig. The old men cackled.

Behind Russell, one of the butchers rolled up the soggy hessian mat. Together, they hoisted the mat onto their shoulders, picked up their buckets and walked off, leaving a trail of blood splashes.

'They fought in the First Gulf War,' said the mountaineer, 'and they're not as old as they look. Early fifties, a bit older than me. They thought we were here about their pensions.'

'And now?'

'They know Hant, full name Arhant, and Hant's mother, Pawnee. Family name is Khetan. Hant is the *Sunko Keta*, the Golden Boy, of Saklis because he was the first person to go to university. Hant's father, Manu Khetan, was also a Ghurkha, but he's dead. A long time ago.'

There were always different ways of doing things, always new things to learn. It had taken some time, but the non-detectives had finally proven themselves, and using methods Rick had never tried. Hero-worship in the case of Kate, and now bribery.

'When? Where? How?' The questions Rick had asked Pemba, Amanda's *sirdar*.

'They don't know.'

'Of course they know, they're Ghurkhas and they live in the same village.'

'Well, they're not saying. They know who I am, but they think you and Kate are British officials of some sort. Army, government, police. The whole village thinks that. They're all suspicious of authority, even the ex-Ghurkhas. That's why nobody's talking to us.'

Rick didn't agree. Like most Nepalese people he'd met, the Saklis villagers were naturally reticent, but Hant's mother had spooked everyone. They weren't talking for a reason.

The Sunrise Guesthouse would look good in a tourist brochure with its terrace well-sited for the morning sun. The L-shaped accommodation half-enclosed the terrace and was designed so that its five rooms opened onto it. The roof was corrugated iron, painted a garish light blue.

The reality was different. Saklis was not Ghandar and the tourist trade was far smaller. The rooms smelt musty, and weeds grew in the cracks of the terrace. The menu was verbal and the *didi* out of practice.

Rick didn't mind. There were no other guests and the three of them could work without worry of scrutiny. He sat on the terrace at a table he'd propped up with a stone. In front of him were a teapot and a large cup of tea and the photos of Hant and the three missing.

At a second table were Russell, Kate and the two boys who'd identified Calix and Hant as visiting Saklis a few days earlier. The two of them were trying to take a statement, a pseudo-statement, to cover the circumstances of that visit. They were breaking all the rules – speaking to the boys together, no adult present, paying their father a fee – but this was a missing person enquiry and only one thing mattered. Finding the missing.

Before Kate had sat down with Russell, Rick had tried. But he'd been impatient and the boys had grown restless.

One of the boys wore Kate's sunglasses and the other her headover. Now it was like a vulnerable persons' interview – Rick could overhear the conversation and occasionally Kate walked over and asked him for clarification. What Rick wanted were the details. Was anyone with Hant and Calix? What did they do? Where did they go? Who did they speak to? Who else saw them? How long did they stay? Which direction did they leave in? Was Calix under any duress? That was the most diffi-cult question, and even adults might struggle.

He drank some tea and looked up at the snowy mountains. How Russell climbed them he had no idea – the steep, icy ridges and gullies looked impossible.

In the foreground a path led east out of the village and down the steep hillside towards the Hinku valley, and Mosom Kharka. From there, it met the main trail, one half heading north to Mera base camp and Mount Mera, the other south to Ghandar and eventually Jiri, the trailhead.

Something caught his eye. A kind of flickering.

Flies?

He swivelled around to have a better look. The shorter side of the guesthouse was built up against an enormous lump of rock, the size of a blue whale, and the flickering was coming from the top of it. He picked up his binoculars. Near the top of the rock was a thick log half a metre long, set on its side and flanked by short walls of stone. On top of the log, and over-hanging it, was a large flat piece of slate. He lowered the binoc-ulars and surveyed the whole rock – three similar constructions spaced across the top.

He put the binoculars back to his eyes and studied the top-most log. The flickering was coming from its centre where there was a small hole, ten centimetres by a centimetre.

Not flies. Bees. The logs were beehives.

Kate walked over.

'How's it going?'

'Slow,' said Kate. 'They jump around a lot, but we're getting there. How formal do you want it?'

'Truth and lies but don't worry about R v Turnbull.'

She nodded and walked back.

Rick looked at the photos on the table. The one of Hant Khetan suggested he was a similar age to Rick, early thirties. Born at the beginning of the 1980s. His mother, Pawnee Khetan, late 1940s. Which together suggested Hant's father, Manu Khetan, died some time after the early 1980s. Manu was a Ghurkha soldier. Had he died fighting? What actions had the Ghurkhas been involved in? The Falklands War in the early 1980s, but apart from that he wasn't sure. Bosnia, Iraq, Afghanistan, anywhere else? Maybe it didn't matter. All that mattered was the crossover with Calix's father, Brigadier Con-iston. The brigadier was now in the MOD but he had been a Ghurkha, and, as the newspaper cutting in his office recorded, he'd won a medal in the Falklands. The brigadier was about the same age as Hant's father.

The ages, the dates fitted. Was the brigadier responsible for Hant's father's death in the Falklands? Did Hant want revenge

216

for his father's death? Hant's full name, Arhant, meant destroyer of enemies.

The hairs went up on the back of his neck.

But, as a motive, it made no sense. The brigadier and Manu Khetan were on the same side.

Rick drank some more tea. A raft of things bothered him. Where were Spencer and Barney? Had they been in Saklis with Calix and Hant, and if not, why not? If a shared Ghurkha history was the reason for Calix to have been kidnapped, then what was the link to the Williams twins? And to Vicky Brant? Were the three of them just collateral? Whatever the reason or reasons for the four to have been kidnapped, why had there been no demands?

He flicked back a few pages and looked at his previous hypotheses. H3, missing in Nepal, seemed increasingly unlikely. Which just left H2a, kidnap then murder, and H2b, kidnap then demands.

Maybe it didn't matter. He only had to find the three missing, and they'd made significant progress.

The boys were describing Calix as a movie star with white hair. Russell was translating, Kate was writing it all down.

Rick stared at one of the log-hives. Bees flitted in and out. He vaguely remembered from a beekeeping course that bees could be kept in different ways, including baskets, and logs. But he'd had no idea they could survive at such a high altitude. His own bees wouldn't.

Kate brought over the statements. Rick put down the binoculars.

'They're pretty much the same.'

'Well persevered.'

'It wasn't hard, they're sweeties. Remind me of Richardson. Kept thinking what he'd remember, what games he plays with his friends.'

My name is Sushil and I'm eleven years old. I've lived in Saklis all my life. The following is true. True means it happened, like this morning we played football with Russell. A lie means it's not true. A lie means it didn't happen, like this morning we flew in an aeroplane.

Yesterday I went to school and hurt my finger in a door. It still hurts. After school I helped my mother with goats. We have seven goats.

The day before yesterday I went to school. After school I played with my friend, Kanak. He's my best friend. We played 'Killer Cars' in Kathmandu. We drive cars around Saklis and kill baddies. We are the cars.

When we played Killer Cars I saw some men stop at a water tap. Three men, I think. I know two of the men, Ram and Hant. Ram lives in Saklis. He's about fifteen years old. He's very strong. Sometimes he comes to my school to help build our new classroom. Hant's in the family of my friend's neighbour. Hant doesn't live in Saklis. He's a grown-up man.

A white man was with Ram and Hant. He was very tall. Not as tall as Russell. The white man had white hair. He looked like a movie star. The white man filled his water bottle and put medicine into the bottle.

The white man smoked a cigarette. He laughed with Hant and Ram.

Hant's mother arrived at the water tap. She spoke to Hant. She was very cross.

Then we played more Killer Cars.

Rick looked up at Kate. Behind her, the two boys were kicking a small ball with Russell. They both watched for a few seconds.

'Killer football,' shouted Russell.

'Good stuff, Kate. Just a bit more on what they were wearing, and what they were carrying. Any weapons? How long did they stay? Where? Which direction did they leave in? Also, why did they mention Ram is strong?'

33

A new day at the cave, and everything was the same. The harsh sun sat high in the azure sky. The snow-capped mountains formed an unassailable wall to the north. The cave was so cold the jerrycan froze at night. Nepalese men chuntered in the cave mouth, and two more squatted on a high rock keeping watch. Marmots scampered across the hillside.

Everything was the same, but everything was different. The Nepalese men were not brothers-in-arms, but guards.

Calix kicked out with his leg. The chain around his shin pulled tight and bit into the flesh. He turned. Suspended in the air, the chain was taut all the way to the ring on the large rock. A second chain led down to Barney. The twin sat on a rollmat, staring at the pieces on Megan's chessboard.

Calix relaxed his leg, the chain clinking as it hit the ground. His leg was throbbing again. And his wrists. He squatted, lit a cigarette and stared at the links in the chain. They were no thicker than the cigarette.

From the stub, he lit a second. Only seven remained. He was unlikely to get any more, but he didn't care. He needed them now, needed the nicotine to help him think. He'd been wrong about getting his hands dirty. Wrong, too, about building a house: it didn't matter if he could, or couldn't, build a house. All that mattered was that he lived in one.

Players didn't get their hands dirty. Being a player meant forcing others to get their hands dirty. Like FIFA and the Nepalese workers. Like Hant and *him*. He'd been played, he'd done Hant's dirty work. He stubbed out the cigarette on the ground. Stood up and mashed it with his heel.

He beckoned to one of the guards on the high rock, and explained what he wanted. If they didn't mind, if they had a minute. Yes, sir, no, sir.

Calix walked back and forth to the grave for half an hour before Barney joined him. As he'd planned. He'd been carrying every lump of rock he could see back to the graveside, and building a new pile of rock. Barney started to work alongside him. Their shackles had been removed. Four guards, compass points in a giant circle, watched.

'I thought,' began Calix. His shirt was stained with sweat.

Barney grunted him into silence.

They ferried for a while, then stopped to share a bottle of water. Together, they lifted the larger rocks.

'Enough,' said Barney after another hour.

They built a large cairn, Barney adding the cross to the top. They sat down, and drank some more water.

'Cigarette?' said Calix.

'What do you think?'

They stared at the cross, and at the guards. They stared up at the cave, and at Hant checking his phone. They looked everywhere, except at each other.

'Are you going to tell me what happened?' Calix glanced at Barney. The twin's eyes were bloodshot and his beard needed hacking back. But he was big, and strong. He'd gripped the spade shaft like Poseidon.

'Are you going to tell me?' said Barney.

Calix flipped a coin, and Barney lost. Of course he did. Playing the twins had been easy, too easy. Hant would be far more difficult.

'It might help,' said Calix.

'Help!'

A minute or two went by. Calix thought about another cigarette. One a day for a week, and that would be it.

'Asthma attack,' said Barney. 'The night you went to Saklis. Spence got wheezier and wheezier. His blue pump was completely empty and his Becotide, the brown one, he'd left behind during the kidnap. He couldn't breathe, he was gasping. Dry heaves, crying, we both were. I didn't know what to do. His last moments...' Barney's voice cracked. 'I held his hand, looked him in the eyes. God! God, it was so fucking awful.'

Barney wept and Calix looked away, up to the cave. Chet lumbered down the slope.

The twin took a deep breath. 'He'd had them before, especially when we were younger. Several times he was rushed to hospital in the middle of the night. Without his drugs and with the altitude—'

'I'm sorry,' said Calix.

Chet wandered over and sat down beside them.

'Ears are an important part of the limbic system,' said Calix, stroking the dog. He waited for Barney's question.

'Now you, Calix. How'd you get involved?'

'I told you – I met Hant at a taxidermy lecture in London.'

'That was the truth?'

'Yes.'

'And Hant's been stringing you along, all this time?'

'Seems like it.'

'Why?'

'I'm not sure. Something to do with my old man and his old man. Amanda mentioned something at the team meal in Kathmandu. The *sirdar* and one of the porters recognised my name.'

'Coniston?'

'Yeah. I asked Ram about it.'

'And?'

'I didn't get anywhere. Just that his old man – his *buwaa* – is dead and Hant is Ram's uncle. His *mama*. Nothing about Hant's *buwaa*.'

'Hant's dad?'

Calix nodded. Beside them, Chet was snuffling.

'How did Ram's dad die?'

'I don't know.'

'When?'

'I don't know.'

A crow landed on the cross. They both hurled stones at it, and it flew off. The stones tinkled down the cairn and fell silent.

'One more question,' said Barney. 'Is your name really Calix?'

'Yeah.' Calix paused. 'My old man went on some army exchange to Westpoint. One of the American generals was called Calix.'

Barney nodded, and threw another stone.

'The way I see it, is that we now have to work together, whether we like it or not.'

'Doing what exactly?'

'Escaping.'

'FIFA might actually do something in Qatar,' said Barney. 'Hant might let us go.'

'They might, or they might not. Even if they do, Hant might not let us go. Two people have died, what's another two?'

'This is about *you*,' said Barney. 'Not me. And you don't even know why Hant wants you here.'

'It's about both of us.'

'How do I know I can trust you?'

Calix smiled. 'You can't. But you don't have a choice.'

'They've got guns, a dog. They know the terrain, they're fit as.'

'You don't need to worry about Chet. You can do whatever you want after ear stroking. Vets use it.' He took out the spoon and pressed it into the first ear. Gently, he pushed it up and down, working the smooth skin and crunching over the ridges of cartilage. He moved lower, to the cavity under the ear, and pressed the spoon in hard. Chet moaned, and went out like a light.

'As for the rest of it, I've got a few ideas.'

Calix stared out. On a distant peak, he thought he could see people – two people, three people, sticking up from a ridge like tiny trees. He looked away, looked back. Not moving, although he wasn't sure. The scale, too, was hard to judge. If they were people, they were giants.

34

Rick watched the *didi* throw corn for the chickens. When they came running, squawking and roughhousing around her ankles, she dived down and grabbed a pair of legs. She turned the bird upside down, placed a foot on its head and yanked the legs upwards. It was a well-practised move. She hung it on the back of the door, and started plucking.

Kate came back with the additional statement. 'Did you see that?'

Rick nodded. 'Quick.'

'Sushil and Kanak didn't even blink.'

My name is Sushil, and this is my second statement. Ram is tall for Saklis. As tall as the shoulder of the white man with white hair. Ram is strong because he helps build our school and carries a big yellow rucksack. Not a basket. His trousers have stars and the letter R at the top. One day I want trousers like Ram. He sometimes wears shorts but I only have shorts.

After I saw the three men at the water tap I saw them one more time. They walked out of Saklis on the path which goes down to the big river and the old village of Mosom Kharka.

Rick put down the statement. 'How's Richardson's cough?'

'Better, he's back at school which my parents are a little too happy about.'

When Russell and Kate had left with the two boys, Rick switched on the sat phone. Nearby, the *didi* clipped off the wing feathers with heavy-duty scissors. Plucking had taken her twenty minutes. There was no blood and no smell.

On the phone, a red light flashed. In theory it had all the functionality of a cell phone. He typed up a summary of the information gained in Saklis in an email and sent it. He watched it go, and moments later felt awed when a sent message popped up. It was 1997 all over again – he was fifteen and he'd been given his first mobile phone. For emergencies, his mum had said. Like your leg's fallen off.

The *didi* eviscerated the bird on a large chopping board. Two plastic bowls were by her side, one for offal, one for waste. He'd witnessed plenty of post mortems where human organs were separated out, weighed, a slice removed for analysis and the remainder stuffed back in. The chest of the cadaver sewn back up. But he'd never seen the insides of a chicken.

He phoned Maggie, and waited for it to connect. Now he could smell the dead chicken.

'Hello, sir.'

'Have you read my email?'

'Reading it now.'

Rick gave her time to catch up. He'd told Maggie about what had happened to *him*. She was the only person he'd told that he didn't have to. Emma was his shrink and Becky was his sister, so neither counted. But Maggie had thrown it back in his face and gone out for a drink with Parry. He wouldn't be telling anyone else.

'Okay,' said Maggie, 'what now?'

'Priority is to re-interview the brigadier. Ask him whether he remembers a Ghurkha soldier called Manu Khetan. Ask him about his service with the Ghurkhas, which campaigns he fought in. He won a medal in the Falklands, so he'll want to talk about that. Any training accidents where Ghurkhas were killed.'

'Yes, sir.'

The word was only small, but was beginning to grate.

'Robbo's here, wants to speak.'

'Good work locating them,' said Robbo. 'But you're now to stay in Saklis until the others catch up. DS Khan and DC Emmett are in Kathmandu and are getting sorted. They've made contact with the Nepalese officers and the Aussie team will arrive tomorrow. They should all be with you in a few days.'

'Okay.'

'You're very quiet.' The superintendent paused. 'I've still got that damn stye. Bloody itchy. Janice's going overboard – I've never eaten so much spinach. Next, I'll be getting a tattoo of an anchor.'

'Robbo—'

'I'll phone you back. Chief super's walked in.'

The chicken sat plucked and gutted. A large blackened cooking pot had replaced the bowls. Using her chunky knife and bare hands, the *didi* cut and broke the bird into legs, wings and misshapen lumps of bone and flesh. All went in the pot, nothing was wasted.

While he waited, Rick studied the log bees with binoculars. He tried another function on the sat phone. *Apis cerana* were commonly known as golden honeybees, and could survive freezing temperatures and live up to an altitude of 3,500 metres. But as surplus-honey-producers, they were poor. He thought it amazing they produced any surplus at all.

The phone rang.

'Right, what is it?' said Robbo. A fat man.

'The crime desk.'

'That again. It's only for six months.'

'Jack could do three.'

'Get Calix back, and the Williams twins, and there may be something I can do.'

Rick scowled.

'That's the world we live in: performance, not people.'

Rick slid the phone onto the table. He went over to the tap and filled his water bottle. He turned off the tap, but too quickly and it cross-threaded. He turned it one way, then the other, but it wouldn't budge. He cast around, and picked up a stone. He whacked the tap back and forth. It moved. He screwed it anti-clockwise and the tap head sheared off in his hand.

'Aargh!'

The *didi* shuffled into the kitchen, shaking her head. The chickens sat around quietly, one or two scratching deeper in their dust-bowls. Feathers blew about, the smell already gone.

Rick walked back to his table. He put the tap head in the ash-tray, and slipped a twenty-dollar note underneath. Next to it, the sat phone beeped the arrival of an email. An alien, scolding noise in the natural world of Saklis.

It was a message from Maggie.

Finally, the kidnappers' demands had arrived.

James Ellson

I want 2 things.

Good work conditons Nepal people Qatar (free travel in & out). And Barney and Spencer free.

Calix father. Then Calix free.

Hant

35

Barney unzipped his jacket. He stood up and leant against the rock where they were shackled. His right leg began to twitch.

'Feeling odd, Calix. Dizzy.'

Calix sat a few metres away, watching.

Barney's face was covered with sweat. His face was pale, his eyes distant. His right leg twitched faster, up and down, up and down, faster and faster, like a sewing machine. The chain, attached to his right ankle, jangled with the movement of the leg, but was, Calix noticed, a fraction delayed. Like thunder, then lightning.

'Calix!'

This time it was a shout. Calix watched Barney's leg. Up and down, faster and faster. It looked tiring, almost like an exercise in a gym. The sweat on Barney's face formed droplets and began to drip down his nose and his cheeks, and onto the front of his shirt. His head jerked back, then nodded, and as if it was finding a rhythm, nodded back and forth. Not as fast as the leg, and more mechanical, controlled even. The leg, though, twitched as if it had a mind of its own.

'Aargh!'

Calix stood up, and yanking his chain, took a step forward.

He glanced up at the cave. Two guards stood at the lip, one watching, and a second talking to someone out of sight.

'Hant!' shouted Calix.

Barney tugged at the sleeve of his jacket. His right leg kept twitching, the chain jangling like a fire-station bell, but his head had slowed. It had looked painful, as if it might give him a headache for days. He ripped his arm out of the sleeve, the sleeve turning inside out. Barney's second leg began twitching, and he fell to the ground like a toppled tree.

Hant appeared in the cave mouth, and a guard sauntered down the slope.

Barney flailed around on the ground. They'd moved the larger rocks, but it was still stony. Barney didn't seem to notice. His jacket worked itself up his back, and suddenly the arm still caught in the sleeve flicked outwards and took the jacket with it, whipping it across the scrub. Both his legs kept twitching, less frequently than when he'd been standing but at random. Random heavy jerks, Barney's brain seemed to be saying.

'Hant!' shouted Calix again.

The guard halfway down the slope turned, and shouted at Hant. The Nepalese leader slotted a pistol into his waistband and headed down the slope.

'They're coming, Barney.'

'Aargh!' The twitching of Barney's legs quickened, and he whipped the jacket around in the scrub. He looked like a beached octopus.

Hant and Kelsang approached.

Barney flailed and twitched and jerked. He whipped his jacket back and forth. He cried out. His shirt had rucked up to reveal the black tuft of hair on his stomach. The shirt was wet and stained. Threads of white spit, like spider webs, stuck to his lips and cheeks, and snot hung from his nose.

Calix took a step closer to Barney, then stepped back.

'Can you hear me, Barney?' he said. 'Try and relax.'

Barney's twitching slowed.

'What happen, Calix?' said Hant. 'You hit Barney?'

The butt of Hant's pistol poked out of his waistband. It was so close – no more than three metres. A lunge and a grab would have it done.

'He complained he was feeling dizzy,' said Calix. 'Then he fell over and started thrashing around. I think it's an epileptic fit.'

Hant folded his arms. It seemed out of place, a British gesture, but then he'd spent a decade in the UK. It reminded Calix of his old man. He folded his arms when he was contemplating – deciding. Maybe it was a good sign.

'First, Spencer,' said Hant. 'Now, Barney. Williams family no strong.'

On the ground, Barney had stopped moving, and lay in wonderful disarray. Self-entangled, like an overloaded coatstand which had fallen over. Calix knelt at Barney's side, and considered the situation. Barney's eyes were closed, and there was a large damp patch around his groin.

'Bad smell,' said Hant.

Calix nodded. He leant a tad closer. 'He's shit himself.' Beforehand, Calix had tried to see it through Hant's eyes, and it had been the one thing he and Barney had argued about. Pissing himself was not enough, Calix had argued. There had to be shit for Hant to believe it, and if Hant didn't believe it, there'd be consequences. Plasticuffs as well as leg shackles. One meal a day. A beating. Calix had won the argument; he was never going to lose.

Calix crawled around Barney, arranging his limbs in some sort of recovery position. Then glanced up at Hant and Kelsang.

They stared at the motionless twin.

'Barney,' said Calix.

There was no response.

'*Bandar ko chaak,*' said Hant.

'Eh?'

'*Bandar ko chaak.*'

'Barney,' said Calix again, louder. He pinched Barney's arm. Still there was no response. Pinching him harder, in addition to everything else, seemed unfair.

'He's breathing okay. Hopefully, he'll be okay.'

Hant scowled, and stared at Calix. His suspicious eyes like black ice.

Calix stood up, shaking his head. He stood for a moment with Hant and Kelsang, all three staring down at Barney. He was tempted to fold his arms, but decided not to risk it. 'Hant, you watch him. I'll find some spare clothes.'

Hant nodded. 'I no want lose him. Then only you.'

Calix shrugged and headed up to the cave.

Under a tangerine sun, Calix sat with Barney at the rock. Barney's trousers and pants lay drying, and he wore only a shirt and a pair of long shorts.

'Quite convincing,' said Calix.

Barney mumbled his reply, trying hard to remain cool towards Calix. But they needed each other; that was the truth.

Between them lay Calix's daysack, and he felt a twinge of hope. Their distraction plan had worked and now with the help of the sat phone, they might be able to extract themselves from the mess.

In the cave mouth, Hant had realised his phone was missing and was searching. There wasn't much to search and it wouldn't take long. Four tents, the cooking paraphernalia, the cave recesses and fissures. The Nepalese leader would quickly realise it wasn't mislaid but taken. Calix wondered what he'd do, who he'd blame.

'Keep a lookout, Barney.'

Calix rummaged in the daysack. Two guards were watching, but he figured they couldn't see what he was doing. He just had to make it look normal. He turned the phone on. The screen flickered and the phone powered up.

'It's working.'

'Okay,' said Barney, a tremor of anticipation in his voice.

Calix pressed a key, and a message appeared on the screen. *Enter PIN code (10 attempts remain).*

Four faint underscores waited expectantly.

He scowled.

'What?'

'It's PIN-locked.'

Calix typed 0000 and pressed enter.

Enter PIN code (9 attempts remain).

He tried 1234. And 9999.

'What're you doing?' said Barney.

'Keep watching.'

It had to be a factory preset. No one PIN-coded their phone – he never had. He tried again. He typed 0123.

The same answer flashed up. *6 attempts remain.*

'Fuck!'

'What?' said Barney.

'Ten attempts, I've tried the obvious presets. Six left.'

'Hant's returned and he's hopping mad. Shouting at Kelsang.'

'I can hear him.' Calix turned the phone off, wrapped it in a sock and put the sock in a plastic bag. 'They'll be down here soon. When they are, whatever you do, don't look at the marmot burrow. Got it?'

'Got it.'

Barney nodded, and Calix wandered over to the knee-high scrub. He dropped his trousers and squatted. Stared into the purple-grey shadows.

The search party arrived. Four guards, and Hant overseeing. The Nepalese leader climbed up the rock and watched from there. He climbed like a mountain goat. Calix and Barney were stripped and each piece of clothing searched and discarded in a pile. Their daysacks were emptied, and the chess set scattered and stamped on.

On the rock, Hant pulled out his pistol and placed it where Calix and Barney could see it. He urinated on Barney's drying trousers in noisy loops, then issued more commands to the searching guards.

They were told to stand facing the rock, but Calix stole glances over his shoulder. The guards searched the ground around the flat stones where the two of them passed the time. It wasn't a fingertip job, but they made up for finesse with energy and destruction. They moved the stones, tore away the scrubby vegetation, kicked things about.

Calix caught Barney glancing at the filled-in burrow. He'd known he would.

Ved the cook-guard found it. He shoved his arm inside and pulled out the weighted bag. Held it up with a triumphant shout. The guards lapsed into smiles and jokes, and Hant climbed down from the rock. More smiles, and more jokes.

As he dressed, Calix watched the guards follow their leader up the slope. He picked up a chessman. It was the black king, unharmed, wearing an eight-point crown, fine robes, and a stoic look.

He sat down and lit a flattened cigarette with the cracked lighter, hoping it would calm his pangs of hunger. There'd been nothing to eat since breakfast because of all the fuss and he was starving. Barney pulled on his wet trousers, still drying after he'd washed them for a second time.

'They're going to come back,' said the twin.

'Of course.'

'This time we might get a beating.'

'If they'd found nothing, they'd have kept searching. They've only taken half our money, and some cigarettes – so what? First rule of war is to spread distrust amongst the enemy. Try to turn them in on themselves.'

'And you're an expert.'

'My old man's always rabbiting on.'

'Except the phone doesn't work. All that effort to steal it – wasted.'

'We didn't steal it,' said Calix. 'We *acquired* it.'

'Same difference.'

It wasn't, but Calix wasn't going to explain. He breathed out a cloud of smoke and watched it disperse. Through it, the vista of snowy mountains reappeared. Stealing was impulsive and for a quick profit.

Acquiring something was different, and often needed finesse and planning. Sometimes took weeks. His art was a two-stage process of acquisition, then merger – combining the old life with the new.

'So what now?' said Barney. 'Have you got a Plan B?'

'Maybe.'

'*Namaste.*'

Calix looked up. Ram was walking down the slope towards them. He'd made himself scarce while the two of them were being searched. '*Namaste.*'

The boy slumped down. His lip was bleeding. Calix touched his own lip, feeling guilty. 'Hant?'

Ram nodded, trying to keep back the tears.

Plan B had come to Calix. Literally. But first, it needed some work. He wanted to ask the boy about Hant's old man. Both their fathers were dead – why? The question would have to wait, and instead, he tried the phrase Hant had used earlier.

'*Hant cha bandar ko chaak.*'

Ram managed a thin smile.

'*Maile bujhina,*' said Calix. I don't understand.

The boy thought for a moment. Then screeched like a monkey and scratched under his armpits and beat his chest. After a few seconds he bent over and pointed at his backside.

Ram laughed, and Calix laughed with him. 'Laugh, Barney, for fuck's sake. He's our Plan B. Now, take him over to the rock and show him our calendar. Let him make the mark for today. Keep his back turned to me and take your time.'

Calix waited until they'd moved away. He went to the area which they used as a toilet when they were chained up. It was at the chain's limit, and marked by knee-high scrub which gave a sense of privacy when squatting. A swarm of flies rose. He scraped away the turds with a stone and dug down into the soil. A little way down, his stone met plastic and he pulled the bag to the surface.

He clanked back with his booty, and re-lit the flattened cigarette. After a long drag he held the cigarette backwards. The smoke blew across his face and hair. Your own shit was one thing, somebody else's quite another.

He smoked down the rest of the cigarette, and watched Ram scratch his name on the rock.

If Ram took a message to Saklis, then he would bump into foreign trekkers along the way. Although Saklis wasn't on the main path, the route from the cave crossed the Jiri to Mera trail at the suspension bridge. Calix expected Ram to take a message without demanding payment, but it was better to be sure.

The question was what? His final wrap of weed? Barney's fancy altimeter watch? The remaining dollars he still had stashed?

The other two walked back and sat down. Calix told Barney about Plan B. Ram sat patiently, listening. He seemed half-asleep, as if he was drunk on the foreign words. His cut lip was shadowed by the reddening bruise. Calix winked at him and the boy closed both eyes as he tried to wink back.

Calix laughed, this time for real. Persuading the boy to take a message wasn't going to be difficult. He found his battered book, ripped out a page and began writing.

TBR

I need your help, big man…

36

It was early, and thick pearly cloud covered Saklis. Rick felt stiff after another night in a sleeping bag, and he wandered out to the edge of the village to loosen up. He stopped at the *chorten*.

A young farmer walked around the monument, a machete swinging in his belt. His basket was already full of firewood. The farmer walked several circuits, each time leaving a stone on the same corner of the square base.

Rick sat on a slate bench and pulled out his notebook. He didn't open it. Hostage demands weren't difficult to remember. Hypothesis 2b, kidnap then demands, had become a reality.

The two demands were mainly good news. Calix and the Williams brothers appeared to be still alive and a line of communication with the kidnappers had opened up. They also provided an opportunity for locating the three missing. The demands had been sent by email and the telecoms unit had established it was from a sat phone. Like cell phones, sat phones could be traced.

He turned on his sat phone. *No service* flashed up. The battery level was fine, and he flicked through the settings. The phone would not work indoors: it needed a direct line of sight to the satellite. But even outside, a solar flare and very thick cloud might affect it.

In front of him, the farmer shouldered his basket and walked off towards the hazy village. The cloud showed no signs of shifting.

Rick's main concern was for the twins – they hadn't been seen in Saklis by the two young witnesses. It was possible they'd escaped, but equally possible they were dead. As for Hant's motives, they appeared to be twofold. Better conditions for Nepalese workers in Qatar, and an unknown issue involving the brigadier.

Rick opened his notebook and wrote 'Hostage negotiation'. Robbo had requested a specialist negotiation team from the centre and they would have their own ideas about contacting Hant. Exchanging Brigadier Coniston for his son was never going to happen. Some small gesture towards better conditions in Qatar was more realistic, although it was likely they would say something had been done when in reality nothing had changed. A fake news item would give credibility. Robbo had made it clear that although Rick was eyes and ears on the ground, strategy would be run from the UK.

Rick hadn't argued. But, negotiating with a sat phone in the middle of nowhere was too fragile a line of enquiry to rely on.

The young farmer returned with an empty basket. He lapped the *chorten* and hurried off down the path away from the village and into the gloom. Rick looked up at the colourful eyes. Russell had told him that not only the eyes but every feature of a temple – the thirteen steps of the tower, the moon and the spike at the top, even the distinctive shapes of its construction – was highly symbolic. Of what, Russell had been less forthcoming.

Rick had a decision to make: stay in Saklis or move down to Mosom Kharka. The statements from the young boys had given clues to the distance and direction for the location of the three missing. The statements had also suggested a way of finding it. Watch out for Ram, the boy who lived in Saklis and was a friend of Hant. Ram, the boy with the yellow rucksack, the letter R and stars on his trousers.

Rick stood up and walked around the *chorten*, placing small stones on the base, like the farmer. The eyes seemed to follow him.

It was cold and he did twenty star-jumps, his breath marking the air. He put on gloves. The sat phone still showed *No service* so he read Maggie's briefing sheet.

The thirteen steps – bhumi – of a chorten's tower signify the ten steps of enlightenment and three higher levels of supraconsciousness. Each stage represents greater power and wisdom. The pinnacle is Buddahood.

In Rick's world, Buddahood was detective superintendent. Not the highest rank, but the highest level in the CID. In the whole service there were only a dozen, each one a goldmine of investigative experience, knowledge and clout. He was only one rank away but he wasn't there yet, and if the Coniston case was a disaster he might never make it. Six months on the crime desk would be going backwards, and quickly.

He looked up again at the eyes of the Buddha, the apparently omniscient and omnipotent Buddha. Maybe he could do with a bit of divine intervention in the search for the three missing. In his personal life, too: Dad to be Dad again, his queen bee to start laying, and finding someone to take to Becky's wedding. Taking Maggie seemed as likely as the *chorten* speaking.

He walked a final circuit, ploughing through the fog like an arctic trawler.

At the Sunrise Guesthouse, Rick sat on the terrace in a duvet jacket, his hands clasped around a bowl of porridge. Cloud still encased the village, and the usual bustle of everyday life was missing. Fewer children, fewer animals, and even the roosters seemed defeated. Like watching a film in black and white with the sound off.

He'd made two decisions. He'd buy a new queen, and they'd move to Mosom Kharka, the abandoned village, and surveil for Ram from there. There was a three-way junction between the path from Saklis, and the main Mera–Jiri route. Following the information from the two statements, it seemed quite likely – as likely as waiting in Saklis – they would see Ram there. They would also be closer to the three missing.

Russell, with Kate's help, was busy organising porters and tents and food. The tents would have to come from Lukla and it would take a day to fetch them.

He needed to talk to Maggie and Robbo and he peered at the sat phone.

No service. Still.

He added more jam to the porridge, and watched the didi fixing the tap.

Everything happened in a wave of small explosions, like the end of a power cut.

The cloud lifted, children and dogs rushed around, two trekkers arrived with a message and the sat phone beeped with updates.

From Maggie.

Can't get hold of you. Can't get hold of Hant. Can't get hold of the brigadier either – Mrs Coniston was evasive on the phone and when I got Bennett to do a knock-on, he wasn't there and still hasn't returned my calls. I'll keep trying.

From Robbo.

Hostage negotiation team now in place here. But they can't communicate with Hant. Back-up still preparing in Kathmandu. They're waiting on the army to liaise with the police, and they will all then fly to Lukla in force. Priority is a confirmed sighting of the Williams brothers.

Stye's gone, thank God.

From DS Khan

We're in Kathmandu. Met up with Aussie plod and we're trying to get things moving. Too many moving parts, so we're not moving.

Rick tried to make a call, but the phone wouldn't connect.

'Excuse me, we're looking for Rick Castle.' A woman's voice.

Rick looked up. On the terrace stood two female trekkers carrying rucksacks. They wore matching jackets, and long shorts. One had a crew cut, the other a ponytail.

'I'm Rick Castle.'

'Police?' said the woman with the shaved head.

'Yes.'

'Oh, that's fantastic, really fantastic,' said the woman with the ponytail, nodding. 'Isn't it, Sam?' She burst into tears.

'We've got a letter for you.'

Rick jumped up, making his chair fall over backwards. At the water tap, the *didi* stopped tinkering. Holding the wrench like a hammer, she stared across the terrace. Rick ignored her.

'I'm listening.'

Sam unzipped a pocket and pulled out a plastic bag. 'We tried not to touch it. We've seen *CSI*.' She put the bag on the table.

Rick delved in his bag for a pair of gloves, and snapped them on.

'Last night we camped down in the valley, a couple of hours

from here. Near a huge suspension bridge. When we were climbing down from the bridge, a Nepalese boy approached us and asked if we could post a letter to someone in the UK. Manchester. He offered us a hundred dollars for postage.'

'Describe him.'

She shrugged. 'Like every other Nepalese boy.'

'Think, it's important.'

Her eyes narrowed. 'You coppers. You're all the bleeding same.'

Rick righted the chair.

'He had a yellow rucksack.'

'Did he?'

'I'm not making it up.'

'I believe you.'

'When he'd gone, we opened it. We thought it was a wind-up – except for the money. But we couldn't do anything because no phone reception. This morning we saw a trekking group heading for Mera, and they had a sat phone. We contacted the British police, and finally, finally managed to speak to a Manchester superintendent.'

'Two am at home,' said her friend. Still sniffling.

'Beth, you can shut up now.'

'Sa-am.'

'You were lucky we got a connection. The cloud's an inversion. Your boss couldn't get hold of you so asked us to bring the letter to you. Said it was urgent and we've hardly stopped. A thank you wouldn't go amiss.'

'Thank you,' said Rick, sealing the unfolded letter and the envelope in an exhibit bag. He ripped off his gloves.

The letter was written on another page torn from Heidegger.

James Ellson

TBR
7A Mount Street
Manchester, UK

TBR

I need your help, big man. I've been captured and I'm being held in a cave – out of Kathmandu (SEE MAP). I know you've got Asian connections.

There are 6 unfriendlies but I'll work on them. I've nabbed their sat phone but it's PIN-locked. Will try and call you.

I'll owe you. Big time.

Keep my round open.

Calix

37

Hant and Kelsang cleaned their pistols at the front of the cave. Chet lay by their feet. The lazy-eyed guard was on lookout, one guard was asleep, and Ved, the cook-guard, was chopping vegetables. One guard was missing, the one with terrible breath – Hant had sent him to Lukla to get a new sat phone.

Calix waited.

Wisps of cloud drifted across the sky.

Barney nodded.

Calix stretched his leg chain around the front of the rock, making sure he kept out of sight of the cave and with his back to Barney. It was the last thing he wanted to do. But Barney had shat himself. It was his turn. He closed his eyes and imagined he was on a beach.

Women in bikinis, lying on towels, an ice-cream seller.

Women in bikinis.

One woman gets up, topless, takes off her pants. He stares and she waggles a finger at him. Beckoning.

The guard on lookout could see, but Calix didn't care. He was a man, would understand. He knelt down in the rocky scrub and unzipped himself. Stones bit into his knees, and he pushed them aside.

Calix closed his eyes again. Tania, the first-year on his corridor who didn't wear a bra, the ITV weathergirl with the ponytail, his sister's friend, Amy. Amy and Tania. All three of them, bending over.

He worked harder. Enough. Some on the ground, but most on the rough Nepalese bog paper.

He'd had the idea when Chet had smelt his crotch. Smells, certain smells in particular, sent dogs wild. Top of the list were bitches on heat. Then cum, any cum. Dog shit. Meat – raw, cooked or cooking. Bitches, cum, shit, meat. Toothpaste may have worked for bears, but it didn't work for dogs. He'd done research and conducted trials. He could give a lecture on the subject – even Professor Steinmann might learn something.

He zipped himself back up, put the bog paper in a plastic bag and put it in his pocket. Now he had to wait.

Calix dragged his chain back to Barney. The twin's straggly beard made him look thirty, his sunken eyes forty. Calix kept going, to the chain's limit on the far side. It reached the stream which flowed down from the side of the cave. At a steepening the guards had built a small rocky dam. The dam created a pool and a spout of water. The pool and the spout were for drinking water, and the stream below was for washing pots, bodies and clothes. He rubbed his hands in the dirt and washed them in the stream.

As he dried his hands on his trousers, he checked on the guards. Four plus Hant. Five.

The sun climbed higher, turned redder, grew fiercer. It harried the wisps of cloud, and burnt them away until there was nothing left. The clouds vanquished, the sun victorious.

Calix waited, staring out through his sunglasses. Watching the watchers.

While he watched he considered the PIN code. He'd lain awake most of the night thinking about it. How people cracked codes. He'd remembered *The Girl with the Dragon Tattoo*. When the journalist had been stumped by Salander's alarm code, he'd tried 9277 on a telephone-type keypad. The numbers spelt WASP, Salander's nickname.

So far, he'd had three ideas for codes.

HANT, YASH, and CHET.

In the cave mouth Ved dropped the jerrycans at Kelsang's feet. Muttering, Kelsang picked them up, and sauntered down the slope to the stream. Chet bounded alongside.

Calix stretched, yawned, and stood up. Grabbed their water bottles, and started walking. He timed it so he coincided with Kelsang at the water spout.

'*Thik chha?*' Okay?

'*Thik chha.*' Kelsang filled up the first jerrycan. He wore desert-coloured boots.

Calix waited with their bottles, his heart thumping. In the fold of his hand he held the sticky bog paper. Over Kelsang's shoulder, he watched Chet chase marmots across the hillside. The first jerrycan spilled over, and Kelsang screwed on the cap.

The guard started filling the second jerrycan. Calix's heart thumped harder. He dropped a water bottle by the guard's boots and bent to pick it up. He nudged Kelsang's calf, and wiped it with the bog paper. The lemony smell was sickly sweet.

Calix stood up, holding the bottle.

'*Maaph garnuhos.*' Sorry.

Kelsang grunted, picked up the jerrycans and plodded back up the slope. When the guard was halfway, Calix whistled. Chet raced up. Calix threw a stone up the slope and Chet ran off in pursuit.

Calix walked back with the bottles and handed one to Barney. He was getting thinner. They both were.

'Is it done?' said Barney.

'It's done.' Calix sat facing the cave, Barney alongside him. He passed the twin the water.

In the cave mouth Kelsang dropped the jerrycans at Ved's feet. Chet padded up and Ved threw him some scraps. The two men started arguing. Chet picked at the scraps and snuffled at Kelsang's legs. The dog bit Kelsang's calf. The guard cried out in pain and kicked out at Chet's ribs. The dog yelped and backed up, but Kelsang ran forward and kicked the dog again. The dog howled and ran off.

'He shouldn't have kicked you during the kidnap,' said Calix. 'It was unnecessary.'

Barney nodded. 'And if he hadn't?'

Calix looked away. He'd have done it anyway. He'd changed sides, and Barney was now on his side, Kelsang on the other side. The opposition. The enemy.

Hant emerged from the back of the cave. Kelsang rubbed his leg, and shouted at Hant. Hant shouted back. Kelsang rolled up his trouser-leg, and pointed a finger in Hant's face. The Nepali was sharp, abrasive, in bursts, like machine-gun fire. Hant drew his pistol and pointed it at Kelsang.

Calix understood one word.

'*Kukur*.' Dog.

He liked dogs, and dogs liked him.

38

Rick raised his binoculars. Two hours in, but as yet no sign of Ram, the boy with the yellow rucksack. He scanned the far bank. He checked the path from the bridge towards Mount Mera, then the opposite hillside – the location of the missing, according to the map sent to TBR. He scanned back across the bridge, up the hillside above him, which led to Saklis, down the hill again, past Mosom Kharka and down the path which eventually led to the Jiri trailhead.

Half a dozen ruined buildings were all that remained at Mosom Kharka. Several of Russell's porters were already there and the first light blue tent had been erected. Russell was directing operations.

Rick let the binoculars hang. Their observation point was opposite the bridge over the Hinku. A swaying ninety-metre curve constructed entirely from wood and wire. There was no concrete, and no steel, and not a single right angle. Fifty metres below crashed the river, its icy waters barely melted. No one, thought Rick, could accuse Nepalese bridge-builders of overkill. A subsistence diet and a belief in reincarnation the only strategy for having to cross regularly.

Kate looked up from her book.

Rick shook his head. No one was in sight, not even a farmer. Surveillance was a waiting game. Waiting and mulling.

'What're you reading?'

She put a finger in the pages and looked at the front cover. '*On Chesil Beach*. Ian McEwan. Maggie lent it to me.'

Rick nodded, and Kate resumed reading.

Maggie. She was always reading. Takes me away, she'd told him. The three books in her bag: a historical by Sarah Dunant, a Christie biography and a thriller.

Books took her away.

Mulling and waiting.

Nearby sat two of Russell's Sherpas, Lok and Uttam. They had a job to do if the boy turned up. They kept up a ceaseless chatter while Lok whittled a spoon and Uttam picked his nose.

Rick pondered the letter from Calix to TBR. No mention of Barney or Spencer. Another fake, like the one supposedly left by Calix in the tent when the four had been kidnapped? The enclosed map showed the missing being held in a cave directly opposite, a couple of hours' trek above the river. A trap?

So many questions. Was TBR involved after all? DCs Bennett and Foulds had been tasked to re-arrest and re-interview him. To brace him.

Unless the two detectives turned something up, he was going to ignore TBR.

Russell joined them. The tents and the camp were all set up at Mosom Kharka. The three of them took it in turns to watch. Half-hour shifts. Russell didn't stop talking. He compared the boredom of surveillance to waiting in a tent at base camp, hoping the weather would break. Both were of unknown duration and carried no guarantee of success, but both also had the possibility of adrenalin overload. The weather clears and a bid for the summit is launched, or a suspect turns up. Or the boy with the yellow rucksack.

Kate put her book away, and talked to Russell. The two of them did a crossword and played word games. It was the usual surveillance nonsense. Rick mulled. Were Barney and Spencer still alive? He watched and he checked that Russell and Kate watched. Surveillance was not difficult, but like driving on the motorway or painting a shed, it required patience and diligence to do well.

Kate passed round a bag of pistachios. Rick turned on the sat phone, and phoned Robbo.

'Has TBR been arrested?'

'No,' replied the superintendent. 'Has the boy turned up?'

'No.' Rick watched three Western trekkers cross the bridge. Laughing and joking, yanking on the handrails. Stopping to take photos. 'What about Hant's phone?'

'Still turned off.'

'Back-up?'

'Still in Kathmandu, finalising terms of engagement. The politicians have become involved, ours and theirs. Chief super's flapping.' The superintendent paused. 'Is this call really about the crime desk?'

'I wanted an update on TBR.'

'I don't believe you.'

Rick threw the phone into his bag, and closed his eyes.

Six months on the crime desk was a life sentence. He'd had a three-hour input on his sergeant's course, and that had been a life sentence. Staring at a computer for eight hours every day. And the job: confirming or changing crime codes, and filing them. Massaging the stats so the division wouldn't underperform in the league tables. Making the chief super look good.

'Rick.'

Rick opened his eyes. Kate was peering down at him

through the gloaming. The grey light had a grainy feel as if it might rain – or snow.

'The boy's turned up?'

She shook her head.

His Puffa jacket had been draped over his shoulders. He shivered. The mountains had disappeared, and he could only just make out the bridge. The two Sherpas looked at him hopefully, a wooden spoon sticking out of Lok's shirt pocket.

'We'll call it a day, the boy *has* to turn up tomorrow.'

39

Day two, Russell on first watch, the clay-coloured sun still climbing. The five of them were enveloped in birdsong, soft Nepalese voices, the constant rumble of the river. In the distance, there was the occasional crash of stonefall, and moments later, its eerie echoes. Rick reached into the paper bag of pistachios.

'He's on the bridge,' said Russell.

Rick jerked up his binoculars, and focused. Two farmers with baskets.

'Climbed back down again.'

Rick ran the binoculars up and down the bridge. Only the two farmers. No boy, with or without a yellow rucksack.

'What?'

'Far side of the bridge. Climbed up the ladder, then climbed back down again.'

'Yellow rucksack?'

'Don't know.'

'Rucksack?'

'Don't think so.'

'You don't think so?' Rick directed the binoculars on the far ladder. No one.

'He'll be back, sure of it.'

'How?! Kate?'

'Didn't see him. Sorry.'

'Come on!'

'Come on yourself,' said Kate.

Rick stared at the far hillside and the approach to the bridge. Nothing moved. He surveilled the bridge. The far ladder was deserted. The two farmers had reached halfway. Empty wicker baskets, large machetes dangling. Small black wellington boots, lean bodies, set faces.

'He's back,' said Russell.

Rick swung the binoculars across. Too far. Back. The ladder – empty. The boy. No rucksack. Wicker basket. More of a man. Stubble. About twenty. Rick scowled.

'What made you think it was him?'

'Small, by himself, not sure really. You did say to err on the side of caution.'

Rick let the binoculars drop. They weighed 650 grams, and the cord was a foot in length. He waited for the jerk.

And it hurt.

He looked away, feeling the stares of the others.

'Yes, you're right, Russell. I did. Both of you, and I don't want to change that. Sorry. It's just, I need this. I need the boy to turn up. The Conistons and the Williamses need the boy to turn up.'

If the boy turned up, then they'd have a chance of locating the three missing – saving three young lives. And if he turned up soon, then he'd be able to find the missing without the back-up. And if he found them without the back-up, then he wouldn't be posted to the crime desk.

'Surveillance is like watching *Citizen Kane*,' said Russell.

'Anything?' said Rick.

The mountaineer shook his head.

'Sure?'

'Sure I'm sure. Check if you don't believe me.'

Rick raised his binoculars. The bridge was deserted, swaying gently in the breeze. He surveilled the far hillside. Terraced fields bordered the river, and dotted amongst them were farmers' shacks. Above the terraces were thick rhododendron forests, and above them the tantalising shapes of mountains coming and going in the morning haze. In every direction great sweeps of hillside led up to snowy mountains. He was beginning to understand why Russell came to Nepal so often.

Kate squirted tea from a giant flask, and handed around plastic mugs. From a cloth, she produced crescent-shaped *momos*.

As he ate, Rick tapped on the sat phone. He'd found a company selling queen bees in Hampshire. Belinda's Bees sent queens in the everyday post, a prominent sticker, 'Bees! Handle With Care', the only precaution. Inside, a small plastic box the size of a pack of cards, and inside that the queen and half a dozen workers to look after her. No water, just a block of fondant to sustain them for the journey. He paid with PayPal.

Midway through the afternoon, mid-morning in the UK, Rick phoned Robbo.

'The boy?'

'No. TBR?'

'Arrested at dawn at his baby mother's. In interview he claimed he didn't even know Calix was in Nepal.'

'Who did it?

'Foulds and Bennett.'

'Did they believe him?'

'Foulds did, Bennett didn't.' The superintendent paused.

'Aren't you going to ask me what I thought? I downstreamed it.'

Rick scratched his chin with the aerial. Robbo wasn't a detective, so no, he wasn't. 'Any news on the back-up in Kathmandu?' He held his breath.

'Sorted themselves out, finally. Will fly to Lukla tomorrow and then head to you. Nepalese police and army, Aussie police, DS Khan and DC Emmett. Wait for them – even if the boy does turn up. Now, yesterday, I think we were cut off.'

'The SMT decision.'

'I knew it'd be this.'

'How did the SMT know about my dad?... Robbo?' said Rick into the silence. 'I thought we were friends.'

'We are – outside of the Job.'

'Dad *is* outside of the Job.'

The phone went dead.

'Anything?' said Rick, looking at Kate.

'No!' Keeping her eyes on the bridge, she said, 'Are you having a row with him?'

Rick shook his head, and ate a pistachio. He flicked away the shell and drank some water. So salty.

'Go on Russell,' said Kate. 'You were explaining *dharma*.'

'There's no direct equivalent in English but a rough translation is a moral code. To many Nepalese people it's an important principle of everyday life. Their moral and religious duty in respect of their family, caste, customs and laws.'

Rick wondered about Hant Khetan. He was Nepalese, probably Hindu, maybe he had a strong sense of *dharma*?

'What do you think, Kate?' asked Russell.

'I like the idea of *karma* but I'm not so sure about the rest of it. Reincarnation and burning the dead.'

'Rick, what do you believe in?'

He was an atheist so no gods or leaps of faith. Darwin, Dawkins, evolution made sense to him. Evidence-based science. But was that the answer Russell wanted? Was evidence-based science a belief? He looked at the mountaineer. At Kate. Both were staring at him, waiting for something deep, or witty. Or just something.

He only believed in one thing.

'Come on, Rick, you must believe in something. Not walking under ladders? Sex twice a week?' The mountaineer paused. 'Justice?'

Rick stood up. 'Death.' He walked away, down the path to the bridge, his head pounding.

It had been a Tuesday.

When he reached flat ground he sat on a porter's bench.

The family of five. Mother, father and their three kids. Triplets, an IVF miracle. Side-by-side in matching cots. Name-plates, like a hospital ward. Martha, Mark and Marissa. They had a mobile with zoo animals on their bedroom ceiling. It had been slowly turning, one way then the other. Blood dripping down onto the white bedding. Each cot a scene of madness. Blood and brain spattered the tiny pillows. A shotgun. Their father – a city banker who went shooting at weekends – had killed his wife first, as she sat on the toilet, then each child in turn. Finally, he'd shot himself. He'd been accused of a massive fraud at work. Licences for all the guns, no criminal record.

Every Tuesday, those three cots. That dripping mobile.

The same thoughts round and round. Anger at the deranged father. Sadness for the unfulfilled lives. Bewilderment at how the combination of evolution and society could conspire in such anomie. He stood up, and kicked at the weeds growing along the foot of the bench. Kept kicking. Kept kicking. Kept kicking.

'Rick!'

Rick looked up towards the others. Russell was waving his arms. Rick waved a hand, and scrabbled back up the hillside. He tried to run but the path was steep and stepped, and he could only manage a fast walk.

Breathing heavily, he arrived at the observation point. Russell was staring at the bridge with the binoculars, Kate, her hand shielding her eyes, also looking. Russell shook his head and handed the glasses to Rick.

'Sorry, false alarm.'

'Another one,' said Rick, booting the bag of pistachios into the scrub. Nuts and shells exploded into the air like shrapnel, and rained down. Lok and Uttam looked up from their cards, and then, in silence, and with studied concentration, resumed playing.

40

Day three, sunrise.

It was not unusual for Rick to be awake. To see the dawn light illuminate the towerblocks and ginnels and scruffy suburbs of Manchester. To watch it reveal cordoned scenes of crime, police vans with rocking cages, spitting prisoners. Early morning was for arrest warrants and house searches. Time spent in custody suites and incident rooms. Frenetic activity. Every minute important.

The mountains and snowfields of the Everest foothills were another world. There were few people, and no vehicles. The people who lived there moved around on foot, and worked together, for common goals. Time moved slower.

Kate passed around tea, and Rick picked up pistachio shells. Miraculously, the nuts had disappeared. He paused to check on the bridge, the far hillside, and the ground below the OP.

The only person in sight walked a local path on their side of the river. The man carried long planks of wood strapped horizontally across his back. Rick raised the binoculars. The planks were attached to a thick band wrapped around the man's head. He passed the bridge, and continued in the direction of Jiri. He wore flip-flops on his feet, and multicoloured hooped socks. Calf muscles solid as bones.

'Come *on*,' said Rick, letting the binoculars gently down.

'I once spent two whole weeks in a tent in Patagonia waiting for a weather window,' said Russell. 'It never arrived.'

Nearby, the two young Sherpas, Lok and Uttam, played dice. Russell had assured Rick they would be ready when the time came.

If it came.

He studied the Shorong / Hinku map. The area it covered was thirty kilometres square. Three permanent glaciers spread down from the top, reaching halfway. They were coloured white, but crossed with so many blue contour lines they appeared light blue.

Rick compared it with Calix's scrawled diagram. It made sense for a hideout to be where Calix had drawn it – close enough to Saklis, but still in the middle of nowhere. But if Calix's map was incorrect, or they'd moved, where were they?

A quarter of the map was white, but it was possible to camp on snow – mountaineers did. They would need water, but the map was covered in a lattice of streams and rivers. There wasn't one grid square without water in one form or another. The area was 900 square kilometres. They could hide out in the hills and mountains for months, possibly years. Like Osama Bin Laden. After 9/11 it had taken a decade for the full investigative might of the American police and military to find him.

'Is there a Mrs Weatherbeater?' said Kate.

Rick looked up. Kate was brushing her hair, pulling the tangles from the bristles and throwing them in the air.

'There's no Mrs Weatherbeater,' said the mountaineer. 'There was a Mrs Beater. Long story, but basically the result of me disappearing on too many Himalayan expeditions. She left me, and took our two kids with her. Just me now, I don't even see the kids much.'

Rick watched a straggle of Kate's hairs, caught on a bush. Scrabbling in the wind, trying to get away.

'What're their names?' said Kate.

'Ella, she's doing her GCSEs, and Jacob, he's A-level year. In a band, wants to be the next big thing.'

'Have you been to see him play?'

'I keep meaning to.'

Rick stared at the map. He was uncomfortable and he fidgeted on the porter's seat. He'd developed piles, for which he blamed not the diet, but stress.

'You've got a son, Kate?' said the mountaineer.

'Richardson.'

'And his father?'

Kate put down the brush and picked up a bottle of suncream. She squeezed some into her palm. She passed it to Rick.

'My ex. We never married.'

Rick had a question. Was Richardson's father paying maintenance? He didn't want to ask. It was too intrusive. He watched Kate rubbing the cream round and round her palm. His *job* was to ask intrusive questions. *Mrs Coniston, did you know your son is dealing drugs? In your worry book, what did you write about your husband?*

'I found out he was having an affair.' Kate stopped rubbing. 'Multiple affairs. Always telling me he was doing overtime. *For us.* I was six months pregnant when I found out.'

Rick felt himself getting hot with anger. Six months pregnant. He put the bottle of suncream down – it didn't seem worth it. If he thought hard about it, nothing was worth it.

In true OP fashion they ate their lunch at 11.30. Cold vegetable samosas wrapped in clingfilm. *Naans*, hunks of cheese, and a fiery homemade pickle. The hardboiled sun directly overhead, the sky baby blue.

Rick surveilled the bridge. '*Come on, come on.*'

Back-up would be massing at Kathmandu Airport. Some of them may have already flown to Lukla, or be in the air, cotton wool in their ears.

'Coffee?' said Kate.

A figure stepped onto the ladder on the far side of the bridge. Carrying not a basket, but a rucksack.

Rick snapped up the binoculars, and stood up. Trained them on the ladder.

'Shut up you two.'

Russell and Kate stopped talking.

'On the bridge.'

They stood alongside Rick, staring out.

'Man with a yellow rucksack. Not a man. A youth. A boy. It's him, it's only frigging him.'

'That's a first,' said Kate. 'For the DCI.'

'Thank Buddha,' said Russell.

Rick swung the binoculars away, then back, just to make sure the sun wasn't conspiring with his mind to deceive him. No, it was a Nepalese boy carrying an empty yellow rucksack. Halfway across, the boy stopped to look over the edge and spit into the water. Rick followed his every step with the binoculars. The boy wore jeans. Rick could see no letter R. The boy reached the near side of the bridge and climbed down the ladder frontways. He drank some water, had a piss, and started to make his way up the steep path towards Saklis.

'Okay, Russell, your big moment's coming up. Make sure Lok and Uttam are ready.'

'I'm ready, they're ready.'

'And let's sit down, we don't want to spook him.'

Rick and Kate sat, and Russell crouched with the Sherpas. Rick held the glasses, elbows propped on his knees. One more close look at the jeans, and then he'd put them down. No letter R. A doubt began to grow and his stomach felt fluttery. Definitely no letter R. He'd read the statements a hundred times, but he couldn't remember whether they said front or back of the trousers. The statements were in his tent at Mosom Kharka. If this wasn't *the* boy, he'd bring them tomorrow.

The boy was making rapid progress, bounding up the steep trail like a gazelle. Rick lowered the binoculars. A second boy with a yellow rucksack. It seemed unlikely, but his stomach didn't settle.

'Okay, Russell. He's nearly reached us.'

The mountaineer stood, gave a thumbs-up to the Sherpas, and walked down to meet the boy. As Rick had ordered.

Russell greeted the boy. They stopped and spoke, and Rick heard laughing. He didn't need an NVC course to know that was a good sign.

The two of them walked up the path towards the OP. Rick glanced around, and was relieved not to be able to see Lok and Uttam.

'This is Ram,' said Russell, turning the boy around and lifting his rucksack.

On the left back pocket of his jeans were large embroidered stars and the letter R.

The boy turned back, and grinned.

'*Namaste!*'

'*Namaste*, Ram!' said Rick, noticing the boy wore an expensive watch. '*Namaste!*'

'And he'll do it.'

Rick felt sick.

Twenty minutes later, Ram was heading back down the trail

to the bridge. There'd not been time to let him sit and stew. If the boy wouldn't answer questions, they would have to hope he understood. Russell's Nepali had worked for everyone else. He was at least heading the right way.

In the boy's pocket were fifty dollars and a message.

Hant

We know where you are.

Release Barney, Spencer and Calix, and I'll stop the army.

DCI Rick Castle, Manchester Police (UK)

Rick watched the boy cross the bridge, descend the far ladder frontways, and head back up the hillside.

He kept watching.

Near the descent ladder, Lok and Uttam emerged from thick vegetation glistening in the sunshine, and keeping the boy in sight, but only just, the two young Sherpas began to follow.

41

Shouting woke Calix up.

'What's happening?' said Barney. Encased in the sleeping bag, his voice was muffled.

Calix rubbed his face, listening to Hant and the guards ping-ponging Nepali. He recognised Kelsang's voice. Hant was angry, and Kelsang was trying to placate him. Calix unzipped his bag and the tent door, and crawled out.

Chet lay in the centre of a large pool of blood. Without the blood the dog would have looked like he was sleeping. He lay next to the fire-pit in the cave mouth. His leonine head rested on the floor, and his front paws pointed neatly at the fire.

Calix slipped his feet into boots and walked towards the dog, dragging the chain with him. Chet's paws were red. The blood had soaked up into the white fur of his body, leaving a stain like a tidal mark. Calix stepped through the blood and bent towards the dog.

Chet's eyes were open, but glassy, all life gone.

'*Chaina,*' said Hant. No.

Too late. Calix grabbed the thick ring of neck fur and lifted the dog's head. A bloody knife wound across the neck revealed the cause of death. The dog was already stiff, and gently, Calix let Chet's head back down. He stroked the back of the head. He stroked Chet's glossy ears with their velvet lining.

Calix stepped back through the sticky pool, and leaving bloody footprints, returned to the tent. There was blood on the chain, on his shirt, on his trousers. There was blood on his hands.

Barney sat in the gloom, pulling on his boots.

He looked up.

'Dead?' whispered the twin.

Calix nodded.

The morning began. Calix and Barney were moved down to the great rock, and from there they watched Ved making tea and heating leftover rice. Smoke from the cookfire swept down and made their eyes smart. Hant squatted with the guards. The Nepalese men ate quickly, shovelling with their hands. Except Hant. He ate with a spoon, but mostly he talked at the guards.

Calix wasn't hopeful, but Barney polished their plates on a sleeve.

Raised voices. Hant and Kelsang. Calix watched with interest. Hant pushed Kelsang, the guard toppling backwards and dropping his plate. The guard stood up, spat, and walked away. Climbed up above the cave and out of sight.

Calix fingered an insect out of his mug, but they weren't brought any tea, and they weren't given any rice.

Ved dragged the dead dog down the slope to the rock, and the same distance again into the scrub. He left a trail of bloody stones and squashed vegetation. Squadrons of flies followed like birds behind a tractor. The cook returned to the cave and washed away the bloody circle which had congealed in the morning sunlight.

Hant walked down the slope. Walked up to them. He had smooth childish cheeks and a goatee that didn't grow.

'Why kill Chet?'

'Us?' said Calix.

'You.'

'It was Kelsang who was bitten.'

'Kelsang say, no. Swear, no.'

Calix shrugged.

Hant kicked their chains, and scowled. The noise echoed around the valley, and dissipated to nothing. He kicked them again. The noise echoed, and died. To Calix, the rattling seemed louder and to last longer than it could have done. Hant stared down the valley towards the bridge, then walked back up the slope.

Lunchtime came and went, but they still weren't given any food. Calix's squashed cigarettes were all gone. Barney produced his last piece of gum, and gave him half. He chewed until his jaw ached and his mouth tasted like sawdust.

The two of them watched a guard dig a hole for Chet. The cloying whiff of raw flesh drifted across. Calix smelt his hands, and his shirt. He stank of the dog. He yanked his chain to the river, and washed his hands with grit from the riverbed. He washed his shirt. Yanked his chain back to Barney.

'You okay?' said the twin.

The harsh white light flooded down. Calix sniffed his fingers, then his nails. Scrubbing had made no difference.

A figure appeared from the direction of the bridge, following the river. He seemed to glide up the hillside. It was Ram, poling the ground with a piece of chunky bamboo.

When he reached the hole and the dog, the boy stopped. He spoke to the guard. Mud flecked the boy's calves, and sweat glistened on his face and hair as if he'd walked out of a shower. He wore Barney's watch on his wrist, and the top of his pack hung loose. He'd not collected supplies which, Calix thought, was odd.

He called Ram over.

'Letter?' said Calix. He pretended to scribble on a pad of paper.

'*Ho.*' Yes. Ram tapped the watch and gave a thumbs-up.

'*Dhanyabaad,*' said Calix. Thank you. Barney put his hands together and bowed his head.

'Chet?' said the boy.

Calix shrugged, and wished he had more Nepali. He wanted to ask about Hant's old man. His father. He tried.

'Hant *buwaa?*'

Ram looked puzzled.

'Hant *buwaa* dead.' Calix used the cut-throat gesture which the boy had used about his own father.

Ram seemed to understand. 'Hant *buwaa* Ghurkha.' The boy fired an imaginary rifle and clutched his breast.

'What's he mean?' whispered Barney.

'Hant's old man was a Ghurkha and was killed. What I don't understand is what that's got to do with me.'

'Ram!' shouted his uncle from the cave mouth.

The boy plodded up the slope. Hant poked the empty rucksack. Poked his nephew in the stomach. The boy passed him a piece of paper. Hant read it, and cuffed the boy around the head. From the cook ledge, he grabbed two Mars bars and tossed them to the boy.

'Carrot and stick,' said Calix.

'Why?' said Barney.

'I don't know.' He watched Ram canter down the hillside. People walked for pleasure, camped for pleasure, climbed mountains for pleasure. They were welcome to it.

'What now?' said Barney.

Calix bit off a nail and chewed it. His stomach hurt. He hurled a rock into the scrub, but wished he hadn't. It reminded him of Spencer.

The note to TBR or the sat phone. But he was losing hope with the sat phone. PIN codes of HANT, YASH and CHET had all failed and in frustration, he'd tapped in a random number. He didn't even know what it was – he'd looked away and tapped it out.

Each time, wah-wah, boom.

Only two attempts remained.

He gripped himself. Megan wouldn't give up. And he owed Barney and Spencer, and Vicky. He owed all of them. Positive thinking. He'd wanted to be a player. He was Calix Coniston, a milkman for TBR, had a parrot called Bird Bird. Two attempts were more than enough.

'It'll be alright,' said Calix, 'I promise.' He didn't believe a word of it.

*

The abandoned village of Mosom Kharka was a good position for their camp, 200 metres downstream of the suspension bridge, and on the Saklis side of the river. A tributary of the Hinku ran down one side. Nepalese prayer-flags fluttered between the dining and cook tents.

Russell and Kate sat at the plastic table in front of the dining tent, and Rick paced up and down. There was nothing they could do except wait. Wait for a reply from Khetan, or for the back-up to arrive. He stood on a chair and raised his binoculars, surveilling the far hillside. The bridge. The far hillside. The bridge.

No one.

He stepped down from the chair, and continued pacing.

Russell was explaining the prayer-flags to Kate, and Rick couldn't help but listen. Five colours. Blue for the sky, white the air, yellow the earth, red for fire and green for water. In the centre of each flag was a horse carrying three jewels on its back. Each jewel represented one of the three central beliefs of Buddhist philosophy. *Dharma* or Buddhist teachings, *sangha* the Buddhist community, and the Buddha himself. Surrounding the horse were hundreds of traditional mantras and the flags ensured that the prayers of peace, strength and wisdom were carried in the wind to everyone.

'Not just Buddhists?' said Kate.

'Not just Buddhists,' said Russell.

The sat phone rang.

Rick heard it like an air-raid warning.

'Quiet, you two. I need to hear, to think.'

Rick picked up the phone from where it was charging in the sun. Kate and Russell said nothing. 'Sorry,' said Rick quietly.

'Castle,' he said on the phone.

'There's been a development,' said Robbo. 'The Nepalese police have arrested a local man in Lukla trying to buy a sat phone. They think he's working for Khetan.'

'What's he said?'

'They're still interrogating him but they've got a sense that Khetan and the three missing are west of Lukla, not east where you are. They think the note and the map from Calix are decoys. They're going to wait in Lukla until they're finished and know whether to head to you in Saklis, or in the opposite direction.'

Rick looked at the prayer-flags, waving in the stiffening wind and slapping against the sides of the tent. They reminded him of the rattling rigging in the marinas of Chichester where Dad had grown up. They'd gone there on family trips when

Rick was a boy, when Dad had not only known his name but every part of a boat.

'They're wrong. The witnesses I spoke to in Saklis indicated east, towards Mosom Kharka. They were in no doubt.'

'They were young kids,' said the superintendent.

'So what?'

'I'm just saying.'

Rick told Robbo about the message he'd sent with Ram, but he didn't mention the two Sherpas who'd lost sight of him in low cloud. Foot surveillance and remaining covert was hard, even on a mountainside.

'We've moved down from Saklis to Mosom Kharka.'

There was a pause and a sharp intake of breath. Unmistakable, even on a sat phone. Rick pictured the fat man at his desk, polishing his glasses and scowling. Eyeing an iced bun.

'Okay, Rick, stay where you are in MK. No further. See what comes of the thumbscrews and the rack in Lukla.'

'And the message I've had delivered.'

'Maggie wants a word. She's had an idea about falsifying newspaper reports.'

There was a brief pause and Maggie came on the line. 'Still no luck, sir, with locating Khetan's sat phone. It may be turned off or out of juice or broken. But, I've had another idea if the missing are where you think they are, *and* you're in contact with Khetan via the boy with the yellow rucksack.'

'Go on.'

'I've sent a runner to you from Lukla,' said Maggie. 'He's bringing you two fake newspaper reports – a red-top and a broadsheet – which I knocked up with Davinda in IT.'

As Maggie explained, Rick pictured her. Pulling strands from her brown bob, and winding them round a finger.

'The articles describe how things have changed in Qatar for the better. How FIFA have started to spend money on improving conditions for the Nepalese workers. How they're going to ensure workers have unobstructed access into and out of the country. Hopefully, they'll show Khetan that his demands have been met. And, as his sat phone doesn't seem to be working, he can't check their authenticity.'

'Worth a try, Maggie. Thanks.' He tried to sound as if he thought the articles might work.

Rick let the binoculars hang. There was no human movement on the opposite hillside, and no fast-moving local coming down the hill from Saklis. He rubbed his eyes. He sat on a plastic chair at MK, waiting. Waiting for a reply from Hant or the package from Maggie or the sat phone to ring. Or something.

It was late afternoon, and the sun was beginning to cool. The cook was chopping onions and garlic and it made him feel hungry. Did piles need starving or feeding?

Nearby sat Russell and Kate. Kate was smoking, the smoke drifting all over. She passed the cigarette to Russell, who took a puff.

Rick shook his head, and looked away.

The ground was scrubby with patches of tiny flowers. Pinks and blues and yellows. Here and there, thick starfish-shaped leaves clustered at the base of a tall stem, the minute flowers well past their best.

'Check this out,' said Kate.

A large party of trekkers was walking up the trail from the south, heading for Mera base camp. Japanese trekkers, each using two walking poles, and their porters carrying huge loads. Four of the porters carried an obese man in a sedan chair. A large camera hung around his neck. The chair was lashed to two long bamboos as thick as drainpipes, and the four porters walked one behind the other. They wore cheap trainers and their t-shirts were soaked in sweat.

Some of the trekkers nodded as they passed, but they didn't stop. The man in the chair waved his cap and took a photo.

'Strange walking holiday,' said Kate.

'He might have no choice,' said Russell. 'I know several companies that take disabled people on expeditions.'

Rick wondered about Maggie's holidays. She wouldn't go anywhere she had to depend on four men to carry her around so Nepal was definitely out. Where did she go? Who with? She'd told him that holidays were ten times more difficult to cope with than day-to-day living.

A relationship with Maggie would be anything but straight-forward.

Impracticable.

Madness.

But?

He stared at the pinks and blues and yellows. A scrap of tissue caught on a stone, waving like a windsock.

'Detective Chief Inspector Castle.'

The voice sounded familiar. Rick turned around.

Three men walked towards them, in arrowhead formation. A porter with a crammed basket towering above him, a second Nepalese man carrying a shiny metal briefcase, and in the lead, Brigadier David Coniston.

42

All three men were sweating like fire fighters, their faces slippery with perspiration, and droplets beading off their cheeks. Salt lines marked their clothes.

The brigadier looked like he was on a military exercise. He wore army lightweights tucked into his boots and a green *Ghurkhas* t-shirt with a dictum in Nepali. A large Bergen hugged his back. The porter, his head at the brigadier's shoulder, was dwarfed by a baggy jumper and sloppy wellington boots. The man with the briefcase wore jeans and carried an umbrella. His boots were shiny, his moustache tidily clipped.

Rick stood up as the trio reached the camp. 'This is a surprise,' he said to the brigadier. He flashed back to the Conistons' rose garden and its well-endowed statue and the first time they'd met, the awkward conversation on the doorstep and worse inside the house. The olive cravat was still neatly in place.

'Robbo said you were underrated.'

On the doorstep it had sounded like a compliment, but Rick hadn't been sure. He still wasn't.

'This is from Maggie.' The brigadier handed over an envelope. 'We intercepted her runner from Lukla.'

Rick took the envelope. 'Why're you here?'

'Now you've found them, thought you could do with some army decisiveness and nerve. Get the job done, and Foxtrot Oscar.' The brigadier slipped his Bergen off. 'Let's get a brew on, you can brief me and we can work out the next move.'

On the ground, the solar panels of the charging sat phone glared in the sun.

*

Calix checked the guards. Hant sat in the cave mouth, scanning the Saklis hillside and the approach path from the bridge with binoculars. The leader had given his orders, and halfway down the hill the lazy-eyed guard and Kelsang were collecting firewood. In the cave Ved was searching the tents. Which left one guard on sentry. Ishwar, whose hair wouldn't lie flat, and was older than the other guards. He sat on a prominent rock, rolling dice.

'Keep watching him, Barney.'

'I am watching.' The twin had washed in the stream and sat with his long pale legs stretched out in front of him. His eyes were red-rimmed and his muscles had lost their definition.

Calix extricated the bag with Hant's phone from his jacket. Condensation misted the plastic, and Calix felt a stab of concern. He slipped it out of the bag and dried it on his trousers. The greater concern was the code, and he glanced around for inspiration. What did Hant want him hostage for? The original demands had been Spencer and Barney in exchange for FIFA taking action in Qatar. But *him*? Hant's *buwaa* was dead, that's what Hant had said. But nothing else. What did they want *him* for? The only thing he was sure about was that if they didn't get what they wanted, both he and Barney would be killed.

His stomach lurched. He was too young to die.

Megan, too. She'd told him she wanted to cycle around the world. Steer well clear of Nepal, he'd have told her. Too many hills. He stared at the ranks of snow-tipped mountains, stretching into the distance like a hall of mirrors.

The sat phone was his – their – only real hope.

Hant's *buwaa*. Hant's old man. The code was Hant's old man. The kidnap was not about Hant, and it was only partly about Qatar. MANU, 6268. It had to be.

Calix turned the phone on, and tapped in the code.

'Are you watching Ishwar?'

'Yes!' said Barney. 'Still rolling his dice.'

Calix looked at the numbers – 6268.

This was it, this was the moment.

He pressed enter, and stared at the screen. Like hearing the news, always disappointing. Inevitable. *Enter PIN code (Final attempt!)* stared back.

'No?' said Barney.

'No.' Calix hid the phone in his jacket, and picked up another stone. Spotting three ants marching along, he jabbed at one with the stone. The ant pushed itself back up and continued. He squashed it with his thumb. Hard. The back legs flailed around.

'Did you kill Chet?'

Calix had been expecting the question, and he looked over at Barney. 'Do you really want to know?'

'Yes.'

'Think about it.' The other two ants circled around and went to inspect the dying ant. Began to haul it away.

'Either one of them is a psycho with a knife,' said Barney. 'Or you are.'

'So?'

'I'm not sure.'

'There you are.' More ants appeared. Calix severed and squashed. 'We're fighting for our lives here.'

'Are we?'

'Aren't we?' said Calix.

'You're talking in riddles.'

Calix threw away his stone of mass slaughter. 'You think your old man's going to come to the rescue? Pull the FIFA levers?'

'Didn't you think that, once?'

'Yes,' said Calix. 'But I was sucked in, like a fool.'

'There's still one more chance with the phone,' said Barney. His voice came and went. Tearful, then less so. 'And there's the letter you sent to the police that Ram delivered.'

Calix grunted. He'd told Barney a white lie. And the letter he had sent, to TBR, had only a chance in a million of reaching Red and spurring him into action.

'You're right, Barney, letter or phone call, someone will come.'

It was another lie. He thought the likelihood of rescue was close to zero. Which meant they had to rescue themselves. The way he now saw things was basic, primeval: fight or flight, hunter-gatherer style. Simple, binary, like carrot and stick. The two of them had to escape. Either that, or they had to fight, and to fight, they had to even the sides up. Numbers and arms. His old man would understand.

He looked at the ground and decapitated another ant.

*

Briefing over, the brigadier supervised the location for his tent and sorted his gear. The porter would sleep in the cook tent with the other porters but the man with the briefcase had his own tent. Rick had asked who he was but the brigadier had parried the question – he'd tell Rick later when they discussed a plan.

Rick was not a trained hostage negotiator, but he knew the basics. Locate the hostages, establish communication and negotiate. Four main tactics. *Calm*: never argue or refuse a demand point-blank, but instead delay, and offer compromises. *Relationships*: build trust and rapport. At home they sent in pizzas and cigarettes, but in Nepal he'd have to be more creative. SERCS were rumoured to have sent in a prostitute. *Prolong*: statistically, the longer it went on, the more likely it was to end peacefully. *Safety* of the hostages was paramount: ensure they have food and medical supplies and ultimately, get released unharmed.

That was the police way of doing things. The army way was bound to be different.

The brigadier had finished with his kit and walked off towards the river that bordered their camp. It was a tributary, but still too wide to jump across, and in places deep enough to submerge a car. At night, the shallows froze.

The brigadier stopped on the near bank. Took off his boots and socks. His trousers. His t-shirt. His pants.

Showing no hesitation, he waded in and disappeared from view.

The five of them gathered outside the dining tent, around the oblong plastic table. Rick, the brigadier, Russell, Kate and Nandan, the man with the briefcase. The case lay under his chair. On the table were mugs of tea, and a map. Behind the tent loomed Mount Mera, an enormous lump in the sky. A patch of cloud concealed its summit.

Rick stood at the head. A police operation. The brigadier

propped up a table-leg, Kate stubbed out her cigarette, and Russell took off his sunglasses.

Rick started with introductions. He had never even met Calix Coniston – minor cannabis dealer, taxidermist, expelled from university. A loner, a dreamer with a parrot called Bird Bird. But he was the brigadier's son.

The lives of Barney and Spencer Williams were also at stake, and they all knew they had to get it right. But there was no right, only decisions to be made and a strategy to be settled. Then time would pass.

Time would reveal.

Time would judge.

Rick unfolded the Shorong / Hinku map and pointed with a stick. 'We're here at MK, our police back-up and the Nepalese police and army are at Lukla, there, and we think Hant and the three missing, Calix, Barney and Spencer, are up there.' He pointed across the Hinku at the hanging valley on the other side – a bare section of map, several hours' walk. He looked around the table. The brigadier's face was lined, more than Rick remembered. The soldier nodded. The other three were impassive. 'Ideas?'

'What's in the briefcase, Nandan?' said Kate.

'He's a doctor,' said the brigadier. 'Used to be one of my medics.'

Kate nodded. 'Does he speak English?'

'Yes, Mrs,' said Nandan. 'Very good.' He paused. 'I think,' he added. He smiled, the big Nepalese smile. Kate smiled back. The brigadier rearranged his cravat. Rick knew the soldier had lied. It wasn't a good start.

Russell stared at the hanging valley and the brigadier stared at the map. Rick explained the four principles of hostage nego-tiation.

The brigadier downed his tea, put his mug on the floor and asked questions. What type of weapons do they have? How many suspects? Can we observe them with binoculars? Can we get onto higher ground and look down on them? Can they be surrounded?

There were no easy answers and no obvious tactical solutions. Russell's mountaineering knowledge helped. There was higher ground, but it was serious mountaineering terrain and would require crampons, ice-axes and ropes. Years of expertise.

Weapons? Almost certainly, probably acquired from the Maoist uprising.

Numbers? Calix had written six, so at least six. No more than twenty.

After an hour they took a break. Russell and Kate shared a Snickers, and Rick took a call from Robbo.

'Got the results on Vicky Brant's PM,' said Robbo. 'Inconclusive: cause of death was a blunt trauma to the head and massive internal bleeding. Nothing suspicious: no defensive injuries, no other injuries, no toxicology of note.'

'What about Khetan's goon, arrested in Lukla?'

'Proving harder to break than they expected,' said Robbo. 'I'll let you know, soon as.'

'The brigadier's here,' said Rick.

'Where?'

'Here – Mosom Kharka. Just arrived.'

'Can you handle him?'

'We'll see.'

They started again, but moved the table inside the dining tent. The five of them sat down. Rick told the brigadier that his boss would miss him at golf on Saturday.

More talking, discussing, pooling their knowledge and expertise. Staring at the map. At Nandan's briefcase.

After two hours, Rick summarised. 'Three options have been suggested and picked apart. Option A, wait here for back-up from Lukla, but take no proactive action. Option B, wait here, but push the negotiation. Option C, an independent and clandestine operation utilising the brigadier's military contacts with ex-Ghurkhas. Questions, or clarifications?'

Rick waited, but no one spoke. 'Okay then. Decision-making may soon be out of our hands, but until then, I think we're all agreed. Option B.'

'I do have a question,' said Kate. 'Why? I mean, I understand the Qatar angle to all this, why Barney and Spencer were kidnapped, but I still don't get it about Calix.' She turned to the brigadier. 'Why has *Calix* rather than anyone else been kidnapped?'

The soldier sat motionless in his chair, staring at the ground. He glanced at his watch and frowned. He unfastened it, held it in his palm and wound it, as carefully as Rick had seen him do at home in Manchester. Taking his time, the brigadier pushed the knob home and re-secured it on his wrist.

He looked up. 'It concerns an incident in the Falklands War when I was a young lieutenant. I will tell you what happened, but I want to tell Calix first.'

'No,' said Rick. 'That's not good enough. I need to know now: it might help me negotiate.'

'It might, and it might not.'

'Let me be the judge of that.'

'I agree,' said Kate.

Russell nodded. He was supporting his chin on his hand, and looked more serious than Rick had ever seen him.

'O-kay,' said the brigadier. 'Hant Khetan's father was in my platoon. Manu Khetan, a young signaller. But that's really as far as I'm going now. I owe it to Calix to tell him first.'

'That might be too late. He might be dead.'

'I've made my decision.'

'What if I said, I'll arrest you?'

'For what?'

'I'll think of something.'

The brigadier scoffed. 'You police are all the same. Hillsborough, Stephen Lawrence, I had you from the start.'

Rick shoved the brigadier back into his chair, and stared down at him.

'We're not all the same. We're all very different, and if you can't see it, I've misjudged you.'

Pushing aside the tent flaps, he went outside into the plumblue twilight. The air smelt fresh, and the mountain-tops sparkled in the last of the sun.

He walked over to his tent, the prayer-flags still knocking like the sailboat masts in Chichester harbour. A military or pseudo-military operation would be a disaster. Keeping their nerve, and humouring Khetan until he gave up, was the best option. The statistical option.

The only option.

He unzipped his tent and crawled in.

It was cold and he could see his breath, but he lay on top of the sleeping bag, too tired to take any clothes off and get inside. His whole body ached from the nights in the tent and his haemorrhoids were killing him.

It was after dark when a reply from Khetan arrived. The messenger threw stones to attract their attention before running off.

A scruffy piece of paper weighted by a stone revealed the message.

Mr Castle

Stop fuck me

Where armee?

Calix buwaa arrive today give him me and I give Calix

H

43

The suspension bridge whispered in the wind. Rick stood at the foot of the ascent ladder with Russell and the two Sherpas, Lok and Uttam. The lowest rung was missing, and graffiti had been carved on the others.

He read the note again.

Hant

Things are changing in Qatar (see newspaper clippings). You are a hero in Kathmandu and many villages across Nepal. It is now time to release Calix, Barney and Spencer. Bring them to the bridge and you have my word we will not cross it. Then we can ALL go home.

Thank you.

DCI Rick Castle, Manchester Police (UK)

Satisfied, he folded the fake newspaper reports into the note and handed them to Uttam. The Sherpa grinned, revealing a mouth of stained teeth.

'Be careful.'

'Yes, *sahib*.'

Uttam gripped the ladder and hauled himself up and onto the bridge. Lok followed and they walked away. Short lean men who looked like they could walk for ever. Each carried a rucksack – cigarettes, food and half the NA medical kit, including a course of antibiotics. Negotiation good practice.

Rick didn't think the fakes would work, but aside from wearing Khetan down, he didn't have anything better. The delay of the back-up was giving him a chance to secure the release of the hostages without them. Save three lives – and avoid Robbo's hospital pass of the crime desk when he got back.

Rick walked back with Russell to their camp, the mountaineer whistling softly. Rick pictured soldiers returning from a battle, carrying their dead.

'Can we rely on those two?'

The mountaineer raised his eyebrows. 'Completely. Their father climbed with me in my early days. We got on well, and after one trip he invited me for a meal at his house. I met his wife and four young children. Lok and Uttam were three and four at the time, and I ended up sponsoring them through their schooling. They're Sherpas, not porters. You understand the difference?'

'Not really.'

'There are four types of people on commercial expeditions: Western guides – people like me – clients, porters, and Sherpas. They can be compared to an aircraft flight. The porters are the plane and the clients are the passengers, enjoying the ride. The Sherpas are like the auto-pilot: they do most of the work. Lead the routes, equip them with ropes, do the difficult climbing and shepherd the clients up and down the mountain.'

'What do you do?'

'Not much. We're like the pilots of the plane: we check on the auto-pilot and the clients and communicate between them. Most of the time, we're unnecessary. The *sirdar* is the head Sherpa and Lok and Uttam's father was my *sirdar* for ten years.

My chief decision-maker. In fact, Rick, I sometimes think that mountaineering is synonymous with decision-making.'

Rick thought the same about policing. It meant competence, or the lack of it, was always on show. And he needed to jolt the investigation forward to prove his. Starting with the brigadier.

At MK, the soldier stood outside the dining tent. He was stripped to the waist, a green quick-dry towel around his neck and white lather on his chin. His torso and shoulders were pale: a t-shirt made by weathering. On the table sat a bowl of water, and, in an organised row, his old-fashioned watch, sunglasses and folded cravat. Nandan sat watching, his briefcase underneath his chair.

'Tell me what this is about, brigadier, why they've taken Calix. It might make all the difference.'

'No. I told you, I owe it to Calix to tell him before anyone else. Even if you do arrest me.'

Rick tried a different tactic. 'What's really in Nandan's case, brigadier?'

'Medical supplies.'

'I don't think so.' Rick whipped the case from underneath Nandan's chair and slid it onto the table. Water slopped from the bowl. He unlatched the case and pushed the top back. Nestling between grey blocks of foam were the parts of a sniper's rifle. Barrel, scope, stock, bipod.

At the far end of the table, the soldier removed a strip of lather without a flicker of emotion. He rinsed the blade in the water. 'Nandan was in my company of Ghurkhas, but he was a sniper, not a medic. He's a good man, completely trustworthy.' He took another pass with the razor.

Rick shook his head. 'Sorry, against the rules.'

'What rules?'

'Rules of engagement while this is still a police-led operation. I had you down as a rule-follower.'

'I am.'

'But?'

'Family's different,' said the brigadier. He put the razor down. 'I thought you'd know that by now. You probably do. But if you don't – not quite, anyway, because you're not married and you don't have children – you will one day when you do love someone that much. When it hurts.' He dried his face with the towel.

Bleating interrupted. On the trail, two boys appeared with a herd of goats, the last goat limping. One of the boys flicked it with a stick. Their woollen hats had long ear-flaps like Russian tank commanders'.

'Maggie maybe, she's a bright young thing.'

They did agree on that, but Rick wasn't going to be side-tracked. 'We couldn't justify it in court.'

The goats wandered about and the two boys sat down. They began to throw stones, aimlessly, flicking glances at the Westerners.

'Rick, the presence or even the use of that sniper's rifle is not going to get to court. I mentioned that I trust Nandan. Well, I trust you too. Trust – real trust – is a rare thing. I'm going off on one, as Calix would say, but it's true – and you only get one chance. Once trust is blown, then it can never be repaired. There's always a nagging doubt.'

The goats slumped down and began to regurgitate what they'd eaten. Russell and the cook wandered over to the boys. A conversation took place and money was handed over.

'Look at it another way,' said the brigadier. 'I hope we don't have to use it, but it might save your life as well as Calix's. Or Barney's or Spencer's, or one of your colleague's. The maniac out there who kidnapped four people has no such compunction.'

'Civilisation falls apart if we don't follow the rules.'

'As I said, family's different, and I include my own life in that.'

'I'll give it some thought.'

The trilling of the sat phone signalled a truce. The soldier leant over the basin and splashed water on his face, and Rick picked up the phone.

'All change,' said Robbo. 'The twins' father, Terry Williams, the FIFA half-a-president, has been jumping up and down and he's got clout at the Home Office. Nepal has stepped up and their army are now in charge. It's out of my hands, and when they reach you, it'll be out of yours.'

Rick watched Russell and the cook walk back, the cook leading the limping goat by a scruffy length of rope. It was bleating again.

'Three companies of Special Forces are being mobilised in Kathmandu and they'll be deploying directly to MK via helicopter in the next twenty-four hours. There may be an advance guard before then, but, officially, you hand over to the ranking officer. When I know his name I'll let you know. Clear?'

Rick shook his head. 'Clear.'

He slid the phone onto the table and took a deep breath. Glanced at the far hillside, then snapped the case with the sniper rifle shut, and threw it back under Nandan's chair.

*

The maimed chess pieces glinted under the rust-coloured sun. Barney scratched his ear, and picked up his bishop. He knocked over Calix's queen, which left only two of Calix's pawns, his knights and his king. Calix was winning. But the rules had changed: they were playing Killer Chess, the aim being to lose all your pieces. It was his idea, sparked by something his old man had once said. *If your enemy has a huge navy, don't fight them on the sea.*

Time dragged as Calix waited for inspiration. Only one more chance with the phone, one chance in ten thousand. No cigarettes, and no toothpaste. His mouth tasted bitter, his teeth furry. He scratched them with a fingernail. His old man again. *A soldier who looks after himself is a reliable soldier.*

He yanked his chain over to the stream. Barney wasn't shaving, but Calix was still doing his best. He pulled his razor out of his pocket. Somehow, he still had it. A blue safety razor, blunt and clogged. From under a rock he pulled out the small dish of cooking oil Ved had given him when Hant wasn't looking. He massaged it onto his chin, pulled the razor through the water and started. He pulled his chin taut and made another pass. It was like cutting a field with a push-mower.

A shadow fell across him, but he didn't look up or stop shaving. The razor was knocked from his hand and a boot ground the blue plastic into the dirt. He'd had his last shave. He looked up to find Hant and Ishwar. Pistols poked out from their waistbands.

'Where's Kelsang?' said Hant.

Calix shrugged and surveyed the scene, counting. Hant and Ishwar. The lazy-eyed guard on sentry, Ved up at the cave. One guard hadn't returned from Lukla, and there was no Kelsang. Which including Hant meant only four. Four plus Ram and the boy didn't count. Four.

He shrugged again. 'Collecting firewood?'

Barney clanked over. 'What's up?'

'Kelsang's missing.'

'Where?' said Barney. He looked guileless and his question was senseless, but he sounded guilty.

'Sit down,' said Hant, removing his pistol and ushering the twin down with the barrel.

He turned to Calix. 'So?'

'I don't know. *We* don't know.' He paused. 'Run away – back to his village?'

Hant levelled the pistol at Barney's chest, then turned to point it at Calix. 'I know you like playing game. Chess. Hide-and-find. So I count five.'

'What – then you'll shoot me?'

'Calix!' shouted Barney.

'One,' said Calix. 'Two.'

His heart-rate spiked. He'd not known he was going to say it. But, it was too late. He'd said it.

'Three.'

If Hant shot him, he couldn't use him to bargain with. Hant wouldn't shoot. Of course he wouldn't.

'Four.'

Calix's heart jabbered like a drill. He stared at the pistol and Hant's brown-black eyes, like two more barrels.

'Lost in Tibet?'

Hant's pistol flashed up, then down across Calix's face. Teeth crunched and blood gushed from his nose, and he fell backwards into the stream. He stabbed his hand down into the icy water to prevent his complete immersion. Pain cascaded through his body, but inside he was smiling. He was getting to them. Like chess, the only way to win was to think several moves ahead. And as he lay there, half in, half out of the freezing water, his overwhelming feeling was not the pain, but guilt. If Hant had shot him dead, he'd have left Barney to fend for himself. He'd got the twins into this, and he was determined to get one of them out. Now, more than ever.

*

After a dinner of goat curry, Rick lay in his tent, listening.

He listened to his breathing. He listened to the thrumming, relentless Hinku, and tried to distinguish its tributary. He listened to the soft Nepalese voices and Russell's booming in the dining tent.

His backside throbbed so he rolled onto his side and closed his eyes. He stared at the dark shapes that appeared. Rectangles, squares. Mauves and magentas. Circles, spheres. All moving. Like being dead? Shapes moving without any rhyme or reason. Not so different to life.

'Rick.'

The voice came again, but louder.

'Rick.' It was Russell's voice.

Rick opened his eyes, shutting off the dark shapes.

'What?'

'We've had a delivery.'

He unzipped the tent and crawled out, knocking ice crystals off its roof. It was almost midnight, but the moon was shrouded. The beam of his head-torch crossed with Russell's and picked out a slant of trodden scrub.

'This.'

Russell passed him a small package with a note. The note had been used as an extra layer of wrapping, but before reading it, before even straightening it out, Rick peered into the package.

44

Two toes wrapped in toilet paper. They'd been placed in a plastic bag and secured with a rubberband. Dirt crammed the toenails and half of one nail was black. Bones stuck out of the severed ends, their whiteness stark against the dried blood. The cuts of both bone and flesh were jagged. A saw of some kind?

Rick couldn't sleep after the pre-dawn delivery and got up. He walked away from the camp, glad of his thick duvet jacket. He flicked up his hood, and pulled on gloves.

Whose toes?

Calix, Barney, Spencer?

Not that it mattered.

Watching his breath freeze in the air reminded him of Christmas: working up an appetite for turkey, chopping up wood with Dad. He wandered towards the bridge, head down. He kicked a stone.

The two toes weren't frostbitten. He – whoever – would, should, still be able to walk.

But, the message showed ruthlessness. And desperation. Time was running out. He booted another, much larger stone.

He came across a clearing. There was a short section of stone wall containing a set of prayer-wheels. Like giant cotton reels, each a foot high, made of wood. A dozen of them were fixed in a row so that if you walked alongside you could spin each one in turn. Russell had told him that spinning them sent prayers, like the flags.

The prayer-wheels were protected from the worst of the weather by a gabled roof but they were old and the intricate carvings had faded. In the light breeze the wooden wheels were trying to turn. Standing next to them, Rick re-read the message which had come with the package.

You must make good work conditons Qatar

You must give Calix buwaa me

No come close

H

Rick put his hand on the first wheel and traced the wood-carver's creations. The shapes and patterns were complex and varied – months and months of work. Now they were fading and one day all would be lost.

'Rick.' The brigadier's voice.

Rick turned around, his hand dropping. He pushed off his hood.

'I'll do it,' said the brigadier. He walked up to the prayer-wheels and touched one. 'Real craftsmanship.'

Rick nodded.

He waited.

'I'll swap places with Calix,' said the brigadier.

'No, David. No way. Absolutely no way.' It would be suicide, and he knew the soldier knew.

The brigadier spun a wheel. They both watched it spinning, rattling on its spindle. Round and round. 'Nothing like a good mechanism – same as my watch. Everything's electronic these days.'

'Back-up should arrive any time now. The army, your lot.'

'Might be too late.'

The soldier spun the next wheel.

'I won't let you give yourself up, David. We need to wait for the back-up. Khetan will be able to see them here at MK and it will heap on the pressure. He'll break.'

'What if he doesn't?'

'Over ninety-nine per cent of these situations end successfully.'

'And if this is an exception?'

The wheels slowed, and stopped, their rattling replaced by the clamour of the river.

'It's a brave thing, David, you're suggesting.'

'I've got no choice. The package settled it.'

Rick recalled a discussion on a CPD course about a runaway trolley which was about to kill five people. Pulling a lever would alter the course of the trolley and send it into a siding where it would kill only one person. There were only two possible choices. Which was the better choice? The moral choice? The less bad choice? The dilemma supposedly originated from a real situation where a railway signalman had to decide.

The brigadier's situation was different. Calix, Barney and Spencer were on the first track, and the brigadier himself was in the siding. Maybe the brigadier didn't have a choice. If they had more time, then they'd have other options. Maybe the trolley was imminent and they had to choose now.

He wondered if it was his moral duty to let the brigadier choose. Or whether he should decide for the soldier.

'*Your* son's not at risk.'

'You're emotionally involved, David. Not the best person to make decisions.'

'Remember what I was saying about family? Well, imagine if it was your son. Or if it was your father having to decide.'

The soldier stared at the hillside, his weathered face creased, his eyes bloodshot. 'Years ago, I taught Calix to snare rabbits – they live in the wood at the bottom of the garden and run across the lawn. I showed him how to skin and gut them, and cook the odd one over a fire; the rest Pat put in pies. Nothing better than rabbit pie. One of the few things we've ever done together.'

Rick noticed the brigadier's porter squatting at the edge of the clearing. From his shirt pocket the brigadier produced a scrap of paper and wrote a few lines. He whistled to the porter and passed the paper to Rick.

H

I will swap places with my son Calix.

Brigadier David Coniston, ex-Lieutenant Coniston, 1st and 3rd Ghurkha Rifles

Rick glanced at the rising sun. It was his choice, *not* the brigadier's. He was still in charge, and with Russell's help he could arrest him, as he'd already threatened, place the soldier in handcuffs and detain him at MK. He realised, however, his choice stemmed not from morality, or from the police manual. But from the fact of one human standing next to another.

'Okay, but I'm changing the note.'

He ripped a page from his notebook, wrote a new message and passed it to the brigadier. 'We're negotiating, not surrendering.'

H

Release Barney and Spencer

THEN I will swap places with my son Calix.

Brigadier David Coniston, ex-Lieutenant Coniston, 1st and 3rd Ghurkha Rifles

The brigadier read the new message, nodded, and beckoned the waiting porter. The man listened to the soldier's instructions, his bobble-hat waving all over. He turned, walked down the line of prayer-wheels, spinning every one, and trotted away.

*

A report like a rifle shot sounded in the mountains.

Moments later came its echo. Then a rumble.

Everyone at the cave looked up. Hant, guards, hostages. Calix.

High on the face of the nearest mountain, the snow slope had developed a huge crack. Hundreds of tons of snow and ice funnelled downwards, picking up speed. The avalanche created a fog of snow in the air, like a car's dust-cloud. It tore down-hill, and when it reached the tree-line, plucked out the trees as if they were matchsticks.

Then it was over. As quickly as it had started, it stopped.

A rush of cold air swathed the lower slopes, including the watchers standing in a line at the lip of the cave. They stood in silence, at one in their awe and their inconsequence.

The cloud of snow settled and visibility returned. The slope looked scarred, like a giant snow-plough had careered down the mountain and buried itself at the bottom. Great chunks of grey-white icy snow revealed the path of the avalanche. Here and there protruded a branch of a tree. At the top, where it had started, the slope overhung, ready to start all over.

Life resumed at the cave. Calix and Barney were unlocked, escorted at gunpoint to the bolt on the rock and chained up. Ishwar and the lazy-eyed guard were placed on sentry.

Hant walked down from the cave to explain. 'One man, one man.' He knocked two fingers together. 'Like football, yes?'

Another day began.

Calix's jaw ached and his tongue repeatedly sought the gap left by his missing tooth. His nose – Barney had told him – was bent and swollen. He had two black eyes. He was a mess, but for a few minutes the avalanche had taken his mind off things.

Fight or flight? They had one more chance with the phone, but if that didn't work, he'd had another idea. The chains. Fat chunky links, but breakable. Everything was breakable, given enough time. People sawed through prison bars with razor blades and escaped, given enough time. He stared at the chains. Barney watched him. Ishwar and the lazy-eyed guard watched him.

'Listen in, Barney.'

He explained what he wanted and together they searched amongst the scattered ammunition thrown by the twins at the effigy. The avalanche slope was still, like a calm sea after a storm. Only the dirty-white ploughed track revealed its passing, and after the first snowfall, that too would be gone.

Barney found it. A wedge-shaped stone with a narrow end that fitted through the chain-links and a thick end that didn't. Once they had that, a fist-sized rock to act as a hammer was easy.

They sat back down, and looked around.

The two sentries were playing dice, but kept sneaking looks at Hant. They seemed more concerned with their leader than with Calix and Barney. Hant sat in the cave mouth cleaning his nails with a knife.

'Good to go,' said Barney.

Calix nodded. The twin was hardening. Better when he was busy, but definitely becoming a more useful second.

He balanced a section of his leg chain on two rocks a few inches apart. Then he jammed the wedge into a link so it protruded into the space below.

'They're playing like children,' said Barney.

'On three.'

'Still a go.'

'Two... three, *bang.*'

On three, Barney threw a rock at a new target, a rock-head with a large charcoal *H.* Calix had been unable to resist.

On *bang*, Calix hit the wedge with the rock-hammer.

The chain held.

They tried again.

They kept trying until one of the sentries shouted.

They looked up, and Calix felt a twinge in his backside as he anticipated another beating. Both men were standing up, pointing not at them but down the hill. Another shout, directed at Hant.

Calix stood, and looked down towards the river. A figure was walking up the hillside towards the cave. The guard who'd gone to buy the new sat phone?

The figure walked closer. Small, Nepalese, wearing a striped jumper. Calix didn't recognise the clothing. At a hundred metres, the man stopped and squatted by a cluster of rocks. He washed his face in the river and drank. Hant shouted orders. The man waited.

Ram galloped down the hill, then slowed to a walk as he neared the rocks.

The boy and the stranger met like animals with young. The man handed something to Ram, turned and ran. The boy jogged back up the hill. In the cave mouth he handed a piece of paper to Hant. Hant pulled out his pistol and fired into the air, which caused an echo to traverse the valley like a Mexican wave.

*

A clap of thunder.

Rick jerked his head up and looked at the sky. There was no sign of bad weather, the few clouds high and puffy-white. He dropped his gaze to the mountains, the other side of the valley. The closest mountain was on the move, downwards. It was miles away and he lifted his binoculars. The snow slope had sheared, an obvious grey line stretching high across it. The line disappeared in a storm of blown snow.

Russell walked up. 'Not much you can do if one of those hits you.'

They stared across the valley.

'Sets like concrete, almost instantly.'

Rick nodded. 'What triggers them?'

'Nothing, usually. Unstable layers of snow can suddenly go, unable to hold the gradient. There can be a trigger. Snowfall, a falling rock, mountain deer, even a bird. The famous butterfly.'

'Humans?'

'Of course. Walkers, skiers, mountaineers.'

'The three missing.' Rick put the glasses down. 'Trying to escape.'

Rick phoned Robbo and told him about the toes and the latest demand from Khetan. He told him about the brigadier's decision and the reply sent with the porter.

'Let me speak to him.'

'He's walked to the bridge to wait for a reply.'

'You can't let him do it, Rick.'

'I can't stop him. He's a friend of yours, you must know what he's like. I'd have to put him in handcuffs. To persuade him, I'd need a viable alternative.'

'You mean the Special Forces?'

'Shouldn't they be here by now?'

'I'll make a call and phone you back,' said Robbo. 'Maggie wants a word.'

'Two ticks,' said Maggie.

Rick heard a door open. 'Hi Maggie,' said someone. She was

moving somewhere else. He was sat in her lap, wheeling down a corridor. He rather liked it. A door closed.

'We're alone,' said Maggie.

He rather liked that too. 'Where are you?'

'Your office.'

He could see her surveying his desk. A photo of Dad, and another of the four of them, his dad's birthday a few years back. He saw a photo of Maggie on his desk, the two of them. In beesuits with his bees.

'Rick,' she said, 'You will be careful.'

It was now or never.

He explained about Becky's wedding, about the familial pressure from his mother and Becky.

She was silent.

Too silent. 'Maggie?'

'Have you asked Kate?' said Maggie. 'Or Amanda? What about speed-dating?' She started laughing.

'Maggie, I'm serious.'

'I know, sorry. I don't know why I said all that.'

He thought he did. She was nervous, which had to be a good sign.

'Rick, there's one condition.'

'Is that a yes?'

'Yes, it's a yes, but on one condition. You said you wanted to know what it's like to be in a wheelchair. The only way to find out is to sit in one, and I've had an idea about that.'

Rick sat at the table, doodling in his notebook. Bees, and a smoker. A football. A gibbet and a noose. The sketch – the thought – had seemingly come from nowhere. Like a dream sequence. Analysis was easy: he was the hangman, the brigadier the sentenced. He could still change his mind, arrest the soldier, cuff him to the table and shackle his legs.

'Back-up from Lukla's here,' shouted Russell.

Rick looked up. Ten or a dozen people, spooling down the hillside from Saklis. He picked up his binoculars and watched them descend. The men reached flat ground and the bridge, and turned towards MK.

They were the advance party, some in the disruptive-patterned blue fatigues and cap of the Nepalese police, some in Nepalese army uniforms. The familiar faces of DS Khan and DC Emmett. Two unfamiliar faces: the Aussie detectives.

Rick shook hands and made introductions.

There was no ranking officer, and he remained in charge. Shielding his eyes from the ochreous sun, he scanned for the helicopters.

45

They waited by the suspension bridge. Rick, Russell, Kate, the brigadier, and the two Sherpas, Lok and Uttam. Trees and thick vegetation encased them, fed by the spray of the huge river. The booming water drowned the noise of wildlife and all but the closest voices.

The advance party waited at Mosom Kharka, Rick not wanting to spook Hant if he did turn up. Back-up in force or not at all. He was still in charge.

He sat on a table-sized rock next to the ladder which led up to the bridge. In front of him, the brigadier paced around, and in a gap in the trees Russell scanned the opposite hillside with binoculars. Kate stood at his side. The Sherpas squatted nearby, smoking and whispering.

Rick stared at the ground. Rocks spattered with the greys and greens of lichens and mosses, like artists' palettes.

'Where's Nandan?' he asked the brigadier. The buckle on the soldier's belt glinted in the sun, and at his side the short scabbard of a knife hung down.

'Do you really want to know?'

'Yes.'

'Up the hill, in position.'

'What happened in the Falklands? It might still make a difference.'

The brigadier took off his watch, huffed on the glass and polished it. He held it up to his ear. 'Listen to that,' he said, passing it over.

Rick listened. 'Ticking?'

'Reassuring, isn't it? Like a heart beating.' The soldier paused. 'I'm sorry what I said earlier about you police being all the same. Heat of the moment.'

Rick nodded. 'Forgotten.'

Kate wandered over. She looked different. Her hair less shiny, her face less made-up. Older, but just as attractive as when he'd bumped into her in the photocopying room and thought about asking her out. He was glad he hadn't, but he was also glad that she was there, in front of him, in Nepal. She'd worked magic in Saklis with the kids.

'You think they'll come?'

It was the million-dollar question – she knew that, they all knew that. He shrugged his answer.

'If they do come, I've got a question. After Barney and Spencer have been released, the brigadier will surrender himself to Khetan, and Khetan will release Calix. But I can't see how that can happen simultaneously. I keep picturing you and Hant holding onto both of them, and very gradually holding one tighter and letting one go.'

'There'll be a delay. The brigadier will deliver himself, and a short time later, Khetan will release Calix.'

'At some point Khetan will have the brigadier *and* Calix?'

'It's how these things work. A ransom is paid and delivered – dropped off or paid into an account. Only then is the hostage released. Usually soon afterwards, but sometimes not for a day or two, and sometimes in a different location. A van will drop the hostage in an underpass or a wood, somewhere there's no CCTV. Then a coded phone call.'

'So why do hostages get released?'

Another million-dollar question.

*

'Clear,' said Barney.

Calix stood up and went to the area of rocky scrub they used as a toilet. He dropped his trousers and squatted. He dug out the hidden phone and slipped it into a trouser pocket. Waited for one minute, as if showing it a mark of respect. It made sense: the phone could get them out. He stood, faffed with the bog roll, and pulled up his clothes.

He dragged his chain back.

'Still clear,' said Barney. 'You had an idea?'

'No, you?'

'Ones. Fives. I don't know, don't try one of them. Please don't. Please.'

'It's okay, Barney. It's okay.' Barney could be solid, but was flaky. Understandable. The twin was hungry and scared; they both were. Barney was also grieving. Each day Calix looked forward to the cold dark, to being asleep, and not being able to think. Fight or flight? The one remaining attempt at the PIN code. 'I'll get us out, I promise.' He was sick of lying, and wanted to blurt out the brutal truth: they hadn't a hope of escape.

'Clear?'

'Clear.'

Calix wiggled the phone out of his trousers. The phone lay on its back. And there it was: the answer. As simple as that.

The numbers 8475 scratched into the plastic.

Barney tried to smile.

Calix checked the guards, then turned the phone on and tapped in the numbers 8-4-7-5.

'I'm in.'

He tapped in a phone number, and pressed call.

*

The brigadier had stopped pacing and was sharpening his knife with a whetstone. He'd done it before.

'You learnt how to make snares in the army?' said Rick.

The knife rasped gently.

'My father. He kept ferrets for a while. Was good with a knife and made very fine snares. Much better than mine.' As he spoke he made rhythmic circular movements.

'And Calix?'

The brigadier added a few drops of water to the stone. 'Takes after his grandfather. Good with a blade. Good with his hands generally. We don't still do it, of course – he prefers his own company. He's more interested now in stuffing things rather than eating them. I've never quite got that.'

Rick opened his policy book and stared at the doodles. At the gibbet. He turned the pages.

Hostage negotiation: 3 phases.

Locate the hostages.

Establish communication.

Termination.

They had reached the last and badly named stage of a hostage situation. There were three possible outcomes: the suspects surrendered, the suspects were arrested after their position was forcibly entered, the suspects' demands were met and they escaped. In all three, the lives of the hostages were at risk. The lives of Calix, Barney and Spencer were not guaranteed despite the brigadier's sacrificial offer.

Invariably with police operations the ransom demand was for money, occasionally for political goals. People exchange was not something the College of Policing contemplated, yet alone advised.

But people exchange did happen.

Usually during a war when both sides exchanged prisoners. There were examples in the Second World War and during the Arab–Israeli conflict. When Hezbollah activists hijacked TWA Flight 847 they successfully demanded the release of over seven hundred Shiite prisoners from Israeli prisons. In return, they released all but one hostage.

There were, Rick thought, two key differences with the situation at the suspension bridge. In a war, if either side reneged on the deal then not only would diplomatic and military weight be invoked, but future negotiations would be jeopardised. If Khetan reneged, there would be no consequence.

There was one even more fundamental difference.

Invariably, people were being returned to their home-side, to smiling faces and open arms. Blankets and large cups of hot sweet tea. A hospital check-up, and hugs and kisses from their families. The brigadier would not be having any of that because he was going in the wrong direction. Ducking under the turnstile.

Rick was *delivering* a hostage to the perpetrators. Perspiration pricked his body.

Would future negotiation courses cite the maverick DCI Castle who delivered a hostage to the hostage-takers? He could hear the instructor, *I know that none of you would dream of doing this,* and the laughter in the background. His policy book seemed to justify it: if the brigadier had not volunteered then the three missing were likely to be murdered. Exchanging the brigadier would save three lives.

The man in question leant back against the ladder leading up to the bridge. He'd removed most of the graffiti.

'You know we had two children?' The soldier tested the knife with his thumb and slotted it back in its scabbard.

'An older girl, cycling accident,' said Rick.

The brigadier nodded. 'Must have told you when you came to the house.' He sat down on the ladder. 'Megan. She's already been gone over a year. Like a dream to me now. I do dream about her, about us as a family when the kids were younger. Happy and carefree.' The brigadier stared down at his boots. 'Before Australia, before this.' He tapped his boots together, knocking off some invisible dirt. 'You never met Megan, but she was affectionate and talkative. Lots of friends, always at the house, and Pat never happier. Now, it's so quiet. Calix has always been different, whatever Pat says.

'But I'm not losing another one. It would kill her. You understand?'

Rick nodded. A question about children. He always nodded.

'Where are they?' The brigadier stood up and stared through the canopy of trees at the opposite hillside.

Rick shook his head. He wasn't sure. He was uncertain even what he was hoping for. A miracle: the three missing delivered to the bridge, and Khetan and his crew to think better about things and melt away into the mountains.

The sat phone beeped.

Rick scooped it up and listened.

'I'll put you on speaker.' He beckoned the others and held the phone out in front of him.

The brigadier moved closer, Kate and Russell walked up, and all of them hunched around the phone as if it was a broadcast on the wireless in the war.

Robbo spoke.

'The Nepalese Special Forces are coming.

'A whole company, over a hundred.

'Now.'

46

'He–hello?' A voice from the stolen phone. Thin, uncertain, but still familiar.

The phone sat on the ground and Calix's head hovered above it. Barney watched the sentries.

'Go, go, go,' said the twin.

'Mum,' said Calix. He stared down at the phone, at the numbers on the screen. At the battery level in the top right corner.

'Calix? Is that you? Calix?'

'Yes, it's me.' He heard the quiver in his voice, felt the hairs stand on his shins, then, like dominoes, work their way up his body to his neck.

'Still good,' whispered Barney.

'Oh, God. Are you okay? Where are you? What's happening out there? Wait, let me turn down the radio.'

'She's turning down the radio,' said Calix. He felt cold all over.

Barney made a choking noise, not quite a laugh, but almost.

'Sorry,' said his mum. 'So, God, are you really okay?'

'I'm okay. Really.' He sniffed through his blood-crusted nose. 'How're you?' Barney patted Calix's leg. Calix shivered.

'Me! I'm fine. Fine. I mean, better now. Are you with Barney and Spencer?'

'Mum, I need—'

'Of course, what? Money? God, it's so wonderful to hear your voice.'

'Mum, is the old man there?'

The screen on the phone faded and disappeared. The transmission light disappeared. Calix pressed the phone back on. It fired up, and requested the PIN code. He jabbed it back in and pressed redial. A message on the screen appeared: *Connecting…*

The screen faded and died.

'What?' said Barney, turning round.

Calix showed him the phone. Barney's face turned ashen. Calix's stomach turned, and he held out a hand.

Barney took it.

They sat there, holding hands like brothers.

It reminded Calix of cradling the Finchams' cat. An accident, the night he'd given Ryan a slap. In the dark and the rain, the cat had appeared from nowhere. He'd hit the brakes, but too late.

*

Rick re-read what he'd written in his policy book.

So much could go wrong. The three missing could die, executed by Khetan before or during the exchange. Even if the exchange took place without incident, the brigadier was likely to meet a terrible end and Khetan likely to escape. The best Rick could hope for was that the kidnappers took the brigadier away with them. Then it was back to square one: trying to secure the release of a hostage, but without a location for Khetan, or a way of communicating with him.

Career-ending?

Six months on the crime desk and a veto on foreign trips seemed the least he could expect. Back to uniform? The greatest humiliation of any detective's career.

Uniform. A flat hat and three pips on each shoulder. Wet-nursing new sergeants and inspectors, supervising industrial accidents and bomb scares, calming neighbourhood tensions and A&E at the weekends. Earlies, lates, and nights. A tightly defined role and responsibilities. No freedom to investigate what he wanted, when and how he liked.

The brigadier crouched next to the ladder, peeling away flakes of wood with his knife.

'Pat doesn't know what happened in the Falklands, does she.' It was more of a statement than a question.

The soldier shook his head. 'Didn't want to make her fret, she's already got a worry book where she writes things down.'

'She told me,' said Rick.

'I don't read it, of course.'

'You're in it.'

The soldier stared at him. 'Me?'

'She thinks you've been bottling something up.'

He jabbed the knife in the wood. 'She's right. I've been married to her a long time. This has always been with me, but recently it's started weighing heavy.'

'You can get help, David.' Rick thought of Emma, his regular sessions at Magenta House. The nondescript building, the old-fashioned lift. Room 331 with its spider plant and box of man-size tissues.

The soldier scowled, and stood up. The graffiti had all been pared away.

'You've probably worked it out. You or Maggie. She's a smart girl but then she should be, she used to be one of ours. A sapper.'

'Oh.' Rick gripped his notebook and looked away. Maggie used to do one of the most dangerous jobs on the planet.

'I can see you didn't know. Sorry.' The soldier fitted the knife back in its scabbard. 'After you'd flown out here, she came to the house and re-interviewed me. The soft-cop approach – she's good at that, too.'

*

Frantic activity took place in the cave. The larger half-burnt logs of the cookfire were rolled away, and the remnants kicked down the slope. Ved stacked his pans. The tents were taken down and packed up. Even Hant helped out.

Calix wasn't going to miss the cave. The dripping ceiling and the puddle on the floor which froze at night, the charcoal wall-painting of indeterminate history, and the ghost of Chet, lying in a pool of his own making.

Rucksacks and wicker baskets were lined up in the cave mouth.

Calix's old man had not wanted him to go to Nepal. He'd wanted him to find a job. At the last minute his old man had relented and helped him pack by producing an armful of useful kit based on his army experience. Diamox tablets for altitude and a quick-drying towel. A neckerchief for the fumes of Kathmandu and the dust-winds on the trails. Gaffa tape to wind around his walking poles so there'd always be some to hand. Calix had taken everything.

The three remaining guards converged on Calix and Barney, and secured them with plasticuffs. They reminded Calix of the kidnap on the football field. The garlic breath of the guard, and the stumbling in the dark. Nothing to worry about – then.

Their leg shackles were removed and the chains coiled up. They were hooded with the reversed balaclavas from the kidnap.

'No talk,' said Hant.

Calix didn't want to talk. He wanted to listen. He rubbed the oozing blister from the leg shackle, and concentrated.

The chains were taken away. Up to the cave. Then moved again. Together with some of the packs. At least one guard stayed with the two of them. Hant's voice stayed close. Not Ram.

'What's happening?' whispered Barney.

'Either we're being moved to a new hideout.'

'Or?'

Calix suddenly felt a touch superstitious, and hadn't wanted to say it aloud – or even think it.

'Or what?'

'Shh.' Surely, Calix thought, Barney could work it out. No reason to be hooded if they were being moved. They couldn't walk if they couldn't see.

'Calix, do you think this is it?'

'Course not. They'd have given us a last meal. Some of that chicken. A final cigarette. Hant's no animal.'

'But you said, either.'

'Did I?'

'Yes.'

'I say, no talk,' said Hant.

Calix heard the dulled slap of a hand, and Barney cry out. He tensed and stepped backwards. Held his cuffed hands in front of his hooded face. Stepped sideways. He could hear a guard moving closer. He swayed his head. He ducked. The guard sniggered. Calix stepped away – backwards, and fell over another guard. More sniggering. Calix scrabbled on the ground, clawing at the hood. He heard a rushing sound, and then felt his head jerk sideways, and his ear mashing into his skull. His head started to pound with a headache from hell and his ear to ring, and ring, and ring.

47

'I can see them,' shouted Russell.

The brigadier ran over to where the mountaineer was standing. Rick shut his notebook and jumped down from the rock.

'They're coming down the hillside. Fifteen minutes away, maybe less. Half a dozen people – it must be them.' Russell passed the binoculars to the brigadier.

'I can see five,' said the soldier. 'Two taller men, white. The first one's Calix. I'm sure of it.' He let out a strange whoop. He wasn't used to whooping. Something Rick and he had in common.

'I've got six now.'

'Seven. Definitely, seven. But only two...' The brigadier petered out.

Rick walked over to the others. He trained his binoculars through the gap in the trees. At first he couldn't see anyone and he took the glasses away. Let his eyes surveil the hillside.

He found them and moved the glasses back. He counted seven: five plus two. He let a minute elapse. There definitely wasn't a third. Nothing in this world was ever straightforward. Nothing.

Rick climbed the short and now pristine ladder onto the bridge. The rails extended above the last rung and, leaning back, he looked to his left and up the hillside towards the village of Saklis. Scene of the butchered cow, the reticent villagers, schoolmistress Kate and the two child-witnesses who liked playing Killer Cars.

His eyes re-focused on the hillside and worked their way back down. He wondered whether Nandan was somewhere there, hidden in the foliage or the folds of the land. Hunkered down, looking at Rick though cross-hairs.

He looked to his right along the bridge, the best part of a hundred metres. A wobbly track, narrowing to its exit with the perspective. Draped along both sides of the wire netting were multicoloured prayer-flags, threadbare and faded in the sun. Ceaseless in spreading their messages of peace and wisdom.

There was a section in the negotiators' manual about arriving first. Watching the opposition set up, noting where they positioned themselves and checking no tricks or surprises were being planned. It was possible that Khetan or one of his men was already there. A sniper, like Nandan, his cross-hairs also trained on Rick. He stared at the far bank, but it was too far to see the detail.

He checked his watch. Three minutes of Russell's fifteen had passed. He tried with binoculars, but the view had gone and he let them hang. They felt heavy. A fly landed in an eye-piece and he swatted it away.

At the foot of the ladder, the brigadier wound his watch. 'Given to me by my father,' he said, glancing up at Rick. 'One day I'll give it to Calix, not that he'll ever wear it. He's in the beeping generation.' He refastened it and rocked up and down on his heels. Next to him stood Russell, still surveilling the approaching suspects. Kate was behind them staring forwards, her face set with worry. Lok and Uttam squatted behind her. Even they were silent.

Eight minutes. Over halfway.

'Still only two, Russell?'

The mountaineer nodded.

Below Rick, the river thundered along. If he listened, it got louder. The fly came back. He trapped it in the eye-piece and jabbed in a finger. It wasn't a good idea. He wiped it out with his shirt.

'Brigadier, you might want to stay out of sight until we know they've got the three of them.' Rick forced himself to say three.

The soldier nodded and he and Kate walked away. The man was rolling his neck and waggling it from side to side, like a boxer limbering up. If only it was a boxing match, or any sporting contest with rules and a referee.

Rick was nervous, his subconscious jabbering away like an idiot. He could only guess how the brigadier was feeling: scared, resolute, purposeful. The soldier had been trained for this kind of thing, trained to keep going forward even if it meant risking his life.

Fifteen minutes.

His stomach turned. There was no sign of them. His limbs felt heavy and he tried moving his feet. Knee raises, slow ones.

'Russell?'

The mountaineer shook his head.

Twenty minutes.

Rick looked at two broken slats a few metres along the bridge. He wondered who was responsible for repairs. Nepalese hard hats who closed them for weeks while they brewed up and decided what needed doing. Repairing the bridge was what they should all be doing, not bargaining with men's lives.

The Trail

*

Fifty metres from the bridge, Calix sat with Barney in a small scrubby amphitheatre. It was a well-chosen hiding place in the thick vegetation of the riverbank: they could not see out and they could not be seen, even from the air. Hant had walked off with the lazy-eyed guard, and he and Barney were being watched by Ved the cook, and Ishwar the oldest guard. They squatted at the lip of the bowl, and between the two pairs sat Ram. He was uneasy, fidgeting with grasses and stones. He was still a boy.

Calix nursed his injuries both old and new. He prodded his swollen ear and wiped pus from his leg. His head ached. At least they hadn't been hooded again.

The river seemed noisy. A bird with a streak of red on its back settled on the lip of the natural crater. It reminded him of Bird Bird. The two guards shared a roll-up, the smoke sitting in the hole.

Calix needed a fag to settle. If he discounted Ram, there were two against two. The best odds yet.

'*Paani*,' said Calix. Water.

Ishwar shoved the jerrycan towards the two of them. It fell over. With the cuffs it was tricky to manoeuvre and Ram helped them drink.

'What now?' asked Barney.

'We're being moved somewhere – maybe.'

'Because of the message – the man we didn't know?'

'It could have been a tip-off from a local hoping for a payout. Someone's seen Ram lugging supplies, or there's a dibble patrol. Or, Hant's posted a lookout at the bridge, or down the trail.'

'Kelsang?'

Calix shrugged.

316

'You said, we're being moved – *maybe.*'

'Don't start that again.'

Calix was equally interested in a second question. Rather than what was happening, what were the two of them going to do? Fight or flight?

'Barney, I want you to practise Nepali with Ram. *Ek, dui, tin,* just the simple stuff. Distract him. Okay?'

Barney nodded, and crawled closer to Ram.

Calix watched and listened as the twin engaged the boy. Distract Ram, distract Barney, reassure the two guards of their inattention.

He ran a hand down the outside of his leg, feeling for the contours of his pockets. The knife was still there. It would cut through the plasticuffs, like one of his scalpels through animal hide. And after the plasticuffs? He glanced across at Ved. The cook had been good to them – leftovers, and cigarettes. Ved caught his eye and offered the roll-up.

Calix nodded, and the cook brought it over. He inhaled, staring into the man's green-tinged eyes. He turned, breathed out, and returned the stub, grunting his thanks. In a fight – a war, his old man would say – you couldn't be on both sides. Ved was the enemy.

The cook sat back down, and Calix fingered the knife in his *khalti.* The pocket within a pocket, sewn in the tiny tailor's shop in Kathmandu. The knife from the crammed shop next door. He worked it up to daylight.

*

Rick wobbled, as if there had been an earthquake miles away. He jerked his head up and stared at the bridge's vanishing point. A man stood there, like a mirage. A small man, a Nepalese man. God, he felt tired. Once, he'd worked two nights without going home and hadn't finished until 11.30 on the Monday morning. Gang warfare had erupted on Moss Side: three shootings, a stabbing and a house fire. Thirty-seven hours straight. That tired.

'Russell,' Rick shouted. But he didn't look around at his friend. Didn't dare take his eyes away from the kidnapper.

'Got your back.'

'Keep David here until I holler.'

Rick set off. His feet felt like lead and he'd lost his sense of balance. He grabbed the handrail on one side. Far beneath him – at least forty metres – the water was pounding along.

'Castle.' A yell from the other end of the bridge. The mirage was real, had legs and arms and was walking towards him, eschewing the handrail.

Dad no longer knew his name, Mum was getting older, and greyer. Becky was getting married. His younger sister. It should have been him first. Had Maggie agreed to accompany him to the wedding? He struggled to remember. The front and side fences of his garden needed replacing. Had he left the vase of bluebells on the kitchen table? *The girl in the middle of the back seat. Pearl. Windscreen glass in her eyes. The sibling jumpers. Parts of them together for ever. Twelve floors. A soggy mess of blood and bone. The children's mobile, gently turning, one way then the other. Blood dripping down onto the white bedding. Each cot spattered with blood and brain. The tiny pillows.*

When was his next appointment with Emma? He gripped the rail and stared into the water. There was no time for this.

Were his bees queening up? Had he asked Robbo to do it? The helicopters were meant to be coming, but he couldn't hear them. All he could hear was the booming Hinku.

His life was flashing past like he was a dying man, but he wasn't dying. He was a stand-in, an imposter, to be substituted at the last minute. Walking the plank – the planks – for some-one else. The brigadier was the dying man.

Rick walked on.

How had it all come to this? One man's life for another. Three others.

On paper it made sense.

On the suspension bridge, nothing did.

48

Calix and Barney sat side by side on the slope of the amphitheatre. They were surrounded by thick glistening undergrowth, damp from the river. Sunlight pierced the canopy of trees and stabbed the ground like a volley of arrows.

The two guards squatted at the top of the crater, smoking, and looking out. Ram squatted lower down, picking at the stitching on his trousers. Calix monitored Ishwar and Ved, biding his time. He saw no sign of their pistols. He whispered instructions to Barney and bum-shuffled closer. The ground was damp and the moisture seeped through to his skin. His ear throbbed.

'Shouldn't we wait?' whispered Barney. 'Find out what's happening?'

'We discussed it.'

'Not really.'

'We've been moved to the bridge. And now it looks like we're waiting for the bridge to free up. So someone can cross it. Someone we don't know about, or Hant, with us or without us. They may have spotted some trekkers, or dibble.'

'We could shout.'

'We could, or we could seize the initiative. There're only

two of them – we'll never have a better chance. Are you with me? You're the big guy. The athlete.'

Barney tried to smile, but it was weak and half-formed. He held out a hand. Calix gripped it, and released.

Together, they turned to observe the two guards.

Ishwar pulled out his wallet, which was attached by a chain to his trousers. It was made of fabric, thin and battered. A teenager's wallet. He ripped the Velcro apart, extricated some photos and showed them to Ved. On all fours Ram scrambled up the slope to join them.

Calix nodded to Barney.

Barney gripped the knife and Calix sawed his hands back and forth. The two guards laughed as they passed the photos. The sawing wasn't working. The knife was sharp, but not serrated and the plastic was bending over, refusing to be cut. He pulled his hands apart so the plastic was taut and sawed some more. He looked up to see Ram point at a photo. There was more laughing.

Calix was free.

He cut the twin loose.

At the rim of the crater, Ishwar slotted the photos back in the wallet and stuffed the wallet back in his trousers.

'Remember,' whispered Calix, 'Keep your hands together until the last moment.'

*

Rick kept going, his legs on auto-pilot, his brain on overdrive. Between the boards he could see the icy river below. At home there would have been a scuba team on standby and paramedics. He'd have worn a life-jacket.

He kept a hand on the wire rail. Unclench, slide, clench.

That way he never lost contact. It was a long way down. He couldn't hear voices – only the river.

Breathe, confidence, one to tell the grandchildren. Unclench, slide, clench.

Khetan stopped, a quarter of the way across the bridge.

Rick closed the gap until it was easy to talk.

Standing in front of him was the man on the CCTV from Barnes Bridge station. His goatee beard was trimmed and neat. He stood in perfect balance, still without a steadying hand on the rail. Dark brown eyes, wells of conspiracy and foreignness – language, religion, culture. The Nepalese man was composed and he was on home turf. A swaying ropebridge miles from anywhere.

'Castle?'

No one had called Rick that since school. He liked it, reminded him of his dad – Mr Castle. Dad was with him on the bridge. He nodded. 'Khetan?'

'No like bridges?'

'Release Calix, Barney, and Spencer, and you can walk away. You have my word.' He still hoped they had missed spotting the second twin.

'What is *word*?'

Rick should have brought Russell. Should have thought. 'Promise. Honour. Deal. Understand?'

Khetan yanked the handrail. The bridge swayed, and Rick grabbed the rail with both hands.

The Nepalese leader snickered. His face was round and boyish. He would never look old. Protruding from the river were enormous rocks, covered in ice crystals. Gleaming teeth in the sunlight, snickering in conspiracy in the rushing water. Tucked into the waistband of Khetan's trousers was the butt of a pistol. At home Rick would have worn a bullet-proof vest as well as a life-jacket. He wondered if a vest would annul a life-jacket.

'Where are Barney and Spencer? Where's Calix?'

'Barney here – bridge, Calix not bridge. Close.' Khetan waved behind him.

'Spencer?'

Khetan frowned and folded his arms. He unfolded them – it gave better access to his pistol. 'Where Calix *buwaa* – David Coniston?' He pronounced it *Con–iss–ton*. Like *hiss*, like a snake.

Khetan's reply was a politician's answer: ask a question to avoid a question.

'Where's *Spencer?*' Rick said again. He was losing hope.

Khetan took a deep breath. 'Spencer dead. Accident. No breathe.' He imitated wheeziness. 'No believe, ask Barney.'

Rick had been dreading the admission, but when it came, it still made his stomach lurch. He forced himself to think.

An *accident* like Vicky Brant? No kidnap, no accident. So obvious. He didn't say it, didn't trust himself with the sarcasm. He thought of his trip to Barnes and meeting Terry Williams, a FIFA high-up. The great view from the flat of the Thames. Lou Williams who'd married her boss and held boat race parties. Someone was going to have to tell them. Or was he jumping ahead – was Khetan not telling the truth? Only part of the truth? Was there more truth to come? Were any of the four missing still alive? They'd seen Barney and Calix walking towards the bridge – hadn't they?

'Bring Barney and Calix onto the bridge.'

Khetan remained impassive. Then, as if he was counting to ten, he released a smile.

'One thing at time. First, David Coniston on bridge.' *Con–iss–ton.*

'How do I know you're not going to shoot him as soon as you see him?'

'You say, word. Nepal, say *dharma*.'

Russell had talked about *dharma*, the Nepalese moral code. A strange ethic that allowed someone to kidnap four people, and to let one of them, if not all of them, die. Beside Rick the prayer-flags fluttered. Through their trailing strings, the snow slopes and mountains glinted in the sun. Nepal was too beautiful a place for such things to happen. They made a grim sense in the ugly housing estates and insipid weather of Manchester, but in Nepal, a mountainous Eden, they seemed aberrant.

'And if David climbs up, onto the bridge?'

'I know you serious. I give Barney.'

'You'll hand over Barney?' Rick didn't want to believe it, and suspected a trap. 'Why?'

'*Dharma.*'

'Then?'

'The soldier come to middle bridge.'

'Then?'

'*When* soldier stand middle bridge, Calix come to middle bridge. Soldier come me. Calix come you.'

Rick took a deep breath. It was a huge risk. Playing with other men's lives, maybe his own. The negotiation course could be a year long, but still be unable to recreate what he was feeling. Tectonic-plate pressure.

He turned around, and stared at Russell. The mountaineer was standing at the top of the ladder, watching.

'Bring David.' A shout, cold and flat as he could. 'Onto the bridge.'

He glanced back at Khetan. The Nepalese man was deadpan, his eyes focusing on Rick, then re-focusing on what was happening behind Rick.

The brigadier climbed up the ladder, and stood with Russell. Two tall rugged men who had achieved on the battlefield or in the mountains, and who would like to tear Khetan apart.

Rick turned once more.

Khetan was walking away. Arms by his sides, surefooted as a goat.

*

Ram climbed out of the crater and walked off. An errand or a piss, it didn't matter. Hant and the lazy-eyed guard would return soon.

'This is our chance,' whispered Calix. 'You ready?'

Barney nodded, looking anything but. Pale, unsure, confused.

'Get ready.' Calix bared his teeth and growled. He pinched Barney hard on the cheek. 'Do it for Spencer.'

Barney did his best to copy Calix's grimace.

'Ishwar, *paani*,' shouted Calix.

He chin-jerked at the jerrycan.

Ved pushed Ishwar towards the can, and the guard with short tufty hair scowled and carried it over.

Barney ran a few paces up the slope, and with a loud roar, threw himself at Ved, half rugby tackle half bear hug. Calix had given Barney a choice, fists or knife. He'd had his own choice too, torso or thigh.

Shadowing Barney up the slope, Calix lunged with the knife at Ishwar, but having had a split-second's warning the guard swerved his body. He dropped the jerrycan and the knife stabbed into his calf muscle. He screamed, not unlike the badger. But with the badger, Calix had used a garden fork and all three prongs went home. The fork had a long handle which helped pin the animal to the ground.

The knife went in and out.

Barney and Ved grappled on the floor, the cook screaming like a banshee. Not the straight knockout Calix had asked for.

Calix held the knife in his hand and looked at the bloody blade. An animal would run away, but Ishwar held his leg, blood oozing through his fingers. He stared at Calix in disbelief and with his other hand felt in his waistband for the pistol. Calix brandished the knife for a repeat.

Three figures appeared at the rim of the crater.

Three figures holding two pistols.

It was over before it had begun.

Hant and the lazy-eyed guard cocked their weapons, and as if in slow motion, Calix and Barney disentangled themselves and withdrew into the well of the crater. Hant snapped orders.

Ved stopped howling. Ram grabbed a jerrycan and backed away, out of sight. Ishwar hauled himself back up the slope, leaving a bloody trail.

Calix's booming heart-rate slowed, but only a fraction.

'Time come,' said Hant.

'Stay strong,' whispered Calix, his heart-rate spiking back. He was telling himself as well as Barney.

49

A young white man stepped off the ladder and onto the bridge, and drifted towards Rick as if he was sleepwalking. Rick raised his binoculars and confirmed it was Barney. Hands tied with rope, and thin as a beanpole. No sign of Khetan or anyone else. Rick glanced over his shoulder at Russell, also watching through binoculars.

The released hostage reached Rick.

'I'm DCI Rick Castle, Manchester CID. You're safe now.'

Barney nodded, but didn't speak. Rick squeezed the young man's arm, which made him flinch.

Rick stepped aside, and let Barney walk past. He'd grown a beard, his face was thin and sunburnt, his expression hollow. Brittle. He looked ten years older than in photos. His shirt and trousers were dirty and hung loose. He smelt of sweat and shit.

'Where's Spencer?' Rick called after him. 'Calix?'

Barney turned around. 'Spencer is dead. I buried him.' His voice was flat, almost robotic. 'Calix is okay. He's not far from the bridge.'

Spencer was dead.

Dead.

Priorities: Barney, Calix, the brigadier – David.

Barney. He was likely to suffer PTSD. Rick had read up on it, and discussed it with Emma. He followed behind Barney, but no longer hung onto the handrail. It seemed unnecessary. No longer did he hear the river or see the rocks or the long drop down. Gone too were the mountains and the snow slopes.

The two of them reached the exit ladder where Russell, Kate, and the brigadier were waiting. Barney climbed down and collapsed on the ground. The mountaineer picked him up, and leant him back against the ladder. The brigadier cut off the rope with his knife. Kate brought mats and a sleeping bag. Hot sweet tea and Mars bars. She held Rick's list of questions.

How many kidnappers?

Weapons? (details: who's carrying? spare ammo?)

How are Spencer and Calix restrained?

Are the kidnappers linked to anyone else?

Are they taking instructions from anyone else?

Have you got any injuries?

Did they hurt you?

Have Spencer or Calix got any injuries?

Whose toes are they?

The questions had to be asked and straightaway. Kate had charmed the two boys in Saklis and Rick hoped she would again. She had a face and a voice that you wanted to talk to.

He searched the petrol-blue sky, but there was no sign or sound of the helicopters.

Barney was safe and looked physically uninjured. A mental assessment would have to wait. Spencer was dead. The surviving twin sat on the ground, legs out in front of him, eyes closed. He shook with shock. Rick wanted to shake him more, to grill him for the answers to his questions. This was not over until it was over – Calix was still alive. Again he checked the sky.

Kate pressed a mug of sweet tea into Barney's hands and unwrapped a chocolate bar. 'Barney, I'm sorry, I need to ask you some questions. Now, before it's too late.'

There was still no sign of Khetan at the end of the bridge. The Nepalese leader had unilaterally released Barney, which was encouraging. But exchanging the brigadier for Calix was a different order of magnitude. If it went wrong then Rick would lose the brigadier *and* Calix *and* Khetan. At least he had Barney. Whatever happened, Barney was safe.

Kate crouched in front of Barney. 'This is important. *Think.*' She sounded insistent. 'You say all four of them carried a pistol, but what about ammunition? People's lives might depend on your answers. *More* lives.' She braced the young man's stick-like arms. 'Come on.'

The brigadier squatted next to Kate. 'Did they hurt you, son?'

Barney nodded. 'Kicks, punches. Slaps.' He sipped the tea. 'It could have been worse.'

'Calix?'

'Same.'

'I have to ask, I'm sorry. We were sent a package, with some toes.'

'They're Spencer's. Taken after he'd died.' Barney's voice was still devoid of emotion. He took another sip of tea.

The brigadier stood, clenching and unclenching his fists.

'Are you absolutely sure about this, David?' asked Rick.

'Let's not go over it again.'

Rick gripped the poles, and hauled himself upwards. He could see First World War soldiers. Climbing ladders in the trenches, the Battle of the Somme about to start. Behind him, the brigadier waited in line. However bad it was for Rick, it was far worse for him. Rick saw more soldiers, going over the top. He could hear their whistles.

Shrill, piercing.

The hairs stood on his neck and goose bumps flared on his arms.

*

Calix couldn't see out of his left eye. His right eye was fuzzy and he blinked a few times without improvement. He tasted blood and he spat out a large reddy-white glob. His tongue reported several teeth out of place – in addition to the one already missing. He was thirsty. An ant crawled across his cheek and he tried to twitch it away.

He wished he hadn't. He had a splitting headache, and his face was on fire. Twitching made everything worse. The ant meandered into his ear.

He lay supine at the bottom of the amphitheatre, trussed up and dumped like an old carpet. Plasticuffs held his wrists and ankles. Ropes pinioned his arms to his body and his legs together. He felt like a Christmas turkey, oven coming up to temperature.

A second ant joined its collaborator in his ear. Revenge for Calix's massacre at the cave. He couldn't brush away the ants or rub his eyes, but he could think. Hant couldn't take that from him.

They had taken his knife and his boots and strip-searched him. Cut off his pockets. Then they had battered him. Kicks mainly – head, arms, torso. His lip was split, his nose was broken, probably a couple of ribs too. His body throbbed and smelt of sweat and piss. His own piss.

But he could think, and he could hear and he could see – a little. And he wasn't dead: they wanted him for something.

Two guards remained, Ved and Ishwar. Halfway up the crater, the injured guard sat with his back against a rock and

Calix's expensive boots on his feet. His leg had been bandaged. He was picking up stones and lobbing them down. He glared and swore and spat. Ved squatted at the lip of the crater, his pistol pointed at Calix. Further favours from the cook looked unlikely.

The others had disappeared. Hant and the lazy-eyed guard, Ram, and Barney.

Barney. Escorted across the bridge?

Sold?

Shot?

Calix stared at his boots. They were clownishly big for Ishwar, but the point was made. Top-of-the-range Gore-Tex boots which mountain rescue teams used. A present from his old man, only a week before he'd left. A peace offering after all the arguments about going.

What would his old man do in Calix's position? His pedantic but practical old man who'd taught him to snare rabbits. His old man was a soldier, trained in escape and evasion.

Calix stared at the boots.

He wasn't a soldier.

He wasn't Houdini.

He felt like the astronaut marooned on Mars having to survive for four years rather than the month he had supplies for. The guy, Watney, had been forced to create his own food and water. Calix had liked the book, liked the self-reliance of one man acting alone. Same with the guy hiking through the Utah canyons forced to cut his arm off. Necessity the mother of invention.

Now it was his turn.

Hant, the lazy-eyed guard and Ram reappeared at the top of the crater.

No Barney.

Calix really was alone now. He'd liked it at home, but in Nepal, in the mountains, it was different. His stomach churned, and he realised he was missing Barney. He hoped, in the end, he'd done alright by him. Even if Barney might not agree.

Fuuuuck!

He had to think of something positive while he still could. Mum. His old man. Bird Bird. Megan.

The two men and the boy stared down at him, Hant smirking, Ram looking worried. The boy's presence gave Calix a small measure of hope. Bad things didn't happen when he was around.

'Ram.' The word came out as a croak, Calix not recognising his own voice.

The boy descended the short, sharp slope in two or three bounds. He peered down at the tied-up, rolled-up white man.

'*Paani?*' Another croak.

At the top of the slope, Hant swore a burst of Nepali. Ram backed away and Hant descended the slope. He also peered down.

Calix ached all over. And he was so thirsty. A hangover from his student days. Torture to listen to the rushing river and feel the wetness of the air.

'Look,' said Hant. Like a magician he produced an egg. 'Look, *andha*.' He tossed the egg a few inches in the air. He caught it again, his hand descending, reducing the momentum. The egg sat there on the palm of his hand.

'Ishwar injure knife.' Hant tossed the egg again. Higher. Calix watched Hant watching. The egg somersaulted, stopped and plummeted. Smashed on the ground.

Calix got it. Basic physics.

Hant and the three guards slipped down the slope. Ved carried a rough plank left over from building the bridge. They removed Calix's plasticuffs and untied his left arm and strapped it to the plank. One cord was tied tightly around Calix's wrist. He wiggled his fingers. They rolled him onto his stomach so his left arm was stretched out in front of him. Like a suspended swimmer.

Ved sat on Calix's back. Calix groaned. The noise frightened him. Ram was nowhere to be seen.

The lazy-eyed guard pinioned Calix's legs and Hant controlled his right arm with a rope.

Ishwar held up a knife.

'Which finger?' said Hant.

Calix shook his head.

50

'Which finger?' repeated Hant.

'Go to hell.' As he said it Calix realised it probably wasn't hell Hant was afraid of. Reincarnation as a dung beetle or a Qatari minister's lapdog.

Hant's face didn't flicker. He wiggled a pinkie. Not so pink. Calix didn't think they'd do it. It was unnecessary, and mean.

Ishwar pressed down with the knife, creasing the skin. Calix felt pressure on the bone. He twisted his body but Ved and the lazy-eyed guard pressed down. Hant stepped onto the plank and hauled on the rope to keep Calix's arm immobile.

Calix set his teeth, wishing he had something to bite on. Was he mean? Did he deserve it? He liked animals and children. He'd come to like Barney, and he'd loved Megan.

Ishwar pressed the knife harder, severing the skin. He pressed harder still, and cut forward and back. Blood seeped. The pain, at first like a bad cut. Then Ishwar cut into the bone. Pain: sudden, raw, searing. Ishwar bent to his task, engaging his shoulder, and forced the knife down through the bone. Calix saw a white light. He cried out. Glanced at the severed finger, separate and bloody. Hant stepped back from the plank.

Calix felt hot and sick. With relief as well as the pain. It was over. 'Aargh. Aaaargh.' Adrenalin and pain coursed his body like an erupting volcano.

From a pocket, Hant produced another egg. He sat it on the palm of his hand.

'Sat phone – dis'pear.

'Chet – dead.

'Kelsang – dis'pear.'

Hant threw the egg into the air and watched it rise, hesitate, and fall. Smash to the ground.

'Which finger?'

Calix looked away. The pain burning like lava. Tried to remember the word for finger in Nepali.

'If you no say, I say.'

'Aargh.'

Hant waggled a thumb.

Ishwar repositioned the knife, and the two guards pinning Calix down, pressed harder.

'Stop,' shouted Calix.

'Stop?'

'Okay, okay, I stole your phone. Of course it was me. Of course I wanted to escape. Wouldn't you have done the same? But, I didn't kill Chet. I swear. I like dogs – you know that, you've seen me. And I don't know where Kelsang is, honestly. When I said he's lost in Tibet, it wasn't a joke, maybe he has gone there. After the argument with you, he killed Chet and ran away.'

It was a long speech, and Calix felt exhausted. And alone. He'd looked out for Barney, but no one was looking out for him.

Hant rocked back and forward on his feet. 'I know you, Calix. You clever man. You gamble man. You think, tell bit truth, I let you off.' The Nepalese leader looked away. At the far hillside, and the empty sky. 'But, you forget egg.'

Hant was right. It was only a part confession. But it was the truth about Kelsang: the guard, Calix was sure, had legged it.

'I fair man,' said Hant. 'Chet and Kelsang I *think*, not know you fault. Ishwar, you fault. Sat phone, you fault. *Ho*, Ishwar.'

The guard bent to his task.

The knife bit into Calix's flesh, and he fought the pain by thinking of lovely Megan being knocked off her bike, and his sister lying there on the warm tarmac, never to think again.

*

The brigadier waited halfway across the bridge. He wore his green t-shirt, army lightweights, army boots. On his back was his khaki rucksack, and in his belt, his knife and army canteen. He held binoculars to his eyes. Every inch the soldier.

Rick waited halfway to the brigadier.

Russell stood at the foot of the ladder.

The mountains were witnesses.

The brigadier rested the binoculars and looked over the rail, straight down into the water. Above his head, prayer-flags flew. He took down a flag, and pulled it taut. Then, threw it over the rail. Rick watched it fall. Quickly at first, but as the flag unfurled it slowed and drifted. It disappeared under the bridge. Rick crossed sides, scanned the air and found it, floating downwards in an ever gentler curve.

At the far end of the bridge there was movement: three people carrying a heavy bundle up the ladder, and a fourth person following.

*

Ved, Ram and the lazy-eyed guard carried Calix to the bridge on their shoulders. He was still a rolled-up carpet. He could see behind him, but not ahead. Hant followed with his pistol drawn.

They manoeuvred him up the ladder and continued across the bridge. The motion of being carried fought with the swaying of the bridge and he felt sick. But it distracted from the burning of the two severed fingers and his throbbing body. His hand was wrapped in the front of his shirt, ripped off and tied by Ved.

The cold air from the river rushed up at him. Why walk any further? They should roll him over the rail and get it over with.

Calix's thoughts flickered. He remembered the lazy-eyed guard in the Dumghat *chirpi*. Playing with his phone like a child. Banana maths with Ram. Homework. At the kitchen table with Megan. Megan – always she was there.

His trio of pall-bearers stopped.

'What have you done to him?'

His old man's voice.

His old man's voice? He knew he must be hallucinating, but he still craned his neck.

He couldn't see.

Hant gave instructions and waved his pistol. The two guards and Ram walked back along the bridge.

The slats of the bridge pressed up through Calix's body and he nestled his head in a space. He rested and breathed. A figure loomed over his head and peered down. A bead of sweat ran off the man's forehead and onto Calix. He knew that weathered face.

His old man cut off the ropes with a knife and propped Calix up against his legs. Leant down, put his arms around him. It felt like a dream. His old man untied the rip of shirt and inspected his hand. Then his old man retied it, scowling. He helped Calix drink some water.

'Barney? Is he—'

'He's okay. He *will* be okay.'

'Is he safe?'

His old man looked at him as if he was a stranger, and nodded.

Calix closed his eyes. All he wanted to do was sleep.

Hant kicked his foot. 'Enough.' He brandished the pistol.

'The exchange is off,' said his old man. He raised his arms in the air in surrender. 'Calix is badly injured, Hant. You've already had more than enough.'

Hant snickered, and cocked the pistol. He waved it at Calix's old man until he backed away. Calix lay back, head again in a space between slats. He listened to the rushing water. *Exchange?*

'You want tell Calix why here?'

Hant didn't know? Nothing made sense. He was so tired. Too tired to work anything out.

'I wanted to tell you, Calix.'

What?

Calix tried again. 'What?'

'Ten minutes,' said Hant.

His old man dropped his arms by his sides and sat down. 'It might take longer.'

He took a deep breath.

'I was twenty-two, Calix, fresh out of Sandhurst. A lieutenant in the 1st and 3rd Ghurkha Rifles, in charge of a platoon of soldiers. Thirty-five Ghurkhas, some younger than me and two old enough to be my father. They included Hant's father Manu, who was only eighteen or nineteen.'

'Eighteen,' said Hant.

Calix looked up at the kidnapper. He'd lowered his pistol. He was listening, concentrating. *He didn't know.*

'Eighteen. Manu was a rifleman, Bravo section. I was

responsible for him, for all of them.' He paused and looked down at Calix, who gave the faintest of nods.

His old man continued. 'In 1982 the Argentinians invaded the Falklands and the First Battalion of the 1st and 3rd was sent there, part of Maggie Thatcher's Task Force. We sailed on the *QE2*. We felt like we were going on holiday. Cabins with floral curtains and bidets. Lots of posing with *kukris* for the media.

'After ten days we arrived at South Georgia. The Ghurkhas were seasick. Your father, Hant, threw up the whole journey. The Hindu Ghurkhas, Calix, are restricted from the sea – one of their traditions. A man I found vomiting into a lifeboat told me he was being punished by the Hindu gods.

'We were all pleased to arrive at East Falkland, but it didn't last. The weather was diabolical. Cold and wet, and it was the middle of winter so only six hours of daylight.

'We just wanted to start fighting.

'Chinooks took us to Goose Green, where the Paras had just won their famous battle. I saw a row of body bags – nine, I counted – and stretchers with wounded soldiers: bloody, moaning, filthy. I remember one man kissing a photograph. Another holding himself, shivering. The POWs looked terrified. The air smelt of burning. I received orders – a ring of dirty faces, stubble, bloodshot eyes. Behind the lieutenant, I saw the man with the photo slump—'

'Take long time,' said Hant. The kidnapper looked over his shoulder, but no one was in sight.

In the other direction, a white man stood halfway to the far bank. Another white man stood at the top of the descent ladder, watching through binoculars.

51

Rick pulled the sat phone from his pocket. He pressed a few keys, and dialled the number Robbo had sent him. The lead helicopter for the Nepalese Army Air Service.

'Leopard 9-0-1.' The voice, Nepalese cut with English public school. In the background, heavy static and the whirring of rotor blades.

'DCI Castle, British police. What's your ETA for the bridge?'

'Nineteen minutes, sir. Do you want the guys on both sides of the bridge?'

Rick stared into the foaming waters fifty metres below. No help from the police negotiators' manual. Three options: the Saklis side, the far side, or both sides of the bridge. Both sides would have the kidnappers surrounded. No one – hostage or kidnapper – would escape. But it might put too much pressure on Khetan, and force him to do something rash. It would be like containing a volatile liquid and shaking it. Khetan might execute Calix Coniston. Underneath the bridge, the glittering water crashed onwards. Shadows from the vegetation stretched across, the colossal dark shapes like primordial beasts.

'DCI Castle?'

'The Saklis side of the bridge. Make contact with the advance party at MK. Tell them to secure that side, and wait for my next instruction.'

'Yes, sir. Eighteen minutes.'

'Thank you.'

'Sir?'

'Yes?'

'Good luck, sir.'

*

Calix glanced at his old man. He looked thin and tired.

'Calix has to understand the context.'

'What is contex?' said Hant.

'The background, the details. You, too. Going to war, being shot at and shooting back feels unreal. If you don't hear everything you won't understand.' There was a slight tremor in his voice.

Hant nodded.

Hant wanted to know.

Calix wanted to know. He was waking up. Two new scenarios were unfolding in his head: his old man fighting in the Falklands and the exchange happening on the bridge. Him for his old man? Left brain, right brain. Right brain, left brain. It didn't matter. Two against one. His old man had a knife, Hant had a pistol. Hopeless. But at least Barney was safe.

His old man forced out a smile and kept going.

'As other British soldiers advanced on Stanley, we were kept back. First at Goose Green and then at Bluff Cove. Waiting was hard. The cold turned the rain to sleet and snow and waterlogged our shell-scrapes. Our boots were rubbish, and it was a miracle we were getting the right compo packs. The

Ghurkhas ate different rations to the rest of the army – lots of *dal baht.*'

Hant's eyes glimmered. Or maybe Calix was mistaken.

'There is an English saying, Hant. An army marches on its stomach.'

Hant nodded.

'Along with the physical hardship of waiting there was the mental. The machine-gunners took potshots at Argie aircraft and the ranks, well they V-signed and moonyed the RAF—'

'What moony?' said Hant.

Calix stared at his old man. First time he'd heard him utter the word. First time for a lot of things.

'*Bandar ko chaak*,' said Calix.

It was his old man's turn to stare at him. Hant, too, leaking a smile. 'How *buwaa?*' said Hant.

'Your father?' The brigadier looked at Calix. A vein protruded on his old man's temple.

Calix nodded his understanding. '*Buwaa* – old man, father.' So much they didn't know about each other. When he got home he and the old man should make a couple of snares together. Like they used to.

If he got home.

'I had thirty-five soldiers to look after.' The brigadier paused. 'Your father, Hant, was doing okay. He'd written a letter home – you've probably read it – but he was a tough soldier, and he was coping well. Both with the conditions and the prospect of battle.'

'More,' said Hant.

'There were victories at Goose Green, Mount Kent, Mount Challenger. I'll never forget the names.

'Then it was our turn. My turn. Your *buwaa* turn. The target was Stanley, a coastal town flanked by hills – a defender's dream. A thousand Brits versus nine thousand Argies, dug in and waiting for us.

'Two nights of attacks. First night, the Paras and Marines took Longdon, Two Sisters and Harriet. The second night was us: Mount William.'

'*Buwaa?*' said Hant again.

'Other soldiers were nervy, but not your father, Hant. He was born to it: he had a strong faith and a belief in reincarnation. He was calm, all the Ghurkhas were. They didn't fear death. Your *buwaa*, Hant, told me that an honourable death is *progress*.'

*

Keeping a hand on the rail, Rick walked a few steps closer, wondering if he'd made the right decision about deploying the Nepalese Special Forces on only one side of the bridge. Ahead of him, the brigadier sat next to Calix, who lay with his head propped up. He was motionless, like a dead man. The soldier was doing all the talking. Khetan and Calix, he presumed, were listening.

Rick also wanted to know. He walked closer still, his eyes on Khetan, ready to back-pedal if the kidnapper got spooked.

The brigadier was a brave man. Would Rick make the same sacrifice for his own son? For Maggie's son? He hoped he would.

He got to within rushing distance, and stopped. Listened.

'Finally,' said the brigadier, 'on Sunday the fourteenth of June at three am we were helicoptered into position, a kilometre to the west of Tumbledown Mountain.'

The brigadier was talking about a battle. Tumbledown sounded like the Falklands. The Falklands made sense.

'That was our Start Line,' said the brigadier. 'The Scots Guards were to attack first, and we were to follow through.'

52

'We de-bussed into another world,' said the brigadier. 'Continuous cracks of rifle fire, long thumps of machine guns. Red tracer bullets and white muzzle-flash criss-crossed the darkness. Men shouting, swearing. One screaming for a medic.'

Calix could see sweat rings under his old man's armpits, staining the t-shirt a darker green. On the front was a Nepali phrase, *Kaphar hunnu bhanda moron ramro chha.* He'd no idea what it meant.

'The barrage started. Hundred-and-five-millimetre artillery rounds and four-and-a-half-inch shells from a Royal Navy frigate. That's their diameter.' The brigadier put his fingers together to make a circle. 'Each shell weighed twenty kilos.' The brigadier paused.

'Our firepower was monstrous. I almost felt sorry for the Argies, most of whom were conscripts.'

'What conscripts?' said Hant.

'Ghurkhas are volunteers. They choose to join the army. Conscripts have no choice.'

Hant nodded.

Something caught Hant's eye behind Calix, and despite the pain, Calix turned his head to look. The white man had moved

344

closer. Calix didn't recognise him, and he didn't look like a soldier. He was too young to be a diplomat. A spy? It didn't matter. The man's face was tight with concern and concentration.
Three against one – perhaps there was hope.

His old man was still going strong, like he'd hardly started.
Playing for time?

'The Scots Guards put in a diversionary attack with light
tanks, and then attacked Tumbledown. Officially it's a mountain, but it's only six hundred and fifty metres, half the altitude
of Kathmandu. To the Ghurkhas it's a small hill, but it was a
tough target. A long rocky ridge running east-west with sheer
cliffs to the north. The southern slopes were gentler but full of
Argie defences.

'At five am it started snowing. I shivered with cold and
excitement. This was it: I was going to war, to lead my men
into battle, to lead Manu into battle. None of us knew if we
were coming back.'

His old man sounded like Rambo. His eyes had lost their
near-focus, as if he was talking to himself. Calix had never
heard him say anything like it. The throbbing of his body had
lessened, and adrenalin was flowing again. His old man's story,
and his own story – the two of them on the bridge.

'We dumped our Bergens and I went round checking my
section commanders and talking to the Ghurkhas. *My*
Ghurkhas. I hoped I would take them all home. I said a few
words, looked into camouflaged faces, exchanged smiles.
Checked they knew the password if there was confusion in the
dark.

'The Ghurkhas were great troops. Not only their stoicism
but also their *kaida*.' He paused. 'Manu most of all.'

Hant nodded. Calix had never heard of it.

'Dad?' The word sounded strange, but it was easier the second time. '*Kaida*, Dad?'

His old man looked at him, and paused. 'Means self-discipline and professionalism.' His old man sounded like a recruitment pamphlet. What was he selling? Or was he buying? Time? Trust?

'Ghurkhas very good soldier,' said Hant. 'Very good people. Do good for Nepal. Send home much money. Much Ghurkhas my family. *Buwaa.* Ram *buwaa buwaa.*'

His old man was selling and Hant was buying.

'I remember your father, Hant. He smeared extra camouflage paint across my face. He grinned at me. He was only a boy.'

Calix didn't believe it. His hand thumped down against a slat. An automatic response of appreciation for his old man. The wrong hand. The pain flooded up his arm and he bit the inside of his cheek.

Hant believed it. Tears ran down his cheeks.

'We set off across the western slopes of Tumbledown Mountain.

'Around us, the ground erupted. The air exploded. We dived for cover as showers of peat rained down. Incoming artillery shells fired from the other side of Tumbledown. Ghurkhas screamed. My NCOs rallied their sections, and we regrouped amongst the rocks. Three soldiers were injured by shrapnel.'

*

Rick had read about the Falklands and seen most of the Vietnam films. As a teenager he'd dreamt about being a soldier, but the brigadier had lived it. Combat was the extreme human experience, even more so than taking drugs or committing burglary. Death at any moment.

Coppering was dull in comparison. He looked around: Khetan holding a pistol, the suspension bridge, the picture-book mountains. The stakes.

Not today.

'One man was looking for his leg,' the brigadier was saying. 'Crawling around, his stump leaving a bloody trail and weeping and singing to himself, *she loves you, yeah, yeah, yeah.* Nearby, a man lay on his back, his chest ripped open and his guts hanging out. A medic was scooping them back in.'

The brigadier paused, and picked out a pebble jammed in a plank. He threw it through the wire and it dropped out of sight. 'War.'

Rick heard the sigh, and the deep breath. The brigadier looked exhausted.

But he continued. 'We set off again. Tabbed in single file behind the battalion commander as he led us on a shepherd's path under the cliffs of Tumbledown. We saw the first dead bodies of our own troops. Each one was marked with an inverted rifle jammed into the rocks. Fear turned to adrenalin. Fight or flight.'

'Fight or flight,' Rick heard Calix repeating. His voice was a croak, and Rick doubted Khetan could understand. Calix stretched an arm towards his father, and tugged at a trouser-leg in a gesture of support.

The hairs went up on Rick's neck.

He had to do something. If he did nothing, the best outcome would be saving Calix, but losing the brigadier. Worst would be Khetan killing both of them, maybe Rick, too.

He reconsidered his options. One, request Leopard 9-0-1 to hover over the bridge, making it impossible to remain standing and causing Khetan to drop the gun. Two, overpower Khetan. If Rick and the brigadier rushed the kidnapper, he would only have time to get one shot away. Maybe two. If they wobbled the bridge, he'd likely miss. Rick's heart-rate notched up. He wasn't a hero. Option three?

The brigadier continued. 'We wanted to fight and to take

revenge for our injured brothers. It was a peculiar sensation, like nothing I'd ever experienced before. The back of my neck and my skin were burning with heat. We speeded up.

'As we rounded the end of Tumbledown the battalion went to ground except for two platoons from D company. One was my platoon. Behind us the battalion's mortar section shelled Mount William. It was ten am and light, but visibility was poor due to mist and smoke – one mortar crew was firing smoke canisters to cover our advance across the open ground between Tumbledown and William.

'I gave the order to fix bayonets, said a few last words of encouragement. Then we spread out. Manu was the nearest man to me. He shouted, *je hola hola.* What will be, will be.'

Je hola hola was not for Rick. Not reincarnation or leaps of faith. Not prayer-wheels or prayer-flags. He was an atheist Manchester detective. He believed in facts, evidence and the rule of law. Free will. Crime and punishment. Policework.

He looked at his watch, then into the crimson-streaked sky. It was empty. Feeling an increasing sense of dread, he extracted the sat phone from his pocket. His fingers were greasy with sweat. He'd made the wrong decision deploying the helicopters. Surrounding Khetan with Nepalese soldiers would force the kidnappers to capitulate. He pressed a key but the phone slipped from his hand, and hit the bridge with a clunk. It skidded between two boards, and disappeared into the void below. Rick's sense of dread ratcheted further and his ears rang.

The brigadier didn't even pause.

'Two sections led out, the soldiers five metres apart in a staggered line. The third section brought up the rear, fifty metres back, also in a line. Me in the middle. A kilometre away was the rocky outcrop of Mount William. A perfect position for the Argies to dominate our approach to Tumbledown.'

Rick edged closer. It was now up to him. Calix looked in

a bad way. One of his hands was bandaged and his face was swollen and bruised. Beaten, if not tortured. Two against one, two and a half including the injured Calix. Something might be possible. He wished he had a Special Ops shield. There'd be collateral. Such a weasel word.

A fly buzzed around Calix's face. He lay on the bridge slats, head on the brigadier's rucksack.

'Stop, Officer Castle,' said Khetan, pointing the pistol. 'Closer, and I shoot.'

Calix craned his neck backwards, and stared up at Rick. As if noticing him for the first time.

Rick stopped.

He was only a metre from the brigadier, who seemed oblivious of his presence. He remembered Nandan. Looking down his sights, lining up the cross-hairs. He wondered if he was spoiling the shot. Nandan gave him an option three. A loose wire on the side netting clinked in the wind. Reminded him of Chichester harbour and his dad. Every time. Even now.

Khetan waved his pistol at the soldier to carry on talking.

'The ground was flat, but heavy going. Soggy peat and huge grassy tufts. Clusters of boulders – good cover if we were fired on. We scanned ahead, searching for the enemy. The mortars kept up a barrage of shells and smoke, and we could only see thirty metres.

'*Dash, down, crawl, observe, sights, fire* – that was what we'd all been trained to do. *Dash* to the nearest cover. Get *down, crawl* into position and *observe*. Check your weapon *sights* and *fire*.

'*Dash, down, crawl, observe, sights, fire.* I repeated it to myself, like a good luck mantra. Like the prayer-flags.'

'Flag no luck,' said Khetan.

The brigadier nodded. Perspiration glistened on his face. A neck ring of sweat matched his armpits.

'You speak now long time. When *buwaa*?'

'Soon,' said the brigadier. 'It's important you know everything.

'The Argies feared the Ghurkhas more than anyone else. They believed that if a Ghurkha unsheathed his *kukri* then he had to spill blood before he could put it away. They even thought the Ghurkhas were cannibals. You know that every year ten thousand Nepalese men vie for the hundred and seventy Ghurkha recruit spots. They're some of the best infantrymen in the British army. And that's an army with the Par—'

'*Bandar ko chaak*,' said Khetan. He sounded angry.

The brigadier seemed to be eking things out, but Rick wasn't sure why. Was the mention of the *kukri* a message? The soldier was going to use his own knife? The stud on the scabbard was undone.

'Enough Ghurkhas,' said Khetan. 'Know very good soldier. *Buwaa*.'

'Okay, okay. Sorry.' The brigadier paused, took a deep breath and continued. 'We walked for fifteen, twenty minutes. Maybe half a kilometre. *Dash, down, crawl, observe, sights, fire.*' He paused again. Then yelled, 'Come on, you fuckers. Or have you all gone home?'

Rick stared at the brigadier. He was gripping the rail of the bridge so tightly that his knuckles had gone white. If the brigadier led, he'd follow. Maybe Calix was less injured than he appeared. Maybe the three of them could do something? Rick should lead. It was a police operation, and he was in charge.

'An enemy shell whistled over our heads and landed somewhere behind me. One of my men screamed and the air fizzed with bullets.

'We were under attack.'

Rick felt it, over and above his own apprehension.

'Take cover, yelled one of the NCOs. I did exactly that, and crawled behind a rocky outcrop. Manu and two or three others shouted, *ayo Ghurkhali.* The Ghurkhas are here.

'Ahead of me, the two section commanders barked at their men to pepperpot. Soldiers in ones and twos took turns to zigzag forward or give covering fire. I shouted to my signaller to let company HQ know. I crawled round to the other side of my cover for a better view.

'That was when the grenade landed.'

53

Calix had never heard this before. The medal story over and over, but nothing about a grenade. Something had gone wrong. His old man had fucked up. His old man never fucked up.

'Talk,' said Hant.

'The grenade didn't roll, didn't move at all. Just landed in the soggy turf, close enough to see the lettering. Not much bigger than a cricket ball.'

Calix stared at his old man. One minute he was a recruitment pamphlet, the next Rambo. His old man was putting on a performance, and it had distracted Calix from his pain. Even the burning in his fingers had receded.

Suddenly, Calix got it. The performance wasn't only for Hant, it was for him too.

His old man drank from his black army-issue water bottle, then offered it to Calix. He held his head while he drank. Calix sloshed it around in his mouth, loosening his dry tongue. He coughed and drank some more. His old man plumped up the rucksack underneath his head. Something rattled inside the pack.

'You'll be safe, soon,' whispered his old man.

'Don't do the exchange, Dad. I… I don't deserve it.'

'No you two talk,' said Hant. 'Talk me.'

Calix's old man – his dad – squeezed Calix's shoulder, and cleared his throat.

'I knew exactly what it was: an M67 fragmentation grenade, used by the Americans for forty years as well as the Argies. Four hundred grams, the average soldier can throw it thirty-five metres. Casualties to fifteen metres. Killing radius of five. I'd been to briefings on it, I'd *given* briefings on it, one on the *QE2*. I knew all that if I'd stopped to think about it.

'But I didn't stop. I picked it up and hurled it. I had one or two seconds at best. Already, I'd been lucky as the M67 explodes on a timer, not on contact. The fuse is four seconds, and the SOP is to count to two and throw it so that the grenade explodes as it lands. But counting takes nerve, and whoever had thrown it hadn't dared. I was lucky – I should have died.'

Calix wanted to scream. It was a war, not the sodding House of Commons. But he said nothing, screamed nothing. He didn't want to attract attention.

When his old man had said, fight or flight, it had jangled Calix's emotions. Something *he'd* thought and said over the last few weeks. He was his old man's son, and he wanted to make him proud. His old man, and his sister Megan.

Castle was dibble. Three against one. Knife against gun.

Hant was in range.

'I should be dead,' said the brigadier. 'Not Manu.'

*

The bridge swayed. A bird flew past, towards Russell. The river smashed along beneath them.

Rick watched Khetan's face, watched his pistol. Watched his trigger finger.

The kidnapper frowned. 'What SP?'

'S-O-P. Standard Operating Procedure. What we're supposed to do – basic instructions.'

Khetan nodded.

Rick had questions, lots of questions, and he expected Khetan did too. Understanding was crucial – the nuances. He glanced around at Russell, and considered beckoning him forward. It was a fourth option, but he dismissed it. Endangering another man's life was futile – and cowardly. It was up to him. He looked higher, up the hillside, vainly searching for Nandan and wondering what the brigadier had instructed the sniper to do, and when. He looked higher still, craning his neck upwards, but still the sky was empty and quiet.

'And that was about it. We fought on, clearing positions, but half an hour later the Argies surrendered. Many of them ran away down the rear slopes. Mount William was ours. Recapturing it was one of the last actions of the war.'

Rick took a half-pace forward. 'So we all understand, David, an enemy grenade which landed near you, and which you picked up and hurled away, killed Manu?'

The brigadier nodded.

'Hant,' said Rick, 'the death of your father was a terrible accident.'

'Accident? You stupid? Why throw *buwaa*? Why no throw enemy?'

'The fog of war,' said Calix, scowling. His voice hoarse.

'Because I had no idea where it came from. I threw it *away from me* – that was all I could do.'

'What is SP for grenade?' said Khetan.

Rick stared at the small Nepalese man. Kidnapper, maybe worse. His spoken English was rough but he wasn't dim. It was a good question: a grenade landing close couldn't be that unusual in skirmishing.

'Kick it into a grenade sump – that's a hole in the ground that will absorb the blast. But sumps – holes – are only practical in defensive positions.'

'No hole, what then SP?'

Rick's question, too.

'Take cover. Crawl away and stay low. Most exploding fragments go upwards.' He pointed at the sky. Clouds were bubbling up from the valley.

Rick glanced at Calix lying at Khetan's feet. The wounded hostage seemed twitchy. Kept glancing back at Rick.

'Maybe crawling away is what I'd have done,' said the brigadier, 'if I'd had a few minutes to think. If I had, it's likely I'd have been seriously injured, if not killed. Along with the platoon signaller and others from platoon HQ.' He stood up and looked over the rail, at the swirling river. A large branch was floating down. 'There are no easy answers, even with hindsight.'

'Hant, I think we can all see that,' said Rick. He felt uneasy. Where, he wondered, were Leopard 9-0-1 and the other Nepalese Air Service helicopters? Khetan was getting increasingly upset, which exacerbated the risk of him panicking and shooting.

'Other choose.'

The brigadier sighed. 'You're right. One final option: dive on it. Not SOP but I like to think if I'd had hours to think about it, that's what I would have done. Having had three decades to think about it, it's what I wish I had done. Most Ghurkhas would have smothered it, and protected everyone else.'

'And medal?' said Khetan.

Rick had forgotten about the medal. There was no way the brigadier would have won a medal if the incident had been reported. Accident or no accident.

'The medal was for taking Mount William.'

'Tell *buwaa* death, no medal,' said Khetan. 'No tell *buwaa* death, medal.'

Rick could only agree with the kidnapper. If the brigadier had told the full truth of that day, he would not have been honoured.

'Probably, yes.' The brigadier looked over the downstream rail. The branch had disappeared. He looked back at Khetan. 'No one said anything about the grenade. There was only one witness, the platoon signaller, and he stayed quiet. It was against his *kaida*. The only person he told was Manu's wife.'

'You *kaida*?'

Rick found himself sighing. It wasn't surprising David hadn't told him.

'Hant, I am truly sorry,' said the brigadier. 'It was the most intense hour of my life and I've regretted it ever since. I was young and I was petrified. Your *buwaa* was a strong, courageous soldier.' He squatted down by his son. 'Calix, is there anything you want to say?'

'You made a mistake in the heat of the battle, and remained shtum for thirty years.' Calix's voice was still a croak. The brigadier helped his son drink. 'I'd have done the same,' whispered Calix. 'Most people would.'

The brigadier stood up. 'Rick?'

'David has told you the truth, Hant. You deserved that. Now, put the weapon down and give yourself up.'

Khetan shook his head, slowly. He laughed. 'You West people. U-S-A, U-K, FIFA. All same. No *kaida*. No *dharma*.'

The river pulsed beneath them, filling the silence.

'I am a fraud,' said the brigadier. 'A fake, a charlatan. I know it, I've always known it. Every day I get up knowing it.'

Calix wriggled his supine body another few centimetres towards Khetan and clenched his fists. Winced with pain.

'You're here now, Dad, aren't you?' Calix's voice was low, but he kept going. 'On the bridge. Prepared to give your life for mine. Forget *dharma*, you're a hero, deserve a Vicky C.'

'You know words you t-shirt?' said Khetan. He waggled the barrel of his pistol.

The brigadier nodded. '*Kaphar hunnu bhanda moron ramro chh.* The Ghurkha motto. Better to die than to live a coward.'

Everything then happened at once.

54

Hearing a faint chopping of rotor blades, Rick looked up into the reddening sky. Five Nepalese Air Service helicopters in formation, heading their way. The back-up he'd long been promised.

'Now, Dad,' shouted Calix, and lashed out at Khetan with his legs.

The kidnapper swayed back, reducing the full force of the kick. Simultaneously, he fired.

Rick's ears rang. For a second he was stunned. But he wasn't hurt, and no one cried out in pain. The brigadier reached for his knife.

Khetan aimed the pistol at Calix, then raised it, and pointed it at Calix's father. The brigadier. Lieutenant David Coniston, 1st and 3rd Ghurkha Rifles. He ushered the soldier forward with the barrel.

The chopping above them was deafening and Rick could no longer hear the river. He watched Khetan glance into the bruise-red sky. It would only be minutes before the heliborne soldiers deployed and swarmed towards the bridge.

The brigadier climbed up onto the handrail.

'No!' screamed Rick.

The soldier swayed on the thick wire, the line of prayer-flags flapping frantically. His hands gripped a vertical cable, one flag sticking against his cheek. He unpeeled the flag, and looked down at his son. Gave the faintest of nods.

Then he jumped.

Rick would always remember David's hands. Bulging blue-green veins, deeply tanned, pockmarked, from decades of military service.

Remaining impassive, Khetan pointed the pistol down at Calix.

Rick hurled himself against the side netting. The wire bulged, and the bridge lurched and began a series of violent wobbles. Violent enough, he hoped, to make Khetan lose his balance. The vertical strengthening wire on the side netting snapped, and whipped back against Rick's cheek. The netting bulged further, and Rick plunged off the wooden walkway, his stomach heaving as if he was in a plummeting lift. But he didn't fall far, caught by the flimsy chicken wire and horizontal strengthening wires. And he hung there, suspended. His body had twisted as he'd fallen, and he stared down into the foaming blue-black waters below. At the strew of car-sized boulders. Bile bubbled up his throat, and into his mouth. Blood dripped from the gash on his cheek onto his hands, and onto the wire, and through the wire and down, and down, and out of his sight. He looked up, and through the hexagonal lattice, could see Khetan lying on the wooden boards.

Rick grabbed wildly at the netting above him.

It gave way.

He grabbed again, higher, further.

More wires broke, and pulled away. He dropped again, his stomach lurching, and became cocooned in the bulge of netting, hanging half a metre down from the boards.

He counted to two, took a deep breath, and heaved his body

upwards and at the same time clutched wildly at the lowest horizontal wire. With the fingers of his right hand he clasped tight. He then grabbed the wire with his left hand. He flicked his feet up and onto the wooden planking. Pulling with his hands and clawing with his feet, he lifted his body upwards and rolled onto the walkway.

'Rick.' A shout from behind him. Russell.

Rick raised his head. Calix still lay on the bridge, and at his feet was Khetan's pistol. *He'd dropped it.* The kidnapper had stood up, but taken a pace back. Rick watched Calix shuffle the pistol closer with his foot.

Rick pulled at the netting entombing his body, and pushed himself upwards. More wires snapped and he rose to his hands and knees. He stood up, blood gushing from his cheek. Staggered forward, alongside Calix, and kicked the pistol off the bridge and into the air, where it dived from view.

He straightened.

'Khetan.' Rick heard the tremble in his own voice. It was a mistake, if an unintentional one. The word was another error. When the kidnapper had called him by his surname he'd liked it – reminded him of Dad. But he didn't want to remind Khetan of his own father, the reason they were all here on the bridge. One word, two mistakes. He needed to up his game, and fast. He tried again.

'Hant.' This time his voice was stronger, as if he was bracing Bennett, or another junior detective.

The Nepalese leader stared at him with cold eyes, and raised his chin a fraction.

'The newspaper cuttings I sent, proclaiming you were a hero in the villages of Nepal, were fake.'

'I no believe.'

'But, you *are* a hero in the villages, and you should be. Your cause to improve conditions for Nepalese workers in Qatar is one I can only commend.' For the second time, Rick felt like a maverick negotiator. Not only had he handed a hostage to the kidnappers, but he was now identifying with their cause. His sympathy was genuine: every two days a worker died in Qatar, a scandal which no one – except Khetan – was tackling.

Khetan's eyes narrowed. 'What, commend?'

'*Dharma.*'

'*Dharma!*' Khetan snorted in annoyance. 'You go home now, take army?'

'No. Your aim may be just, but your method is not. Kidnapping, manslaughter, torture. The pointless death of the brigadier – David. No *dharma.*'

He stepped forward. 'Hant Khetan, you're coming with me. You're under arrest.'

As if in a choreographed dance, Khetan stepped backward, then turned and ran. Rick gave chase, and together they bobbed up and down with the bridge.

At the descent ladder Khetan didn't turn but slid down frontwards, like the boy with the yellow rucksack.

Planning to hurl himself onto the fugitive, Rick reached the top of the ladder. He glanced down.

Three of Khetan's men emerged from the bushes. Their pistols were drawn and they pointed them at Rick. Khetan walked forward to his men, and turned. His men fanned out either side of him.

Rick showed the palms of his hands.

'No gun.'

Khetan smirked. 'I live London ten year.'

'But up there,' said Rick, pointing at the hillside behind him and keeping his eyes on the Nepalese leader, 'I have an army sniper with his sights trained on you. If I give the signal, he will shoot.'

'Why no signal before?'

'Because I'm not a soldier. I'm a British police officer. We arrest, and ask questions. Courts decide.'

'*Bandar ko chaak.*'

Rick had no idea what the words meant, but he understood the gist. It gave him a second or two to think and decide. Nandan would be in position, and would, he had no doubt, be training his cross-hairs on Khetan, and although they had no pre-arranged signal, he also had no doubt, if he screamed Nandan's name, the sniper would shoot, and if the marksman was half as accurate as David had said, then Khetan would die. Compensation, if not justice, for the families of Vicky, Spencer, and David. He would, he thought, probably have their votes. But he was police, not army. Police, not god, Hindu or any other type, and police believed in the rule of law. Which left him one final card to play.

'If you surrender to me, Hant, I will ensure you have a fair trial in London. You'll have the eyes of the world on you, and be able to promote your cause. And, there is a very strong chance of real change in Qatar.'

Almost imperceptibly, Khetan started nodding.

Finally, he smiled. 'I like believe.'

The kidnapper slowly surveilled left and right – at his three men, pistols trained on Rick.

He shook his head and laughed. 'You crazy.'

Rick felt crazy. But he was a police officer – all he'd ever wanted to be, ever since Dad had taken him to the football, and he'd seen the dog-handlers.

And he wasn't reneging on that commitment now. He stood rail-straight, like the brigadier – like David – and watched the Nepalese men disappear into the hard-edged shadows.

Epilogue

Sunlight streamed through the high windows of the South Manchester sports hall. Across the wooden floor, wheelchairs screeched and rumbled. Fast, slow, circling, one way, then the other.

The klaxon sounded for the end of the first quarter, and Rick wheeled to the cluster of players gathering on the sideline. The game was the end-of-case social, delayed six months because Russell had been leading trips in Tanzania.

The mountaineer thundered over. 'Great idea of yours.'

'Not his idea. Mine,' said Maggie, swiping Rick's water bottle.

'Like an old married couple already,' said Kate.

Rick smiled. He couldn't help it.

'How're the bees?' said Russell.

'Disaster. My new queen disappeared and laying workers took over the hive. Have to start again next year.'

'And the case?'

'Not much to report,' said Maggie. 'Coniston's still on remand for conspiracy to kidnap, although he was allowed out for the brigadier's funeral. Khetan's on GMP's Most Wanted list.'

'There is Marrakech,' said Rick. 'Following an Amnesty report on immigrant workers in Qatar, a revote on them hosting the 2022 World Cup was proposed.'

'The kidnap actually made a difference – I can't believe it.' Russell climbed out of his chair, and bounced up and down on his haunches. 'No offence, Maggie.'

'I haven't finished,' said Rick. 'Last week in Marrakech, Blatter guaranteed there wouldn't be a revote on hosting. Thereby killing any leverage FIFA had on Qatar to improve things for the workers.'

'No great surprise,' said Russell. 'They're bent as ice-axes.'

'The death toll in Qatar's over four hundred. It was a scandal, and it still is.'

'You sound like you sympathise with Calix Coniston.'

'His aim was laudable.'

'But all for nothing.'

'Not so for Khetan,' said Rick. 'He wanted revenge – and he got it. Effectively, he murdered David Coniston.'

'Meaning?'

'It's complicated. Think of it like a drunk driver who kills a pedestrian. The driver didn't intend to kill, but usually gets charged with manslaughter. It'll be a decision for the CPS but I think there's enough.'

Rick knew there were further problems – jurisdiction and the lack of an extradition treaty with Nepal – but they could wait. He wriggled in his chair. His piles had long since cleared up, but he really did want to stand up. 'I'll get Khetan for something. Even if it's non-payment of his taxes.' It sounded like a joke, but he meant it.

Robbo walked up – another cheat. His face the colour of ripe plums. He leant closer. 'Did you see the news last night? The Derbyshire quarry collapse?'

'No.'

'Superintendent Bransby was on.'

Rick was thinking of the pictures in his lounge, and what Maggie thought of them. What her taste in art was.

'Sorry about all that. The decision to post you to the crime desk was foisted on me, then reversed.'

'What are you two whispering about?' said Maggie. She threw Rick the ball. He bounced it and threw it back. She threw it at Russell. 'How was your Kili trip?'

'Not quite as exciting as trekking with Rick and it got me thinking, I should join you lot.'

'Leave NA?'

'Not regular. Special.'

'You serious?' said Rick.

'I've got the forms. I've given a lot to Nepal over the years, and I want to give something here too.' He spun the orange ball in his hands. 'But it's not only that. Actually quite interesting what you do.'

If Russell was serious then it was a win all round. Maybe he could have the odd beer with the mountaineer. Tell him about Maggie.

He liked talking about her. About the two of them. She'd met him at the airport and in a concourse café they'd held hands over cups of coffee. It had felt unreal. It still did. When he'd asked her about the honey metaphor in the briefing sheet, she smiled and pecked him on the cheek. He'd surprised everyone by taking her to Becky's wedding. She'd been a hit. She'd tried on a beesuit and veil and he was a regular at wheelchair basketball. They were spending New Year together and planning a canoeing holiday.

Together nearly six months.

Only one thing to dwell on. She still hadn't told him what had happened when she'd been in the army. Not telling him meant she was unsure about him. About the two of them.

Play resumed, and Rick drifted up and down the court with the others. He circled, raced, trundled. Caught the ball, threw the ball. Hot pink faces flashed past him, shouting urgently and gesticulating. A motorbike backfired in the car park.

He was back on the bridge. Prayer-flags flapping, and below, far below, foaming water and behemoth rocks. David.

'Come on, Rick.' A voice from the viewing gallery.

He glanced up.

Becky was there – with Dad. Dad was waving and calling his name. Dad had remembered his name.

Rick closed his eyes, rueing the decision to put Dad in a nursing home. It was only temporary, to give Mum a break.

He wheeled to the side of the court, unclipped the straps, and climbed out. The chair skittered and stilled. He pushed through the doors, negotiated the busy reception, and went outside. The air was cold and goose bumps flecked his arms. He leant back against the wall, the flat of his foot against the brickwork, and stared out into the velvet twilight. A squirrel clicked in the trees, and in the distance a siren wailed.

He'd go and see Dad tomorrow. Take Maggie with him.

Lexicon

Nepali	English
aamaa	mother
aath	eight
andha	egg
ayo Ghurkhali	the Ghurkhas are here
buwaa	father
bandar ko chaak	(inf.) monkey's bottom
(das) bajyo	(two) o'clock
baliyo	strong
biyara	beer

chaa; jaaro chaa	cold; it's cold
chaar	four
chaina	no
chha	six
chhora	son
chineu	recognise
chirpi	toilet
chiyaa	tea
chorachori	children
chorten	Buddhist temple
daai	(elder) brother
dal baht	rice and lentils, Nepalese staple meal
das	ten
dhanyabaad	thank you

dharma	moral code (Hinduism); teachings (Buddhism)
didi	elder sister (lit.); friendly term for women of same generation
dui	two
ek	one
gaai	cow
garam; garam chaa	warm; it's warm
gompa	Buddhist monastery
ho	yes
(Mera) jaane bato kata parcha?	which is the way to (Mera)?
je hola hola	what will be, will be
kaida	(no direct translation) instinctive self-discipline and professionalism
kati bajyo?	what's the time?
kera	banana
khalti	pocket
kukri	curved knife, carried by Nepalese men

369

kukur	dog
lung ta	powerful horse
maaph garnuhos	sorry
maile bujhina	I didn't understand
mama	uncle
mani	wall or stone carved with prayers
momo	similar to dumplings, contain meat or vegetables
naam	name
naan	a flat round or oval bread
namaste	hello / goodbye
naramro	bad
paanch	five
paani	water
paani parchcha	it's raining
piro	spicy
rakshi	whisky (local)

ramro	good, pretty
roti	a flat round bread
saat	seven
sadhu	an individual on a spiritual search
sahib	sir
sangha	the Buddhist community
sano; sano Nepali	small; I speak little Nepali
sirdar	chief guide
Sunko Keta	Golden Boy
thaahaa chha	I know
thaahaa chhaina	I don't know
thik chha? / thik chha	are you okay? / yes, I'm okay
thulo	big
timro naam ke ho?	what is your name?
tin	three
topi	traditional Nepalese hat

Acknowledgements

I would like to thank Simon Nicholson for early encouragement. Nick Archer, Dr Emma Coleman-Jones, and Dr Rachel Bray for feedback on the first draft. Lakpa Doma Sherpa for checking the Nepali. My tutor Joe Stretch and my creative writing workshop classes at Manchester Metropolitan University. My writing group, especially Michael Conroy and Dan O'Sullivan. Xander Cansell, Caitlin Harvey, and the team at Unbound. My editors Eve Seymour and Mary Chesshyre.

Unbound is the world's first crowdfunding publisher, established in 2011.

We believe that wonderful things can happen when you clear a path for people who share a passion. That's why we've built a platform that brings together readers and authors to crowdfund books they believe in – and give fresh ideas that don't fit the traditional mould the chance they deserve.

This book is in your hands because readers made it possible. Everyone who pledged their support is listed at the front of the book and below. Join them by visiting unbound.com and supporting a book today.

Marcus Brueton
Anthony Businelli
David Butcher
Phil Chapman
Allen Chubb
Mike & Christine Clarke
Emma Coleman-Jones
Ian Conolly
Ashley Coups
Robert Cox
Terry Crompton
Claire Crook
John Davies
Bill Delaney
Matt Dobson
Jenny Dowding
Pam Elliott
Margaret Ellison
Vivian Emerson
Jennie Ephgrave
Deirdre Ezzell Stables
Baskeyfield Family
Lisa Fergusson
Paula Fitzmaurice
Helen Fletcher
Anthony Fletcher
Simon Foster
Helen Garforth
Kurt Gengenbacher
Jane Germany
Richard Glynne-Jones
Joel Goldstein
Peter Gray
Salman Haider
Paul & Heather Hardman
Melanie Harris
Deborah Harris
Peter Haspel
Kirstie Hawkins
Will Hawtin
The Royal at Hayfield
Adam Heppinstall
Sue Hill
Colin Hill
Patrick Hill
Andrew Hooper

Rob Hooper
Mary Horlock
James Hume
Michael Hunter
Sara Jagger
Laurie James
Sam Jardine
Stephen Jay
Graeme Jeffery
Laura Jenny
Duncan Johnson
Adrian Jolliffe
Paul Jones
Nick Jupp
Helen Kaye
Richard Kenyon
Peter Keymer
Anne Kitchen
Chris Langton
Mike Lawrence
Eva & Richard Lawson
Simon Lefevre
Clive Lewis
Alison Lomas
Margaret Lovett
Sam Lucy
John Mantel
Laura Marschall
Bruce Marshall
Linda Mawdsley
Ewan Mclellan
Andy McMeeking
David Mellor
Edwina Mendes
Peter Milhofer
Jo Minogue
Simon Morris
Daniel Nardiello
John Nathan
Carlo Navato
Joan & Kevin Nelson
Simon Nicholson
Dorothy Nightingale
Wendy Oakes
Jane Orchard
Clare Padley